ALSO BY NIKKI TURNER

The Glamorous Life

A Hustler's Wife

A Project Chick

Girls from da Hood

The Game: Short Stories About the Life
(contributing author)

TALES FROM DA HOOD

NIKKI TURNER

PRESENTS

STREET CHRONICLES
TALES FROM DA HOOD

ONE WORLD

BALLANTINE BOOKS • NEW YORK

A One World Books Trade Paperback Original

Street Chronicles copyright © 2006 by Nikki Turner
"Big Daddy" copyright © 2006 by Seven
"360" copyright © 2006 by The Ghost
"No Mercy" copyright © 2006 by Akbar Pray
"Thicker Than Mud" copyright © 2006 by Y. Blak Moore

Published in the United States by One World Books, an imprint of The Random House Publishing Group, a division of Random House, Inc., New York.

ONE WORLD is a registered trademark and the One World colophon is a trademark of Random House, Inc.

Library of Congress Cataloging-in-Publication Data

Nikki Turner presents Street chronicles : tales from da hood.
p. cm.
Contents: Big Daddy / by Seven — 360 / The Ghost — No mercy / by Akbar Pray — Thicker than mud / by Y. Blak Moore — Street chronicles / by Nikki Turner.
1. Short stories, American—African American authors. 2. African Americans—Fiction. 3. Inner cities—Fiction. 4. Gang members—Fiction. 5. Street life—Fiction. 6. Gangs—Fiction. I. Title: Street chronicles. II. Turner, Nikki.

PS647.A35N55 2006
813'.04083552—dc22
2005049872

ISBN 0-345-48401-0

Printed in the United States of America

www.oneworldbooks.net

6 8 9 7

Book design by Lisa Sloane

THE BIRTH OF STREET CHRONICLES

FIRST, I WOULD LIKE to thank God for giving me the strength and patience to put such a powerful project together. Having a dream is one of the hardest things to sell to someone else because at the end of the day, it's your dream and your dream alone. But sometimes, dreams do come true, such as going from a career as a travel agent to becoming a bestselling author.

There were only a few people who genuinely believed in me, and those are the folks who I continue to thank in every book. Getting people to look outside of the box is hard. I know firsthand the stress it takes to break through any industry's door. So when those who have supported me asked me for a chance to let them shine by publishing their work, and giving their dream a chance to come true, I knew I had to do something. But what?

The letters and the calls kept pouring in. Upcoming authors had stories that needed to be heard through a vehicle that the streets respected. There was nothing for me to do but pray, and that's when God gave me the vision, the Street Chronicles series.

To the many authors in the various volumes, I came to you with a vision and each of you embraced it. In one single phone call you were just as excited about the manifestation of this project as I was. The enthusiasm rose like a tidal wave even though I didn't know how I was going to fund the book, print it, or get distribution for it. Having come to you with nothing but an idea, I thank you all for believing in me, in my potential, and in the editorial process from the beginning.

From conception to birth, I knew it wouldn't be a smooth ride.

There were some authors with me early on who, when the waves got too high, didn't have the patience to hold on and fell by the wayside. I wish you the absolute best in your future endeavors. But to those of you who rode it out with me on the high tide to the calming still waters, taking pride in your work by accepting any input I shared with you about your story, you make me proud to be able to put my name on this project. Thank you! Together WE DID IT, BABY!!! We're in the major leagues, being published by Random House, the same publisher that published Bill Clinton's books. If that isn't God's grace and mercy, I don't know what is.

All in all, this is only the beginning for you. You're not diamonds in the rough anymore. Continue to shine as stars do. The sky is the limit for you!

Craig, you will never know just how much I love you. You were the first person I shared my desire with and you stepped up to the plate, offering to fund the project for me without even knowing anything about it. You always keep me afloat, whatever the storm is in my life. Marc, my agent, I love you simply for being you. Melody, thanks for being one of the first professionals to assist me with this idea. You gave me a safe and sanitized place for the labor and delivery while you continued to encourage and believe in me. Thanks! Nicey B, my secretary from day one, thanks for only accepting Red Lobster lunches as payment for all you do to keep me organized. Kells, my best friend, for being there around the clock for me. Wayne, Drack, Robinette, Cool, Chelsea, Claudie, and Dre for reading through all the submissions. Pat, thanks for listening to all my tantrums and introducing me to yoga to escape from it all, but most of all, just for doing what you do best, be you! Joy, the official godmother, consultant, prayer partner, et cetera, I am sending you some black dye for all the unwanted gray hair I might have given you. Thank you for always holding me down or picking me up as you do. I know the industry hasn't been nice to either one of us but somehow we always seem to make it through with a smile and a laugh. My Shay-Shay, never think I don't see you or appreciate you. To every one of you reading this, I cannot thank you enough for being avid supporters of my work. I appreciate you taking my babies (novels) into your home and loving them, and introducing them to as many people as you have. This is a book of short stories, so I need to keep this short and sweet. I apologize if you are not mentioned here, but I would like to thank everyone who played a part in the prenatal process, delivery, and nurturing of this baby. Charge it to my head, not my heart.

Peace and Love,

Nikki Turner

WORD ON THE STREET

A NOTE FROM NIKKI TURNER

NIKKI TURNER, NUMBER-ONE BESTSELLING AUTHOR, looked long and hard, high and low, in every prison, ghetto, ditch, crack, and crevice all over the world for the hottest street writers on the planet to assist her in composing this masterpiece exploring every aspect of street life. With a powerful introduction by Kwame Teague, "Big Daddy," "360," "No Mercy," "Thicker than Mud," and "Gotta Have a Ruffneck" make up the first volume of an ongoing legacy guaranteed to change the game of urban fiction as we know it. These five uncut and uncensored urban tales chronicle subject matter that has yet to be told and are penned by five authors whose original voices demand to be heard.

The Queen of Hip-Hop Fiction presents a Nikki Turner Exclusive, the first volume of a series, *Street Chronicles: Tales from da Hood.*

INTRODUCTION BY KWAME TEAGUE

Diamond in the back, sunroof top . . .

Digging the scene with a gangster lean.

FOR MANY, this is the summation of the American Dream, that piece of the pie that young men and women everywhere aspire to obtain. They are raised with the ethic that if you work hard, you will succeed. If you go to school and get an education, you'll get a good job, a beautiful wife, and a picket fence surrounding nice green grass to water on Sundays.

But what happens when your school is a war zone, nothing more than a fashion show, and the only education you get is from a teacher who doesn't see you as a person, but as a problem, and therefore treats you as such? What happens when your job pays a slave's wages but the cost of living is a king's ransom? And even if you do have a degree, a piece of paper confirming you've been educated, just the fact of being young and black is considered a liability instead of an asset. Under these circumstances, the only fence a man's wife sees is the one around her project complex or the prison her man is bidding in. So, by the time you see that nice green grass, it's in the manicured lawn of the cemetery, your final resting place.

The American Dream has been deferred, so those who realize this have chosen another avenue to success, another road to riches, a darker but parallel path. This is the way of the gangster, the one who makes his own list of rules and enforces it. His word is his gun and his silence is law. Violations are dealt with swiftly and, by the code of the streets, justly. This is the world where loyalty and honor really mean something because anything less can cost you your life.

D.B.D . . . TWIN . . . (DEATH BEFORE DISHONOR)

THE GANGSTER KNOWS he isn't living the American Dream, he is a part of the American reality. He knows that this country was built on the same principles that he ruthlessly enforces. He knows the pilgrims were pillagers who conned the natives out of their country, and when the natives got wise, those pilgrims raped, burned, and slaughtered all who stood in their path. So while you eat turkey on Thanksgiving, the American tradition, the gangster celebrates the biggest takeover this country has ever seen, a real thug holiday.

But it doesn't stop with what the English took from the native. The Americans took from the English with common thug tactics and a "fuck you" attitude. When Patrick Henry said, "Give me liberty or give me death," he might as well have screamed, "Ride or die!" Because that's what he meant by today's terms. The Americans ran England off their block and we celebrate it every Fourth of July. We even sing its praises before major sporting events and salute it around the country. The American flag, its colors, red and blue. These same colors have split the streets, literally ripping them in half, making half our hoods Bloods and the other half Crips. Yet, however you cut it, red and blue are the American colors, but *white* is the American Power.

The gangster sees this, understands it, and so he applies it to the world in which he dwells. He turns the UN into the five families, the Geneva Convention into a gang peace treaty, and instead of invading countries, he invades neighborhoods, spreading the same violence, poison, and corruption on a smaller scale. He destroys lives, creates illusions, and sells dreams. All the while profiting, until one day the very law he created backlashes and destroys him. Then another man, disenfranchised by the mainstream, steps up, being even more ruthless, violent, and cunning than his predecessor. And the cycle continues. But don't blame the man. Don't hate the game because, you see, it's the American way. We are products of our environment so the only question left to ask is "How far are you willing to go?"

Following is a collection of stories that tell you just how far some people went . . . how far they continue to go, the results, and the lessons to be learned. These are not fables. They are not fairy tales. They are not manufactured commercial gangstas that BET, the source of Clear Channel Communications, tries to create for your entertainment pleasure. The set is Harlem, Compton, Chicago, or Newark . . . not Universal Studios. There are no stunt doubles or rehearsals so no one will cry out "cut" because these are the uncut versions. They are stories by men and women who lived the life, who live the life, and who have starved and bled, took it in the blood, won or lost. In short, these are the chronicles of gangstas that lived them.

Yes, these are only a few of the eight million stories, and tomorrow there will be probably eight million more. What we present is like various snapshots of a continuous riot, some faces laughing, some crying, some bloodied in the custody of the police, some fleeing the scene, arms wrapped around a stolen plasma TV set. Nevertheless, the riot continues and it will continue until we realize that we have two options. Either we play the game all the way out, or get all the way out the game. Take the hustle, the grind, and the gangsta to a whole new level.

The Street Chronicles are a testament to that whole new level the writers in this book are examples of, and of what the power of expression can do. We as artists, as writers, are using our voices in diverse ways to articulate what the streets are feeling. This is for the beautiful women who do ugly things, for the intelligent brothers who make dumb decisions, and for the next generation of ghetto kids who need someone to look up to and an ideal to believe in. From the streets to the books, from books to beyond, the world is for those with the courage to claim it and the wisdom to maintain it.

HOW FAR are you willing to go?

IN CLOSING, remember to take what you see and hear, use what you can, and discard the rest. But by no means allow yourself to become just another story to tell, just another name to be remembered on walls or T-shirts, just another face lost in the riot that is the streets.

I've said all I'ma say. Turn off the lights and close the door when you leave. . . . One Love!

Kwame Teague,
Author of *The Adventures of Ghetto Sam*

TALES FROM DA HOOD

BIG DADDY

Penned by Seven, but lived by many

ONE

IT'S A SLOW NIGHT, not too many cars cruising up and down Second and Broad for a Friday. This is partly due to the fact that NASCAR is at Richmond International Speedway, and most of my clients are old white men who enjoy that type of shit. I'm slowly losing my patience with Vanessa; the bitch is walking at a slow, nonchalant pace instead of strutting her phat ass up and down the block like I've taught her to do. I'm standing with my back and one foot up against the wall by Eggleston's Restaurant, thinking about how badly I'm gonna choke the shit out of her if she don't make me at least $300 tonight. Tonight the stakes are raised because business has been slow due to the races: I'm charging $40 for blowjobs, $50 for ass licks, and $125 for the total package. Golden showers are going for $30 'cause Nessa's piss makes a nigga ass feel warm and fuzzy.

Twenty minutes ago I made up my mind that I wasn't gonna

give her tired walking ass anything. Can you believe it? The bitch had the audacity to turn down a trick because he was Mexican. Talking about she could smell bean burritos and shit on his breath. I punched the bitch hard enough to frazzle her, but not hard enough to bruise her—couldn't chance having my moneymaker look tore up. I told her ass I didn't give a fuck if she smelt dog shit on his breath, she better had fucked and sucked his dick until the mutherfucker couldn't come any longer. This lazy-ass ho of mine ain't getting shit, not one copper penny tonight. She's lucky if I still take her ass to get her wig smoked, but it wouldn't benefit me if I don't. There's money out here to be made, and I got to keep my bitch looking good at all times. Right now, I've got to go remind this trick bitch who's in charge.

"Bitch, you better pull that goddamn skirt up over your ass and stop these mutherfucking cars out here. You think I'm fucking play-ing with you?" I get up close and personal in the bitch's ear, like she is deaf or something, but she needs to hear loud and clear that I'm not on joke time.

"Daddy, I'm tired, my feet are hurting and so is my back. I told you not to buy these cheap-ass shoes from Payless," Nessa cries, as she stands with one hand on her hip while the other hand holds her strappy patent leather $9.99 buy-one-get-one-free high-heeled hooker shoe.

"Bitch, don't you ever back-talk me," I say, raising my hand like I'm gonna backhand her ass.

"I'll buy you whatever the fuck I want your ass to have. I run this show. You will wear, eat, say, and do whatever the hell I say. Is that understood, bitch?" I scream at her as I jack her ass up by the collar of her shirt.

It suddenly dawns on me: What the fuck is she doing wearing an oxford shirt in fucking July? I let go of her shirt and stand back to get a better view of her attire. Then I realize the bitch don't look like a hooker. Her ass is out on the ho stroll looking like a goddamn Sunday school teacher. I grab the ho by her hair weave, yanking her to my chest.

She cries, pleading, "Daddy, let go of me, please, Daddy, don't do this." She covers her head with her hand 'cause she knows I am about to go upside it. Man, I am mad as hell. Here it is hotter than the Fourth of July and this bitch is on the ho stroll in a mutherfucking long sleeve, pink oxford shirt, revealing absolutely no cleavage. I smack the bitch so hard, she falls to the ground. I stomp her ass with my black Timbs. I never rock the butter ones when I'm working 'cause I don't wanna scuff them shits up. Vanessa's ass is balled up in a knot, crying about how much she loves me and asking why am I treating her this way.

Then the bitch jumps up and begins running toward Broad Street. I know that if she gets away, I won't see her ass for a minute. Oh, she'll stay gone for a day or two, but she always finds her way back home to Daddy. The bitch needs me like a crackhead needs crack, like Kool-Aid needs sugar, and chitterlings need potato salad. Nessa couldn't survive the streets of Richmond without Big Daddy, 'cause for real, every ho needs a nigga like me. I made that bitch who she is today. If it wasn't for me, she'd be homeless, hungry, and ugly as a mutherfucker. Truth be told Nessa ain't all that pretty, but the bitch has the baddest body in Richmond, and she sucks a mean dick. She's five feet seven inches with a caramel complexion and a 36-24-36 shape. Yeah, she's a straight brick house. Her ass is so phat, I like to hit it from the back, doggy style, and man, oh man the bitch's pussy is vicious. Granted, Nessa has a white liver and loves to fuck, but nobody can hit that g-spot like me.

Nessa is running in and out of traffic. *Beep-beep-Beep*, cars are blowing their horns for her to get out of the street. The bitch is running like Flo Jo in the Summer Olympics. Then I realize she's heading toward the Slip at Shockoe. I don't know why but I keep running behind her. Since we aren't the type to hang in the Slip, I can't understand why Nessa is willing to die to get there. Maybe she knows a nigga there she can turn a quick trick with; whatever the reason, I ain't gonna stop chasing the bitch. Besides she's wearing the skirt I bought from Rainbow and the track of weave I got her ass from Ruby Red. If I have to snatch my shit off her ass, I will. The bitch is straight up disrespecting me; the more she runs the hotter I get.

When we get to the front door of the club, the bouncer motions for us to go in. Nessa is about two people in front of me, but he knows we're together. He's a big fat mutherfucker from Nine Mile Road. He used to do security at the convenience store over there, so I just nod and he knows what time it is. You see, he's tricked with Nessa before and he knows she's my ho. I give his fat ass a half smile as I look at him. I remember Nessa telling me how that nigga wanted her to put her finger in his ass. She told me she was able to get two fingers in at one time. She said that big nigga moaned in sheer delight as she shoved them shits in his ass. He must've been used to taking it in the rear. He paid Nessa $35 for a finger fuck. Now he standing at the door, acting like he the mutherfucking man and shit. I got no respect for da nigga. Nigga lets us in for free, 'cause he ain't want his secret to get out.

By the time I get in, Nessa is sitting at the bar. Her shoes are back on and her shirt tail is hanging out. I walk over to the bar and whisper in her ear, "It's okay, baby. Go fix yourself up." Nessa stands and walks toward the back to the restroom. I scope the room, seeing wall-to-wall drug dealers, a couple college cats, and a bunch of low-life bums who ain't doing shit with their lives except throwing them away. You can tell who the niggas from the streets are because they never dance; they just flex their gear, represent their hood, and nod their heads to a few rap songs. The college niggas is up dancing around to house music, that shit that Baltimore gets down with, and the slum-ass niggas, man, they whack asses is always on the dance floor at the Slip, dancing harder than the broads. Me, I just sit back and chill. I order me and Nessa a couple Alizés, and wait to see what's up.

When she returns from the back, she doesn't even look like the same ho. Nessa has wrapped her shirt around her waist and tied that mutherfucker in a perfect bow. I don't know what the fuck she did to the collar; she must've tucked that mutherfucker under or something cause that shit was gone. She's combed her weave out and that shit is looking jive sexy. Her lips are shining. I guess she borrowed some lip gloss from one of the chicks in the bathroom, 'cause I don't remember seeing any in her Dolce & Gabanna bag.

The Slip at Shockoe has an interesting set-up. There are tables and chairs for eating, a place in the back for taking pictures, and a small dance floor. There's a long glass mirror on the wall so people can look at themselves as they dance. I am sipping on my Alizé when suddenly I hear a nigga yelling, "Damn, man, that bitch is bad." As I turn to look, Nessa has taken over the dance floor. She is jamming with all eyes on her. I notice a lot of chicks standing and watching, trying to take in a few slut moves. Nessa works that ass like something you've never seen before. Her skirt is well above her hips and her ass and thong show every time she bends over. The DJ is spinning "Rump Shaker," the jam by Wreckx-N-Effect, and Nessa is making that songwriter proud. My shit gets hard just watching her move; Nessa's ass moves like waves in the ocean. I see a few niggas holding their dicks, as if they want to hit. Then I spot Turk.

Turk is a big-time drug dealer from Churchill. He gets paid out the yin-yang. Turk grew up in Mosby Court and had moved his family out to Chesterfield County, way out in the suburbs. He is pushing a 1993 Lexus Coupe and is dating the baddest hairdresser in town. Shit, with his drugs and her clientele, them niggas was getting paid. His girl, Lil Mo Sumptner, works at the salon on Second and

SEVEN

Leigh, near the spot where the prostitutes work. Her clientele is so big she works seven days a week, six A.M. to ten P.M. I wonder when the fuck did Turk have time to hit that. Lil Mo is bad, too; she's a short cutesy momma, about five feet one, 125 pounds, light-skinned with long silky hair, hazel eyes, and a nice round ass. She reminds me of the chick that played Ronnie in *Menace II Society*, except her hips and ass are a lil bit thicker. Niggas say she came to the city out of nowhere and hooked up with Turk in a matter of days. Don't nobody know where she came from, but I sure as hell knows where I want her ass to be. I wouldn't mind making her my ho, but Lil Mo got too much class for that. She would never trick, as fine as she is; she never would have a reason to.

"What up, dawg?" I say, walking over to Turk and smacking hands with him.

"Ain't nothing, playa. I see you still holding it down with the ol' girl and shit," he says, as he stretches his arm out so his ice can shine.

I don't know if he is asking a question or making a statement, so I just shoot back at him, "Yeah man, bitch ain't going nowhere, she getting it too good with me."

I poke my chest out proudly. I have to make it known that I am still holding it down on Second Street.

"So, dawg, my girl told me she be doing your hooker's hair?" he asked in a matter-of-fact tone.

"Yeah, Turk, yo people's jive all right. She be hooking Nessa up, helping to keep that money in my pocket, you feel me?"

By this time Nessa has walked over to us, with her hands in the air, snapping her fingers and moving her body just a little. I ask if she's ready to leave. She says no, 'cause she still needs to make my money. Turk asks me to step away for a minute. He says he has a proposition for me.

8

"Man, let me book yo ho for the night, her ass is phat to death, she got my dick harder than a rock," he says, grabbing his crotch and biting down on his bottom lip.

He looks hungry for Vanessa, and I intend to make sure Nessa is hungry for his ass, too. I ask how much he's paying for the night, and he says, "Five hundid and I'll even stop the bitch by McDonald's in the morning."

"Bet, but I have to go lay down the rules with her. Meet us around the corner by First Virginia Bank on Main Street."

I stroll off real hard, like I'm the hardest nigga in the Slip at Shockoe. Walking over to Nessa, I outline the plans for the rest of her evening.

"Nessa, baby, don't fuck this one up, this is big money right here. If you fuck him good, I guarantee he'll be back for more." I say this with a serious look, nodding my head straight up and down to let her ass know that fucking up isn't an option.

"Damn, his girl be doing my hair and now I gotta go fuck her man? Oh, well, ain't like I don't do this shit every day," Nessa says as she licks her lips with excitement.

"Oh, and one last thing, Nessa. Give him the Vanessa Del Rio tonight. His fine black chocolate ass is worth it, and them pockets are tight. Shit, if I wasn't straight pussy, I would probably fuck him myself," I say half-jokingly.

"Girl, you are so crazy. I'll see you in the morning." She blows me a sexy kiss and steps off.

"What the fuck did you just call me?" I ask as if she has called me something that I'm not.

"Sorry, I meant Big Daddy." Her left shoulder flinches in fear as she apologizes.

"Oh, I ain't gonna hit you. Just make sure you don't ever call me *girl* again, you feel me?"

"Yeah, Big Daddy," she answers.

"All right, now go make my mutherfucking money, bitch! And remember. Swallow it!"

TWO

IT IS TEN the next morning when my alarm clock goes off. I turn over to see the sunshine coming in from the bedroom window. Nessa is nowhere to be found. I jump out of bed, find my way to the bathroom, brush my teeth, and splash water on my face. I throw on a pair of old denims and a T-shirt and make my way downstairs. Momma is in the kitchen, sitting at the table reading the newspaper, without her usual cup of coffee.

"What up, Mom? Why you ain't got no coffee?" I ask as if I don't know the answer.

" 'Cause we ain't got no goddamn money to get no food, let alone mutherfucking coffee," she shoots back at me.

"Well, as soon as Nessa gets here, I'm gonna go shopping and get my favorite girl some coffee and danishes," I say as I peep out the kitchen window.

"Oh, Nessa called. She said she was on her way." As my mother gives me the message, she never looks up from the newspaper.

"I'll be sitting on the porch waiting on her. Call me if you need me."

I throw on my socks, grab my Adidas flip-flops, and pull the door closed behind me so the cool air blowing from the fans won't escape. In the pj's we don't have air-conditioning, and you can only get the window kind if someone in your house has a medical problem. Ain't nobody in my house sick, so we just shit outta luck. I sit on the porch, gazing into the hot-ass fog. At only 10:15 it's already

90 degrees. I think about staying in today, but there's money to be made, and I need some coca.

I get up and walk up the block to see who is out hustling this bright early morning. I want to wait on Nessa so we can get our shot on together, but she's taking too damn long. I find La-La in the cut and book some boy from him. La-La's the most committed project hustler I know. He seems to work twenty-four/seven; it's just a matter of time before that nigga becomes a millionaire. He's smart because he saves his money. He is frugal with his spending, still rocking Lee jeans and K-Swiss sneakers, but for real, everybody knows that nigga getting paid. He doesn't buy cars, jewelry, and clothes like most niggas do when they getting paper. Whenever somebody asks what the fuck he doing with his money, the nigga always say, "Saving for a rainy day."

Well, today it ain't raining. It is sunshine outside like a mutherfucker, and I need to get high real fast. I have a $100-a-day coke habit. La-La usually lets me book when I don't have the funds straight up. I pull out my ace of spade card from my back pocket, he lays some shit out for me, and I get busy. I snort so much that my mutherfucking nose starts bleeding, but it feels good just to get high. My shit starts getting hard; I always get horny when I snort good coke. I can't wait to fuck the shit out of Nessa when she gets home.

I walk back down the block and wait on the front porch. By the time she pulls up, I am so fucking high that I don't even see whose car she gets out of. All I see is the Mickey D's bag she grippin'. Nessa comes running up to me, waving a blue torn-off piece of paper.

"Turk gave me his car phone and pager number; he told me to call him whenever I need to be fucked by a real nigga," she says while shaking the paper in my face like she's just won a scratch-off ticket from the Virginia Lottery. I smack the bitch's hand away from my grill.

"Bitch, carry yo ass upstairs and take a bath," I order.

"But Daddy, I already took a shower at the hotel," Nessa said, standing there looking like she's surprised or offended that she was being ordered to take another one.

"All right then," she says. "I'll take a birdbath just to ease your mind." Shittt, Nessa knows I don't like touching her unless she is extra clean. But then again, who am I fooling—just how clean can a trick bitch get?

"I'll be done in a minute, and then I'll tell you all about my night." I didn't care to hear about her fuck session last night. As long as I had my loot, I didn't give a rat's ass about what happened with her and Turk. My business is to put her ass to work, that's it, that's all, but she always feels obligated to give me blow-by-blow details, especially when it comes to the big-time drug dealer customers like Turk.

Before climbing the stairs, Nessa hands me a thousand dollars. She says Turk paid double for me trusting him enough to put the money in her hand. Trusting my ho and my clients is all part of the game. The way I see it, if you let your ho think she has a little power, then the bitch will stay happy and keep the ends flowing, and if you don't make your clients pay up front, they more than likely will give a fat-ass tip. And if either one of 'em fucks up, then that's when Big Daddy is gonna have to bust a cap in somebody's ass. Hey, but that's just my way. Every nigga has his own way of running they shit. I kick $200 to Moms to go grocery shopping; that way I can get my swirl on while she's out of the crib.

"Hey, baby, you all right?" I ask Nessa, pulling her close to me and stroking the back of her hair.

"Yeah, I'm good. What about you, Daddy? Did you miss me at all?" Nessa asks as she leads me to the bedroom. She knows what time it is. It's time for her to take care of Big Daddy. She is back at Daddy's house, and it is time for me to get mine. She jumps in the bathtub and in less than ten minutes she's out. I am chilling, laid back on the bed, coked up out of my fucking mind, waiting to be sucked and fucked by the best ho in town, and those ten minutes are five minutes too long.

I lay Nessa on her stomach, so the sun is shining through the bedroom window on her big round voluptuous ass. I rub her butt; her ass is beautiful, like a work of art. It's just as beautiful as the painting of Mona Lisa. I start kissing and squeezing her booty. She lays stretched out, spread eagle, her face down. Then I get on top of her; I want to feel her phat ass on my shit. I massage her back as I hump up and down on her ass. My shit is pulsating, as I make slow circular moves. The shit feels so good, I want to come, but I can't 'cause I haven't put my dick on yet, and if I come without my strap on, then I am just another bitch. I reach over to the nightstand and pull out my dark black dick and strap it on.

Nessa gets on her knees in the doggy-style position, and I stick my dick in her asshole and start fucking. I'm feeling good as shit, my head is tilted back farther than a Cadillac seat. I think I'm in heaven, and if heaven is this good, then I know goddamn well I ain't wanna go to hell. Nessa is working that ass like the professional she is. I pull my dick out and Nessa sucks it as I watch her lick my pussy secretions on the ten-inch friend that I bought from the X-rated shop at Belvidere and Broad. I tell Nessa to turn over and spread her legs. Nessa's clitoris looks old and worn out, 'cause she has been fucked by well over three hundred men, but I don't care; there is something about her pussy that I just can't get enough of. I slide my tongue inside and begin to lick; she tightens her pussy muscles, which excites me more. I rub her breast as I eat her out.

Nessa moans and cries out, "Oh, Daddy, I love you, I love you," with her eyes rolled to the back of her head. The more she talks, the more I want her.

I say, "Yeah, bitch, say my name," as I shove my middle finger into her pussy. Nessa then pulls me up and flips me over on my back; she begins sucking my chest. 'Cause for real, I'm a nigga. I ain't got no mutherfucking titties, let's keep it real. She straddles across me and begins bumping her pussy against mine. My shit is throbbing, I want to come but I'm still not ready. I want more. Nessa slides off me and starts giving me head. The bitch licks my shit like nobody has ever licked it before, not even her. She presses down on my midsection with one hand, like I'm gonna try to raise up and run or something. Sheeett, run from this? Man, I ain't going nowhere!

We stand up and walk over to the window. I tell Nessa to put both hands on the windowsill and to back that thing up for me. She bends over and I drop to the floor and start eating her asshole. I spread her butt cheeks and stick my tongue in and out, in and out, as Nessa works that ass in slow motion. I grab my dick again, strap on, but this time I hit the pussy from the back door. I hook my arms underneath her until they land on her shoulders. I'm tearing that ass up! I raise the shade all the way up, so the sun will shine in. In the pj's we don't have mini-blinds, just one shade that stretches across the whole window. We are butt-ball naked, fucking in front of the window. Man, I am fucking the shit out of Nessa; she leans on the glass with her left hand while her right leg is propped up on the radiator. The radiator in the pj's is always by the window. The radiator used to get hot as a bitch in the winter, but it serves as a good ass prop in the summer. I start coming; my body starts shaking and jerking, and I moan in a masculine tone, "NOW, BITCH, NOW." I snatch the strap from around my waist, and Nessa turns, drops to her knees, and starts eating my nut. Her head is buried between my legs as I stand with them spread apart. I grab onto her hair and look down at her while she pleases Big Daddy. My cum shoots out like water from a faucet. I come all over her face.

When she's finished licking, she gets up from her knees and we both lean against the window, our bodies pressed against the glass. Nessa rolls a joint and laces it with coke; we smoke it while watching the neighborhood wake up. It's now two o'clock and people are starting to come out of the house. Kids are riding bicycles, and La-La has moved his operation down the block near my crib. I look into the street, and suddenly, there is Momma holding a brown paper bag in her hand and looking up at my bedroom window while Mr. Arnold, who charges less than Yellow Cab for a ride to and from the grocery store, stands outside his van, looking up at us with a perverted smile on his face. We've been caught; we are still standing butt-ball naked, in the window, in the middle of the day, in the sunshine.

THREE

TIME FLIES FAST when you're having fun. Half the day is gone and I need to get to the mall to get something fly to wear for tonight. I tell Nessa to run my bathwater. Then I call La-La to tell that nigga I'm gonna have to pay my tab later. That nigga told me this morning I owed him six hundred. Fuck that nigga, I ain't bout to pay up when all I got is $800 in my pocket. I'm going shopping. The new Jordans came out today, and I have to get me a pair. I have this bitch name Ayanna who works at Foot Locker in Cloverleaf Mall holding them for me. That bitch be jockeying me hard. I thought about asking her ass to use her discount, but I ain't really trying to fuck with her like that 'cause bitches be getting too attached. I told Nessa's ass last night, she wasn't getting a mutherfucking thing, and I still mean that shit!

I step into the bathroom and Nessa is standing in the tub waiting to wash Big Daddy off. I step in and sit down. The bitch has my water a little colder than usual, but I figure I'll let it slide, since she worked so hard last night. Nessa grabs the Dial soap and starts washing my back. She tosses around a few bubbles, trying to be playful, but I'm really not in the mood for no goddamn rub-a-dub-dub two-bitches-in-the-tub type shit. I am thinking about where we're gonna work tonight. The races are still in town, so I know the ho stroll on Second will be slow. I stand up for Nessa to wash between my legs. As she is scrubbing me down, she's telling me how beautiful I am. I get mad and smash her face with my soap-filled hand, and the bitch's head hits the back of the wall. I've told Nessa's ass numerous times not to talk to me like I'm a bitch, but she keeps forgetting that shit.

See, my looks be throwing muh-fuckers off. I'm five feet eight inches, 160 pounds, medium brown, with long hair and chestnut-colored eyes. People say I look like Spinderella, Salt-N-Pepa's DJ, so niggas be asking me all the time why I like pussy. They say I can probably get any man I want if I learn to be feminine. I tell them niggas that pussy is all I know. I'm twenty-three years young, and I ain't never had a dick in my life. Never wanted any. I been liking pussy ever since Momma used to leave me over the next-door neighbor's house. I was about eleven and Cookie was twenty. Momma used to be hanging out at that goddamn Devil's Nite Club and shit. Cookie was bad as hell. She had a baby and a six-year-old daughter by this nigga that sold heroin. Them mutherfuckers used to hide the dope in the baby's Pampers and push the stroller up and down the street, using the baby to transport. The Feds got hip and caught the nigga Tom one day with the baby and locked his ass up, and Child Protective Services took the lil shorties away. Only way that bitch Cookie kept her project was 'cause she had breast cancer and shit.

Anyway, she used to keep me when Momma would go out. One night she was crying and shit, talking about how she missed Tom. She told me to get in bed with her, and before I knew it, she was kissing all over my innocent little body. She told me we was playing mommies and daddies. I told her I was too old for that doll-baby shit. I was young, but I wasn't stupid. Man, Cookie turned my young ass out. By the time I was thirteen, I was head over heels in love with her ass. She was the one who taught me how to eat pussy. She used to demonstrate on her little girl's It's Alive doll baby. CPS had left the little white cracker doll behind. Then one night, she made me put this fake dick in her pussy; the shit was pink plastic and battery operated. She came all over the muh-fucker. Then she stuck her middle finger in her pussy, pulled it out, and told me to sniff then taste it. I sniffed it and then I sucked her cum off her finger. I been hooked on pussy ever since.

We was kicking it till I was bout fifteen. Then one day I saw this nigga coming out of her house and I got mad as hell. I knocked on the door and asked Cookie who that nigga was and she told me that he was her new sugar daddy. Man, I was so mad, I had smoke coming out my ears. That muh-fucker was bout fifty years old, with gray hair and a big-ass potbelly. I couldn't believe she was fucking round on me for that old-ass nigga. I grabbed her by her hair and punched her in the face. She grabbed the broom and started swinging that mutherfucker at me. Man, we was going hard. I was slinging her ass all around the living room, knocking over and breaking up some of that expensive shit that Tom had put in her crib. The next thing I know, that old nigga came running back in the house, and him and Cookie tried to bank me. I was handling mine, until Momma came and broke the shit up. When Momma asked why I was fighting Cookie, I told her that Cookie had been fucking with me since I was eleven. Momma was ticked off, so she reported her ass to CPS. Then, about a week later, Cookie died. She ain't never get locked up for sexing me, although they was investigating her ass.

So for real, I can't stand for a muh-fucker to talk that "you're pretty" shit to me. That's why I keep my hair cornrowed straight to the back, or pulled back in a slick-ass ponytail like them niggas on the West Coast. I wear my jeans big and baggy and my shirts triple X. Yeah, I stay rough and ragged, just like the average nigga out here. Niggas better know what time it is.

I jump out the tub, throw my jean shorts back on, and tell Nessa to get dressed. I have to get to Cloverleaf before that broad in Foot Locker puts them Jordans back. I decided while Nessa was washing me off that tonight we gon' go up on Broad Street and Allen Avenue. I really ain't wanna go there, 'cause that's transvestites' turf, but what the hell, I heard the block was hot. They say a lot of straight niggas, hustlers, and out-of-town muh-fuckers be rolling through, paying punks to suck their dicks. I like Second and Broad 'cause straight women work that block. I really ain't tryna be round no mutherfucking niggas selling their asses, but my clients are all busy at the track, watching cars crash and shit. So, whatever is whatever.

I'M RUSHING and shit trying to get up the block before Mr. Arnold leaves with the van. Nessa is behind me, moving slow like a mutherfucking turtle again. It never ceases to amaze me; it always seems like I have to put my foot in her ass for that bitch to get some energy behind her. My shorts keep falling down, 'cause I ain't ever liked wearing belts. I keep yelling behind me, "Keep up, bitch, don't make me miss this muh-fucking ride."

When we get to the top of the hill, everybody is out on the strip, all the hustlers, hoochie mommas, and junkies. There's a crowd around La-La, who has just finished beating the fuck outta this young dude who works for him, name Smitty. I heard Smitty fucked up another package and now was five g's in the hole. I ain't have time to stay and watch that shit. Besides, I done seen that nigga

La-La beat plenty niggas' ass. He don't fuck around when it comes to his scratch.

We catch Mr. Arnold just in time.

"Yo, Mr. A, I'll break you off a dove if you take us over Southside to the mall," I say as I'm walking over to him.

Mr. A heads toward the van, walking lopsided and shit, and says, "Shit, I'll do it for free if she sucks my dick; there's plenty of room in the van, you know."

I laugh at his old ring worm-having ass, then I tell him, "Nah, Mr. A, a blow job is gonna cost you fifty dollars."

"But I don't have fifty dollars, Demetria. I haven't made that much money today playing taxi," he says as he pulls both pockets inside out.

"Man, let's go." I brush him off 'cause Mr. A was starting to act like I was supposed to feel sorry for him 'cause he ain't have no money to trick with. I open the passenger doors for me and Nessa to get in the van.

I pull out a dove and hand it to him. "Here you go, Mr. A, twenty dollars for the ride, and when you get the money for a blow job, let me know, all right?"

"Demetria, keep the twenty dollars, and let me pay you thirty dollars later." He starts begging. I push the money back at him.

"Nah, Mr. A, I'm not booking my ho's blow jobs, so stop tripping and drive the van." I kinda yell at him 'cause I'm starting to get pissed off with him. That old nigga must be crazy, fuck he thinks he gonna get his dick sucked for credit. The entire ride to Cloverleaf Mall we have to listen to this nigga try to sing the O'Jays and Temptations. The nigga is whining and shit; he sounds more like Keith Sweat. That old gimp-leg mutherfucker is getting on my nerves. He pulls up to the front of the mall and turns down his music and says, "Do you want me to wait for y'all?"

"Hell NO!" I scream at him and jump out of the van. "Come on," I say to Nessa. "We all right," I tell Mr. A, knowing I didn't have us a ride back, but ain't no way I was bout to listen to that noise for another minute.

The mall is jam-packed. It's Saturday, and everybody is out shopping for club gear. I walk through the mall, checking out the gals and shit. I'm well known in the city. Everybody knows me, 'cause I am the baddest butch they have ever seen. I am smooth with my shit. Bitches come up to me, trying to strike up conversations just to get up on me. Lot of muh-fuckers have been asking am I all right since my baby bro was killed a year ago.

I run into my nigga, Rome. Rome is running shit over Hillside Court; nigga has the coke and heroin market on lock. Shorty is one of the thoroughest niggas in Richmond without a doubt. If he tells his crew to kill a nigga, they ask, "Should we kill the nigga's family, too?" That nigga's presence alone can shut a whole mutherfucking block down. Rome walks over to me, with bout five niggas trailing behind him and shit like he's John Gotti.

"S'up, dawg?" he asks, reaching out his hand to show me love.

"Ain't nothing. Chilling," I respond, grabbing hold of his hand and throwing my chest up against his.

"You all right? Heard anything? You know I still got you," Rome says, reminding me of the conversation we had at my brother's funeral. Nigga told me outside Manning Funeral Home that if I had to go to war with the chump that killed my lil bro, he had my back.

"Nah, Shorty, niggas still ain't talking, but I'm straight," I say, giving him an easy answer 'cause I ain't wanna look weak to another nigga.

"All right then, you know where I'm at if you need me," he says as he and his men walk off.

But for real, shit ain't been the same. I started getting high after KaQuanza was murdered. I'm still tryna find out who killed him, and when I do, I'ma smoke the nigga like a Newport. Muh-fuckers ain't talking. You know how that shit goes. Niggas be on some ol' bitch type shit. Even niggas you fuck with, they be knowing shit, but they be too scared to get involved. Man, I miss my lil nigga, me and that nigga was getting paid together and niggas couldn't handle that shit. Young dude and a female? Niggas wasn't having it. So some jealous-type muh-fucker figured they had to put a stop to us. They caught him out one night in the cut and blew his head off. Niggas was saying that whoever blasted him was mad 'cause he won all the nigga's money shooting crap that day and was talking shit.

I hate thinking about that shit, man, makes me wanna lose it, but I gotta stay strong for Moms. I been holding it down for me and Moms, 'cause she can't get no assistance since I'm too old. I had a nice stash put away, over twenty-five g's but I went through that shit so fast it ain't funny. Then Momma made me promise I wouldn't sell drugs again. I stopped selling, 'cause she was all stressed out and shit and seeing a shrink. That's when I came up with my new hustle, selling this ho bitch behind me that's still walking muther-fucking slow.

"Bitch, what the fuck is wrong with you? Pick up your goddamn feet." I turn to see what the fuck Nessa is doing. I am halfway down the mall and that bitch is behind me window-shopping.

"Daddy, I'm walking as fast as I can. I'm trying to find me a dress for tonight," she says as she peeps in the window of Victoria's Secret.

"You gonna spend your own damn money 'cause I ain't buying you shit. The next time a Mexican mutherfucker come up to you, you gon' remember this here shit," I say, pointing my finger toward the floor as if the shit last night happened at Cloverleaf Mall.

I step into Foot Locker and notice Ayanna behind the cash register. As I walk over to her, she starts grinning from ear to ear.

"Hey, Mommie, what's happening?" I ask, flirting with her.

"You, that's what's up," she says with a sexy look. Her coworker, an ugly chick in need of a fresh perm and a facial, gives her a look like, *I know you ain't feeling another bitch*, and walks off. Ayanna puts her head down as if she's embarrassed. I reach behind the counter, lean over, pull her chin up, look her dead in the eye, and say, "Mommie, your coworker bugging. She's the same ugly bitch that tried to give me her number when I saw her undercover ass in Colors, the gay spot downtown. She hating on you, baby girl, that's all." I let go of her chin and raise back up.

Ayanna starts laughing while Nessa stands there with her hands on her hips, watching us kick it like she owns me or something. I pay for the Air Jordans and get a Chicago Bulls jersey. I stop by Cavalier's and cop a pair of jean shorts. Nessa buys herself a sexy black minidress from Limited Express. She says she gonna work that mutherfucker to death. Since we're going on new grounds, we both know she has to be on point.

We get something to eat from the food court and just as we're about to leave the mall, we run into Lil Mo. She is looking good. She has on a pair of stop-traffic Tommy Hilfiger coochie cutters and a Tommy halter top. Them muh-fucking shorts are squeezing her thighs so tight, I think that any moment her circulation is gonna be cut off in her legs. Every nigga in the mall that walks by stops dead in they tracks to look at her fine ass. Man, shorty is rocking a pair of white on white Flavs. Flavs are Nike sneakers. The niggas in Richmond named 'em Flavs 'cause you can get them in all types of colors. White on white, white with blue stripe, white with yellow, white with green, or whatever. Niggas up north don't know nuthing about Flavs. That's Richmond, Virginia's shit. We've been rocking them muh-fucking Nikes for bout 150 years. Lil Mo walks over to holler at us since Nessa is her client and shit.

"Hey, Nessa, what's up?" she asks, looking at me but talking to Nessa.

"Ain't nothing, girl. Me and my man in here shopping for tonight," Nessa says, holding that goddamn Dolce & Gabanna bag under her arm like somebody wants to steal it or something.

"You know the club on Broad Street reopens tonight," Lil Mo asks, or makes a statement. It reminded me of my conversation with her nigga Turk. Them mutherfuckers be talking stupid and shit. You fuck around with them, you don't know if they asking you or telling you something.

"Yeah, shorty," I jump in, 'cause I don't plan on being in the mall all night talking to Lil Mo's ass. "Are you talking about Ivory's?" I ask her directly. See, I know how to phrase a muh-fucking question. I don't know what the fuck her and Turk be doing.

"Yeah, baby, Ivory's, just like the soap, and I'm gonna get my man tonight 'cause Turk ass is out of town and I'm on vacation for a week," she says, skipping around like she's in a reggae video or something. I'm checking shorty out, and it is obvious she is interested.

"Well, we might check it out if we ain't doing nothing," Nessa says, though she knows damn well her ass is gonna be busy even if I'm not.

Lil Mo offers us a ride back to the pj's, and I accept. She's pushing a 1993 Silver Isuzu Rodeo, and the broad has replaced the wheel cover on the back of the truck with a spray-painted picture of Turk. I think to myself, This is some 'Bama ass shit right here. No wonder muh-fuckers be thinking Richmond country and shit. Muh-fuckers like this give the city a bad name.

I jump in the backseat, 'cause after that shit with my lil bro, I just don't trust anybody, so I never ride shotgun, no matter who the fuck I'm riding with. Rule in the streets, you don't ride shotgun with people you don't know well enough to trust. Lil Mo pumps up the AC and cranks up the sound system. She plays "Baby Got Back" by Sir Mix-A-Lot, and her and Nessa have some type of girly competition, singing, ".I like big butts and I cannot lie, you other brothers can't deny . . ."

Lil Mo is humping up and down while holding onto the steering wheel. Then she raises up out of her seat and starts shaking her ass while driving. I laugh to myself 'cause I know she's putting on a rodeo show for Big Daddy. I sit up and peep over Nessa's seat to see if the truck is an automatic. I get my answer, then sit back and slide down in the chair, thinking to myself, Yeah, this bitch can drive a stick.

FOUR

I GIVE NESSA a serious pep talk before we get to Broad and Allen. I hold her chin in my hand, look her dead in the eye without blinking, and say, "Look here, Nessa, I'm not putting up with that slow-walking shit tonight. You better strut yo ass like you're a mutherfucking runway model or else I'ma beat your ass down to the mutherfucking ground out that mutherfucker! Now do you understand?" I let go of her chin after giving the bitch her last and final warning.

I'm rocking my new shit, and Nessa has on the tight black minidress and a pair of sexy-ass black sandals with stiletto heels that she purchased from Saxon Shoes. We reach our destination, and, man, there are so many transvestites out there it is unbelievable. Them niggas is looking better than the average bitch. But I don't give a fuck what anybody says, a nigga should still be able to tell a nigga from a bitch. Straight up! Niggas be using that shit for an excuse to get they gay on. Talking about they couldn't tell the difference.

I stand back on the wall and wait for the show to begin. Nessa blows me a sexy kiss like she always does before showtime. Before I know it, Nessa is strutting down the block like Julia Roberts in *Pretty*

Woman. Her legs are long and sensual, and her phat ass is bouncing and behaving. She looks good enough to eat and tempting enough to swallow. I stand back, half cover my mouth with my hand, and yell, "That's right, baby, make that muh-fucking money for Daddy, get that money, baby."

A black Mercedes-Benz pulls up. Nessa sticks her head in the car and says a few words to the driver, who is a middle-aged black man dressed in a suit and hat. She turns to me and nods the okay signal. I jot down his license plate number in case Nessa turns up dead or something. They pull off; I stand on the wall and wait while checking out the other prostitutes. I have to give them niggas they props; cars are rolling up left and right. Hustlers, white men, black men, and a few college cats even walk up on foot. Them niggas is turning tricks right in the alley. I'm chilling; Nessa has thirty minutes to be back.

About then I see this shim out there named Shanté. I know Shanté from Richmond City Jail. Our paths crossed 'cause they put that nigga in the wrong holding cell at the lockup. They thought he was a girl and shit. Shanté turned a few niggas' ass out in jail. Niggas caught him up under the sheets with William Braxton. Big Willie had just gotten knocked off for killing two niggas outside the twenty-four-hour McDonald's on Broad. That gangsta nigga killed the muh-fuckers, then said, Fuck it. He sat on the curb and waited for 5-0 to come get him. He was fucking Shanté while he was waiting to be transferred to a maximum-security prison. Shanté spots me and comes over to talk.

"Hey, baby, long time no see," he says, all the while twisting and poking his ass out for the cars riding by.

"Word," I answer, trying to keep the conversation short and simple. I wasn't out there to be lollygagging. I was out there to get paid; I didn't have time to be fucking with Shanté.

"I'm just waiting on my Saturday night special," he says. Shanté looks good. His real name is Sam Oliver Brown. That S.O.B. is bout five feet ten, 210 pounds. He wears a long red dress and red hooker shoes: red plastic criss-cross type strap across the front and a fat-ass three-and-a-half-inch-wedge heel. His hair is up in a French roll, and he's wearing this "fuck me" red lipstick.

"Is that right?" I say, trying to be polite, but I am already feeling uneasy with Shanté all up in my space.

"Oops, got to go," he says and takes off running to this white Honda Accord.

I look to see who his client is and I be damn, if it wasn't La-La then my goddamn name ain't Demetria. I check the license plate and the tag starts off with an R, which means rental. Mutherfucking La-La has been hitting faggots. I start tripping 'cause I think about what my cousin Melody said about him. She had told me that their sex life wasn't hitting on two cents. La-La has been fucking with my cousin for about five years and is hustling out of her house in the pj's. She only puts up with the nigga 'cause he keeps her hair and nails done and supports her dope habit.

Nessa comes back and passes me our first $75 of the night.

"Hey, baby, did everything go okay?" I ask.

"No, that tight-shirt-wearing-ass schoolteacher only tipped me five dollars," Nessa says while standing with her hands on her hip and her face balled up in a knot.

"What service did he get and how do you know he a school-teacher?" I ask 'cause it was obvious her ass wanted me to.

"He paid for a blow job and a golden shower, and I know he's a teacher 'cause his little dick ass taught me sixth grade," Nessa says.

"Did you piss on the nigga?"

"Nope, I sucked that little dick and he came within two minutes. Then we waited for about ten minutes for me to work up some urine. When it was time for me to pee on him, I straddled him and sat on his dick. But as soon as I starting peeing, I jumped off his dick so fast, you would've thought lightning struck my ass. Piss ran all down the seat of the car. That limp-dick nigga was trying to lick the piss up from the leather interior," Nessa says, imitating the man. I'm bout to die laughing out that mutherfucker. Then I smack her on her ass and tell her get back to work.

The next car that drives up is a pretty red Corvette with a black ragtop. A white man in his thirties wearing a baseball cap with long stringy hair hidden underneath is driving, and a punk-rock-looking female is on the passenger side.

"Two goes for a hundred dollars straight up." I walk over and force my head in the car. I have to get involved with them complicated-type situations. "What you want?"

"My girlfriend wants to eat her out, and I want her to suck my dick," the man says, sure of himself.

"Okay, but no extra shit. Nessa, do you understand that this is a one-at-a-time?" I ask just to be clear, 'cause sometimes Nessa's ass be getting amnesia and shit.

"Yeah, I got it," Nessa answers as she squeezes her way in between the couple, landing sideways on the white girl's lap.

"All right then, everybody listen up." I squat down low so I can be at eye level with them. "This is how it's going down. Nessa, you gon' let this white chick eat you out first, then you gone give ol' boy the best blow job he ever had in his life." I pause for a moment, 'cause I need to be sure they asses is listening to what the fuck I'm saying. When I realize all six eyeballs on me, I continue on like I am coaching a Little League baseball team. "Look here, gang, I'm serious as a heart attack about this one-at-a-time deal. There will be no muh-fucking double-teaming, gang banging, getting in the bed for any reason, no penetration, no titty sucking, ass licking, none of that, this here is not a mutherfucking ménage-a-trois type deal! Mat-o-fact, fuck it. Nessa, I want you to stand up while the bitch eats you and, player, you gon' stand up while Nessa sucks your dick. I'm telling you now, dude," I say, and nod my head back and forth to let 'em know I ain't playing, "if you want a fucking threesome tonight, it's two hundred dollars. If not, follow my rules, 'cause if you try to run game, I'll find your redneck ass and slit yo throat. You got it, buddy?"

"Yes, sir." the white man salutes me like I'm a sergeant in the United States Army.

I pat the hood of the car and order, "Be gone."

Nessa comes back in about forty-five minutes. She hands me $100 in small bills.

"Daddy, them crackers was crazy as hell. They drove me around the corner to their house on Cary Street."

"Is that right?"

"Yeah, and when we got inside, the chick turned on some heavy metal music and started jumping up and down like she was fucking crazy. I told her ass I didn't have all night. Daddy, that bitch dropped to her knees and said, 'Spread 'em open, you sexy black bitch,' " Nessa says, walking back and forth trying to keep up her pace.

"What happened next?"

"So, I stood with my legs far apart and when that bitch starting eating me, I felt something sharp on my clit. It was her tongue ring. I was about to tell her she had to take it out if she wanted to eat me, but before I could even say 'eat me,' the bitch had thrown the ring across the room. She looked up at me with them dark-ass mascara eyes and said, 'I've been waiting all my life to taste dark meat.' Uhm, uhm, uhm. Daddy, that bitch ate me out so good, my goddamn knees buckled. I had to take a break before sucking her boyfriend's dick," Nessa says, fanning herself 'cause the memory was just that hot.

"Did you take good care of ol' boy?" I ask. I need to know if we have made a lifetime customer.

"Oh, yes, I did. I sucked it so good, the skin peeled off that tiny pink mutherfucker. They said they didn't have any extra money to tip tonight, but asked if I could provide services to them on a regular and said we could stop by his store on Monday if we need anything."

Nessa hands me the man's business card; he is a general manager at Kinko's. I toss the card in my back pocket, thinking, What the fuck does he think I need a photocopy of?

The next car that rolls up is a young black cat in his early twenties. Nessa struts over to the car, makes a sharp turn to show him her rear end, then swings back around and leans, asking, "You think you could handle this, baby boy?" He's pushing a black Acura Legend, with tinted windows and chromed-out wheels. His windows are rolled down so you can hear the bass from his stereo. He's blasting "Nuthin' but a 'G' Thang" by Dr. Dre. The nigga is leaning to the side and bopping his head off track five of the Chronic. When he opens his mouth to talk, his gold teeth sparkle.

He whispers, "I want the total package."

Nessa jumps in, and I yell, "One hour." It is already ten P.M. and Nessa is rolling. I walk over to the Exxon Gas Station to get me a pack of Newports, a Snickers bar, and a Mountain Dew. It's gonna be a long night and I need a sugar rush to keep my ass up.

As I cross the street, I see Shanté getting out of the Honda. I'm tearing open the pack of cigarettes with my mouth, and by that time I am right up on the car. La-La's eyes meet mine, and that nigga speeds off: *Screeeech*. He has to be pushing eighty down Broad Street. I go back to the alley to wait for Nessa. Shanté comes over.

"Heyyy, I'm about to roll out," Shanté says while tucking his money into his bra.

"Damn, so soon." I try to give da nigga a blank statement so he'll keep it moving.

"Hmm, after my Saturday night special, I'm done," he says while sounding all lisp tongue and shit.

"Oh yeah?" I shoot back. I didn't want to ask shit about La-La but I felt a story coming. One thing's for sure, if you fuck a shim, them muh-fuckers gon' tell it sooner or later, and one thing about it, they don't ever lie on a nigga's ass.

"Hmm." He sucks his teeth. "You see that nigga I was with? He picks me up every Saturday night at the same time, and we go to the hotel on Chamberlain across from Burger King. And trust me, I lets the nigga have it his way." He strokes his hair and continues. "Baby, I gets four hundred dollars a whop. Oh yes, baby, that nigga fucks the shit out of me. I asked him if I could hit him one time, but he don't trade off." Shanté rubs up and down his girlish figure, straightening up his tight-fitting body dress.

"See ya." He waves good-bye and heads toward Feldens, where each and every Saturday night the drag queens perform. He was sashaying like Naomi Campbell on the runway. I thought about hiring him to give Nessa some touch-up lessons, but I just flat-out refuse to pay a nigga to show a bitch how to work it.

It's now eleven and Nessa's ass isn't back. Broad Street has a party atmosphere. Cars are going up and down, back and forth. I see the same cars ride by me so many times that I get dizzy as hell just from being out there. Carload after carload of muh-fuckers is making they way to Ivory's. My pager goes off with a 5-0 code. I know then that the gold tooth–wearing nigga that Nessa left with was the po-po. I jog over to Exxon to the pay phone, only to realize that there ain't a phone in the cradle. So I walk down to Mickey D's to use the phone out there. I close the door to the booth behind me and call Momma.

"Ma, what up?" I ask, knowing very damn well what time it is.

"You know, don't play games with me, Dee," Mom says, sounding irritated and sleepy. "That girl said come get her first thing Monday morning. She said her bail is three thousand dollars, which mean you ain't got to pay but three hundred dollars to get her out."

"Tell Nessa if she calls back that she ain't make three hundred dollars tonight, and even if she did, her commission is only twenty percent. So tell her ass I said to turn a couple tricks with some of them RoboCop guards like she did last time to get up the money to get her slew-foot ass out."

"You don't make no damn sense. Every time that gal gets locked up, you leave her in there for days and weeks at a time when she could be out there tricking for you," Momma says. Momma is overstepping her boundaries by getting in my business.

"Ma, I'm gone, just tell her what I said if they let her call back."

"All right then, and what time are you coming home?"

I hang up when Momma asks that question. I don't like it when Momma asks me about my business. My business is my business. Shit, I don't be all in her business when she's at that goddamn Purple Pit Nite Club acting like she's fucking sweet sixteen and shit. Wearing them short-ass miniskirts with them ugly-ass knocked knees.

I decide to go check out Ivory's to see what all the hype is about. I walk down Broad, and bitches are yelling and shit out the car at me like I'm Denzel Washington.

"Hey, Dee, Dee baby, what's up?"

I'm walking cooler than a penguin on ice. When I walk, I glide. I just know I'm the baddest mutherfucker in Richmond and nobody can tell me shit. I'm gonna take that club by storm. I tell myself on the way there that I am gonna run that mutherfucker. I'm used to going to gay clubs, but tonight is different. Every hustler, hood rat, killer, baller, skeezer, hoochie, player, nobody, and everybody from every project in Richmond is gonna be in that mutherfucker 'cause Armani's is closed, and I'm prepared to make Ivory's my own.

The line extends down the sidewalk. I notice the bouncer from the Slip at Shockoe working the door. He sees me and motions for me to come to the front of the line. I walk past the crowd, pimping and shit like I got clout. This punk nigga in the back of the line mouths some ol' foul shit at me: "Look at that fake-ass nigga."

I yell back at him, "Yo bitch Keisha loves this fake-ass nigga." That nigga's mouth drops. He looks surprised that I know his girl's name. I look over to the crowd and say, "Yeah, I fucked that bitch two months ago, but she wasn't cool with Massengill, and any bitch that don't fuck with Massengill can't fuck with me." Everybody in line falls out laughing.

I keep it moving and walk into the club. I ain't sweating that weak-ass nigga.

Ivory's isn't like any other club I've ever seen in Richmond. Them muh-fuckers have the scenery all bubbly and shit. Everybody walks around sipping on champagne, compliments of the club owner. This is the grand reopening and niggas is representing. Everybody in the joint is acting Hollywood. I notice all the ballers kicking it, and the sack-chasing girls circling around the niggas with money in hopes that they ass is gonna be the chosen one for the night. Oh yeah, Ivory's is definitely off the chain.

The DJ is kicking that old joint by Doug E. Fresh, "All the Way to Heaven," and man, oh man, people is bout to lose their damn minds. Then that nigga starts spinning "Push It Real Good" by Salt-N-Pepa, and the girls on the dance floor start showing niggas just how hard they can push it. I'm not feeling that shit, 'cause I keep thinking bout how muh-fuckers compare me to Spinderella. I walk over to the bar to get me a straight shot of Henny, 'cause for real, that Champale and Andre shit is for bitches.

Lil Mo stands at the bar, ordering a Courvoisier and Coke. She spots me and walks over with her drink in hand, stirring the ice around with her finger.

"Where's your girl? You mean to tell me she let you off the leash tonight?' she asks with a sarcastic smile, then sucks on her wet index finger.

"She's out working, like she 'sposed to be. And what about your man—you mean to tell me he let you out of the house in that dress?" I down my shot of Henny. I set the empty glass on the bar and grab a small napkin, not to wipe my mouth with, but for writing the numbers down that I know I'm gon' get.

"Like I told you in the mall today, Turk is out of town on business. He will be gone all week," she answers, moving closer to me.

"All right, I'll holler at you later," I say in a very friendly tone. Then I walk away and make my way through the crowd.

Lil Mo looks so good, I want to drink her bathwater. Her long jet-black hair is spiral curled. She's wearing a short black spaghetti-strap, doll-baby dress that accents her small, round phat ass, and every time she moves that dress moves with her. Her dress dips low in the front, and you can see the butterfly tattoo on her breast. Her titties are sitting up nice and high. She has on these tall black sandals; looks like some shit Mary J. Blige would wear, but them shits is tight. She has a big-ass tattoo of Cookie Monster, Ernie, and Bert riding a bicycle over her left ankle and LIL MO is tattooed on her right arm. From all the tattoos and shit on her body, I know her lil ass could handle pain.

I stand up against the wall nodding my head to the music and checking out the ladies. There are some bad-ass bitches in Richmond and I'm imagining myself fucking every ho in the joint. I look behind me and see Lil Mo talking to Cynthia. I know Cynthia from Colors; she's the bartender there on Wednesday nights. Cynthia is gorgeous. Asian, black, and Creole, about five feet five with big wide hips and a badunka butt. With her copper-toned complexion and light brown slanted bedroom eyes, that bitch is so muh-fucking bad that I tricked with her ass one night. I thought she was fem, but she carried her shit straight butch, but I ain't know it until we got to the hotel room. Cyn ass ate me out, sucked my toes, licked my asshole, my armpits, my navel, that bitch even ate the wax out of my ears. She licked and sucked every fucking crack and crevice on my body. I was feeling so good that when the bitch told me to turn around and put my ass in the air, I did it. I had forgotten who the fuck I was, until I felt a flabby dick at the entrance of my ass. I jumped up and yelled, "What the fuck you doing?"

The DJ been throwing down so far, then his 'Bama ass plays that goddamn "Push It Real Good" again. I can't understand what the fuck is up with that shit. Then he announces, "I have a special request from Lil Mo." I turn around and see Lil Mo's ass heading toward me. She comes up to me singing, "Ooooh, baby, baby be, baby baby be, get up on this." Before I know it, her leg is in the air and around my waist, and her arms are hung around my neck. She wants me to get up on it, and so fuck it, I do. I start grinding back on her ass. People are looking and shit 'cause everybody know Lil Mo is Turk's girl. But sheeett, I'm saying to myself, if Lil Mo is his bitch, then it's that nigga's responsibility to keep his ho in check.

For the rest of the night, we kick it. Every time I turn around her ass is at me. I think, I'ma hit that tonight.

When the club party is over, I walk back down to McDonald's to call Yellow Cab to scoop me up. Before the cab arrives, Lil Mo pulls up with this chick name Tasha riding with her. She offers me a ride home and for the second time in one day, I accept. Tasha lives in HoneyBrook Apartments, and Lil Mo lives in Lakefield Mews. She says she'll take Tasha home first, then drop me off. That shit doesn't make sense to me since they live closer to each other. But I know what time it is, so I ain't ask no questions. On the way home, they gossip bout niggas in the club. Who's fucking who, who's snitching, who got evicted, who's getting high, which projects is beefing against the other. They know all the baby mommas baby daddies drama. They all up in everybody's business. I sit in the back-seat tripping. Lil Mo keeps looking at me through the rearview mir-ror, smiling and tracing her lips with her tongue.

As soon as Tasha gets out, Lil Mo drives out of the complex, turns around, looks at me, and says, "You know what I want." She pulls over and parks on a dark deserted road. She turns off the truck and removes the key from the ignition. She gets out of the driver seat, walks to the back door, opens it, and climbs in back with me. She shuts the door behind her, straddles me, and sticks her tongue dead down my throat. She tongues me hard. I never tongue-kissed anybody except Cookie.

Then she starts sucking on my neck and humping up and down on me. I feel good, so I start humping back. She pulls my jersey over my head, then removes my white tee and starts sucking on my chest. I throw her off of me, pull up her dress, and realize she isn't wearing any panties. I stick my middle finger in her pussy, and she starts squirming around, fucking it. Then I remove my finger and slide my tongue in her pussy. It's dark and I can't see, so I reach up front and turn on the interior lights, 'cause I need to see what the fuck I am eating. Man, her pussy is pretty and pink. Looks like that has never been tapped into. I eat her out for 'bout fifteen minutes straight without raising my head. When she's about to come, she tells me to get on top of her, she wants me to hump her. I don't have my strap with me, so I get on top of her and we are straight fucking like two bitches. We kiss and grind and suck each other's necks. I can't remember the last time I felt that good. It's different from when I'm with Nessa; I am feeling some shit I ain't never felt before— passion. We both start coming at the same time, our bodies shaking and jerking in unison. I hold on to her tight. I never want to let go of the MoJo.

FIVE

IT'S FOUR A.M. on Sunday, and I tell Lil Mo to drop me off in front of Oakwood Cemetery. I'm feeling good but need to get high to calm my ass down 'cause, for real, Lil Mo had a nigga on cloud nine. I walk through the cut, looking for La-La's night-prowling ass. It's so quiet round the way that you can hear a pin drop. I ain't see the nigga, so I go and knock on his door.

"Yo, who is it?" he yells.

"It's Demetria, man," I yell back, as I look around to make sure niggas ain't outside, waiting to catch a nigga out. I can hear him fucking around with the door and shit. Seems like the nigga is nervous or something 'cause it takes his ass a minute to open up.

"Fuck you want, nigga?" he asks me with bass in his voice. Its four in the morning and the nigga opens the door with a bowl of Kellogg's Frosted Flakes in his hand.

"Man, let me get a hit," I say as I walk past him, reaching into my back pocket for my ace of spade.

"Shorty, you need to pay your tab. How the fuck you think you gon' keep booking shit off me and don't pay up?"

"Man, you know I'm good for it, why you tripping?" I ask him like I have an open line of credit.

La-La walks back into the kitchen and sits down to finish his bowl of cereal. I look around the apartment and notice that there isn't shit in the living room except a big-screen television with a Rent-A-Center sticker attached to the side and a couple card-table folding chairs. In the kitchen is a glass table with four chairs—the type of chairs with the black-and-gold-specked seats that everybody in the fucking pj's seemed to have. They ain't got no curtains at the kitchen or living room windows. La-La continues eating his Frosted Flakes, paying my ass no attention as I stand over him with money in my pocket and credit on my mind.

"Man, I got to take a leak, can I use your bathroom?" I ask while twitching my legs together 'cause I had to pee bad as shit.

La-La nods his head. "Yeah."

I run upstairs and shut the door behind me. There isn't shit in the bathroom except the sink, bathtub, and toilet. They ain't have no shower curtain up, no rugs on the floor, or no soap in the god-damn soap dish. By this time, I'm pissed with my cousin for letting that nigga live up in her house and they ain't have nothing in it. I finished pissing and was about to stand up when that nigga came bursting through the door. *Bam!* he kicked that mutherfucker in with his foot.

"Man, what the fuck is wrong with you?" I ask, and cover myself with my hands.

"Any nigga who knocks at this door without my permission is bound to get whatever the fuck I got waiting for 'em. Why the fuck you think it was all right to knock at my shit?" He stands at the door staring at me with rage in his eyes. I don't notice the burner in his hand until he put the mutherfucker up to my head.

"Raise up off the muh-fucking toilet, nickga!" he orders as he presses the black 9mm directly at my temple.

"All right, dawg, I'm moving," I say as I stand up and start to pull up my black-and-red Joe Cool boxers.

"Nah, nickga, leave them bitch-ass boxers and shorts at yo knees and get the fuck in the bedroom."

I step out of the bathroom, holding my shorts with my hands, while my boxers are still at my knees. La-La walks beside me, never moving the gun from my dome.

"Man, what up?" I ask as I make my way to the bedroom with the black lacquer bedroom set. We pass by the children's room, and I notice they ain't have no beds, just two pissed-up mattresses on the floor.

"You owe, nigga. Pay up now or I'ma smoke your ass right here, right now!" he yells.

I reach in my back pocket, my hands trembling and shaking like a pipehead phening for crack. I start counting. "Twenty, forty, sixty, eighty, one-twenty."

The nigga snatches the money from my hands and says, "Nigga, this ain't enough to keep you breathing." He throws the money on the bed.

"But you ain't count all of it," I say, when I know damn well it ain't enough to close out my tab. La-La is tripping, but I know it ain't about the money. The nigga is flexing on me 'cause I caught his ass out last night. He's trying to prove to me that he's still a real nigga 'cause I found out that he likes hitting faggots.

"You got a choice. You can either suck my dick or let me fuck you. You got one minute to decide," he says while kicking off his flip-flops and dropping his shorts to the floor with his available hand, while the other is still holding the gun to my head. My eyes grow big. I can't believe this is happening. I'm thinking, if only I had taken my cokehead ass home, I wouldn't be here right now dealing with these ultimatums this nigga giving me.

Suddenly, my heart starts beating fast: *thump thump, thump thump, thump thump*. I could see it pumping from beneath my shirt. Then I start sweating; I can feel the perspiration settling on my forehead. Then I think, Let's see, I was born a woman so if I let him hit, it wouldn't be too bad, but if I suck that nigga's dick, I might never be able to look at myself in the mirror again.

"All right, time's up," La says, holding his dick in his hand.

"Let's fuck," I say, as if it didn't faze me, 'cause I'm planning on fighting the nigga once we get in position.

"Nah, I changed my mind, you don't get to choose. You gon' suck my mutherfucking dick, nickga," he says with a sinister laugh, swinging his dick from side to side like it is his muh-fucking most prized possession. "And if you make one wrong move I'ma blast yo bitch ass. Drop to yo knees now, nickga." He moves the nine from my temple and points it between my eyes.

I drop to my knees, but I ain't sucking; his dick is just resting there.

"Man, where is Melody and the kids, 'spose they walk in on us?" I pull my head back and try a scare tactic so he'll let me go.

"Melody is wit' yo momma at the Purple Pit and the kids is with they country-ass daddy in Charles City. So, nickga, shut the fuck up. I know what you tryna do but it ain't gone work."

Bam! The nigga hits me across the head with the gun, not hard enough to knock me out, but hard enough to motivate my ass. I wrap my sweaty hands around his dick and start sucking slowly; the nigga is fucking my mouth like he is in some pussy. After about three minutes, the nigga pulls out of my mouth and looks down at me.

"I'm getting ready to come," he says and looks at me like I know what time it is. I try to rise up but he knocks me back down. "Suck my nut, bitch, or I'ma split yo muh-fucking head open!" La-La then forces his dick back into my mouth. This time he holds on to the back of my head with his left hand. He pumps and pumps until he busses off.

"I'm coming, I'm coming," he announces. "Oh yeah, nickga, yeah, I like this shit, ooh yeah, ooh yeah, don't stop, keep sucking, nickga."

I want to jump up and fight the nigga, but La is stronger than me, and I know there is no win. The big muh-fucker is cock diesel; he's 6 feet 5 inches, 240 pounds, and cut up like a mutherfucker. The nigga jerks off in my mouth and then tells me to get the fuck out of his house. I run to the bathroom. I'm humiliated, violated, and some mo shit. I shut the door behind me.

He yells, "Yeah, bitch, wash your mouth out."

I sit on the toilet for a minute trying to compose myself, 'cause I am hurt like a muh-fucker. I'm already thinking of ways I'm gon' get back at that nigga. I stand up and open the medicine cabinet to see if Melody keeps toothpaste or Listerine since I don't see shit lying around. I'm throwing shit out of the cabinet, which looks like it ain't never been cleaned or wiped out. That's when I come across a ring with the initial K on it. It's a diamond cluster, and one of the diamonds is missing from it. There was only one nigga in the hood that wore a ring like it, and that was my lil bro, KaQuanza.

I wonder, what the fuck is Quanza's ring doing in Melody and La's crib. Come to think of it, La-La's night-prowling ass is the only nigga that would be in the cut at four in the morning. And that nigga gambles every fucking day. Mat-o-fact, I saw that nigga at Food Circus with one of them dudes from Fairmont the same day Quanza died. Yeah, everybody knows them niggas from Fairmont love gambling. I wonder if La ass was out there with them, too. Man, I know this nigga ain't the one who pulled the trigger on my baby bro.

I sit on the toilet then stand up again, sit on the toilet, then stand up again. My mind is racing. It's going a hundred miles an hour. I start pacing back and forth in the confined quarters of the bathroom. My heart starts beating fast again and sweat pours down my face. I start thinking about all the crazy shit me and Quanza used to do when we was little, like playing "knock on people's door and run." I think about how we used to make signs like we was homeless and stand in front of the Daily Planet Homeless Shelter on Canal Street holding signs that read HUNGRY ORPHANS, CAN YOU PLEASE SPARE A DIME? just to collect money so we could go to the Kiddy Disco at the Ebony Island Club. Then I think about the time we used Uncle Lee's driver's license to get Quanza's ass in Club Tropicana, and how that nigga got pissy drunk 'cause his ass was a forty-five-year-old man that night and was able to buy liquor. I'm vexed. I think to myself, This nigga done killed my brother and made me suck his dick!

Man, I lose it. I swing open the bathroom door and run downstairs. La-La is sitting back at the table finishing off the box of cereal, his burner on the table beside him. I slam the ring down in front of him. He looks up from the bowl, still eating and wearing nothing but his boxers and says, "And what, nickga?"

"So it was you, dawg?" I'm not crying. I can't cry. Besides, the teardrop tattoo underneath my left eye takes care of my pain for me.

"Fuck it look like? You a smart girl, figure it out," he says, reaching for his burner. He ain't fast enough. I grab the gun and stick it in his face. I back up to the refrigerator and I'm about to blast that nigga when Melody comes through the front door.

I yell, "Lock the mutherfucking door and get your fat ass in here." Melody walks in and I don't give her a chance to say shit.

"So you knew too, bitch?" I point at the ring on the table. Then point the gun back and forth at them.

"I told La he shouldn't have done it, but he said KaQuanza disrespected him in front of them dudes from Fairmont. He said Quanza called him a faggot lover or some shit like that."

"We *fam*, Mel, how you gon' look at my mom knowing that nigga killed her son?"

La-La sits there like he don't give a fuck. So I shoot the nigga in his head. *BAM!* He falls out the chair and hits the floor.

Melody starts screaming.

I bite my bottom lip and say, "Shut the fuck up, bitch. Where's the loot?"

"Upstairs," Melody says, whining like a baby in a pissy-ass diaper.

"Take me to it." I point the gun to her back and follow her upstairs. She goes to the bedroom where the nigga made me suck his dick. She steps into the closet and pulls out an old raggedy suitcase full of money. As I'm sliding it in the hallway, her ass reaches for the phone like she's gonna call 5-0. Man, I snatch the phone out of her hand. Then I jump up and drop kick her ass in the stomach. *Wham!* She falls over from the pain. When she stands up, I shoot her ass twice in the head. *Boom boom!* The bitch falls to the floor.

I drag her ass down the steps and into the living room. Then I drag La's ass from the kitchen and lay him out beside her. Fuck it, them niggas was rolling together, so I made sure they died together. I'm so fuckin' mad I can't feel nothing. I put them both on their backs, and I cross their hands in front of them. Melody's eyes are wide open, and I leave them big Popeye mutherfuckers just like they are. I take the mop from the bucket and clean up the blood from the kitchen, the bedroom, and the blood trail that leads from upstairs to down. I change into one of that nigga's T-shirts 'cause my shit was all bloody. Before I leave, I walk over to La-La's body and kick the nigga in his head and tell the nigga, "So much for your rainy day, *nickga.*" I leave them muh-fuckers spread out on the living room floor just like John List did to his fam back in the seventies.

I peep out the back door to make sure the coast is clear. There isn't a soul in sight. I fired three rounds, and nobody heard anything. If they did, they didn't pay them shits no mind 'cause that's just how it is in the pj's. Niggas be shooting all day and all night so people get used to the sound. It's kinda fucked up when you think about it, 'cause for real, there's been many times when a nigga ass really needed emergency help 'cause a nigga done come through and smoked they ass. But folks be in the house chilling, while a nigga's ass out there dying and shit 'cause ain't nobody responding to the familiar sound of gunfire.

I make it home without anybody seeing me. I jump in the tub and take me a bath. When I get out, I count the money from La's suitcase—thirty g's. I didn't have time to worry about getting his product; all I wanted was the nigga's scratch. I call Lil Mo to ask if she wants to go out to eat and to the movies. She says she down for whatever and that she will scoop me up around five. I get into bed and fall off to sleep. I feel a whole lot better since my brother's killer has also been laid to rest.

SIX

I WAKE UP at four P.M. and get dressed for my date with Shorty. She picks me up near Carolina Barbecue, and we drive to Three Lakes Park. I sit on top of a picnic table, and Shorty stands in between my legs with her arms wrapped around my neck like I'm her nigga for real.

"So what's up, Shorty? Why you come at me like that last night?" I ask as I lie back on the table and place my hands behind my head.

" 'Cause I've been wanting you for a long time," she answers, and climbs on top of me. She kisses me in my mouth and continues, "I used to see you outside of Club Tropicana. I was too young to get in the club, so I used to sit outside on the hood of my friend's car and wait for the club to let out so I could check out the fellows. I still remember the first night I saw you, I said to myself, 'One day I'ma get that fine-ass nigga.' "

"Is that right?" I'm blushing hard as hell.

"Sheeett, everybody knows you the flyest nigga in town," she says, boosting my ego even more.

"Have you ever fucked with a nigga like me?" I ask.

"Well, I used to be in love with a girl name Ann, but she was fem."

"Why did you stop fucking with her?"

" 'Cause we was having money problems. We used to have an apartment together, but Ann started getting high and fucking up our money," she answers.

"Oh yeah, so where you from?" I ask 'cause I never saw Shorty around town until she started doing Nessa's hair.

"I've lived a little bit of everywhere, but I lived with Ann in Petersburg."

Since I'm straight butch, I don't know why she likes me, but then again, she's fucking with that nigga Turk and he's one of the hardest niggas in Richmond.

"So what's up with you and Turk?"

"T is too possessive, and his ass is starting to get tight with his money. I only started fucking with him 'cause his ass was getting paid. I've been tryna stick it out with him until I can save up enough money to move to Atlanta."

"Word. Have you ever been to Atlanta before?"

"I plan on moving there and opening up my own hair salon," she answers. Then she gives me another soft kiss on the lips, slides off me, jumps down off the picnic table, and starts running toward the truck.

We decide not to go to the movies. We drive down to Virginia Beach and get a room. Once in the room, she gives me a full body massage, complete with hot oil. Then we get in the sauna together. I hadn't brought my strap with me 'cause she said she wasn't ready for that. I'm satisfied with just locking and bumping pussies with her. Man, Shorty is so muh-fucking bad that I allow her ass to revoke my butch card. I'm spending money like it ain't funny. She is used to being wined and dined by Turk so I have to keep the broad in her element. Our three-day escape from Richmond includes Virginia Beach, Norfolk Naval Base, Busch Gardens, Water Country, Captain George's Seafood, Colonial Williamsburg, and shopping at the pottery and outlet stores in Williamsburg. We have so much shit in the Rodeo when we return to Richmond that it is ridiculous.

When I get back, Momma is sitting on the porch with a frown on her face, like she pissed off or something.

"What's wrong, Ma?" I ask 'cause I don't know what the fuck her problem is.

"Demetria, that damn Nessa called all day Monday and Tuesday. She say the city jail don't have no air-conditioning and that her bronchitis is acting up."

I still had $25,000, but I meant I wasn't gonna go get her ass until I was good and goddamn ready.

"Ma, Nessa faking. She say that same old shit every time," I say as I walk past her and make my way into the house. Momma follows me in, still bitching about Nessa being locked up. As soon as I sit down at the kitchen table, Sneaky Pete comes knocking at the back door.

"Come in, man," I invite, but I stand right there beside the muh-fucking refrigerator. I point to the spot where I want the nigga to stand. Niggas call Pete ass Sneaky Pete 'cause that nigga would steal the drawers off yo ass, yo clothesline, or from wherever, then go sell yo shit so he could get high. That nigga is so cruddy that one time he sold me a radio and when I went upstairs to get the money for the nigga, he had stolen the radio back from me. I came back downstairs, gave the nigga the $20, and put his ass out of my house. Man, when I went to go hook the shit up, I realized that the nigga had beaten me out of my money and the radio. The shit was so funny, I couldn't do nothing but laugh. Me and Pete go way back, so ain't no way I was gonna beat that nigga's ass over a dove. Pete used to be cool as shit, but the nigga got caught out there and started oiling.

"What up, Pete?" I ask 'cause I want his visit to be brief since I don't trust the nigga round my shit.

"Yall know they found La-La and Melody dead as two doorknobs, right?" He asks slowly, nodding like he bout to rock the fuck over. "At first everybody thought Smitty ass came back, but Shorty ain't do it, 'cause he was in MCV and shit; his girl stabbed him the same day La-La beat his ass." He scratches his arms and chest and continues on, still leaning with his eyes closed and talking slow as molasses.

"Demetria, man, guess what niggas saying about La ass?" he asks.

He is ready to gossip like most dopeheads. Them muh-fuckers be gossiping and expecting a nigga to pay they ass for hot and juicy project rumors. Gossip in the projects is free, but them junkies be getting that shit twisted. Always tryna act like they know more than every fucking body else. Then, after they finish running they mouth, they always never seem to forget to hit yo ass up for a few dollars.

"Man, they say that nigga La was fucking with faggots and that one of them followed him home, and robbed and killed him and Mel."

Sneaky Pete gave me the lowdown, then added "Demetria, man, let me get two dollars from you?"

"Ain't got it, Pete," I lie to him.

"All right, I'm gone." Pete wipes his face with his dirty face towel and exits through the back door.

I'm happy to know that people ain't on to me. I call Lil Mo when Pete's gossiping ass is clearly out of sight. She says she has some errands to run and asks if I want to hang out with her for the day. I tell her yeah, to come back and scoop me up, which she does. We go to Eastgate Mall and she gets a pedicure and manicure. Then we go to DMV to pick up her tags, 'cause her thirty-day ones expiring on Friday. For lunch I treat her to Kabutos, the Japanese joint on West Broad. They stir-fry the food right in front of us and shit. Then I take her to Cary Town and buy her a Versace dress from this boutique that only them white hos out in the county shop at. For dinner we go to Skilligalee on Glenside. We sit in the booth next to each other, feeding each other and making out like teenagers on a first date. I pull up her skirt and play with her pussy hairs. She sucks on my neck, giving me a passion mark. She sucks so hard that I scream out loud and the manager orders us to leave. We run out of the restaurant, holding hands and laughing. I'm enjoying my new young tender ronni. Lil Mo is only eighteen, she's five years younger than me, and she has my nose wide open. I quickly forget about Nessa's ass locked up in the city jail.

The next day Lil Mo says she has something important to tell me.

"What's up, baby?" I ask, 'cause I'm curious to know what's on her mind.

"Well, I thought you should know that I found a three-bedroom apartment in Innsbrook. The apartments are renting for nine hundred dollars a month, and—"

I cut her off and ask, "Why are you moving way out there?"

"Well," she continued on, " 'cause we need to get away from the inner city." I notice the *we* so I question further.

"Who is 'we'?" I ask with a puzzled look on my face.

"Well, Dee, I'm gonna break up with Turk when he gets back in town on Friday, because I want to be with you," she answers with a serious look.

I'm delighted to hear this, so I nod and say, "That's cool." I think to myself, If that nigga wants beef he can bring it.

The professional movers are hired and it don't take long to get shit packed up. Lil Mo dances around the apartment singing the Jeffersons: "Well, we're moving on up, moving on up, to the East Side, to a deluxe apartment in the skkyyyyy."

That night we get a room at the Embassy Suites on Broad. We order room service and watch movies on cable. We talk about our families, and she tells me that her entire family is dead. She was in and out of foster homes her entire life. I tell her about KaQuanza, and she says she had heard about his death. We doze off and suddenly we hear a phone ringing. We both look at each other, 'cause neither one of us told anybody where we was gon' be. She answers the hotel phone and slams it down when she realizes that its her carry-around car phone that's ringing. She answers it, then lips to me that it's that nigga Turk. I put my ear up to the phone so I can hear what the nigga's saying. He's arguing with her about me.

"What the fuck is this shit I'm hearing about you in Skilligalee with that bitch-ass nigga from Nine Mile?" Turk screams at the top of his lungs.

"I don't know what you talking about," Lil Mo responds, sounding nervous as hell.

"Bitch, don't lie to me. I know for a mutherfucking fact you been with that nigga, and I hear you was all up on that nigga in Ivory's, pushing it real good," Turk says, his voice echoing through the phone.

"No, baby, I was with Vanessa, my client. You know that's Vanessa's man. I love you, Turk, I wouldn't fuck around on you." Lil Mo starts crying as she tries calming him down.

"I don't wanna hear that bullshit; I'ma beat yo ass and kill that bitch-ass nigga, watch me! I'm done talking, just have your ass at the spot over Jarrett at ten sharp on Friday night so we can finish this conversation," Turk said.

"All right, baby, I'll be there," Lil Mo says with tears rolling down her face. She hangs up the phone and sits up in bed with her back to the headboard.

"Are you all right?" I ask, 'cause I jive like felt sorry for her. She has just told me about her family being dead, and now this shit. And that nigga Turk ain't buying that shit she was tryna sell him. He's vexed, and I can almost feel the ass-whipping she has coming.

"I'm scared, you just don't know, Turk is crazy. Whenever I don't wanna have sex with him, he holds me down and fucks me in my ass, or he beats me and then makes me suck his dick. I wanna leave him so bad, but he keeps threatening me. I would have left him alone a long time ago, but he paid for me to go to Flair's Beauty Academy to get my cosmetologist license, and he put eight thousand dollars as a down payment on my truck," Lil Mo says, crying hysterically.

"Do you have the key to the crib in Jarrett?" I ask, 'cause I'm gonna take care of my baby's problem.

"Yeah, baby," she answers as she wipes the tears from her eyes. "Are you gonna get rid of him for me?"

I look at her and tell her to lie back down. I rub her back and tell her, "Big Daddy got you."

SEVEN

FRIDAY MORNING we walk over to Shoney's to eat from the all-you-can-eat breakfast bar. We eat, and then Lil Mo goes back to the room to get more shut-eye. I find a spot on West Broad to get my hair cornrowed. When I get back to the room, my girl is sitting on the edge of the bed crying. I run over to her and kneel down.

"What's wrong, baby?" I ask as I stroke her face with my hand.

"Turk took the truck from the parking lot."

"How do you know he took it?" I ask.

"Because he called my car phone after he did and told me he had."

"That's all right, baby, 'cause after tonight you won't have to worry bout that nigga." I need her to know that I got her back.

"Okay, boo, and just to let you know, he keeps his drugs and some of his money in the apartment out Jarrett."

"Word," I say to let her know that I know what she's getting at.

We call Enterprise and rent a car for the rest of the weekend. I tell her that on Monday morning we gonna go and get a car from J. P.'s Auto Sales. This is where all the moneymaking niggas get their rides.

I leave her in the room while I go bond Nessa out. When I get to the lockup, they tell me Nessa ain't there. I say to myself out loud, "Damn, I guess her Aunt June got her out."

The clerk hears me talking to myself, and says, "Ma'am, we haven't had nobody name Vanessa Tinsley down here at all."

I say, "Excuse me, but she been down here since last Saturday night." The lady asks for Nessa's social security.

I run it off, and the lady says, "Sorry, but you may want to try Chesterfield and Henrico." I stop by my house to call around, and Nessa can't be found anywhere. I even call all the surrounding counties, and all the jails say the same thing: "Sorry, but we haven't had anyone lately by that name."

Momma is upset when she walks in. She asks me if the jersey found in Melody's house belongs to me. I thought I had put that mutherfucker in the suitcase with the money, but I slipped up and left that Chicago Bulls shit behind. I ignore her question. She never asks me if I killed Mel, 'cause for real, I don't think she wants to know the answer. She says 5-0 wants to talk to me. I ask if I was suspect with the niggas in the pj's and she says La-La's cousin from the West End has been out there asking bout me. For a minute, I get kinda nervous, 'cause them niggas from the West End go hard. If one nigga in the West End got beef with you, then all the niggas in the West End got beef with you. That's just how them niggas roll. Then I think, Let them niggas bring it.

I drive back to the hotel and get in bed with my baby. I'm waiting to hear from Nessa, 'cause at this point, I'm not sure if the bitch is dead or alive. At nine Lil Mo gives me the key and I drive back across town and wait for the nigga to show up. I let myself inside and turn on all the lights so he'll think Lil Mo is waiting on him, and then I hide in the extra small bedroom closet. The nigga comes in alone, just like Lil Mo said he would. He drops his keys and yells, "Where you at?"

I step from the closet and bounce around the wall. The nigga throws his hands up when he sees me; nigga knows what time it is.

"Get the fuck down," I yell as I point La-La's 9mm at his head.

"Yeah, nigga, who's the bitch now?" I say as I rumble through his pockets. The nigga doesn't say a word; he gets on the floor like I order his ass to do. I reach for a pillow and that's when he realizes that I'm not just there to rob him. He scrambles to get up, but I smash the pillow to the back of the nigga's head and pull the trigger. *BOOM!* The nigga's body jerks for seven minutes before he dies. I stand over him and watch until there is no more movement. Then I ransack the apartment. I get two kilos of coke and sixty-five g's from a safe that was left wide open. He was smart when it came to getting paper but dumb as a muh-fucker when it came to protecting his shit.

The next day we don't get up until about three in the afternoon. I still haven't heard from Nessa. I call home to check on Momma.

"Hey, Ma, what's happening? You all right?"

"Demetria, Nessa called and said she's still in the lockup. How come you won't go get the girl out?" Momma asks, getting all in my shit again.

"Ma, did she call collect?" I ask, 'cause I am confused as hell about Nessa's whereabouts. I didn't tell Momma that I had gone to get her and that her ass wasn't there.

"Nah, she ain't call here no goddamn collect, she been calling all week on somebody's three way," Momma says like she had a fucking collect call block or something on the line.

That explains why I didn't see any pay phone calls on the caller ID whenever I checked it. I tell Momma I'm gonna go shopping and buy her some new clothes and shoes.

Me and Lil Mo get dressed and go to Regency Square mall to get me some new gear to wear to Ivory's. Lil Mo says she's gonna wear the Versace dress that I bought her. I cop a pair of green on white Flavs, a pair of Polo Jean shorts, and a green-and-white Polo shirt. I'm gonna rock green 'cause that shit is money. We go to Outback Steakhouse for dinner; then we go back to our room to rest up for the night. Mo says she wants to give me a special treat for getting rid of that nigga Turk. She takes a shower and comes out of the bathroom wearing a black satin thong. She has a black feather boa around her neck and a pair of glass slippers with black feathers on them. Her hair is pulled up in a bun, and she has on a pair of dangling diamond earrings. She must've borrowed a CD player from the hotel while I was gone, cause Shorty came out teasing me with the boa while swirling her ass off around the joint by Mary J. Blige, "You Remind Me."

I feel like I'm gonna lose my mind. But her perky-ass breasts sitting at attention is enough to keep me focused.

"Let me make love to you one more time," she says, unzipping my pants.

"Fuck you mean, one more time?" I immediately become defensive 'cause I'm thinking she's tryna diss me after I had killed that nigga for her, and all that black shit she's wearing makes me think her ass is in mourning or something.

"One more time before we go to the club tonight, silly," she says, hitting me with the pillow.

We get into a pillow fight and then we make love. She pours hot vanilla oil over my entire body and licks me from head to toe. Shorty makes my toes curl, and for the first time since I been wit' her, I have multiple orgasms. I pull off her panties and spread her legs apart as far as they could go. I lick her clit until the tip of my tongue goes numb. She comes twice and then we doze off into a deep sleep. When I wake up, it's ten P.M. and she is up and ready to go. I take a shower and then throw my shit on. I toss my money green headband around my cornrows, and we leave the room with over $80,000 in cash, and God only knows how much them two kilos is gonna bring.

When we get to the club, there is a rack of muh-fuckers waiting. I take my girl by the hand, and we walk to the front of the line. The fat-ass bouncer is standing there, and he nods for us to go in. The club is already packed like sardines, so I know all them niggas outside ain't gon' make it in.

I order drinks for everybody standing around the bar. Niggas is checking me 'cause I'm looking good and spending money left and right. Lil Mo is all up on me and shit. The DJ is playing Tupac's "I Get Around," and, man, that is my shit. I start grooving, my girl is in front of me, and I'm dancing behind her with my arms around her neck and singing along. Niggas is checking me 'cause I'm with the baddest girl in the club, and she belongs to Turk.

Then I see that 'Bama-ass nigga from the week before that fuck with Keisha. The nigga walks over to me with his boys and gives me a hard-ass look, then spits that same ol' comment out his mouth, "Look at that fake-ass nigga." Him and his boys start giggling like lil bitches. I lean over Lil Mo and get up in the nigga's face and continue singing my man's Tupac shit: "Cuz hos they sweat a brotha majorly, and I don't know why your girl keeps pagin' me."

Next thing I know, me and this nigga is going toe to toe. I'm feeling myself. I done gunned down three muh-fuckers, been off the coca for a minute, and my pockets is fat like they used to be. Man, I rock that puny-ass nigga. I jab him in the face three times: *Pap, pap, pap.* That nigga's head wobbles back and forth. I jump back and throw my hands up to protect my grill. I start rocking back and forth. I tell the nigga, "Bring it."

I wait for him to show me what he's got, but nigga ain't have no fight in him. He comes charging at me with his head down, so I cuff him up and flip his skinny ass over. I hold the muh-fucker upside down for a minute, and then I drop the nigga. *Wham.* His boys stand by and watch 'cause this shit is one-on-one. I start stomping his bitch ass. Girls are screaming, "Break it up, break it up." But his boys are saying, "Nah, let them fight."

Then security comes and breaks it up. Security throws them niggas out of the club. The shit was wild 'cause the DJ never stopped playing the music, and people was still dancing and shit. It only took me about three minutes to prove to the nigga that I wasn't no joke.

I go to the bathroom to fix myself up 'cause my headband has slid all around my neck and shit. When I come out, some of Lil Mo's girls are standing around, and I overhear them telling her that Turk's boy just found him dead in the apartment out Jarrett. They tell her that we should leave 'cause niggas is saying that I killed him over her. My girl walks over to me and whispers in my ear, "I'll go pull the rental around. Meet me in front of the club."

"All right," I say, looking around 'cause I'm not too sure if skinny dude has gotten back into the club and is planning to steal me. I walk to the bar to get me another drink before I roll out. This nigga name Duke from round the way walks up to me.

"Man, you know niggas talking. They say you killed La-La, Shorty. You need to lay low for a minute," he informs me as he checks the room like he ain't want certain niggas to see him hollering at me. He continues, "Man, five-oh been talking to the maintenance man, and the nigga say he seen you leaving Melody's house when he was out on an emergency call. Be careful, man, cause La's people from the West End came rolling through deep today and they was asking questions bout you."

I smash him off a $100 bill and tell him, "Good looking out."

I walk outside and wait in front of the club for my baby to pull up. It is still just as many people outside of the club as inside. Cars are lined up and down Broad Street and music is blasting from just about every car on the strip. Niggas shooting dice on the corner like it's legal. I see my nigga Rome standing across the street with his crew, so I start to make my way to him when all of a sudden I hear muh-fuckers screaming, "They got guns."

I hear the fat bouncer say, "Run, Dee, man, run." I hear a car speed off so I haul ass running. I run down the street, and somebody is gunning behind me. *Pop, pop, pop, pop, pop, pop.* I turn the corner, but them niggas is right up on me. One shot hits me in the leg—*pow*—and then three hit me in the back. *Boom, boom, boom.* I keep running until I can't run anymore.

I collapse in Hardee's parking lot. I hear the car stop and the car doors open. Somebody is coming over to me. I think, Oh my God, these niggas gonna shoot me in the head now. I close my eyes, 'cause I ain't wanna see death coming. Somebody stoops beside me. I smell vanilla. It's Lil Mo.

She drops to her knees and gets up close and personal in my ear and says, "By the way, Cookie didn't die from breast cancer. She committed suicide 'cause your butch ass told your knock-kneed momma that she fucked you and your momma called CPS, and they wouldn't let her get me and my sister back." She says this without stopping to catch her breath. "Remember the baby with the dope in her Pampers? Well, that was my baby sis Iesha, and she was thrown down the stairs and killed by our foster mother. Remember the six-year-old? Well, that's me, you forgetful-ass mutherfucker. If I didn't tell that Momma was fucking me, why did you tell? If it wasn't for you, Momma would have gotten us back, and my sister would be alive, and Daddy wouldn't have hung himself in prison. Oh, and one other thing—here is your practice toy. You need it 'cause you don't eat pussy all that great."

She tosses the It's Alive baby doll at me and runs off, still holding the .38 caliber in her hand. I don't hear the car pull away, so I turn my head to see where she is. Then I see another muh-fucker coming toward me. It's Nessa. She leans down, gets up close and personal in my ear, and says, "You thought you left me for dead in that hot-ass jail, but I was in New York for a week, getting fucked by a real nigga." Then she tosses the blue torn-off piece of paper with Turk's car phone and pager number at me. Before she walks off, she turns and says, "Oh, and one last thing, we don't like dick, we like pussy."

Then Nessa stomps my ass in the stomach one good time and spits on me. *Thoof.* Her spit catches me between the eyes.

I am slowly losing consciousness, but I roll over on my side so I can see her. She walks slowly in her same usual nonchalant pace, carrying the goddamn Dolce & Gabanna bag. She and Lil Mo are wearing the exact same silk wrap Versace dresses. Then I realize she is walking to the silver Rodeo that Turk had supposedly taken from the hotel parking lot. Lil Mo is now sitting in the driver's seat. She yells out the window, "Vanessa Ann Tinsley, come on, pick up your mutherfucking feet, you slewfoot-ass bitch!"

Nessa runs to the truck, opens the passenger side, jumps in, and closes it behind her. As the truck drives off, I notice that Turk's picture has been replaced with a picture of Nessa and Lil Mo, taken at King's Dominion. They are snuggled in each other's arms and the date on the picture is July Fourth. I glance down at the Atlanta license plate and the tag spells DYKE. Suddenly I remember the day I met Nessa. The bitch approached me telling me that she had just quit her janitorial job at an all-girls group home in Petersburg. Man, I can't believe it; those dyke bitches set me up. Then I think about the day I fucked Nessa by the window in the sunshine, then I think about Lil Mo and how I had let that bitch revoke my butch card. I'm mad as a muh-fucker 'cause I ain't never get to hit it. But I know Nessa's ass is gon' miss me! Fuck that, Richmond is gon' miss me cause I'm the baddest mutherfucker that ever walked them streets.

That's right, me, Big Daddy, Demetria, Dee, or whatever the fuck a nigga wanna call me—I was the baddest nigga that muh-fucking city ever seen.

Soon the clubgoers start gathering around the Hardee's parking lot. The parking lot is well lit, so niggas is all in my face and shit while I'm stretched the fuck out. The lights make it seem like sunshine but suddenly a dark gloom comes over the crowd. It starts to drizzle; small droplets of rain fall on my face, and Nessa's saliva slides down my nose. I can hear bitches crying, "Somebody call for help," and niggas saying, "Man, that's Dyke Demetria from Nine Mile." Then it starts pouring, the rain drowns out the lights and niggas start running 'cause they soft asses is scared of getting wet. I'm wondering where my nigga Rome at 'cause by now that nigga should've come blasting. Shit, man, niggas ain't never round when you need 'em. But I'm jive all right, 'cause a nigga like me ain't 'sposed to be scared to die. I'm glad that it's raining on these fake-ass muh-fuckers that's out here looking down on me. I arch my back, take in a deep breath and yell out, "That's right, niggas! Ain't gon' be no muh-fucking sunshine when I'm gone!"

Then I close my eyes and take my last breath.

360

Written by The Ghost, experienced by many

ONE

IT WAS THE LAST NIGHT of bike week at Myrtle Beach and the scene was off the chain. The hotel parties were off the hook and the women were fascinating. There were phat asses in thongs all over the place. Everybody was out trying to get their last night of riding, drinking, smoking, and fucking on, but not necessarily in that order.

Cojack and his partners, Maniac, Fisher, and a couple other dudes from the hood, weren't any different. They had spent the entire week partying and acting a fool in Myrtle Beach. Myrtle Beach, with all the half-naked women running around and niggas willing to spend cheddar to get the women fully naked, was surely something to write home about. Cojack and his crew must have spent well over $5,000 on pussy alone. But that was nothing to a true baller. Most cats were there to trick up some dough anyway.

The Strip was one of the biggest attractions. This was the spot where some of the best motorcycle riders performed remarkable stunts. If a person's skills weren't up to par, then they were definitely out of place.

It was the last night of bike week and Cojack was determined to go out with a bang. Cojack, his best friend Mason, aka Maniac, and his crew were all up in a strip club ballin' out of control. Although they knew it was all part of the business, broads talkin' shit in order to get cats to buy them hundred-dollar drinks, their attitude was "Fuck it!" They were all sipping bubbly with Mr. Cheeks from The Lost Boyz and paying strippers for lap dances when two cats from Atlanta approached Cojack about buying some weight. Cojack slipped them his digits and told them to hit him in a few days. Cojack was typically leery of dealing with strangers and ol' dudes from the ATL would be no exception.

After giving out his digits, a few minutes later Cojack made note of Mason leaving the table and chatting with the ATL cats. Cojack wondered what Mason was telling them, but he didn't care too much. If they fell for Mason's game, then that was their bad luck.

After leaving Magic City, Cojack, Mason, and the crew rolled up to Solid Gold. The place was jam-packed and the music blasted through the speakers. A gang of stars lounged in VIP. Shaq and Alonzo Mourning were at a table having drinks while being entertained by a group of cuties engaged in an ass-shaking contest. There was a group of rappers at a table in another section of the club smoking purple haze. Cojack knew one of them personally from a show his partner promoted a few years back. After a brief conversation earlier out at the races where bikers were going over a hundred miles per hour, Busta and Cojack planned to hook up later at the club and have a few drinks.

That's exactly what they did, drank half the night while flirting with beautiful females. By the time they reached the hotel it was five A.M. The crew crashed out in their suite for a few hours and woke up ready to head back home. Just one hour before they were about to leave, Mason's cell phone chimed.

"I won't be but a minute," Mason said before answering it, heading out the door. He was followed by Fisher, flashing one of his characteristic smiles.

An hour later he came back, flashing a roll. Cojack figured the guys from Atlanta were raising hell right about now. Mason was known to sell one brick of coke along with a couple of other bricks that were just old videotapes wrapped up in plastic. Mason was as grimey as they came with a million-dollar smile and an awesome talk game, in total contrast to his ace, Cojack. He was a baller in the truest sense: a regular pretty boy who not only had his way with women but knew how to stack that paper. Cuties were entranced by his six foot three towering frame, dark wavy hair, and the hypnotizing brown eyes that complemented his smooth chestnut skin.

As Cojack and most of the crew rode in the trailer with the motorcycles attached behind, Mason and Fisher followed. Along with Fisher, Mason was pushing a cream Q45 with eighteen-inch Pirelli wheels. Mason knew his friend would disapprove of his actions, which was why he drove his own ride instead of riding with everyone else in the trailer. He didn't realize that Cojack knew all along what he was doing. But Cojack wasn't the type of person to push too much into someone else's business, especially someone who would kill at the drop of a dime for him. Friends that had your back like that were hard to find.

TWO

THE VERY NEXT MORNING Cojack opened his eyes to find his mother standing over his bed. He wiped sleep from his face as he took in her small frame adorned with her usual pink-and-white housecoat. She held out the cordless phone and said, "Telephone."

"Tell whoever it is I'm sleep, Ma," Cojack replied with a yawn.

"It's Mason, boy," she said, tossing the phone on his bed. "He said it's important." Then she walked out of the room.

Cojack sighed, watching his mother turn and head toward the door. Then he picked up the receiver.

"Yo, what up?" he said after clearing his throat. He listened for a few seconds. Suddenly, he was wide awake. "I got you. Just calm down. Give me a minute and I'll be there. . . . I said I'm coming!" Cojack hung up.

"Shit!" he mumbled as he jumped from his bed like a firefighter going to put out a blaze.

Ten minutes later, Cojack was racing down the stairs. The pleasant aroma of bacon and eggs hit him instantly as he flew to the kitchen to say bye to his mother.

"Smells good, Ma, but I gotta run," Cojack said, stealing a slice of bacon off of the paper-towel–covered plate.

"What that boy done got himself into now?" she asked without even turning around.

"I don't know, Ma. I gotta go get him, though."

"You not gon' eat breakfast first?"

"Gotta go, Ma. I'll see you later," he said, and shot out of the kitchen.

Outside, Cojack hopped in his Lexus and sped away. In less than twenty minutes he was rolling up in an apartment complex. It was just a little after nine in the morning. Cojack dialed a number into his cell phone as he slowed for a speed bump. He passed a swimming pool and then drove ten or fifteen yards down, turning left into another duplex. Before he could park, he caught sight of Mason rushing toward the car. Mason was wearing a black velour hoodie, blue jeans, and tan Timberlands. What really got Cojack's attention was the bandanna covering his face. What the hell was that about? Cojack immediately became alert, lifting the .40 caliber from under his seat. Something about this scene just didn't look right.

As Mason approached the car and got in, Cojack's gaze swept the surroundings. He turned and looked at his partner. "What was the bandanna for? What the hell on your mind?" Finally, Mason removed the scarf from his face. Cojack wasn't prepared for what he was seeing.

"What the fuck?" Cojack asked in shock. Mason's face was lumped up, both eyes swollen and a trace of blood on his lip.

"Give me the pistol right quick," Mason instructed him excitedly.

"Hol' up, nigga. What the fuck going on?" Cojack said, twisting up his mug at the sight of Mason's face.

Mason took a deep breath, then told Cojack how he had been asleep in some chick named Kenya's place when her jealous baby daddy snuck inside and caught him there. He described how the guy punched his lights out and slung him around like a rag doll.

"I was sleep, man," Mason said bitterly. "Nigga caught me out, Jack." Mason had tears in his eyes. "Give me the gun, man. The bitch still in the crib and his sister in there, too. I swear to God I'ma slump both of them bitches."

Cojack watched as tears fell from his boy's eyes. Mason never cried. And he knew without a doubt that if he gave up the pistol he'd do exactly what he said. Cojack did a quick evaluation of the situation. It was nine-thirty in the morning and he was driving a hot-ass Lexus. There was no way he could go out like that. Mason was obviously not thinking clearly.

"You don't wanna do that, playa," Cojack said, giving Mason a supportive pat on the shoulder. "Trust me."

Mason knew Cojack was right, but he was still mad as hell. He pulled the hoodie back over his head.

"I'ma take you home," Cojack said. "That fool will have his day."

Cojack threw the car in reverse and backed up. He peered out the corner of his eye at Mason and thought, Damn! My nigga is fucked up. It was not a laughing matter, but Cojack couldn't help from smiling on the inside. Time and time again he had warned Mason about playing these broads so close. First of all, Mason didn't have his gun, which was unlike him. Fisher had his car. The reason for that was because Mason didn't want it parked at the apartment complex. He had a girlfriend, Trina, one of those who, if he stayed out, would undoubtedly ride around searching for him. As they rode in silence, Cojack thought of the two girls back at the apartment. They had not a clue as to how close their lives were to being over. Cojack felt pity for them all. The guy and the two females. Mason would not forget.

THREE

THREE DAYS LATER, as Cojack cruised the Richmond streets in his 'Bama Ford pickup truck, he couldn't help from reflecting back on the spectacular time he'd had at bike week.

In the back of his truck was his dog, Killer, a red nose pitbull whose specialty was sinking teeth. Killer was a nutcase and would bite anything in his reach. Whenever Cojack made his moves, he would bring along his dog.

Cojack pulled into an Amoco gas station on Broad Rock and was relieved to see his customer, Rob, already there, parked in the end car wash. It was dark, and the place was crowded as usual. Music blasted from a SEL 500 Benz, royal blue with chrome eighteen-inch Lorenzos. Porsha, the cutie behind the register, had her weed customers in and out all night.

"What up, partna?" Rob said as he hesitated at the sight of Killer standing upright and sizing him down.

"He tied up, cuz," Cojack said to Rob.

"You sure he can't get a loose, man? And why the fuck he so mean anyway?"

"He supposed to be," Cojack said, then, getting down to business, "Ay, you know that thang was five hundred dollars short last time, right?"

"Damn, that's my bad, Jack. I'll straighten it on the next one."

"A'ight," Cojack answered, holding the dog as he growled at the stranger. "Look in the passenger floor. You can weigh it, too. The scale beside it."

Rob crept past the dog and got in the truck. Cojack played with Killer while watching the street. He surveyed the entire scene and saw nothing that looked unusual. For over a year now, he'd been serving cats at that same spot and so far had no problems. Cojack punched numbers into his cell, spoke a few minutes, and hung up. He restrained his dog as Rob exited the truck.

"Everything good, Jack. The money in the floor," Rob said.

"A'ight, playa. Holla back, shit should be smooth for a minute."

"Good," replied Rob. "I'ma step it up next time anyway. A half a bird or somethin'."

"Just give me a ring." Rob attempted to shake his hand but saw Killer's teeth and changed his mind. Cojack laughed as Rob walked off, got in his car, and drove away. Just as Cojack hopped in the truck, his phone chimed. He rapped for a minute then sparked his Black & Mild. After he pushed end on his cell phone, he turned up the volume on his radio and the sounds of *All Eyez on Me* by Tupac filled the speakers. With a brick and a half left and two more people to see in another thirty minutes, he'd be on his way.

It was after eleven P.M. when Cojack left the gas station. Forty-five thousand dollars in an hour; he couldn't complain. He drove back to his house in Northside. After he put Killer back in his pen, he pulled out his LS 400, all black with smoke gray tint and factory wheels. His first stop was the projects, where he'd find his boys shooting the breeze about their weekend. Mason was also among the crowd. The swelling around his eyes had gone down, and he now had a black ring under the left one. Cojack had been talking to him ever since his unfortunate incident, trying to prevent anything drastic from happening.

You could never tell what was on Mason's mind. He was unpredictable. Still, Cojack loved the crazy muthafucka. How could he not love someone who would kill for him at the blink of an eye, no questions asked?

Actually, now that he was thinking about it, Cojack knew exactly why he was so devoted to this lunatic. It happened long ago when they were just teenagers. Even as a youngster, Cojack was someone who all the little shorties looked up to. One day he and a group of guys were shooting dice when a royal blue minivan pulled directly across from them and opened fire. The bullets weren't intended for Cojack but he was shot once in the back along with two others. One guy died at the scene from a single shot to the head. While Cojack was in the hospital, Mason, one of his young admirers, saw one of the guys involved and shot him on GP. Cojack and Mason hardly knew each other before then. By the time Cojack was released from the hospital, he'd learned what Mason had done for him. After that incident, they became the best of friends, bonded for life.

"So what you gon' do about Kenya's baby daddy?" Cojack asked Mason as the two stood away from the crap game, in between two buildings. Cojack was smoking his Black & Mild and Mason his blunt.

"You know how I get down," Mason said, taking a pull. "You

don't even have to ask me that shit. Muthafuckas gon' pay. You can best believe that."

"I know how you can get sometimes. You be doing some ol' unnecessary shit, so check this out," Cojack said. "Only go after the guy responsible."

"Fuck that!" Mason said, looking at Cojack as if he was crazy. "That bitch, Kenya, could have woke a nigga up, warned me or something."

Cojack sighed. "Promise me, just the dude who did it."

Mason didn't respond. He just twisted up his lips as if to say, *Yeah, whatever, man.*

"Cool?" Cojack said. "You wit' me on that one?"

Mason just stood there for a moment, then agreed. "Yeah, yeah, I'm wit' cha and shit, dawg."

"I don't know why you give a shit bout that bitch Kenya, anyway," Mason said. "You got a soft spot for the females, huh?" Mason began to snicker. "Speaking of females, that cutie, Robbin, rode through earlier and asked about you."

"Oh, word?" Cojack said, nodding his head, thinking he'd have to catch up with her.

Before Mason could respond, the conversation was cut short as a squad car came cruising by with two white officers flashing what they hoped were intimidating stares. Police got a kick out of the fear they saw in the dealers when they arrived. That was Cojack's cue. He jumped in his ride the minute they were out of sight. He was constantly harassed by the law, especially the ones who knew him by face. The ones who often stopped him just to say hello.

Cojack decided to go check out Robbin. It took him twenty-five minutes to reach Willow Oaks Apartments, where Robbin lived. As Cojack punched in the code, the gate ascended into the air. He drove through, made a left, slowed for a speed bump, and then rode another ten or fifteen yards where he parked beside Robbin's gold J30.

Cojack got out of his car and headed toward Robbin's apartment. He immediately noticed Robbin standing on the balcony. The mere sight of her brought a smile to his face. She was absolutely stunning, standing five feet six inches with skin the color of cinnamon.

"Hey, sexy," Cojack yelled up to her.

"Right back at ya," Robbin said. She walked into her apartment and went to the front door so that she could greet Cojack. By the time he got to her apartment, she was standing in the doorway waiting on him. Her skimpy shorts and sports bra, revealing a set of firm nipples, aroused him instantly as he stepped toward her and kissed her gently on the lips.

They had met six months ago at a party Mason hosted at Pier 7 Night Club for Cojack's birthday. It was in the VIP section that Mason led the attractive female to his friend and introduced them. They hung out a few times and had been good friends ever since. Robbin was real cool, and out of all the women he was involved with, she was the most fun. For one, she never asked for anything other than his time, which was a plus. She had her own car and her own place. Baby girl had it going on. Plus she had the prettiest smile, not to mention a body that could stop traffic.

She led him into her bedroom. The only light came from the television. Robbin smiled as Cojack kicked off his Wallies and sat down on the bed.

"Did you have fun in Myrtle Beach?" she asked, standing there smiling at him.

"Yeah, it was a'ight," he responded as if it wasn't a big deal.

"How many hos did you fuck?" Robbin had a way with words and always spoke her mind.

"Girl, you say anything out yo mouth. Why you gon' ask me somethin' like that?"

"Stop frontin'. I know how y'all niggas do. Bike week ain't nothin' but a freak fest." Robbin had seen a lot in her twenty-seven years and had been to the event on numerous occasions. She knew all too well about the nude women and freak parties. But none of it really mattered to her. She did her thang on the side every now and then and she figured the less fuss she made with Cojack, the less fuss he would make with her. But she enjoyed teasing him nonetheless. Cojack was her boo.

"Girl, why you looking all crazy? You high, ain't chu?" It was more of a statement than a question.

"Of course I am," she answered with a bit of a slur in her tone. "You know how I do." She bent down and began unfastening his belt. "I'm horny, too," she said in a husky voice. "Why you got on all these clothes? You know what I want."

Cojack doubled over in laughter as she continued to talk shit about how horny she had gotten while waiting on him. Robbin was on fire. Her juices oozed through her pink lace panties around her crotch and down her inner thigh. It was that way whenever he came near. Cojack dragged on his cigar as she kneeled down in front of him. She unbuttoned his belt and unzipped his Guess jeans, pushing them down to the floor.

"Lay back," she instructed, retrieving the cigar from his hand. Robbin motioned to the dresser and was back with a folded dollar bill. She pulled out his dick and began caressing it and watching it grow in her hand. Robbin licked her lips while sprinkling a white substance on the tip of his head. Cojack looked up at her curiously.

"Shorty, what the hell you up to?" he asked.

"Just lay back and let me drive this car. I wanna try something new." He observed the powder on his penis and shook his head.

He'd heard that freaks put coke on the dick to numb it up, but just 'cause he sold it didn't mean he ever tried it.

"Now just relax," she said as she commenced to licking the head of his cock until the substance was gone. She then let her tongue travel up and down the length of his penis, watching it swell. A deep sigh escaped from Cojack as he felt his muscle go deep inside her mouth, the head touching the back of her throat. Robbin was now sucking hard, and from the look on Cojack's face, it was evident he was enjoying himself. She had never sucked his dick so good before. Robbin could feel the bitter cocaine taste in her mouth, which only turned her on more. Drenched with the excitement, she slid out of her shorts and panties, kissed his head, and hopped on his dick. In minutes she was moaning and screaming out his name.

"Baby, damn! It is sooo good. Aw . . . oh I missed this dick," she exclaimed in an emotional outburst.

"Shit!" he responded as convulsions shook him. "Damn, boo. I'm ready to come," Cojack gasped and took hold of her shoulders, slamming every inch of his meat in her.

"No, Cojack, no. Please don't," she cooed. "Not yet, baby." Robbin felt his body tremble beneath her as a mother lode of seed filled her insides. She rode him faster, determined to get what she'd been longing for the whole night.

"Naw, you not getting soft on me," she said, her voice full of disappointment. She was angry and out of breath. "Shit!" she cursed and collapsed on top of him as he slipped out of her wet coochie. "I can't believe you did this to me again." She stared at him, waiting for an explanation. Cojack returned a dumbfounded look.

"Damn you!" She rolled off of him. "What's wrong with you? Why can't you stay hard, Cojack?" she said angrily.

He sat up, pulling at his member as if it would rise to the occasion.

"Damn, shorty, I don't know what the fuck is up."

"You not leaving me like this," she stated with a pout. He knew she was serious but couldn't help laughing.

"What the hell so funny?" She sucked her teeth and rolled her eyes. "I don't see shit funny. I'm sick of this shit," she stated in a fury. "Cojack, I told you what you need to do," she added, slightly blushing.

"Shorty, you should already know the answer to that. I don't get down like that."

"It ain't gon' hurt you, Cojack, dag. I been doing it for years and ain't nothin' happened." She pulled at his limp dick. "Baby, please. I need it so bad."

"Before I sniff dope, I'll get a bottle of ginseng," Cojack stated, laughing in a way that only infuriated her more.

"That shit don't even work! Live a little, boo. I know you'll like it. Just this once," Robbin begged.

What the hell is wrong with me? he wondered as he gazed at her disappointed look. Cojack hated the fact that he couldn't stay up after busting a nut. It was this way with all his female friends, but Robbin was the first to ever complain. She continued to nag him about the dope. Cojack shook his head, but in his mind he was seriously contemplating the idea. She had some good pussy and he wanted nothing more than to give her what she needed. She began kissing between his thighs, enticing him with long broad licks up his dick.

"Please, boo, just one time," she said, nibbling on the base of his shaft. "Don't I always give you what you want? I always please you, Cojack."

Ain't this a bitch! As much as he tried, he couldn't resist any longer. His eyes gazed over her perfectly shaped buns as she lay there blowing him. He knew a lot of cats would call this a straight-up sucker move, which he could not dispute. But tonight it didn't even matter. His only concern was knocking sparks from Robbin's fine ass for about two or three hours straight. "Fuck it," he finally said. "Where that shit at?"

She gave him a rolled-up dollar bill and some white powder. Without even looking at it, Cojack snorted.

"Damn, baby, that wasn't no coke," he said, sniffing.

"No," she said. She explained that it was heroin and that it would make him stay hard longer. At first Cojack was mad. It was one thing to snort a little coke, but he would never do something as stupid as sniffing heroin. But it was too late now, and with Robbin sucking his knob he didn't seem to care anymore. Everything just felt good—real good.

FOUR

THE NEXT DAY Cojack had important business to take care of. He had to meet a couple of his best customers and unload some product. The love for Cojack in the projects was tremendous. Under him were a gang of loyal adolescents who would do anything he asked without question. In a way he kind of felt responsible for his foot soldiers, because he had taken on such an authoritative role in their lives. He was the father of those who didn't have one. Aside from the hustlers, he really prided himself on the little kids who dwelled in the small confines of the ghetto. They were so precious, so innocent. He invested a lot of time in them.

Every other weekend he was taking them somewhere. Last week it was the Skateland, the girls' choice, of course. He'd rent three or four utility vehicles and squeeze as many children as he could in them and move out. It didn't take long for his partners to get involved after noticing how much attention they received from females as a result of their good deeds. King's Dominion was the most fun. In fact, Cojack had met many of the girls he was seeing when he was out with the kids. It warmed his heart to know their mothers trusted him the way they did. Most of them were single parents who were more than happy to see someone like Cojack doing nice things for their kids. A lot of the mothers were fiends and too high to keep up with their kids anyway. Cojack knew this and was saddened at times.

It was a warm Sunday afternoon, a perfect day for a cookout. Bellmeade Community Center was swarming with project kids. The parking lot was filled with cars and so was the street. Cojack had outdone himself as always. He had purchased pounds of hamburgers, hot dogs, and chicken for the grill. There were dozens of coolers full of soda and juice, as well as bag after bag of chips and cookies.

He and David, the event coordinator, were good friends. Over the years Cojack had donated money toward team uniforms and football equipment. At least twice a month they would get together and do something nice for the inner-city youth. Some of the mothers even volunteered to come out and assist with the cooking.

Several picnic tables were set up on the basketball court. The grills were burning and the place was swarming with folks happily indulging themselves in the free food and drinks. Alcohol was not allowed, at least not on the premises. But every now and then Mason, Fisher, and a few guys would dip off from the crowd for a quick sip of a forty and a chronic break. Cojack was too involved with the kids to think about dippin' off even for a second.

"Yo, little man," Cojack called to one of the boys who played on the football team.

"What's up, Cojack," the youngen said as he gave Cojack a five.

"What's been up? How are things going?"

"Things is cool."

"What about school? How's your grades?"

"They a'ight," the boy answered.

"A'ight don't get you in college," Cojack said in a serious tone. "A'ight don't get you out the hood. You know what I'm saying, little man?"

The boy put his head down and nodded. "I'm just having problems with math is all. I can't do those fractions and shit." Cojack sighed. "I mean stuff."

Cojack stood there and thought for a minute. "What if you had a tutor? Would that help you out?"

The boy laughed and sucked his teeth. "My moms ain't got no money for no tutor."

"I didn't ask you all that, now did I? If you had a tutor would that help you?"

"Yeah, I guess," the boy said, shrugging his shoulders.

"You guess?" Cojack asked.

"Yeah, it would. I can get better with some help."

"Then what do you say maybe twice a week after school you could come here to the rec and work with a math tutor?"

"That sounds good," the boy said.

"Cool. Then I'll hook it up."

"Damn, thanks, Cojack," the boy said. Once again Cojack sighed. "I mean, dang, Mr. Cojack, sir. Thank you."

Cojack laughed, then patted the kid on the head. "No problem. Now go on and eat up some of this food."

"Okay," he said, running off.

Cojack watched him run off and just stood there with a smile on his face. But then a gorgeous chick walked by and he stood there watching her ass instead.

Females crushed the party in packs. They wanted to be wherever the hustlers were. It was such a good day, but something was different for Cojack. Something was missing. His mind was distracted and all he thought about was going to see Robbin again. He remembered the way he had felt the night before, like he was some kind of superman. Maybe it wouldn't hurt to try some more of that stuff she had.

FIVE

TWO WEEKS after the picnic the sun was blazing over Richmond's streets, bringing people out to the Midlothian Car Wash in droves. It was more like a car show, the way drivers lined up their whips in front of the car wash for everyone to admire, everything from Hummers, Corvettes, and Escalades to souped-up old-school Caddys.

The chicks were hawking all of the fellas in an attempt to find their flavor, whether it was a dude in a snugly fit wife beater that outlined his cuts and a body covered in tattoos or a clean-cut dude in a Rocawear button-up with khakis.

Cojack cruised up and saw Mason's Philly cap hung to the back as he stood talking to two cuties in a forest green Land Cruiser. Cojack got out of his Lexus. His iced-out chain and Rolex glistened in the strong rays of the sun. Immediately, three girls cleaning out a red Tracker began flirting with him as he stopped to chat with a few of his buddies from the Ave. Finally, he made his way over to Mason, who was with two familiar faces, this woman named Mesha that Cojack sometimes ran with and her friend Kim. Cojack chuckled to himself at the look Mesha shot him. After giving his man dap, he faced the glaring female.

"Damn, Mesha, when we get there?" Cojack asked as he looked her up and down, admiring her toned physique. He almost quivered thinking about the last time the two of them had hooked up. Whether he came too quick or not and she never got hers, she got excited off of the mere fact of pleasing him.

"Why you ain't been callin' me?" she said, rolling her eyes.

"I can't even lie, shorty. A nigga been rippin' and runnin'.'"

"Unh-hunh, I bet," she replied.

"So what up, though?" He smiled and squeezed her cheek. "You gon' spend the day with a nigga or what?"

"And where we goin'?" she asked, snappin' her neck.

"For real, for real, I'm tryin' to lay back in an AC somewhere. Shit, we can hit the pool and chill. It's too hot to do anything else."

"That sounds like fun," Kim jumped in. Mason seemed to like the idea as well.

"So how you gon' act? You gon' chill out wit' your boy or what?" Cojack asked, giving her a pat on the behind. He stepped closer, observing her long bronze legs, thick hips, and a set of breasts that seemed like they would burst out of her one-size-too-small blouse if she breathed too hard.

She finally agreed but said they had to run up to Cloverleaf and get something out of layaway. That worked for Cojack because he had to make a quick run. He produced a bankroll, peeling off a crisp hundred. "Get the room after you handle your business," he said, handing Mesha the money.

"Anywhere specific, baby?" she asked in a sexy and drawn out tone.

"Anyplace with a pool."

Days Inn was located directly across from Chesterfield Towne Center. Mason and the girls were already in the pool when Cojack arrived. The foursome played around in the water for over an hour, dunking each other and simply enjoying themselves. Cojack and Mesha were the first to leave. He was answered at the expression on the white woman's face as he exited with a rock-hard penis. Her face turned a reddish pink and she started rubbing her neck as if she had become hot. He and Mesha laughed all the way to their room.

Inside, no time was wasted as Cojack and Mesha stripped themselves bare as if they couldn't wait another second. He rained soft, heated kisses on her neck and then laid her across the bed. Mesha looked in awe at his large penis. It seemed to have expanded a few inches since their last session. After ten minutes of foreplay, Cojack propped her legs on his shoulders. With her pretty manicured feet resting on his collarbone, he commenced to stroke her nice and slow.

Almost two hours later, Mesha had experienced three major orgasms, a record breaker for her. Cojack was sweating like a Hebrew slave and hadn't climaxed once. What the hell was his problem?

"Please come, baby," she begged. "You killin' me." There was no response as he turned her slippery body over like a pancake and began pounding her from behind. Twenty minutes later, Cojack said fuck it and faked his orgasm, collapsing on top of her. Soaked in each other's ecstasy, she looked at him nearly out of breath. "Did you come?"

"Yeah," he responded between breaths, lying through his teeth.

"Oh my God. Damn," she uttered and turned to him with a surprised expression. "You ain't never fucked me like that before. Have you been drinking or something?" He nodded, tired and drained, lying again. Luckily, it was a room with double beds because the bed they had fucked on was destroyed. Thirty minutes later, after regaining his strength, Cojack led her into the shower and picked up where they left off.

SIX

THE ROOM SEEMED to spin in front of Cojack as he sat in the corner of Pier 7 Night Club watching the dance floor. He had just left the VIP section after buying out the bar. Now he was standing close by the restroom, feeling like he'd puke any minute. The fellas had set up so much pussy for after hours that it was hard to pick and choose.

Cojack felt so twisted after leaving the restroom that he changed his mind and decided to call it a night. Plus he felt strange and very uneasy. He had a paranoid feeling that he couldn't dismiss. Maybe it was just being in the company of so many strangers. Or maybe he was just stoned out of his fucking mind. At any rate it was time to go. Everyone stayed back except Mason, who wanted to make sure his man got home safe.

Cojack felt more alert once the fresh air hit him. A lot of party-goers stood around in the parking lot, goofing around and passing time. As they proceeded on their long journey to the car, their attention quickly turned to a dispute fifteen yards away between two men and a female. Everyone in hearing distance tuned in as one young guy, obviously drunk, pulled out his penis and urinated a couple feet over from the pair.

"Ay man, you don't see the lady right here," the other guy stated.

"So? Fuck that bitch! I gotta piss. Tell her to turn her head," replied the young cat.

"C'mon, baby, don't pay him no mind," the woman suggested, tugging at her man's arm. He hesitated for a moment, staring at the youth.

"Got a problem or somethin', slim?" the youngster asked, zipping up his fly. He knew the man was pissed, but still, if he knew what was best for him, he'd take his girl and step.

"What!" the youngster barked, lifting up his shirt just enough for the other guy to see the pistol strapped to the side of his waist.

"I don't want no problem, man," the older guy said, then turned to his woman. "Get in the car. Let's go."

"Huh? That's what I thought," the drunk said as he turned and walked off. Suddenly, the sound of a gun being cocked brought him to a halt. The young drunk never got chance to pull his pistol.

Boom! The overconfident youngster was dead after the first bullet slammed through his brain. The last three were simply for general principle. The deafening vibrations echoed through the entire parking lot, sending people ducking for cover.

"Oh shit! Did you see that?" Cojack asked in disbelief, staring at the speeding car as the guy and his woman fled the scene.

Mason shook his head and replied, "I ain't see shit. C'mon, let's get the fuck outta here." They scurried through the parking lot, glancing at the riddled body stretched between two cars. After pulling off, they wound up out on the Ave, shooting dice.

The block was nearly deserted except for five or six young hustlers at the top of the corner getting that early-morning cash.

Dukey, a veteran in the projects who used to get money back in the mid-eighties, waved the Lexus down, flashing a bankroll, hollering, "What the dice hittin' fo?" The stranger he had with him was a dopehead, but he had a pocket full of cash. It was two in the morning and these cats had been going at it for an hour straight. Mason stood on the curb smoking a blunt while watching for the rollers.

"Don't cover the dice no more, Duke. This the second time you done pull that shit," Cojack warned.

"Nigga, you crazy," Duke replied, lying as usual. Everyone who gambled with him was aware of his slickness when it came to dice. It was just a matter of time before he did something to piss off his opponent. The stranger, whose name was Stan, told the men to stop arguing. "C'mon, baby, let's gamble," he said.

They continued and shot hard for another thirty minutes until Duke did it again. An argument erupted. Mason had to intervene by stepping between his homeboy and Dukey before a punch could be thrown. It had gotten so out of hand that Mason snapped.

"Y'all niggas wanna argue? Tell you what," he said, scooping the dice up and throwing them into the dark night. "Ain't no mutha-fuckin' body gamblin' then!"

Dukey and Stan looked at him, surprised, while Cojack simply laughed. He knew when his man was mad and so did Dukey. As for Stan, he grinned and said, "I got some more, baby. Don't worry." He was slurring, his head kept rolling, and his eyelids were getting heavy, making it obvious that the heroin had him feeling nice. Mason's eyes lit up as Stan pulled out a box of dice. Stan took three out and shook them in his hand before letting them fall to the side-walk. "One monkey don't stop no show," he stated, telling his two players to come on.

In one fluid motion, Mason pulled a chrome "four pound" from his waist and cocked it, catching everyone by surprise, including Cojack.

"Whoa, whoa. Playa, what's this about?" Stan stood, scared shit-less.

"Nigga, didn't I tell you the game is over?" Mason growled, aim-ing his weapon. Stan looked at Dukey for some type of assistance only to receive a dumbfounded look.

"Get the fuck from around here, muthafucka!" Mason threat-ened.

"A'ight, man. Please, I'm leavin'. I don't want no problems." Stan was so nervous that he stuttered out every word. Duke stood silently, zoning as if he were living a nightmare.

"You ain't moving fast enough, nigga," Mason yelled.

Boom! Mason fired a slug at Stan, causing him to fall against a nearby car.

"Please!" Stan screamed, clutching his wounded leg. "Don't kill me. Please don't," he hollered, moving swiftly, half walking and half limping. Dudes at the corner observed the action and quickly cleared the block, knowing the police were on their way. Mason laughed and fired off three more rounds. Stan grunted, catching another in his left biceps. He kept stepping in an effort to make it out alive. When Stan was out of sight, Mason turned his attention to Duke.

"You started this shit, so go ahead and blame yourself for what just happened," Mason said.

The old head didn't respond, scared that he'd say something to get himself killed. He knew Mason was half crazy and, if provoked, wouldn't think twice of offing him.

Just two years earlier Mason had slumped a cop for running up on him at the wrong time. He'd just left Cojack and had two kilos in a bag in the backseat. Luckily, he was stopped on a backstreet a couple blocks over from Midlothian Village. As soon as the cop walked up to the car, Mason just unloaded his entire clip, giving him several head shots to make sure he was dead.

Cojack cursed him the whole walk to the car for cappin' Stan. They drove away from the projects and Mason snickered as they passed the wounded man sitting on a porch across from the projects.

"You's a fuckin' nutcase, cuz," Cojack said as he made a right turn on Jefferson Davis. When they stopped at a red light, he looked over at Mason and asked, "Why you do that crazy shit, man?"

"He disrespected me," Mason replied. "Who the fuck is he to pull out some dice? Nigga ain't even from round here. He lucky I ain't merk his ass. You know I could've."

Cojack sighed and shook his head. "Now we gotta worry about this nigga comin' back. Or even worse, sending the police at us. You ain't think about that, did you?"

"Damn," Mason muttered, realizing that Cojack had a point.

"And you know Dukey. He ain't nothing but a snake. Now we gotta look out for this nigga, too." Cojack had to take a deep breath to calm his growing anger. He continued, "How the hell you expect to get money and be gangsta at the same time? You tryin' to live up to that maniac shit for real, ain't chu?"

Mason laughed and replied, "I feel you, man. But for real, for real, I done seen plenty gangsta niggas get money."

"Oh yeah, and how long they last?" Cojack asked.

"Not long," Mason answered, gazing out of the window. "But see, most of them dudes didn't know what the hell they was doing."

"And you do?" Cojack said.

Mason nodded and said, "A lot of niggas just be out there in the way. It ain't what you do, Jack, but how you do it."

"Look, cuz, all I'm saying is we coulda handled the shit another way." Cojack paused for a second. "You don't think, man. You just act and I'm telling you now, shit like that is what brings heat. Fuck the stupid shit. I'm tryin' to get this paper."

"Yeah, you right, man," Mason agreed. They rode in silence listening to Jay-Z's *Reasonable Doubt*. Cojack dropped Mason off at his Village Green apartment and then hit the highway and headed home.

Despite his long-standing loyalty, Cojack was beginning to question Mason and he wondered if Mason's actions would eventually impact his paper.

SEVEN

A WEEK LATER, Cojack pulled into a busy Southside Plaza on a balmy Friday evening. Light drizzles were whizzing through a cloudless sky as he parked and hurried up to buy some liquor before the weekend. As he approached the store, Nation of Islam members were posted outside selling bean pies and the *Final Call* newsletter. As usual he was greeted with a smile; then a brother waved a newspaper at him.

"I got you, brotha," Cojack said. "Let me run in here right quick." No matter where he bumped into these distinguished brothas, whether at functions or in the middle of traffic, he always supported their cause.

He was in and out of the liquor store in no time. After purchasing three pies and a *Final Call*, he made his way over toward his car. The champagne-colored Maxima parked beside his Lexus instantly caught his attention. The female behind the wheel stared at him. Damn, he thought, shorty girl is fine as hell. She was alone. At least it appeared that way. Cojack glanced around as he approached his ride and opened the door.

"Hey, is your name Cojack?" she asked. Cojack shot her a puzzled look as he turned around.

"I don't know, who is you?" he curiously inquired.

She blushed, then answered, "April."

Cojack put the bag inside the car and walked over to her ride. "I don't believe I know you, do I?"

"No, you don't know me," April said, before drawing a long sigh. "Look, Cojack, I'm here for my cousin Kenya."

"Kenya?" he uttered. "Kenya who?" He was totally lost. She flashed a timid smile that only puzzled him even more.

"Kenya used to see your friend Mason."

"Oh, that Kenya," Cojack said, recalling the female. "What the hell goin' on?" Cojack's whole demeanor changed. This was the same chick that crossed his man up. At least that's how Cojack saw it. How else did her baby daddy get inside the apartment? April claimed that her cousin needed to speak to him. What the hell could she possibly have to say? Was she trying to save her kid's father? Did she think he could change Mason's mind? Baby girl had another thing coming.

"Tell Kenya I don't have nothing to do with that," Cojack said. He turned on his heel, got in his car, and drove away. The moment he left the Plaza, he picked up his cell phone and tried to contact Mason but wasn't successful.

Darkness had covered the sky by the time he reached the projects. By now, Cojack had forgotten all about telling Mason about Kenya sending her cousin to holler at him. Cojack went on about his usual business.

The block was wide open as usual. A group of girls stood on the corner puffing ganja. They all hollered simultaneously as the Lexus whipped around the corner. Cojack honked the horn and kept it moving. There was so much going on that Cojack quickly parked directly behind an Acura Legend. Three or four flatfooters trying to come up was pushing crack through the window of a white pickup truck that they had surrounded. Cojack stood chatting with one of the baseheads when he noticed several of his partners standing in a cut in front of Pearl's bootleg spot. There was a lot of commotion, whooping, and hollering. Immediately, Cojack sensed a bad vibe. It was a bunch of them gathered together. The whole scene just seemed strange. Cojack told the fiend he'd see him later and started over toward the group.

Cojack reflected back on his strange encounter with the chick at the Plaza. He wondered what Kenya had to say. Did it have something to do with Mason? Where was he anyway? Everyone was there except him. Cojack was within thirty feet of the clique when Fisher turned and looked at him. His eyes were tiny dark beads. His expression startled Cojack so bad that he paused in his tracks. What the hell happened? Then everyone looked his way and had the same face. It was then that he realized they were all crying. They had drinks in their hands. Tupac's CD was blasting from Pearl's stereo. Where the hell was Mason? Cojack felt his insides shift as intense pressure began to build up. Was it a coincidence that a stranger approached him about Kenya?

Finally, he was there, standing before fifteen or twenty of his people. Their eyes were bloodshot red and he could see murder in them. He almost didn't want to ask, but he had to.

"What the hell is goin' on?" he asked, looking at all the faces around him.

"They killed him, man," Davo cried out.

"What? Who?" Cojack said. "Where?"

"Tupac, man," Fisher interjected. "Mutherfuckas just announced on the radio that he died." At this point Mason appeared in Pearl's doorway and Cojack exhaled a little. He had never felt so happy to see this muthafucka in his life. Then it hit him.

"Tupac died?" Cojack asked as if he hadn't heard it the first time. Cojack suddenly felt empty inside. No one there knew this guy personally, yet these cats were shedding tears and pouring out liquor as if a real homey had died. Who was this man? This shit was not a game. These dudes were not squares. They were real life hustlers and killers ready to go all out.

Now that Tupac was gone, who would be their spokesperson? Man, it was a sad day. Someone great had just departed this life. Cojack went and grabbed his liquor from the car, got some cups, and set out in front of Pearl's door while Tupac's voice trailed through the night.

EIGHT

IT WAS APPROXIMATELY 7:30 A.M. as Cojack got off the expressway ramp on the Chippenham Parkway exit coming to a complete stop at a red light. He breezed through the light traffic on his GSX-R1100 turning left toward Town & Country Apartments, where Mason lived.

THE GHOST

Mason's apartment was laid. The floor was covered with wall-to-wall carpet and triangle mirrors hung on the walls. An oak wood coffee table with built-in glass holders sat in front of a black circular leather couch with matching armchairs. The sixty-inch flat screen was the best part. Mason's girl practically had to drag him to bed because he'd sit in front of the TV until he fell asleep.

As Mason trotted down the stairs, he looked like a child who'd just been awakened for school. "Wake your ass up, cuz. Ain't nothin' gon' come to a sleeper but a dream," Cojack said.

"Damn, nigga. You up early as shit," Mason said, sprawling across from him on his cozy long couch.

"Yeah, cuz. This how I been doing it for the past few days. I know you gon' think I'm tripping, but I swear to God I can't sleep worth a damn anymore. And my back is aching. I been feeling bad, but going to bed don't help."

Mason just shook his head.

"Jack, you need to leave that dope alone, man. How much of that shit you been sniffing?"

"Nothing for a few days."

"You dope sick," Mason said. "Got a little bitty habit going."

"That ain't it," Cojack said. He knew he hadn't been that stupid.

Their conversation came to a halt when Trina appeared at the top of the stairs fully dressed in her work attire. She sauntered down and kissed her man, not speaking to Cojack on her way out. As the door slammed behind her, Mason chuckled. "Shorty in her feelings."

"Yeah, I could tell she was mad when she opened the door," Cojack said.

"She'll be a'ight, though. I usually hit her off before she go to work." Mason smirked. "When you gon' settle down with something?"

"No time soon," Cojack answered. "I got ninety-nine problems, and a bitch ain't one. I rather stick and move, playa."

"That dope enough problems," Mason said, and shook his head. "Shorty musta put something real tough on you to make you start sniffing that shit." Cojack gave him the "I've heard this sermon before" face. "You ain't trying to hear that though, are you? You the one used to tell me not to fuck with it." Mason met his gaze. "Remember what you said, fucking with dope ain't but one route a nigga can go and that's down!" Mason reminded him.

Cojack took a long drag off his cigar and released a cloud of smoke. "You finish yet, playa? I ain't come over here for that. I'm up early in the morning, taking care of business. Do it look like I'm slackin'?" Cojack flashed a perfect smile. "I'm on toppa my game."

"It's yo world, cuz," Mason admitted.

"Here," Cojack said, pulling a package from his book bag and passing it to him. "It's a bird. This gon' be it for a minute. I talked to my man and he saying it might be a month or two before he be back on. I'ma break the rest of this shit I got down. The price still the same for you but I'm gon' tax the rest of them niggas."

"It's all good 'cause I'ma get me an extra quarter key off this shit." Mason snickered. "Yeah, I'ma blow this shit right on up."

Cojack rose to his feet, securing his backpack over his shoulder. "I'ma be runnin' all day. Let everybody know I'll be through when it gets dark."

It was nearly six P.M. when Cojack left the barbershop. The sun was down and night was approaching. He planned to stop by Willie's Record Store and pick up a few CDs, but he was interrupted by two pages from his mother. Already an hour late from dropping her off some cash for the light bill, he hopped on his motorcycle and headed straight across town.

For Cojack, a kid was the furthest thing from his mind. He

didn't have a steady girlfriend. At twenty-six years old, he lived by the motto "Never get attached to anything you can't leave when it's time to go." Cojack had plenty of females he enjoyed being around but hadn't found that special one who could make his heart skip a beat.

As he turned into his neighborhood he beeped his horn at Keisha, a cutie he'd knocked off a few times. He drove up the hill and parked behind his mother's Ford Explorer, which he had purchased just last year for her birthday. On his way to the door he stopped beside the truck, noticing it could use a wash, then hollered at Killer in the backyard, who was standing on top of his doghouse having a fit at the mere sight of his owner.

The house was soundless, which was very odd. He yelled for his mother, "Ma," but received no response.

"Hell she at?" he mumbled, calling for her again. "Ma!" Still no answer. Strange, he thought as he tossed his bag and helmet on the living room chair. Cojack paused for a moment trying to think of where his mother could be with her truck still here. Just twenty-five minutes ago he received two pages. Then it dawned on him, she was over Ms. Penny's crib across the street, probably running her mouth. With them two together, it was no telling how long she'd be gone.

Cojack proceeded into the den. That's when everything began to go in slow motion. First, the turned-over end of the couch got his attention. Then his heart fell to the floor as his mother came into view in the corner of the room. Her mouth and hands were duct-taped and her feet tied together. Panic gripped his entire being as he bolted toward her only to be struck over the head.

"Get the fuck up!" a strong voice demanded from above. Cojack's vision began to blur from the incredible blow as he struggled to his feet. Suddenly, another figure came into view. Dressed in all black with a ski mask, he aimed the .40-caliber gun at Cojack's mother's head.

"Please, man, don't hurt her," Cojack pleaded, tears clouding his eyes. His heart ached as he gazed at her horror-stricken face. "Just tell me what you want," he said to the man holding him at gunpoint.

"Shut the fuck up. You talk when I tell you to, you dig?" *Crack!* The tall gunman leveled the butt of his pistol across Cojack's head. Blood leaked into his eyes as he clutched at the throbbing pain. Was this all a bad dream? Please God let it be, he prayed to himself.

"Where the money at, nigga?" the gunman said. Nope, it wasn't a dream. "Don't play with us, muthafucka!" The man's voice was full of hostility as he pressed the cold barrel against Cojack's cheek. "I'ma ask you one more time."

"Homeboy," the man called across the room to his partner. "If he don't give us what we came for, I want you to blow that bitch's brains out, you hear?" His man nodded toward Cojack's mother and cocked his burner.

"Wait! Please. I got it upstairs," Cojack said. He couldn't believe this was happening. He tried desperately to place the voice but couldn't. "Don't hurt her. God, please don't. That's my mama, man. It's over two hundred thousand dollars upstairs. It's yours, every dime, just don't hurt her." Cojack was trembling and didn't really care about nothing but protecting his earth. How could this be? The woman who gave him life sat there duct-taped as if she was nothing but an old box.

As the gunman pushed Cojack up the stairs, keeping the pistol in his back, Cojack turned to catch a glimpse of his mother. Their eyes connected for what seemed an eternity. Was this the last time he would see her alive? Would they take the money and kill them both? Damn! Where did I go wrong? he wondered.

"He not gon' hurt her, is he?" Cojack asked.

"If your word is good, we'll leave here in peace. But if you fucking with us, I promise, both of you will die right beside each other. Now move it!" the gunman said, shoving Cojack forward.

The hallway was long and narrow. Both sides of the walls were decorated with expensive paintings. His mother was an art fanatic, always visiting art galleries. Her favorite pictures showed scenes of oceans and waterfalls. She was just so intrigued with beauty.

Cojack came to a complete stop in the hallway. He swallowed hard, not because his mouth was dry. It was just something about having a gun to his back and his mother downstairs scared shitless. Cojack pointed to a huge abstract painting in a gold frame and said, "It's right there."

"Where?" the gunman asked. Cojack took the picture from the wall. An instant smile covered the guy's face upon seeing the built-in safe. When it opened, his eyes lit up like Christmas tree lights. "Damn, you full up. I knew you was strapped," he said excitedly as he handed Cojack a bag for him to load the cash in.

Back downstairs the masked gunmen tied up Cojack's hands and feet good enough for them to make it out of the neighborhood. After they left, Cojack struggled with the ropes and finally freed himself. He reached for his mother, hugged her, and asked if they had hurt her.

"No, they didn't hurt me. I didn't give them no reason to hurt me," she said.

The turned-over sofa was just a mask. One of the guys did it to throw Cojack off. Both mother and son sat and cried.

"I'm sorry, Ma," Cojack said over and over.

Cojack spent the next thirty minutes calling friends from the projects. He couldn't reach Mason. The others offered to come over but Cojack declined the offer. It was no use. He had no clue who his assailants were. He even called Keisha to ask her if she had seen anything unusual in the neighborhood. She said no and then asked when could they hook up. That's when she got the dial tone. Pussy was the last thing on Cojack's mind.

"Baby, how much did they take? It wasn't what you said, was it?" his mother asked.

Cojack finally sat down. His nose was running as he clutched at the pain in his stomach.

"What's wrong with you, boy?" Momma asked, shooting him a curious look.

"They took everything, Ma, two hundred thirty thousand dollars."

"Oh my God," she whispered. "I'm sorry, baby," she said in between sobs.

He took her small frame in his arms and kissed her. "Don't apologize, Momma. It's my fault."

NINE

ROBBIN SLOWED UP in front of the house, checked the address in her hand, and drove into the driveway. She got out of the car and walked up to the door and knocked. As she waited for someone to answer the door, she wondered if this was where Cojack lived. In the past he was always so secretive about anything he did. Her heart pounded as the door was opened by a small woman who appeared to be in her late forties. No one had to tell her that this was Cojack's mother. She had his same exact features, the high cheekbones and spacious eyebrows. She wore a long turquoise housecoat and had suede slippers on her feet. Robbin cleared her throat and asked if Cojack was in.

"And what's your name?" the woman asked.

"Robbin," she replied.

"Well, I'm Cojack's mother," she said, opening the screen door. "C'mon in. He's waiting on you." Momma hardly ever got a chance to see any of Cojack's friends, so in spite of how the day had unfolded, she still acted kindly toward her. Robbin followed her into the kitchen and waited while she poured two large glasses of lemonade. "He upstairs in the last room on the right." Robbin accepted the glasses from her outstretched hands and then went upstairs.

She took a deep breath and tapped lightly on the door. The first thing she noticed upon entering was the chrome Glock on the dresser. When they had talked on the phone, she could sense in his voice that something was wrong. After placing the drinks down, she joined him on the end of the bed where he sat staring out the window into the dark night.

"Did you bring it?" he asked bluntly.

"Yeah, it's in my purse. What happened to your head?" Cojack grabbed her hand as she attempted to touch it.

"Nothing, it's a'ight," he replied.

"Why you got that gun out like that? Is something going on?"

"Get that for me and stop asking so many goddamn questions." The turbulence in his tone was evident. Never had she seen him so distant, so rude. Had he lost his damn mind? She started to say something but decided not to.

Robbin opened her purse and passed him a folded dollar bill. "I like your momma. She's real nice," Robbin said, trying to ease the tension. Robbin watched in awe as he sniffed the entire pill of dope.

"Take it easy, boy, damn!"

Cojack looked up, a trace of powder still on his nose, and asked, "You gon' stay with me tonight or what?"

"If you want me to," she replied, sitting down beside him. "You sure you all right?" She gazed at the deep cut on his head. "I think you might need stitches."

"I'm a'ight, shorty," he said. "Make yourself comfortable." Cojack fell back across the bed as she proceeded with his request. The heroin did its job, causing him to sink into a deep trance. He reflected back on his horrible day. *Where did I go wrong? Where did these muthafuckas come from?* A lonely tear trickled down his cheek as he pictured his own mother held at gunpoint. It was the worst thing that could happen. Why him?

"Two hundred thousand dollars," he mumbled bitterly. He felt weak and didn't want to see or talk to anyone. Robbin was only there because she had what he needed. He could've gotten it from someone else but she was more convenient being that he didn't have to leave. Plus she kept good dope. He thought of his best friend and their conversation this morning. "Heroin will only bring you down, nigga," Mason had said.

Cojack gazed at the beautiful woman as she cuddled up under him and mouthed a quiet "Damn, I can't believe this shit."

TEN

A FEW DAYS LATER, Cojack sat inside Harvey's Barbershop on Hull Street getting a cut. It was a Thursday evening and the place was about half full. Sabrina, the beautician, had a handful of walk-ins. From the back she had been observing Cojack since he arrived. Actually, the entire shop was looking at him perform like a true dope fiend, nodding and scratching terribly. Children laughed and pointed, while adults whispered among themselves.

What started off as a trick to keep his dick hard turned into a habit right underneath Cojack's nose. He found himself taking a hit here and there throughout the day like it was nothing. He kept telling himself that each time would be his last time, but it never was.

James, his barber, caught hell cutting his hair. He woke him up twice to tell him to keep his head still. But it was no use. The heroin was just too strong. If it wasn't for Cojack being a regular, James would've been upset. They were like family, though. Cojack was a seven-year veteran at the barbershop.

Cojack finally awakened. James was just putting on the finishing touches when a thunderous blast startled the hell out of everyone in the shop. Parents pulled their kids close and held them.

"What the hell was that?" asked Kevon, one of the barbers.

"Probably a car backfiring," James answered. Kevon walked to the door and looked out. Everything was normal, regular busy Hull Street traffic. He retreated back to his chair to tend to his customer. Just as Cojack was about to call Mason to see where he was, the phone chimed in his hand.

"Yo, what up?" Cojack answered.

"Jack, I'm outside. Come out now. Hurry up," Mason said.

"What—"

"Don't ask no questions," Mason interrupted. "Just c'mon."

Cojack hung up and quickly pulled out a knot of cash and peeled off a twenty. James observed his trembling hands as he accepted the bill.

"You a'ight, playa?" James said, looking curiously at Cojack as he scrambled toward the entrance. There was no response. Cojack waved and left out the door. The Infiniti pulled up directly in front of him. Mason pushed the passenger door open, and Cojack jumped in.

"You almost made the six o'clock news," Mason told him as he pulled away.

"What you mean?" Cojack asked, confused as hell. A smile appeared across Mason's face as he peered up into the rearview mirror, then made a quick detour back toward the barbershop. When they were within a block of the building, Mason instructed him to look in the parking lot once they were there.

"Oh shit!" Cojack mouthed at the sight of a body sprawled out between two cars.

"I know you heard the shot," Mason said, and pressed the gas pedal.

Cojack could recall the loud blast he heard that broke him out of a deep nod while in the barbershop. Hold up, he thought. What the hell was Mason saying?

"You did that?" Cojack asked.

"You slippin' like hell, nigga. Hell, yeah, I did it. That woulda been your high ass if I wouldn't have showed up when I did."

"Fuck is you talking about, man?" Cojack asked.

"That was the nigga I shot awhile back at the crap game, remember?"

"Get the fuck outta here." Mason just nodded. "You mean the dude that was with Dukey that night?"

"Yeah," Mason said, stopping for a red light at Hull and Midlothian directly across from the gas station. Mason described how he watched the man walk to the window, look in, and then retreat to this Pontiac Bonneville. The guy did this act twice.

"I know it was risky in broad daylight and all, but I had to get him, Jack. The nigga was laying on you, man. Least we ain't got to worry about him no more."

ELEVEN

AFTER A COUPLE MONTHS passed, Cojack couldn't seem to get it right. There was still no word on his assailants, and the dope became his pain reliever. People who saw Cojack in the street couldn't believe it was him. Even the females who used to follow him around were talking bad, surprised at how drastically he'd fallen in such a short period of time.

The only good thing going for him was his connect, a cat black as midnight from Nigeria who supplied half of the city with coke.

He gave Cojack two kilos on the strength of his word and simply told him to spend the money he made back with him. So Cojack wasn't completely broke, still holding six figures, but now he had a monkey on his back that would soon get the best of him. He sniffed more heroin than usual and had begun to push all the weight on Mason.

The temperature dropped suddenly, a sure sign that fall had arrived.

Cojack and Robbin were sitting in her gold J30, waiting to meet Mason at Captain D's. Mason pulled up and nodded to Robbin as Cojack got out and staggered to his passenger door.

"Nigga, you high as a bitch," Mason mumbled under his breath. Cojack ignored him and sighed once he was inside as if something terrible had happened.

"What's up, man?" Mason asked with a concerned tone.

"Cuz, we got a problem. Don't you know? This sucka-ass Nigerian talking bout he ain't gon' sell me no more coke after this week."

"Get the fuck outta here, you serious. But why?" Mason asked.

Cojack chuckled. "This muthafucka gon' tell me I'm washed up. Nigga say I don't want no money. Do you believe that bullshit? All the cake I done made this bitch!" Cojack was furious. Mason observed him closely. He hadn't stopped scratching since he got in. Both men sat in silence for a moment. Then Mason faced him.

"This is fucked up, man. What the hell we gon' do now?"

Cojack looked straight ahead, a smile stretched across his face. "We gon' rob his bitch ass. That's what we gon' do." Mason shook his head as if he wasn't pleased with the response. "Fuck the nigga, cuz. He in the way."

"You know what? I think you done lost your goddamn mind. Listen to yourself, Jack."

"Fuck is you talkin' bout, cuz?" Cojack replied. "Nigga, this ain't no game. You think I'ma let this nigga play me like that. Two hundred thirty thousand dollars muthafuckas rob me for and this sucka talking bout cutting me off. I made this nigga millions!"

"Calm the fuck down, man," Mason said as he noticed a few people leaving the restaurant looking their way. A white family had heard as well. "Cojack, you gon' fuck around and get us killed fucking with these Nigerians. I can't go out like that."

"Oh, you scared? Not my nigga. Don't let me find out you scared. Here, jump in my pocket then."

"Fuck you, Cojack. You know goddamn well I ain't scared. I'll take it to any nigga's face! I'm King Kong out this bitch! Don't get shit twisted," Mason said in his defense.

Cojack smiled. "Yeah, now that's my nigga. That's what the fuck I wanna hear!"

"Look, Jack, you know I got your back, but damn, man. Who the fuck gon' have mine? You getting high as a bitch, cuz. I—"

"Is you going with me or what, man?" Cojack interrupted.

"Check this, man. It ain't nothin' I won't do for you. But you ain't you no more. This ain't the nigga I grew up with, the flyest nigga I know. Damn, I sho miss that nigga." Cojack just listened, realizing it was all true. Mason continued, "Now say we rob these niggas and come off. We gon' have to burn 'em. That ain't even a question. But what's the use, Jack, if you still gon' get high?"

"You right, cuz," Cojack said, nodding his head.

"Do you know how much it hurt to see you on that shit? You like my brotha, man. Know what though," Mason paused. "Before I see you destroy yourself, I'll kill you myself." A long silence fell over the car as Mason's words sunk in.

"Nigga, is you serious? Fuck you mean, you'll kill me?" Cojack said, surprised at his boy's words.

"Jack, I swear to God on my dead momma, before I see you turn into a dope fiend, I'll burn you, cuz."

Cojack stared out of the window in a trance. He really didn't know what to say. "You's a wild muthafucka, cuz. But you ain't gotta worry about that. I fell off but after we take care of business, I'll get back. So you rolling with me or what?"

Mason hesitated, but he had always had his boy's back and what would it look like if he didn't continue to? He finally agreed with a nod of the head.

"How much you think we can come off with?" Mason asked.

"I'm looking for him to be loaded for real. He gotta see a lot of niggas. I was supposed to have five keys coming to me so ain't no tellin' how much shit this sucka gon' have. He a flashy nigga, too. Last time I was with him he showed me over fifty birds. He'll be in town this weekend. I already know we gon' come off whether it be coke or money. The only problem is that we gon' need at least two more heads. Some thoroughbreds. You need to get at the crew. Think you can handle that?"

"Yeah, I got somebody," Mason replied.

"Good. Well, I'll call you tomorrow. I see this broad over there grillin' me."

"You need to lose her ass," Mason suggested as they exchanged daps.

Cojack laughed. "You the one brought her to me."

"I regret I ever did that stupid shit, too."

"You's a wild boy. Talk to you tomorrow," Cojack said as he got out.

The weekend was approaching and in another twenty-four hours Cojack's plan would be put into motion. Mason recruited two young gunners who'd been dreaming of an opportunity like this. The Nigerian was in town and the hit squad was just waiting on Cojack's call. It was nothing for this cat to unload fifty to a hundred kilos in a week's time. He moved weight all over Virginia and never stayed in the same spot for too long. The three dudes that stuck to him like glue would be the only obstacle. They were mean-looking muthafuckers who seldom spoke unless Bam, their leader, asked for assistance. Cojack made it clear that there wasn't to be any half-stepping. Shoot first and ask questions later. That was pretty much the plan. Run in the spot, cut these cats down, and take the goodies and bounce.

Mason and two young members of his crew, Sam and Fisher, were held up in a hotel on the outskirts of the city waiting on Co-jack. Growing restless, Mason punched in his digits. On the third ring, a voice said, "What up?"

"You tell me," replied Mason. "Any word yet?"

"I just hung up with the nigga," Cojack said. "It ain't gon' happen until tomorrow night. The same spot I was tellin' you about though. We gotta get there an hour early, a'ight."

"I hear you. Just keep me posted." Mason pushed end and turned to his friends in the room. "Tomorrow, y'all."

"I can't wait," Sam said eagerly. "I don't like Nigerians anyway." Mason observed his two buddies as they laughed, giving each other high fives. They were too damn excited.

"Look, man," Mason said, getting their attention. "We gon' do this work sober. That means no weed, you hear?"

"What!" Both men bolted simultaneously. "You gotta be joking, right," Sam exclaimed.

"Do it look like I'm joking? Ain't no room for slipups, man. Ain't nobody smoking and that's final. This ain't amateur night. We fucking with some sho nuff niggas."

Sam looked Mason dead in the eyes. "You need to be telling Cojack this shit. He the one getting high as a kite."

TWELVE

THE URGE FOR HEROIN had become a constant nagging feeling that Cojack couldn't dismiss. It was a fixation he couldn't quite get away from. He could remember watching some of the best players around the city fall victim to this monster, but he never thought it would happen to him. Man would rather die than experience the pain felt when that shot wasn't on time. The white devil had become his new love.

He arose from his sleep with a runny nose and stumbled to the dresser, retrieving the pill of heroin Robbin left for him the night before. She had been an occasional user but now she was also getting high whenever they were together. Lately, she'd been trying to distance herself from him, but she was his connect and he didn't let her stay away for long.

Cojack exhaled as he caught the drain he was looking for. He made a face as the bitter taste came up in his throat, but it soon passed and he began to feel the soothing effects of the drug.

I got a long day ahead of me, he thought to himself as he gazed in the mirror at his reflection.

"Damn," he swore. He could see himself deteriorating right before his eyes. He was thin and his eyes were glassy with deep, dark circles around them.

"Fallen off, playa," he reminded himself of his friend's words as he splashed water on his face. After washing up, he threw on the same Polo sweatsuit he had worn the night before and was on his way. Thirty minutes later he was cruising through the early-morning traffic along with his dog on their way across town to meet Charles, a dude from Farmville he saw once a month who purchased nothing under a half of a key. As he drove, puffing on his cigar, he couldn't help thinking about the guys that robbed him. He even saw them in his dreams. Their evil eyes under the ski masks and the deep voice often woke him out of his sleep.

He felt like a damn fool. Was it the heroin that caused this to happen? And what about the guy that caught him slipping at the barbershop? While he was in the chair nodding, this cat had been back and forth just waiting on him. How did he know? He got a call from his barber that same night. James said it was a good thing he left because someone had been shot outside the shop. He then added he remembered the man's face from earlier that day. Cojack's thoughts bounced back from the barbershop scene back to the guys who robbed him. They had to have been clocking him for a while to come to his home and duct-tape his mother.

"Muthafucka!" he cursed, bitterly coming to a complete stop at a red light at Broad Rock and Hull. His eyes fixed on two black guys driving a dark blue Quest minivan. For some odd reason he just knew the robbers were still watching, looking for another opportunity.

"Damn, I'm 'noid as shit," he mumbled. Cojack had even brought his mother a .38 special, instructing her to go nowhere without it. He noticed a black sedan cruising beside him, the driver peering over in his direction. Were they the dudes who robbed him? How would he know? One thing for sure, he'd never forget that voice. It seemed everybody was watching. He noticed his paranoia when he wasn't high and he wasn't high now. The heroin he snorted earlier that morning was all that kept him from getting sick.

Finally, he arrived at his destination. As he drove up to the Amoco gas station, Killer barked at a white couple holding hands near the pay phone. Cojack was pleased to see Charles parked at the vacuum, cleaning out his car. He pulled into the middle car wash as always. After retrieving the coke from the toolbox he placed it inside the truck, and thoughts of his connect entered his mind. He couldn't wait to rip that sucker off.

"Washed up," he recited the man's words. "We'll see who gon' be washed up after tonight, Nigerian muthafucka!"

Charles pulled his Nissan Sentra into the car wash beside Cojack. His kid's mother, a sexy brown-skinned chick with hazel eyes, was in the passenger seat. The exchange was quick as usual. They shook hands afterward, and Charles got in his ride and drove away. Cojack glanced at his Rolex Presidential and noticed that it was nine A.M. Willie's was about to open and he wanted to stop by and pick up the new Makaveli CD. From there he was going to pay his barber a visit. He jumped in his truck and no sooner had he put it in drive than the strangest thing happened.

A Quest van pulled in front of him while at the same time a car pulled up tight behind him. The white couple he'd spotted at the pay phone when he first arrived appeared from out of nowhere, pointing guns and flashing badges while yelling for him to throw up his hands in surrender. When he looked closer, it was the same van from earlier with the two black guys. The sedan was at the scene as well. What the hell was happening? Killer barked hysterically as ATF jackets surrounded him in the truck. The commotion was so loud that Cojack could barely make out what the agents were saying. Cojack kicked his Glock under the seat while Killer held the agents at bay. They threw a cover over the dog to restrain him and then ordered Cojack out of the truck. People slowed down in their cars. Employees from the gas station even stepped out to catch a glimpse as agents escorted Cojack in handcuffs to the waiting van.

They drove him to a white and gray brick building. He had never been locked up before but it was something about this place that spooked him the hell out. There was nothing but woods surrounding the area. No houses or apartments. Not even a business in the vicinity. He'd heard many stories about the Feds and how they had their own private offices somewhere hidden in the city. A person could ride past them a million times and never know they were federal processing stations.

His urge for a sniff was steadily increasing as he sat in the lonely interrogation room, cursing Charles for setting him up. He observed his surroundings for the first time since he arrived. The small room was dingy. The walls looked dirty and the light was dim. There was one door with a huge glass window that he stared though, wondering if they were watching him.

"Bitch muthafucka!" Cojack stated in fury. "I can't believe this shit. I got the worse fuckin' luck in the world," he said dejectedly.

What was happening to his life? Was someone trying to tell him something? Suddenly, the door opened and a black guy walked in holding a Ziploc bag in his hand.

"Look familiar?" the man said, flashing a grin as he dropped the coke in front of Cojack.

"What the hell is that?" Cojack backed away as if a snake was in front of him.

"It's yours. I'm Agent Boston," he said.

"Ay, you need to get that shit from round me. It ain't mine," Cojack announced. Boston roared in laughter as he sat on the end of the table watching the remarkable performance. He glanced over his shoulder at someone behind the glass.

"Mind if I call you Cojack?" He chuckled. "Look, man, cut the shit. Your buddy in the other room talking so much we had to put a sock in his mouth." Cojack dropped his head just as a cleaned-faced white guy walked in. The same dude he saw at the pay phone with the lady.

"My man Cojack, finally we meet. I'm Agent Whitehead." Cojack stared at both men and couldn't help feeling as though he'd seen them before. "You don't remember, do you, Cojack?"

"Remember what?" he asked puzzled.

Boston looked at his partner and grinned. "Pier Seven about six months ago." The agents shared laughs as if enjoying some type of private joke. "I meant to thank you for the drinks but you had to rush off." Boston smirked. "You weren't feeling too well that night."

Whitehead cleared his throat. "Yeah, man we've been watching you for a little over a year now." He seated himself in a chair across from Cojack, his blue eyes beaming directly at him. "We know all about your crew."

Cojack started to say, If you know so goddamn much, who the fuck robbed me then? But he decided to keep his thoughts to himself.

"This here is a lot of time," Boston said, holding up the bag. He flashed a devilish grin. "Crack, too, not to mention the currency and the gun we found in the truck."

"You looking at a shitload of time, man, no bullshit," Whitehead interrupted. "Got any kids?"

"Naw, I don't got none of them," Cojack replied.

"Well, hell, you may have twenty to thirty years in you."

Just the thought of doing time gave Cojack stomach pains. There was no way he could go to prison, especially with a dope habit.

"So, Cojack, what's it gonna be? You gonna play ball or go hard?" Boston asked.

"I can't go to jail, man," Cojack answered.

The agents exchanged pleased expressions. "You're a smart man," Whitehead said. "So what do you have? Must be something real good for us not to lock you up."

"Tell me something," Boston interjected. "Did you see who killed the guy outside the club that night? You and Mason were . . ." The agent paused to observe Cojack's expression at the sound of his friend's name. He continued, "You two left around the time of the shooting."

"Naw, I ain't see it," Cojack answered.

"By the way—" Boston glanced in his partner's direction. "—I think it's only fair to inform you that Mason and the others will be picked up, too. We have units on them."

"Look, man," Cojack cut in. "Let me work the streets and keep my niggas out there."

"I don't know about that, Cojack. I mean, that's a lot of work, man. We got four of you on conspiracy charges. Let's not forget the gun." Boston shook his head, looking at the other agent. "That's one heavy load."

"I don't care," Cojack said, his nose running profusely. "Look, I got niggas who will sell me five keys. Nigerians, man. Just put me back on the streets and let me work. Don't nobody know I got arrested." The agents looked at each other as if they were pondering the thought. "Look man, I'll put on a wire or however you wanna do this."

"When is the soonest you can make a buy?" Boston asked.

"Tonight, but you gotta let me go." Cojack told the agents how the Nigerian only came around once a month. They agreed to work with him but said their superior had to make the final decision. As they left the room, Cojack's mind worked overtime trying to think of a good lie.

Think, nigga, shit! I gotta tell these niggas something. The connect got arrested. Naw, I can't tell 'em that, he reasoned with himself. He had to go out of town for something. Cojack sat there in a deep trance trying to decide. Yeah, that might work. The robbery was definitely off. The pains were growing sharper by the minute and perspiration was building on his forehead. He felt like crying out. "Goddamn, I need some dope," he mumbled.

Thirty minutes later his head lifted at the sight of the two agents.

"All right, Cojack, it's your lucky day. You'll be working closely with Agent Boston and myself." Whitehead explained that he'd have to wear a wire so they could monitor the transaction.

"Is there a problem?" Boston asked, observing the concerned look on Cojack's face.

"Y'all not gon' arrest him while I'm there are you?" Cojack asked with a slight degree of concern.

"Of course not, Cojack," Boston replied. "We wouldn't put you out there like that."

"If all goes well, you and your friends get to stay on the streets," Whitehead added.

"How soon can I get back out there?"

"We gotta get your fingerprints, sign some paperwork, and the necessary BS. You all right, Cojack? You don't look too good," Whitehead said. "A little shook up, huh?" He grinned. "Well, don't be. It's always this way in the beginning. You'll do well." Cojack's mind drifted off, thinking about how good he'd feel once he had some heroin in his system.

"Let me warn you, Cojack," Boston said. "Don't cross us or you'll be back in custody before you can blink." He snapped his fingers to emphasize his point.

"Just trust me, man. I got you. Whatever I gotta do, it's done. Long as me and my niggas out there, fuck the rest," Cojack said sincerely.

"That's the spirit," Whitehead stated. He glanced at his partner, winking his eye. "I guess we're about ready. C'mon, buddy. Let's sign some papers and get you printed so you can be on your way."

Later that night Cojack drove across the Chamberlayne bridge. The radio was off so all he could hear were his thoughts that seemed to drown out everything else. Feeling the wire attached to his chest, he couldn't help from laughing.

"Ain't this a bitch!" In just a matter of months his life had done a 180-degree turn for the worse. He began to contemplate the many possibilities. What if something went wrong? Did anyone he knew witness the arrest? What if the Nigerian wanted to search him?

You trippin', nigga, he thought to himself. He turned on his music and tried to relax. He thought of Mason and knew he was upset about the robbery being called off. He hated that he had to lie to his boy, but if only he had a clue Mason'd probably thank him. Even still, he didn't like having to lie to him. Cojack decided to pick up his cell phone and call him just to make sure things were still cool.

"Yeah," Mason said, answering the phone.

"What's up, man?" Cojack asked. "I was just calling to make sure you was cool. I could tell you wasn't feelin' the shit being called off and all."

"I'm good," Mason replied.

"I'm just as pissed. But ol' dude had to leave town for a family emergency. Shit happens. But don't worry. It will all work out," Cojack said in an attempt to give Mason some reassurance. Mason didn't trip so he figured it worked.

"It's all good."

"Alright then."

"Holla."

"Peace."

When Cojack arrived within two blocks of the detail shop where he'd purchased drugs on numerous occasions, butterflies began to surface.

"Just stay cool, man. Everything gon' go smooth," he assured himself. The place was located directly across from Burger King, behind a run-down motel. Cojack parked on a deserted side street and got out. He knew his man was there because the burgundy Maxima was parked in the alley as always. He observed two Nigerians posted up at the entrance, smoking a joint and speaking a language he couldn't understand.

A seven-foot-tall black brother led him inside and instructed him to wait. Cojack took a seat with three other dudes in front of the TV, watching soccer. Neither of the men spoke English and it kind of bothered him. He wondered what they were saying. Were they talking about him? Almost twenty minutes later, he heard his name called in a familiar Nigerian accent. He got up and trotted to the back room, where he was greeted by his connect.

Bam and another cat were seated at a table smoking weed while a money machine counted a table full of cash. It had to be over a quarter million. Cojack fumed with anger, wishing the Feds hadn't intervened and spoiled his planned heist. As Cojack handed Bam $75,000, he told him how fucked up it was that he would simply cut him off after their long business relationship. Bam laughed.

"C'mon, Cojack. I was just joking, man. You didn't take me serious, did you?" Having been in the States for so long, Bam spoke the language exceptionally well.

"Get the fuck outta here," Cojack said in surprise. "You mean it was a joke?"

"Yeah man. How could I cut you of all people off? You one of my best customers. Just to show you everything is still love, I'm gonna match the five kilos 'cause I wanna see you get back on your feet."

Cojack could not believe his ears. He wondered how long the Feds would wait before they picked him up. Hopefully they'd give him enough time to stack some real paper. He would definitely keep a few kilos for himself.

They started loading the bricks up when suddenly a thunderous blast sent the men careening to the floor. Bam yelled something in his native language to his partner, who leaped up clutching the longest Desert Eagle Cojack had ever seen. Bam's bodyguard let off several rounds just to let the intruders know they were packing, then slammed the door. Immediately, Cojack began to think the worst.

The Feds. *Muthfuckas lied to me! What the hell did I get myself into?* Cojack thought.

Slugs were tearing through the walls. It sounded like machine guns.

"Cojack, help me put the money in a bag," Bam said in a desperate tone, his eyes full of horror. "It's a back door. We can get out through there." They moved swiftly, staying low while clearing the entire table. They stuffed the cash in a leather Gucci bag. The Nigerian bodyguard had the door covered. Through the commotion, Bam and Cojack, with both of their hands full, broke for the back door that led to the alley where his car was parked. Cojack just knew agents had the place surrounded. His plan was to throw up his hands in surrender to avoid being killed once he was outside.

When Bam opened the door, Cojack's heart nearly jumped from his chest at the sight of the ski-masked figure standing before him. It was as though he was living in a horror movie, watching in awe as the man leveled his weapon at Bam's head and squeezed the trigger, taking the top of Bam's skull completely off.

Cojack dropped his bags and retreated in the opposite direction only to run into another dude dressed in similar attire. He stopped in his tracks and threw up his hands but it was all in vain. The first slug struck him in the chest. Another ripped into his midsection before he could hit the floor. Suddenly, the shots had came to a screeching halt and all that he could hear were voices. One voice stood out over all the rest as he ordered his men to clean the place out. At that moment Cojack realized these were the same dudes who had robbed him. He could feel himself losing consciousness; labored sounds came from his heaving chest as he pressed his hand against his torn flesh. Eyes clouding with tears, he saw one of the men stand over him and aim his weapon.

"Please don't kill me," Cojack droned out in a weak tone as he stared down the barrel of the Glock. He begged for mercy through pleading eyes.

"Let's go!" a voice ordered from across the room.

Cojack's breathing increased and his eyelids were becoming heavier by the second. A picture of his mother entered his mind as he imagined her crying over his casket. Then he thought of his good friend Mason. He should've listened to him from the start. Was this the way he would go out? Cojack opened his eyes and found no one there. Then he passed out.

THIRTEEN

THREE DAYS LATER, Cojack opened his eyes in the hospital room, feeling the pull of the IV line stuck in his arm.

"Thank God, Corey Anderson," Janice called out to her son. Cojack strained his weak eyes and saw his mother smiling down at him. She kissed his forehead. "Boy, you scared me to death. How do you feel?"

"Weak," he replied. "I'm a'ight though. How long I been here, Ma?"

"Three days," she leaned over and whispered. "The police been back and forth up here since you got here."

Cojack tried to sit up but couldn't because his body lacked the strength.

"You all right? Need me to do anything for you?" his mother asked. Cojack thought for a minute, then shook his head. The door opened and a white petite nurse walked in followed by two men in suits.

"Hello. How do you feel?" the nurse asked in a friendly voice. Cojack just nodded. "I'll bring you something to eat shortly. You must be starving."

Cojack felt his stomach turn but not from hunger; he needed a sniff. The morphine the doctor ordered him to be shot up with was wearing off. The nurse adjusted his bed so that he could sit up and then glanced over her shoulder at the two white men.

"Looks like you have some company," she said with a smile. Cojack caught the men's stares and knew off the top that they weren't regular cops.

His mother leaned over, giving her son another kiss. "Are you sure you all right?"

"Yeah, I'm a'ight, Mama. Did Robbin or anybody call?"

"Sho did. She called twice and came down here when you first got shot." His mother snickered. "Boy, you had all types of girls comin' down here. People I didn't even know walked up and was giving me hugs. It was so crowded that the nurses started putting people out."

"Call Robbin and have her come up here," Cojack told his mother.

"Okay, baby. I'll go call her. I'll give you a chance to talk to these police officers." She kissed him again and said she'd be back in an hour.

As soon as the room was clear, one of the men closed the door while the other, a chubby dude, introduced himself as Agent Tucker. He flashed his badge and nodded to his partner. "This here is Agent Scott," Tucker said, stroking his beard. "You're a very lucky fella. I don't know if you're aware or not that you were the only survivor. Everyone else died at the scene. Guess you're the last man standing."

Scott interjected, "Cojack, we know that these homicides were drug related." Agent Scott looked at his partner and continued, "We need to hear in your words what happened."

Cojack struggled to get a better position in his bed as a grimace covered his face. "Why should I tell y'all muthafuckas anything!" he growled. His response brought a puzzled look to the men's faces. "I wanna talk to the muthafuckas that almost got me killed. Get me Agents Boston and Whitehead," Cojack demanded. The two agents returned dumbfounded stares.

"What the hell are you saying?" Tucker asked. Cojack gazed at both men as if they were insane. He was in pain and his patience was wearing thin. The last thing he needed was more agents trying to bullshit him.

Cojack drew a long breath. "You mean to tell me y'all don't know the agents I'm talking about?" he asked, looking from one face to the other.

"We don't have anyone with those names working for our agency," Scott answered. He saw the fire in Cojack's eyes and cut him off before he could speak. "Why don't you just explain to us what happened?"

The nurse entered with a cup in one hand and medication in the other. After he swallowed his pill and the nurse left, Cojack settled back and began his rendition of his arrest and how he was taken to a building near Staples Mill Road.

Tucker interrupted. "Where on Staples Mill?" he asked curiously.

"Man, this shit was in the boonies. It was like a warehouse or something. I'll remember it if I see it," Cojack said. He then went on to tell them about the deal he made with the devil. The conspiracy charges, the wire, and the setup with the Nigerians. The whole nine.

"We found the wire you had on when you were brought in," Scott said. "Mr. Anderson, it wasn't even activated."

"What!" Cojack bolted. "It wasn't activated? What the hell that mean?"

Tucker whispered something to his partner, who then pulled out his cell phone and started punching in numbers. "Calm down, sir," said Tucker. "We're trying to get to the bottom of this. Something is obviously wrong. The place you said they took you doesn't exist. I'm certain of that because it's too close to our agency for me not to know."

Scott hung up the phone. "Davis is on his way," he said. The agent looked at Cojack. "We're going to need you to take a look at some mug shots. I don't know what's going on but something is definitely not adding up."

The nurse walked in with a tray in her hand. Cojack's stomach reacted instantly to the aroma of scrambled eggs and bacon.

"You put something in your stomach. We'll be back," Tucker said. The two agents left.

As Cojack sipped from a cup of orange juice, the nurse began to talk his head off about how lucky he was to be alive. Cojack listened while trying to eat his meal. Suddenly, thoughts of the shooting started to play back in his mind. All the money and coke they got away with, not to mention his $230,000. Who the fuck were these dudes?

He was more upset with the agents than he was with the robbers. How could they send him into a situation like that with no protection? A wire that wasn't even activated? "Muthafuckas!" he shouted, losing his appetite. The connect was dead. What the hell was a nigga gon' do now? Cojack knew Mason would have questions. He could hear him now saying, "For one, what the hell was you doing there in the first place when Bam supposed to had been out of town?"

Damn, I fucked up big time, Cojack thought. "The sweetest connect in the city. I gotta call this nigga," he mumbled as he stretched over to grab the phone.

The door opened before he could pick up the phone. Tucker and Scott walked in followed by a short nerdy-looking white guy who they called Davis. In his hands were two large mug-shot books. After the introduction, Scott moved the tray to the side while Davis placed one of the books in front of Cojack.

"We need you to go through these photos and see if you recognize any of the men who supposedly arrested you," Tucker said.

"This gotta be a joke, right?" Cojack said. He observed the faces in the room. "For what? Why would ATF agents be in here?"

Scott shook his head and replied, "Look, Mr. Anderson, we have reason to believe the people who arrested you were con artists masquerading as agents."

"Get the fuck outta here, man!" Cojack gazed at the other two agents. "Y'all can't be serious."

"Just look through the photos and we'll explain later," Tucker insisted.

Cojack opened the book. The room was soundless as he leafed through the pages scanning each face carefully. After five minutes, he passed the book to Agent Scott.

"Nope, they ain't in there," he said.

Davis gave him the next one, instructing him to study the faces closely. Cojack shot the agents a curious gaze and then turned his attention to the book. He studied every face thoroughly before turning the page. "Who are these people I'm lookin' at?" Cojack stopped and asked.

"International con artists from all around the world," Davis said. "Keep going."

Cojack did as he was told. Halfway through the book he blurted out, "Oh shit! It's them."

The agents grabbed the book to catch a glimpse. "Well, I'll be damned," Davis stated. "I knew it."

"The Lynch Mob," Tucker uttered.

"The who?" Cojack asked, confused. He took the book and studied the faces. It was all of them. Whitehead, Boston, the other black guy, plus the white girl who was at the scene when they arrested him. Agent Scott spoke.

"Mr. Anderson, these four individuals are a gang out of California. They're notorious for sticking up. They travel around the globe posing as ATF, FBI, regular cops, you name it, shaking down hustlers. Law enforcement in California named them the Lynch Mob because they left bodies wherever they went." Scott nodded his head. "When you first told us what happened, they were the first to come to my mind." The agent put his hands in his pockets and said, "Richmond is the last place I thought they'd come, though."

Tucker cut in, "They're wanted on all types of charges ranging from murder, extortion, racketeering, a list of shit, you name it." He cleared his throat. "Usually, the way these guys operate is they will come to a city targeting major players, trying to hook into a drug connection. Sometimes they will purchase drugs and often times they'll even pay some mediocre hustler to do it. Let me ask you something, Mr. Anderson. Is this your first encounter with these guys?"

Images of his mother with duct tape over her mouth entered his mind. He didn't want to give up information that would incriminate him further. Plus he didn't trust these guys as far as he could throw them. Who knows? Maybe they weren't the real deal either. Maybe the pictures and these agents were just an illusion. Who could he trust?

"Naw, I ain't never seen 'em before," Cojack said.

"The reason I ask is because usually the way they work is similar to real FBI procedures. They'll stake out their victim for months before they even make a move. Look, Mr. Anderson, we know you're a drug dealer. Obviously either you or the Nigerians were the target." Scott flashed a devilish grin. "We're not here to hurt you, Cojack. We want to help you."

Cojack chuckled. "How the hell can you help me?" A painful

smile escaped. He felt like a rape victim, totally violated. His bank-roll diminished, short a connect, how the hell were they gon' help him? Cojack thought of the way he sung like a bird for those fake agents. All for nothing. He was made a fool of and couldn't possibly see how these muthafuckas could do anything for him. On top of all this, he wanted some heroin so bad that it crossed his mind to ask one of the agents if they could get some.

"Mason Fuller," Agent Tucker said, bluntly flashing a smile similar to a serpent. "Name ring a bell?" Silence fell over the entire room as the three agents waited for a reply.

"What about him?" Cojack shot back.

"We've had him under surveillance for quite some time now, trying to build a murder case against him." Scott cleared his throat. "I'm sure you're familiar with the police murder a couple years back."

"I don't know what you're talking about, man," Cojack stated angrily.

"Sure you do, Mr. Anderson. He's your best friend, right?" Tucker said.

"Hol' up, man. What the hell is this? How y'all jump from the Lynch Mob to Mason? Them the muthafuckas y'all need to be worried about. Got me in this bitch shot the fuck up!" Cojack was fuming. A sharp pain shot through his belly, a sign that he needed to settle down.

Davis rose from the chair holding a large manila envelope. Cojack watched him closely as he whispered something to the other two agents and then handed over the contents. Agent Scott stepped up and said, "Mr. Anderson, please believe we understand your concerns." He gazed down at the envelope in his hand as if its contents were something sacred. "I want you to take a look at these photos and tell us what you see."

"More pictures, huh?" Cojack uttered, taking the 8½ x 11 photo in his hand. It was Mason and Robbin, which was odd. He knew his friend didn't care for her. Cojack stared at the picture for almost a minute trying to make something of it. He gave the picture back. "So what is this? They know each other," Cojack said.

Tucker interjected. "Doesn't it look strange to see them together like that?"

Cojack shrugged. "Man, that's nothing. Look, y'all wasting your time. I don't got shit else to talk about."

The agents exchanged gazes. Then Scott held out another photo. Cojack took it. Now this was strange. It was Mason and two guys he never saw before. Or had he? The faces were familiar but he couldn't place them. What did this mean? They were just regular dudes. He didn't keep up with everybody Mason hung out with. Cojack passed the picture back.

"Perhaps you'll find this one interesting," Scott said, handing him another photo. Cojack sighed, growing irritated and nearly snatching the pictures from Agent Scott's hand. As his eyes fixed on the faces in the picture, they grew large with surprise.

"What the fuck is this?" he asked, looking at the agents.

"You don't know, Mr. Anderson?" Tucker said. "It's a picture of your main man, Mason; your sweetheart, Robbin; and a couple of Atlanta dudes we've tied to our buddies the Lynch Mob. This one did the time in a federal penitentiary with the ringleader from California," Tucker said, pointing at one of the men. "We just now put it all together ourselves. Is it registering in your mind now? Are you getting the picture? I forgot to inform you one of the Mob's greatest tools is infiltrating cliques. They got to Mason. How? I don't know."

The air seemed to seep right out of Cojack's lungs as he gazed at the picture in disbelief. His best friend and the Lynch Mob meeting secretly. The same muthafuckas who duct-taped his mother and nearly killed him. What part of the game was that? "Damn, my nigga," he droned in a disappointed tone. He looked up at the agents, trying his hardest to hold back tears that felt like they would come at any minute. "I need some time alone, please," he pleaded, returning his attention to the photo. The men exchanged glances and then slowly headed for the door.

"We'll be back," Tucker said.

As the door closed, Cojack could feel the pressure intensifying. Voices drummed loudly in his head.

"Why would he do this to me?" Cojack said to himself. "One of the only niggas I truly loved." His mind began to work rapidly, searching for any small hint. Robbin crossed his mind. What part did she play in this? He thought of the first time that he saw her. "Damn, it was Mason that introduced us." Cojack gazed down at the picture, his senses buzzing. Then suddenly it hit him like a ton of bricks. "They worked me. My own nigga."

Now it was all clear to him: the jealousy, the deceit, and the hidden hatred. It had always been there. Mason was always trying to outdo him in some type of way. He thought of the time he purchased his Rolex Presidential. A week later, Mason had the same exact watch. But that wasn't the half. Cojack was the first out of the crew to buy a motorcycle. Two weeks later, Mason bought a bike. And at bike week, when those two dudes wanted to buy a couple bricks off Cojack, Mason had snuck around and sold them some bullshit, undercutting Cojack at every chance.

He never thought nothing of it until now. Then there was Kimberly, a VCU college student Cojack was seeing. Mason tried to hit on her but she was so hung up on him that she didn't give Mason the time of day. When Cojack asked him about it, Mason's reply was, "We don't love them hos. Only reason I did it was because I knew you didn't care."

It was all a setup and Robbin was a stinky bitch! He thought of the first time he used heroin and the story she threw him about doing it just to stay hard. Cojack bit down hard on his bottom lip. "I fell right into the trap. Ain't that a bitch!"

It hadn't registered then but now it did. Mason had talked to his mother minutes before her assailants abducted her. Every nerve in his body seemed to go slack. It was like someone had reached inside his chest and squeezed his heart.

He recalled the conversation right after Mason shot the dude over the crap game. "How the hell you expect to get money and be gangster at the same time?" he remembered asking Mason.

"I done seen plenty gangsta niggas get money" was his reply. "A lot of these niggas just be out there in the way. It ain't what you do but how you do it."

A tear burned down Cojack's cheek. How could he have known his best friend was speaking of him? His mind drifted back to a few days before the shooting and how Mason had portrayed the concerned friend. "I'll kill you myself before I see you turn into a dope-head," Mason had said.

He gazed at the tall black guy in the photo. It was him, the same dude from his house as well as the one who spared his life at the detail shop. Memories flashed through his mind of him and Mason coming up. All the good times they shared were now in the past. The fake loyalty was an illusion. It was not real. One can only love or hate. Two and the same is impossible. A man can't have two hearts. Cojack understood this now. He wiped his moist eyes as the door opened and his mother walked in. She took one look at him and knew something was wrong.

"What is it, baby?" she asked with concern. Cojack just shook his head. "I tried to reach Robbin but ain't nobody answer."

"Don't even worry about it," he said.

"Oh, I almost forgot," his mother said as she opened her pocket-book and pulled out a white envelope.

"What's that?" Cojack asked curiously.

"Some girl I ran into when I left the first time asked me to give this to you." Cojack accepted the envelope, which had no name or address.

"She didn't tell you her name, Ma?"

"Nope, sure didn't. Say it was important though. Probably one of your little girlfriends."

Cojack opened the contents and pulled the letter out. It read:

Dear Cojack,

It's good to know that you're alive and well. After I learned about your accident I felt the need to contact you by any means necessary. Lord knows I've been trying. Where do I begin? I'm still confused about this whole ordeal but something is definitely not right and I had to leave town because I feared my life was in danger.

Your friend Mason and I had a little thing going. The night you all got back from the beach, Mason came to my apartment. A little after midnight, someone knocked at my door. I asked who it was and the person said your name. Of course I opened it not even thinking first. It was two guys wearing ski masks. One grabbed me and covered my mouth to prevent me from screaming. Three or four more came in and went back to the bedroom where Mason was. They beat him, then brought him out into the living room where I was. I don't know what happened or what was discussed but I could almost bet that it was behind money. Something he may have done, I don't know.

What was very strange to me was after they beat him, he told me he was all right and not to worry. They went back into the room and talked some more. Then they left as if nothing ever happened. Mason made me promise to not say anything about it. We sat up the whole night and that morning he called you to pick him up. Cojack, I don't know what story he gave you but this is the truth, I swear.

Like I said, I'm not in Richmond anymore. That night I took my kids and we're now staying in another city. I've been sending you messages, but you wouldn't talk to me. Cojack, I really need your help. I wasn't prepared to move but felt I had to because maybe I saw something I wasn't supposed to. My money is low and I really need a loan so that I can catch up on my bills. I will contact you again very soon when I feel it's safe.

I hope this information has helped in some way. Or maybe this is old news, I don't know. I just felt like I should tell you. I'll be in touch.

Kenya

When Cojack was done reading the letter, he looked over to find his mother staring at the photo.

"What's this?" she asked, holding up the picture. Cojack began to explain his latest discovery.

"That can't be true, baby," she said, tears running down her face. But she had to know in her heart that it was true. The picture and the letter were all the proof she needed.

It all added up. Now Cojack understood why Mason was so anxious to rock Kenya to sleep that morning. The baby daddy drama was all a front. The Lynch Mob and their two friends had beat him up that night. Now he remembered—sipping the bubbly, slipping his digits to the tall dude with the crazy-looking eyes. That was him. And Mason was his front man.

The three agents reentered the room a few minutes later. Cojack sat in a trance. They greeted his mother and then focused their attention on Cojack.

Taking a deep breath, Tucker spoke. "Reality can be really harsh, Mr. Anderson. Your buddy Mason betrayed you. As for the Lynch Mob, well, they're long gone. Probably to another state to find more prey. Trust me, you'll never see them again. Hopefully, sometime in the near future, they'll be picked up. On the other hand, Mason is gonna fall. We know he killed that cop. The officer called in his plates before he stopped him. But that's not enough to charge him."

"Why don't y'all just get the fuck outta here," Cojack said, looking away. "I'm tired of talking."

Scott interjected, "What are you gonna do, Cojack? Settle it in the street? Then both of you end up in prison. Is that what you want? Haven't you been through enough already?" The agent looked Cojack directly in the eyes. "This is your time now. Help us take him down."

"And what's in it for me? Do you realize how much I've lost, man? You have no fucking idea." Cojack buried his face in his hands.

Tucker took over. "We'll make it worth your while. We need to close this case, Cojack. A cop has been murdered. We found two hundred fifty thousand dollars cash in the trunk of a Maxima that belonged to one of the victims. It was probably your money anyway. So, how does a hundred thousand dollars sound and a house in another state? Your choice."

Cojack glanced over at his mother, who simply shrugged her shoulders. She was just as angry as he was and wanted Mason to pay for his actions.

"It's a deal. But I want something on paper," Cojack said.

"That won't be a problem," Scott said. "You just give us Mason. All you have to do is get him to admit to the murder. Then you're outta here. And if you're smart, you'll clean up your act. Get into something legitimate. Stop putting your mom here through hell."

Cojack didn't need any lectures from these fools. But it would be good to get a clean start somewhere else. The two agents walked out of the door. They'd gotten what they wanted. Cojack's mother kissed him on the cheek, sat with him for a while, then headed home to get some rest.

After everyone was gone, Cojack sat in the dimly lit hospital room watching television while strategizing his scheme. He wondered if Mason knew about him cooperating with the Lynch Mob. It didn't really matter. He only did it to keep his friends out of prison. His number-one priority now was to get Mason to speak about the cop's murder, which wouldn't be hard. They had discussed the matter on numerous occasions and Cojack knew the story as if he'd been at the scene. Mason was a talker; a little ego stroking over a couple blunts and a drink and he'd be singing war stories the whole night. The barbershop murder even crossed his mind. It was amazing how well Mason played the role as a true soldier, a "ride or die" nigga, when all along he was simply setting up smoke screens to conceal who he really was. But it was okay because what goes up must come down.

It took the Feds less than an hour after Cojack got Mason to talk to bust in on his spot, and when they brought him out, hands cuffed behind his back, Cojack was waiting right there with a smirk on his face that only said one thing. From the moment Mason looked into his friend's eyes, he knew that he had been set up. "Love is still love, my nigga. My friend to the end," Cojack muttered.

Mason cut Cojack with his eyes, spat on the ground, and continued on as he was escorted into the back of a police car. It had been tormenting for Cojack to sit there in Mason's apartment and kick it with him over a few drinks. Everything in him wanted to inform Mason that he was onto his rat ass. Fuck what the Feds were going to do to him—Cojack wanted to blow his brains out. But he just sat back cool, thinking about the aftermath. Later Cojack planned to run up in Mason's spot and take every goddamn dime he had. He wouldn't even have enough to pay his attorney. There was no doubt in his mind that Mason had come up big time from working with the gang, his $230,000 and the Nigerian hit. Yeah, this nigga was strap for sho. But first Cojack had other business that needed handling and he needed to take care of it before Mason was allowed any phone calls because Cojack put everything on it that he knew exactly who Mason would call. So just as soon as Cojack watched Mason ride away in the back of a police car, men mugging him down until he was out of sight, Cojack jumped into his car and headed off to take care of his next order of business.

Robbin was none the wiser when Cojack showed up at her apartment acting his normal self. He had given himself a pep talk before entering her apartment, telling himself that no matter what he wouldn't put his hands around her neck and squeeze the life out of her, not taking his eyes off of hers until every ounce of breath had exited her body. Cojack entered and she began her normal flirting routine. He had pretended that he had just done some heroin and that he wanted her to be high too when they had sex. Cojack had prepared a package especially for her. It was uncut, raw, strong. Robbin didn't know what hit her when it started taking effect on her body. It would be days before she would be found in her apartment bed, dead from a heroin overdose.

"Yeah, muthafuckas, two can play at that game," Cojack said to himself as he sat at his living room table counting all the money he had jacked from Mason's spot as an episode of *The Sopranos* played on his big television. He laughed as he thought about the expression on Mason's face once he found out that he didn't have shit. "What goes around comes around, the law of life and nature itself." He laughed again.

As far as Cojack was concerned, it was on and muthafuckas was about to feel his wrath. He didn't feel pain no more. He didn't need heroin no more. He had a new high. He was born again in a sense. Yes, he fell, but now it was time to get back up. He would beat this monster called heroin. It had been a long time since he felt so much excitement. Now he could feel the same anticipation Mason experienced in the course of perfecting his plot. He exhaled as he picked up the remote control. As he flicked through the TV channels, a smile covered his face. Relaxing his head against the soft pillow cushion of his couch, he gazed up at the ceiling and mumbled, "Ain't no fun when the rabbits got the gun!"

NO MERCY

Put down by Akbar Pray, picked up by many

ONE

IN THE BACK of a dark brown UPS van, the three checked their gear. For the third time Furquan looked in his carryall to make sure they had not forgotten the duct tape, handcuffs, or rope. His movements were quick, and his eyes darted around nervously. Although Malik assured Furquan that they probably would not need the guns, Furquan put a round in the chamber, engaged the safety, and hid his nine in the small of his back.

Malik was husky, about six feet two inches, with a quiet air of authority. "All right," he said as he turned the ignition and started the van. "I'm gonna pull up to that phone booth down the street. DuJuanna, hop out and make the call. Then we on from there."

Sitting across from Malik and Furquan, DuJuanna rolled up her long hair into a bun and tucked it under a brown cap that also had UPS stenciled across the front. She handed a cap to both Malik and Furquan and put on a pair of black aviator sunglasses that hid her green eyes. Built like a brick house, she filled out the UPS uniform perfectly.

As the van moved down the street, Furquan's mind drifted back to his and Malik's last caper and the short money they had come up with.

"Yo, Malik," Furquan said as soon as DuJuanna had gotten out of the van. "You sure your cousin is sitting on forty or fifty thousand and this ain't some more yeast shit like that last caper we rode on?"

"Listen, Fu, if you starting to get cold feet, nigga, just say so. I don't be doing no perpetrating. The nigga sold drugs in the Seth Boyden projects for years before he opened his video store. He's sitting on at least that," Malik growled with a hard edge to his voice.

"Nigga, I don't know what cold feet feel like and I ain't scared of nothing that shit between two humps and that includes a Silver Back," Furquan retorted, screwing up his face.

"Yo, I hope y'all don't start that arguing shit again," DuJuanna remarked as she climbed back into the van and looked at their faces. "Let's just get this shit over with so I can take off this fuckin' uniform."

"Let's do this then," Malik said as he turned the ignition and pulled away from the curb.

JANET DAWSON spotted her two boys placing bulbs on the Christmas tree and smiled to herself as her younger son, Antwan, came stumbling toward her, carrying a candy apple red Christmas bulb. She reached down to pick up her son and thought that life could not be better.

Carl Senior had just put the down payment on a second video store, she was expecting their third child, and both her boys had bright futures. They would never have to deal drugs the way their father once did. They would never have to live in the projects and hustle out on the streets. She and Carl Senior had made sure of that.

"Daddy, you want me to get the presents out of the basement?" little Carl Junior asked as he stepped through the kitchen's open door and walked hurriedly toward his father. Carl Junior was the spitting image of his dad, whereas Antwan had his mother's features.

"Hold it down, shorty," Carl Senior said to his son, faking anger before smiling. "Do you want your little brother to hear you?"

"Nah, Dad, I just wanted to help you and Ma," Carl Junior replied, looking up at his father. The phone rang and Carl Senior picked it up.

A few minutes later, Janet came into the kitchen and asked, "Baby, who was that on the phone?" She rubbed her slightly protruding belly as Antwan clung to her skirt.

"UPS," Carl replied, replacing the wall phone in its cradle. "They wanted to make sure we were home and that they had the right address. They said they were only a few minutes from here and would be dropping off a package that we need to sign for."

"Did they say who it was from, baby?" Janet asked.

"No, but I guess we'll find that out when they get here. I bet it's a present for the boys from your crazy-ass aunt."

Janet laughed. "Well, tight as things are this month, a few extra presents wouldn't hurt."

Carl Senior stood up and kissed her. "I know I had to put a lot down on that second store, but it'll be worth it. Wait and see. I'm gonna leave a video store empire to my sons."

Janet pulled back from him and glanced down at her belly. "And maybe your daughter, too," she said.

"That's right," he said, putting his hand on her stomach. "All my kids."

* * *

"ALL RIGHT, WE'RE HERE," Malik announced as he pulled into the driveway of the Dawson house. "DuJuanna, put your sunglasses back on and get the clipboard. Fu, you ready, man?"

"Nigga, I was born ready," Furquan responded, putting on his aviator glasses and checking the gun tucked at his back.

"Yeah, yeah, man, whatever. Just make sure you got all of them handcuffed and blindfolded before I come in. Click the porch light on and off when y'all ready for me."

Fu exited the truck with a package in hand and headed to the Dawsons' doorstep. DuJuanna followed. Once they reached the doorstep, Fu knocked. Janet looked through the peephole and saw two UPS carriers. This must be the package Carl was talking about, Janet thought to herself as she answered the door.

"Ms. Dawson?" Fu asked as he set the box down with DuJuanna close behind him.

"Yes. Do you mind bringing it in the hallway?" Janet asked. "I'm expecting, and I can't pick up anything too heavy." Just then, Antwan approached his mother bashfully. "Antwan, stop. Come from behind Mommy's dress." Janet turned to the deliveryman. "I'm sorry about that. My son is acting so weird. He's generally not afraid of strangers."

Antwan came from behind his mother and ran to the back of the house.

"Carl, your package is here," Janet yelled as DuJuanna handed her the clipboard.

"Coming," Carl said, heading toward the front of the house with Carl Junior walking in lockstep with him.

As Carl walked into the front hall, he saw two UPS agents talking to his wife. He noticed that the UPS girl was attractive, and then thought it was a little odd that there were two deliverers. Must be a heavy package, he thought. He was about to smile as he came abreast of the male agent, but something about the firm set of the agent's jaw and his aggressive body posture pulled him up short. His street instincts kicked in, and he realized that something didn't feel right. Too late, Carl also noticed the delivery guy had one hand behind his back, a hand that suddenly came forward holding a gun.

"All right, muthafucka, put your hands up and get against the wall," Furquan snapped as he pointed the gun at Carl Junior's head.

"Oh my God, what do you want?" Janet screamed, reaching out to grab little Carl by his hand and drawing him to her side.

"Shut the fuck up, bitch, and get your ass against the wall," Furquan hissed, "before I slap the shit out of you."

"Man, what do y'all want?" Carl asked and faced the pair.

"Nigga, turn your ass back around and face the muthafuckin' wall," Furquan commanded as he slammed the butt of his nine against Carl's forehead.

Janet screamed as she watched Carl sink to the floor, where a pool of blood began forming from the open gash on his forehead.

"Oh my God, what are y'all doing?"

"Daddy!" Little Carl shouted, running to his father, Carl Senior was sprawled out awkwardly in the small vestibule. "Daddy, get up. Get up, Daddy," Little Carl repeatedly screamed with tears rolling down his face.

"I'm okay," Carl murmured as he tried to clear his head while wiping away the blood that was flowing into his eyes. "Go back over there by your mom."

DuJuanna took out four pairs of handcuffs and a roll of duct tape.

"Stand up and put your hands behind your back," DuJuanna demanded. Carl struggled to his feet. "That goes for you, too, Ms. Thang. Put your hands behind your back and face that wall," she instructed Janet.

* * *

MALIK SAT in the van nervously puffing on a Camel cigarette. It felt as if Furquan and DuJuanna had been in the house for hours. He looked at his watch and realized it had really been less than ten minutes.

"Shit, they still should be finished by now," he muttered to himself while glancing up and down the street and then back at the house. Maybe something went wrong, he thought. He took a short drag on his cigarette before putting it out. Just as Malik was about to get out of the van to go inside and check on things, the porch light flashed on and off.

DuJuanna stood in the doorway with the screen door slightly ajar as Malik walked up the short path leading to the house.

"We got all three of them downstairs in the basement tied up," DuJuanna said as they walked to the back of the house and down the small flight of stairs leading to the basement. In the middle of the floor near a green felt pool table, Carl, Janet, and Little Carl lay on their stomachs, blindfolded, with their mouths duct-taped and their hands cuffed behind their backs.

"Where's the baby?" Malik whispered to DuJuanna.

"He ran when we first came in, but I don't think we have to worry about him, he don't look to be no more than two or three."

"All right, fuck him, let's get started and get the fuck outta here," Malik replied.

Furquan walked around the pool table, stopping between Carl and Janet, bending down so that he was talking almost directly in Carl's ear.

"Listen, nigga, I ain't gonna say this but one time, where the muthafuckin' money?"

"Yo, man," Carl began, trying his best to steady the tremor of fear in his voice. "All we have is our weekend receipts from the store. You can have that, man."

"Bitch, do you think I'm a goddamn fool? We know you was

rolling, nigga, and we know you got bank," Furquan hissed in Carl's ear. He turned and kicked Janet sharply in the stomach. Janet's muffled scream escaped the duct tape and sent shivers up Carl's spine.

"You think we fuckin' around, nigga?" Furquan shouted, standing up straight and kicking Janet again in the side. "You must be trying to get your bitch kilt."

"Listen, please don't kick her again," Carl managed to mumble through his duct-taped, swollen lips. "I have some jewelry, man, plus my wife's wedding rings and the money from the store. Man, just take all of that and leave her alone." Tears seeped from behind the blindfold and ran down his swollen cheeks as he muttered his plea.

"Nigga, what you think, we from the Itty Bitty Committee?" Furquan said. "We ain't here for no kibbles and bits. Your black ass is sitting on fifty thou, and you gon' unass that shit fo we leave out here."

It had been years since Carl had that kind of money. He didn't know where this cat had gotten his information from, but they were way off. After buying the house, opening up the store, buying a family car and a car for himself, plus putting a down payment on a second store, he was lucky to have six thousand in the bank.

"Listen, my brother," Carl began, "I—"

"Hey, nigga, I ain't ya fuckin' brother, so don't try to play that brother shit on me," Furquan spat.

Furquan, Malik, and DuJuanna had been in the house for over thirty minutes. Janet, who was semiconscious, was curled up in a fetal position, moaning. Malik, standing off to the side through the beatings and torture, was impatient. He walked over to Fu, touched his shoulder and motioned for him to follow him to the far side of the room.

"Listen, Fu," Malik began as soon as they had gotten out of earshot. "This shit ain't gettin' us nowhere."

"You sho this nigga sittin' on that kinda bank?" Furquan asked, his UPS jacket drenched with sweat and dried blood.

"Yeah, I'm sure. Listen, I know my cousin. The nigga is caked but the muthafucka is cheap and stubborn as hell. Thing is, he loves Janet but he worship that little boy. You got to make that nigga believe you gon' kill Little Carl. That cheap muthafuck will come up then.

"Let me step back out of the way, then take the blindfold and the duct tape off, put the gun to Little Carl's head, and act like you gon' kill the kid. The nigga will up them duckets then."

Furquan put his black aviator glasses back on and walked back over to where Carl and his family lay sprawled out on the floor. "Listen, nigga, I see you think this shit is a joke."

"Yo, I don't think—," Carl started.

"Shut the fuck up. You must be trying to get your fuckin' son killed," Furquan said as he knelt down next to Carl and took off his blindfold.

Furquan then pulled out his nine and placed the barrel against Little Carl's head. Little Carl had tried not to cry during most of the ordeal, but he visibly shook as the cold steel rested against his temple. He tried to maintain his composure, to be a man even now, but he couldn't stop his body from trembling or stop the beads of sweat from running down his forehead.

"Now, nigga, I'm gon' ask you for the last time, where is the muthafuckin' money? I'm not fucking with your bitch ass, nigga. Where's that muthafuckin' cheddar?" Furquan demanded as he placed the barrel of the gun firmly against Little Carl's head.

"Man, I don't have—," Carl began.

"Fuck this shit," Furquan hissed. He pulled the trigger. A deafening sound exploded from the barrel of the gun and a bullet smashed through Little Carl's head. Little Carl's body jumped nearly two feet from the force of the large-caliber bullet. Thick warm blood splashed onto Furquan's face, covering the aviator glasses and much of his UPS uniform.

Janet began to moan and move slowly.

One loud and prolonged screeching sound came from Carl's mouth. It seemed to begin in the depth of his soul and went straight to the heavens.

"My son, my son," he screamed, tears running down his face.

"Oh my God," DuJuanna said, backing away from the pool table toward the stairs.

"Where the fuck you think you going, bitch?" Furquan growled, grabbing DuJuanna roughly by the sleeve of her jacket.

"I'm getting the fuck out of here, Fu. I'm not down wit' no killing shit," she said.

"Bitch, you ain't going no fuckin' where. We gotta finish this shit now," Furquan snarled as he looked across the room at Malik, who hadn't moved since the explosion from the gun.

"What the fuck did you do that crazy-ass shit for, Furquan?" Malik shouted, walking out of the shadows, heading toward Furquan, his eyes blazing fire.

Furquan raised the gun and pointed it at Malik. "Nigga, don't be calling my fuckin' name," he spat.

"Mafucka, don't ever point no muthafuckin' gun at me," Malik replied coldly, walking past Furquan and continuing to the other side of the pool table where the lifeless body of his cousin's boy lay.

"Y'all done killed my son," Carl whined. "Y'all killed Little Carl."

"Come on, Malik," DuJuanna begged, tugging at Malik's arm. "Let's get the fuck outta here. You wit' me?"

Malik paused then sighed. "We can't," Malik said, looking first at Janet and then at Carl. "We can't. Fu is right. We gotta finish it."

Janet lay in a pool of blood, shaking violently and sobbing uncontrollably.

"Where's your gun, DuJuanna?" Furquan asked, wiping the wet blood from his glasses and face.

"Why?" DuJuanna asked, stepping back from Furquan.

"Shoot him," Furquan said, pointing toward Carl.

"Shoot who?" DuJuanna asked, eyes wide with apprehension and fear. "I ain't shooting nobody, Fu." DuJuanna once again backed toward the stairs.

"Bitch, I ain't playing. We all in this shit together now. Shoot that muthafucka or I'm gonna bust your ass," Furquan roared, stepping forward and pointing the gun directly at DuJuanna's right eye.

"Malik, talk to Furquan," DuJuanna begged, glancing furtively at Malik, who was staring at the lifeless body of Little Carl, shaking his head.

"We gotta finish it, D," Malik said, meeting DuJuanna's gaze with a determined but distant look in his eyes. "We gotta finish it."

"Now shoot him, bitch!" Furquan demanded, stepping close to DuJuanna, still pointing the gun toward her face.

DuJuanna pulled out the .38 she had in the bottom of her carry-all. She began shaking as she pointed the gun at Carl. The first bullet caught Carl in his shoulder. Carl screamed in pain and tried to roll out of the way but three more bullets rang out of the gun in rapid succession, the last one landing in his neck at the base of his skull. When the shooting stopped, DuJuanna stood in the middle of the room shaking. There were now two dead bodies on the floor. Janet was lying next to them, rocking in a fetal position, waiting for whatever fate had in store for her.

"This one's on you, Malik," Furquan commanded as he looked across at Malik, who was still staring at the lifeless body of Little Carl. Malik had never intended for this shit to turn out like this. Now he was in too deep to turn back. The shit had started out as a simple robbery. Now it was about to become a triple murder. He knew he didn't have an option. If he was locked up for this shit, he would be lucky to escape the death penalty and was certain to get life without parole.

"Go upstairs and get the money and the jewelry from the bedroom," Malik said as he jacked a bullet into the chamber and stood over Janet's trembling body.

As DuJuanna crept along the wall around the bodies toward the stairs, Malik fired the first shot. "No mercy," Malik said as the bullet hit Janet's cheekbone, ricocheted off, and broke the bridge of her nose. Janet screamed and in the same instant, DuJuanna heard a noise come from the pile of toys and quilted blankets in the corner. She looked closer and realized that she was staring into the prettiest, yet saddest, eyes she had ever seen in her life. The eyes never blinked. They didn't tear up. They simply stared at her in pain, confusion, and fear. Malik fired into Janet's body again and again.

DuJuanna knew that she could never reveal to Fu and Malik what she had seen. He's just a baby, she thought as she rushed upstairs to get the money and the jewelry.

TWO

Little Antwan's eyes were glued to the bad man who just kicked his mommy. He tried to scream but no sound came out. The bad people had tied up Mommy, Daddy, and Little Carl. He didn't like them from the first moment he saw them. When the big man and the pretty lady came in the house, he had run to the basement and hid behind his old toys under two quilts. Looking out from under the quilts, he watched as the bad people hurt his mommy, daddy, and brother.

ANTWAN WAS on the bottom bunk in his fourth foster home in a year. He moved restlessly in his sleep as he did most nights as nightmares of his family's murder tormented him. Tears rolled down Antwan's face and drenched his pillow. Though tears flowed, no other sound ever escaped. When Antwan woke up he promised himself once again that one day he would get the people who killed his family.

In the years since the murders took place, Antwan had not spoken once. Now eight years old and in third grade, he was a good student. His teachers, aware of his problem, never called him to the front of the class or to answer questions aloud. He listened intently, did his homework religiously, and became an avid reader. He had no friends and usually sat in back of the classroom.

One day Antwan placed his head on his desk and fell asleep. The same nightmare plagued him, but this time one thing was decidedly different. His mother's body, which had been lying perfectly still for what seemed like hours in the dream, suddenly began to move. Antwan held his breath under the quilt as his mother rose up on her knees and the handcuffs that had bound her from behind suddenly slipped off. Slowly she turned toward him. Blood and maggots oozed out of the holes where his mother's eyes had once been. She stretched out her arms and started walking toward him, stumbling awkwardly but still walking directly toward him. When Antwan looked up, she opened her mouth to speak and maggots poured out.

Antwan's scream was as if a long-dormant volcano had erupted. It pierced his dream state and shattered the calm of the real world. The screaming didn't stop as Antwan's scared classmates ran to the front of the class. His teacher ran to the nurse's office.

"Antwan screamed! He actually made a sound," she said breathlessly to the nurse. The nurse stared at her in shock and then reached for the phone.

*   *   *

A FEW MONTHS LATER, Dr. Shaw entered the office of Dr. Milton, his superior, and sat down heavily in the brown leather recliner directly across from Milton's desk.

"So how's that boy, the one who didn't speak for all those years?" Dr. Milton asked, turning toward the window to stare out at the panoramic view of the New York City skyline.

"He's still getting used to hearing his own voice," Dr. Shaw answered. "You know, Dr. Milton, even though the kid had not spoken a word in five years, he's bright. I've been in his room talking with him for most of the day. Still, getting more than two or three sentences at a time out of him is like pulling teeth."

"Well, Shaw, you have to give him time. As you yourself said, he's seen and been through a lot."

"Yes, I know, but I get a bad feeling when I talk to him," Dr. Shaw said, shaking his head and sighing. "He's suppressing a lot of hostility and anger. In most of the clinical studies, in cases where kids have been severely traumatized, they've suppressed those memories so deeply and for so long that sometimes they've buried them completely and can only recall them under hypnosis. This case is totally different. It seems as though he relives that day during almost all of his sleeping periods and sometimes while he is wide awake." Dr. Shaw paused briefly and then continued. "But there's something else I can't ignore that makes me worry."

"What?" Dr. Milton asked curiously.

"When I ask the kid what he wants to be when he grows up, he looks me squarely in the eyes and says 'a killer.' "

THREE

ANTWAN RODE to Watson Avenue on the back of Rah Rah's black Ninja motorcycle. Big Farook had given the sixteen-year-old two more contracts in addition to the work he'd done for him down in the Mercer Street projects. On Mercer Street, Farook had wanted a nigga shot in both legs and had given him $500 for the work. This time he wanted a nigga slumped and had given him a thousand dollars up front and another thousand was promised when he completed the work. Antwan planned to give Rah Rah, his best friend, $200 to ride him to the spot where the mark hung out and wait for him while he put his work in.

Over the last two years Rah Rah and Antwan had been inseparable. Never had Antwan allowed anyone else to get close to him, but there was something about Rah Rah that he found intriguing from the moment he saw him.

Antwan was fourteen years old when he was walking up the alley one day and an altercation between two boys caught his attention. From what he could tell, there was an older boy hemming up a smaller boy for his sneakers. After the smaller boy took a few hard blows to the mug from the older boy, he kneeled down in defeat to remove the sneakers from his feet in order to relinquish them to the older boy.

As the older boy stood directly over the smaller one waiting for him to turn over the sneakers, the smaller boy caught him off guard. As hard as he could, the smaller boy rammed his head right up into the crotch of the older boy. The older boy keeled over, grabbing his privates. That's when the smaller boy stood up and began throwing uppercuts until the older boy fell to the ground. Antwan watched intently as the smaller boy got on top of the older boy and began ramming his head into the concrete with all of his might. After the older boy's head banged against the concrete about fifteen times, his body went limp.

The smaller boy slowly got up, nudged the older one with his foot, then proceeded to walk away heartlessly. When he turned to walk away, his eyes locked with Antwan's. Antwan didn't budge as the smaller boy came toward him, not taking his eyes off him once.

The closer the boy got to Antwan, the clearer it became to Antwan that even though the boy was smaller than the one who had just tried to jack him for his sneakers, he was bigger than Antwan was. The boy was only a couple of years older than him, but bigger nonetheless. Still, Antwan could hardly wait for the boy to approach him. He wanted to look into the eyes of the person who had so callously taken someone's life. As the boy approached Antwan, he was surprised by the look he found in Antwan's eyes. It wasn't the look of fear he had expected. It was a look of admiration. The boy knew then that standing before him was his very own prodigy.

Antwan swallowed. Though he never spoke to anyone first, and barely spoke even if he was being spoken to, he couldn't keep the words from spilling out of his mouth.

"Is he dead?" Antwan asked. "Did you kill him?"

The boy looked over his shoulder at the lifeless body lying in the alley behind him. He nodded and then replied, "Yep."

Antwan looked over at the body, paused, and then gave a simple, "Oh."

"He deserved it though," the boy said in his defense. "Fool try to get me for my sneakers."

Antwan looked down at the fresh new pair of Air Jordans the boy was wearing.

"Yeah, them some phat shoes, too," Antwan said as if to let the boy know that he didn't blame him for killing ol' dude.

Just then there was a sound of sirens. Neither boy knew where the sirens were headed, but just in case they were headed their way, they knew that they had to get out of there.

"You hungry, kid?" the boy said to Antwan.

Antwan overpowered the smile that wanted to creep across his face. He thought it was funny how the boy had taken a life and all of sudden felt like a man, calling him a kid and shit.

"Yeah," Antwan replied.

"Then let's go around the corner to KFC and grab something to eat."

Antwan sucked his teeth. "I ain't got no money."

"Damn, that's right," the boy said, snapping his finger as he had a sudden thought. "Hold up."

The boy ran back over to the body and proceeded to go through the dead boy's pockets. The closer the sound of the sirens came, the faster Antwan's adrenaline rushed. His little peter was tingling in his pants.

The boy walked back over to Antwan with a fistful of crumbled bills that panned out to be nothing but $1 bills. "Good lookin' out. I almost forgot to check that fool's shit in. I would have forgotten if you hadn't mentioned money." He continued unfolding and counting the money. "Only twenty damn dollars. No wonder dude was trying to take my shoes and shit. Broke-ass nigga can't afford to buy his own. What a dude that ain't got nothing but twenty dollars in his pocket got to live for anyway?"

Antwan just stood there with envy as he looked at the boy. Here he had been brave enough to stand up to someone bigger than him who was trying to take something from him, something that was his. If only Antwan could have stood up to those three people who had tried to take something of his, who did take something of his.

"Here you go, kid," the boy said to Antwan, handing him ten dollars of the twenty. "Let's go eat." They headed off out of the alley toward KFC. "By the way, I'm Rah Rah," he said, extending his hand to Antwan.

"Antwan," he replied, shaking Rah Rah's hand. The boys continued walking. Again, Antwan looked down at Rah Rah's shoes, the shoes that had cost another boy his life. "I know your moms had to work hard to get you those shoes. I would have killed anybody who tried to take them from me in a heartbeat."

"Oh these," Rah Rah said nonchalantly, looking down at the shoes. "I just jacked some clown yesterday for these." Rah Rah looked down at Antwan's beat-up sneakers. "After we eat we gon' go find you a pair, too. You wit' it?"

Antwan just looked up at Rah Rah, the boy he knew was to be his new best friend, his only friend, and replied, "I'm wit' it."

From that point on they started doing stickups together. It had started with gold chains, sneakers, and whatever money a victim happened to have. Later they graduated to sticking up the dope kids off Clinton and Avon Avenue. They had done their first contract work for Big Farook in December of last year.

"Yo, Rah Rah, slow down. That look like green-eyed Hassan standing over there in front of the record shop," Antwan shouted over the roar of the bike's engine. Rah Rah slowed down to get a better look.

"Yeah, that's him, Antwan. What you want me to do?" Rah Rah asked as he slowed the bike down even more, waiting for his instructions.

"Just let me off, pull around the corner, and be ready to roll as soon as you see me bend the corner coming back."

Green-eyed Hassan was a stickup kid. He'd been sticking up the crackhouses in Seth Boyden projects and the Little Bricks projects, then camping out in the North Newark projects until shit blew over. Three weeks ago he had stuck up a crackhouse run by Big Farook's people on West Kinney Street. Big Farook had put a contract on him, and Antwan had gotten the work.

Hassan and some girl were leaning against a green Acura Legend when Antwan walked around the corner and headed casually in their direction with his motorcycle helmet still on and his hands in his pockets. Antwan sang a song that was on the radio all the time.

Slight of build, and weighing little more than 130 pounds, Antwan didn't appear to be anybody's idea of a contract killer. When Antwan was directly in front of Hassan and the girl, he stopped.

"Yo, Has," Antwan greeted Hassan as he eased his hand behind his back.

Hassan looked up at the young face peering at him from under the helmet and was about to smirk until he noticed that the kid was holding a .38 short.

"Yo, what the fuck?" Hassan gasped as the girl with him began screaming as she ran up the street. The first bullet slammed into Hassan's upper shoulder, knocking him into the car door.

"Hold, hold up for a minute, man," Hassan said as he stared into Antwan's hard, angry eyes. "What the fuck did I do, man? Yo, man, please."

"No mercy, nigga," Antwan snapped as he fired the next five shots into Hassan's face. "No mercy!"

During the next seven or eight months Rah Rah and Antwan committed three more contract hits, six shootings where they capped the dude in both legs, and one robbery at the Parrow Lounge where Rah Rah shot some cat in the ass for trying to buck.

"Yo, Antwan," Rah Rah said with a mouthful of food as he took another bite from his corned beef sandwich. "What's the fucking deal with you saying that 'no mercy' shit every time we have to slump a nigga? What you think, you some kinda serial killer or some shit? Remember nigga, like they said in the movie *The Godfather*, the shit ain't personal. It's business."

"Yeah, I know it's business," Antwan replied, staring off in the distance. "But it seems like every time I'm about to bust a nigga, I get mad as shit. Especially if one of them muthafuckas be lookin' at me like they expect me not to smoke their ass. So I just started telling them niggas 'no mercy' right 'fore I put them hot balls in they ass. Anyhow, Rah, why you asking a million questions and shit?

Fuck you s'pose to be? Some kinda black Sigmund Freud or some shit?"

"Nah, I'm just wondering," Rah Rah replied. " 'Cause sometimes you seem like your ass be tripping the fuck out. Anyhow, nigga, let's roll. We got work to do. Niggas couldn't go put in work on an empty stomach."

Antwan smirked as the two went to handle their business.

THE NEXT TWO YEARS flashed by in a series of shootings, car chases, stickups, blunts, and freaking with some of the project girls in the backseat of Rah Rah's car or sometimes at the Stinkin' Lincoln Motel downtown.

One Friday in March, Rah Rah, a couple of other cats, and Antwan rented a minisuite at the Lincoln to celebrate Rah Rah's twentieth birthday. They bought twelve forty-ounces, an ounce of weed, and a bottle of Dom, and they invited some girls from Seth Boyden projects. The party had been going on for hours when Antwan decided he'd had more than enough to drink and went next door to crash for a minute.

Fully clothed, Antwan lay across one of the double beds in the room and soon he was sound asleep.

Once again in his dream he watched from under the quilt as the two men and the pretty lady marched his handcuffed mother, father, and brother down into the basement. Once again he watched and jumped as one of the gunmen placed a gun to his brother's head and pulled the trigger. But this time he was no longer the traumatized little boy looking up from under the quilt, shaken and scared. This time he saw the carnage with the eyes of an eighteen-year-old and the faces were not mere blurs. He could see their faces. Their features and images ingrained themselves into his memory as if they were being burned into his brain. The dream, however, had yet another dimension, one that had escaped his years of therapy, consultation, and even hypnosis. This time he could discern exactly what the killers were saying. He could hear his mother's moans and his father's pleas to the killers to leave his wife alone. And more important, he could hear the voices of the killers themselves.

"Listen, nigga, I see you think this shit is a joke. You must be trying to get your fuckin' son killed," the tall dark-skinned killer said as he leaned over Antwan's father. "I'm gon' ask you for the last time. Where is the muthafuckin' money?"

Antwan stared out from under the quilt, his heart pounding like a drum as he watched the gunman put the gun to his brother's head and pull the trigger. With tears pouring from his eyes even as he slept, he jumped as the bullet tore through his brother's head, pushing brains and blood into the blindfolded face of his mother. He heard his father's scream of pain and anguish as he watched his son's lifeless body slump from the force of the bullet.

He stared as a familiar face stepped from the shadows of the room and one of the other killers addressed him by his name: Malik. With tears flowing from his eyes, Antwan watched his father's face contort in dismay and confusion as he tried to make sense of what was happening to him and his family. All of this was at the hands of one of the killers, Malik.

Antwan trembled with emotion as Malik stood over his mother while she was begging for mercy and uttered the words that had been imbedded in his subconscious for fifteen years. . . .

"No, Janet," Malik said in a low and distant voice. "No mercy."

When Antwan woke up his clothes were drenched in sweat. He looked around the motel room slowly, trying to get his bearings, trying to figure out exactly where he was. Then he heard the music coming through the walls from the room next door and everything began to make sense. For the first time in his life, so did the dream. He knew who the killers were, every one of them. He heard their names clearly and saw their faces. A smile danced at the corners of his mouth. He knew for certain that he would finally get what he had been praying for since he was a little boy. He was about to get revenge.

FOUR

WHEN RAH RAH NOTICED that Antwan was missing from the party he went over to the room next door to check on him. He found his friend in a cold sweat, coming out of the nightmare.

"Antwan, how you so sure that the nigga's name is Malik?" Rah Rah said, after listening to Antwan tell him about his dream. "Don't tell me just 'cause you dreamt that shit you ready to go slump any nigga wit' that name." Rah Rah tried to make sense of it all. "And you saying that you remember one of them, some Malik cat, saying he was your peoples? Your cousin and shit?"

"Listen, Rah, you either with this shit or you ain't," Antwan said. "All I need is a muthafucka to watch my back. I don't need no nigga to hold my hand if I'ma slump a nigga. Especially a muthafucka that slaughtered my whole family."

"Yo, my nigga, that's not what I'm saying. You know I'm down for whatever. I'll slump the nigga for you in a New York second. You like my family and your family like mines, but if we s'pose to be downing three cats, I just wanna make sure we got the right mutha-fuckas fo we get three bodies on the house. You feel me, Antwan? This ain't about no cold feet shit. 'Cause you know I slump a muthafucka soon as I look at him. But it's yo call, my nigga. You call it. I'm wit' it," Rah Rah said.

"First, I gotta find out who this nigga Malik is. I don't really know none of my dad's or mother's people. You know I was raised in an orphanage and in foster homes and none of them muthafuckas reached out for me. But I know they had family in the city. I heard my aunts and uncles sold off the business, split the proceeds, and went on about their lives," Antwan said, shaking his head. "Nonetheless, I don't think it's gonna be but so hard for me to find this nigga."

"All right, Antwan, whatever and whenever," Rah Rah said, reaching in his pocket for his room key. "Holla at me when you ready to roll."

"Yo, Rah, let me get the keys to your ride. I'm too hyped to sleep right now. I'm gonna just drive. I'll pick you back up before checkout time."

"All right, nigga. Don't leave me hangin' in the front of the motel waiting on your ass like you did the last time you took my car," Rah Rah replied, smiling as he tossed Antwan the keys.

Antwan caught the keys with one hand. "Man, would I ever leave you hangin'?"

"Hell, yeah. Didn't you just hear me say you did, fool?"

"Don't worry," Antwan said. "I'll be back."

OVER THE NEXT FEW weeks Antwan and Rah Rah tried to track down the people from Antwan's dream. They had so far checked on seven or eight guys named Malik, but none of them, to the best of Antwan's knowledge, was in any way related to him.

Friday night at the Zanzibar, Antwan kicked it with an old head who knew his peoples and schooled him on what he knew about his cousin, Malik. He told him that back in the day Malik used to be a vicious stickup kid. The old head said that maybe fifteen or sixteen years ago, Malik suddenly hung up his guns, and the last he had heard he was a deacon in the church, living somewhere in Belleville.

Sunday night, Rah Rah and Antwan had tracked that Malik to a duplex on the Belleville-Newark line, where he lived with his wife and two sons. Every night Malik would go to work on the night shift as a security guard at a Secaucus warehouse.

Rah Rah and Antwan were sitting in the car down from Malik's house passing a blunt back and forth when the porch light came on and a man, who didn't look to be a lot older than forty years old, stepped out on the porch accompanied by a caramel-colored woman who kissed him on the lips and then stepped back into the house as he proceeded down the steps.

Antwan and Rah Rah had already flattened the back tire on Malik's Camry. Antwan planned to make his move once Malik got out to change his tire. Antwan, who was lying on the backseat in Rah's car, had disconnected the car's interior light so he could ease out of the car and come up from behind Malik as he jacked his car up.

Except for one streetlight, which sat at the end of the block, Gray Street was almost completely dark. Malik started the car and had driven less than three feet before he felt the *thump, thump, thump* of a flat tire.

"Damn," Malik said aloud as he backed the car back into his space while hitting the trunk release button in the glove compartment. Except for a lone car that was stopped at a traffic light two blocks down, Gray Street was deserted. Malik was jacking up his car, humming his church's signature hymn, "Mary, Don't You Weep," when he heard light footsteps approaching.

Malik turned around and saw Antwan standing over him with his hands behind his back. Malik looked into the large, pretty, yet angry, eyes of the young kid who stared at him, unsmiling.

"Can I help you, brother?" Malik asked slowly, looking around and trying to make some sense of the situation.

"Yeah, cousin, you can help me," Antwan retorted, never smiling, never budging, never taking his penetrating stare from Malik's face. "I need something from you," Antwan continued, without changing the tone of his voice.

"Do I know you?" Malik asked nervously as a car door opened and quietly closed and another kid walked slowly in their direction. "Listen, brother, I don't have any money," Malik began. "I'm just a security—"

"I don't want any money, Malik," Antwan said, cutting him off, "and I'm not your fuckin' brother. I'm your cousin," Antwan snarled, pulling his pearl-handled .38 special from behind his back and aiming it at Malik's face.

"Hold it a minute, brother," Malik cried, throwing up his hands to cover his face. "I don't have any money, man."

"I told you, nigga, I ain't your brother. I'm your cousin. Look at me, Malik. Look good and think back."

Malik's mind raced back over the years as he looked into the large angry eyes of the kid pointing a gun at his face. The eyes, the eyes, he thought to himself. I know those eyes. Then it all came crashing down on him, and it felt as if he was being snatched into the mouth of a storm. Yes, they were the eyes of his dead cousin's wife. They were Janet's eyes, the woman he had killed those many years ago!

"Oh my God. Oh my God, for the love of Jesus," Malik pleaded, his voice trembling, his eyes wide with fear. The barrel of the gun now touched his forehead. He knew that this was little Antwan, his dead cousin's remaining child.

"Listen, Antwan. Listen to me for one minute, please, son," Malik begged, the tremor in his voice making his words barely audible. "Tell me what I can do. I know I can't bring them back." A current seemed to move through his body and he trembled un-controllably. "Please, Antwan. For the love of God, please have mercy."

"No, nigga. No mercy," Antwan spat while pulling back the hammer on the .38. "No mercy," Antwan repeated, pulling the trigger. The first bullet shattered Malik's forehead and exited the base of his brain.

"No mercy," Antwan repeated to Malik's lifeless body, which was now slumped down against the car. He fired five more shots into the mangled face.

WITH ONE DOWN and two to go, Antwan and Rah Rah were back on the grind a few days later. Tracking and finding Furquan didn't prove to be nearly as hard as tracking Malik. Furquan was still in the game. In fact, he had really blown up. A respected old head, Furquan now controlled building 178 of the Spruce Street projects. He had it locked down. His crew ran the spot wide-open twenty-four/seven and clocked between ten and fifteen thousand dollars a day. Furquan had purchased a $400,000 split-level home in South Orange, drove a big-body Benz, and wore a black diamond female-skin ranch-mink coat that he bragged he'd paid $10,000 for. Furquan also owned a detail shop on Peshine and Clinton Avenue. His bodyguard, a pitch-black nigga named Ali Mu, walked with a limp and had just beaten a double homicide the previous year.

"I'm telling you, Antwan, if we gonna knock Furquan's ass off, we gotta down Ali Mu first," Rah Rah explained as the waiter in Copper's Deli brought over two corned beef sandwiches. "If we gotta wait for a minute 'fore we get Furquan's ass so we can get at Ali Mu first, then man, we just hafta wait. I ain't trying to get in no blazing shoot-out with Ali Mu's 'noid ass if he suspects we mighta had something to do with offin' Furquan. Plus that nigga been death-struck ever since them cats from Hawthorne Avenue ambushed him and left his ass for dead."

"Yeah, I'm up on all that, Rah, but I been waiting on this nigga for what seems like forever," Antwan replied, staring out the window with a pained and angry look on his face.

"I'm feeling you, Antwan, and I know I'd be feeling the same way if I was you but think about it: Knocking off Ali Mu first will give us the ups on Furquan, 'cause without him the nigga gon' be buck naked. Antwan, I know he killed your family, but the nigga ain't no killer for real. He ain't gangsta like that. He don't put in no work like that. That's what he got Ali Mu for. "

"All right, Rah," Antwan said, turning from the window, placing his sandwich on the plate. "I been waiting this long. I guess I can wait long enough to do the shit right. But how we gon' get up on Ali Mu?" he asked, turning from the window and facing Rah Rah. "If the nigga is as 'noid as you say, I don't know how we gon' get within twenty feet of him."

"Me and the nigga stuck up a couple times together back in the day. The nigga is 'noid as shit, but he ain't gonna be on no super 'noid shit around me. Plus the nigga likes to sniff dope. He loves that P dope."

Antwan was quiet for a minute. He stared out the window, watching two kids play-fighting in front of the store. Finally he spoke. "You know, Furquan and Big Farook is s'pose to be beefing, and I hear Farook is got some paper on his head. Since we gon' knock Furquan's ass, we might as well touch base with Farook and get the work. Shit, we'll be killing two birds with one stone," Antwan stated, turning away from the window to face Rah Rah.

"That's why I scooped your young ass up when I first met you," Rah Rah responded with a wide smile. "You got something going on in that big-ass fuckin' head of yours."

* * *

ALI MU WAS STANDING in front of the movie theater when Rah Rah pulled up across the street in a car, waving at him and smiling.

"Yo, what's up?" Ali Mu shouted as Rah Rah waved him over to the car.

"Man, I got something I need to kick with you," Rah Rah replied, hitting the door locks when Ali Mu came over.

"What's up?" Ali Mu asked, sliding in as he adjusted the nine at his waist. He leaned back in the seat to face Rah Rah.

"I got some work, Mu, if you down. It's like for between eight and ten grand and probably a half a brick. The shit is a piece of cake. But its gon' take two people. Some West Indians over in North Newark projects is slinging outta building twelve. My cousin is the doorman for them. He searches everybody that comes in to cop to make sure they ain't strapped. He's gon' let us in. The rest of the shit is cake. I got a little kid who's my cousin. He'll do anything I tell him to do. He gonna sit in the car and wait out front for us. All we got to do is give him a couple hundred dollars apiece. Plus, I told his little dumb ass we'd buy him some Michael Jordan pumps when we come off. So the little nigga is hyped," Rah Rah said, looking at Ali Mu, who was hanging on to his every word. "So what's up, Mu? You trying to get with this lick or what?"

Without hesitation, Ali replied, "Yeah, I'm down. The shit sounds proper. When you wanna handle it?"

"We can ride out there tonight and take a peek at the area. Then we can handle the shit tomorrow night after it gets dark."

"All right, my nigga. That's money," Ali said, looking out the passenger window as they drove up Springfield Avenue. "But, nigga, you ain't got no dog food?" Ali asked, turning again in his seat to face Rah Rah.

"No dog food?" Rah Rah repeated with a puzzled look on his face.

"Yeah, nigga. No dog food, no P?" Ali asked angrily like Rah Rah was the dumbest cat he knew.

"Yeah, I got eight bags," Rah Rah smirked, reaching into his pocket and passing the rubber band–wrapped package to Ali.

Rah Rah and Ali rode, sniffed, and swapped war stories for nearly two hours before they drove out to the North Newark Projects to take a look at the spot they were supposed to hit the next night. Before getting out of the car in front of the Magic Johnson Theater, Ali cuffed the remaining three bags of P, smiled to himself, and stepped from the car.

"Tomorrow night, round ten?" Ali hollered over his shoulder as he crossed the street and headed in the direction of the theater.

"Cool," Rah Rah said as he drove away.

The next night Rah Rah and Antwan pulled up in front of the Magic Johnson Theater and Ali Mu was out in front waiting. When Rah Rah pulled to a stop, Antwan hopped out of the car to allow Ali Mu to sit up front.

"What the fuck you hopping in the back for?" Ali barked as he approached the car. "I don't want no muthafucka I don't know sitting behind me." Screwing up his face, Ali lifted the seat to climb in the back.

"You got any more of that dog food?" Ali asked as he settled into the backseat.

"Yeah, I'm straight," Rah Rah responded as he waited for the light to turn from red to green. "But I don't like to be riding through the city, sniffing with all of us strapped. Wait till we get on the highway or till we get in front of the building."

Ali was sniffing the last corner out of the $10 bag when Rah Rah eased his car into the parking lot behind building twelve.

"Let me get that last bag fo we go up," Ali said as he adjusted his pistol in his waist and waited, with an annoyed dope fiend grin on his face, for Rah Rah's slow-ass cousin to hand him the last bag of P.

"Hand him that last bag," Rah Rah told Antwan, who reached in his pocket and began to pass the blow over the seat. As Ali reached for a blow of the P, Rah slid a gun from under the armrest and raised it. Ali Mu stared in disbelief and groped for his nine, but before he could reach it, Rah Rah fired at point-blank range into Ali's face.

NOBODY WAS particularly shocked when Ali Mu came up murdered. Although nobody had any idea who did the work, the general consensus was that it could have been anybody. At Sensations Disco a group of cats, all former victims of Ali's at one time or another, hosted a "Thank God, he's dead!" celebration in the back of the club. As word of his death began to spread like an electric current through the club, most niggas felt that Ali Mu getting killed was like the chickens coming home to roost. He lived by the gun, most reasoned, so evidently it was his fate to die by the gun.

Most everyone shook their heads and went on about their business. Everybody, that is, but Furquan. Furquan was scared shitless. Ali Mu had been his back, his spine, and his trigger nigga. Ali Mu never asked why when there was work to be put in, he only asked who. Now that Ali Mu was gone, Furquan knew that he had to be extra careful. Plus, there was still that open beef he was having with Big Farook. Furquan decided it was time to pull back.

As a result, he seldom left his home in South Orange, and when he had to go to the projects to collect his money, he rarely even got out of his car. But like most people, Furquan had a weakness. Furquan was in love with a nineteen-year-old chickenhead named Shanaynay.

Shanaynay was coming out of building 178 when Rah Rah spotted her. She was walking fast, heading toward Furquan's car, which was idling at the curb.

"Yo, Antwan, check it. Ain't that that nigga Furquan's burgundy Benz Shanaynay just hopped in?" Rah Rah asked, sitting up straight in the driver's seat.

"Yeah, that that nigga," Antwan stated, taking off his sunglasses as he put out his blunt in the ashtray.

As soon as Shanaynay closed the passenger door, Furquan pulled away from the curb, driving to the corner where he turned left.

"Follow his ass, Rah," Antwan said. "He's probably taking that bird home. Somebody said he bought her a condo in Metuchen or down the shore."

Furquan got on the parkway heading south.

"You're too close," Antwan told Rah Rah. "Stay at least four lengths behind him, man, so that he don't make the car. Then come off the exit with him."

After fifteen minutes on the parkway, Furquan put on his turn signal, pulled into the right lane, and drove up the exit ramp at the Metuchen exit. Then Furquan drove eight or nine blocks and turned left in front of an apartment complex that read Tree Top Village.

"Don't follow him in there. Just keep driving straight," Antwan told Rah Rah as Furquan pulled into the complex entrance. "We can slide back and ride through the parking lots after he's gone into the house."

"That's money," Rah Rah responded as he watched Furquan's car go about thirty or forty yards and then turn right.

Antwan and Rah Rah drove to the parking lot of a 7-Eleven convenience store three blocks from Tree Top Village and strategized a plan for getting at Furquan.

"He don't know what neither one of us look like," Rah Rah said, passing the forty-ounce bottle of Red Bull to Antwan. "We could go to the door, ring the bell, and say we have a special delivery. When they open the door, we pull our burners and down the fool."

"The shit might work, Rah, and it might not. But you know if we do it that way we gon' hafta down his bitch, too, and for real— for real I ain't wit' killing no innocent muthafucka if I don't have to. Plus Rah, you know Little Man is ol' girl's baby daddy. And that little muthafucka gon' be heated," Antwan said, rarely taking a breath. "Shit, we might have to end up blasting his ass if we dump her when we take care of her nigga."

"Then it looks like we gon' just hafta wait on his bitch ass and get at the nigga another time," Rah Rah snapped as he reached for the forty.

"Fuck that, Rah. We been stalking this nigga forever, and this is the first time in over a month that we even spotted his ass. I'm not passing this nigga up," Antwan shouted.

"Listen, Antwan," Rah Rah retorted, raising his voice to match Antwan's. "If we ain't going in the house to get at him, and he sho ain't gon' come to us, how the fuck you think we gon' take care of this shit tonight? We sho can't use the same move we used on Malik 'cause this ain't that kinda neighborhood. It's bright as shit in front of that nigga's house. Plus all the muthafuckas out here keep they fucking porch lights on."

Antwan was silent for a moment. He just stared out the window in thought. When he finally turned from the window and looked at Rah Rah, he was smiling.

"I think I got an idea, Rah. It might sound like some cowboy shit, but Rah," Antwan said, his smile now disappearing, "I want this muthafucka so bad that I can taste his bitch ass."

"I'm feeling you on that, Antwan, but what's up?"

"You know Furquan is married," Antwan began. "But he's been knocking that ho he wit' now boots for over a year now. Her cousin says that the nigga never spends the night. He goes home every night. That means that the nigga gon' be leaving out of there before the morning."

"And," Rah Rah said, picking up on Antwan's idea but still a bit perplexed, "what the fuck does that get us? What we gon' do? Follow the nigga home then camp out there?"

"Nah, nothin' like that," Antwan said. "We just wait until it gets dark, then around eleven or twelve o'clock, we'll drive back around to the complex and pull up next to his car. His parking space is down from his town house. When we get there, pop the trunk, and I'm gonna get the jack out of the trunk. I'm gonna act like I'm bending down to change the tire on his car but I'm gonna loose the lug nuts on both his front tires. When the nigga comes out we gon' follow him. It'll still be dark out and there shouldn't be too many folks out there on the road. By the time that nigga gets on the parkway, one, maybe both, them tires gon' fall off. When the nigga gets out the car to see what the fuck happened, all we gotta do is ride by and wet his ass up."

"Nigga, you talking about a fuckin' drive by. I'm a muthafuckin' professional. I don't do that wack-ass California kinda shit," Rah Rah spat.

"Well, nigga, you ain't got to spray," Antwan retorted heatedly. "I do my own work. Just drive."

"If we gon' ride, nigga, we rides together. I ain't on no fake shit. I'm down, my nigga, from the womb to the tomb. But you know how I like to rock a nigga to sleep then slump his ass, but if this is how the shit gotta go down, then fuck it! I'm down for whatever."

AT FOUR in the morning, Furquan pulled out of his parking space to start his thirty-five-minute drive from his and Shanaynay's spot to his home in South Orange. Furquan hadn't been driving ten minutes when he noticed a hard shimmy coming from the front of his car. The car began to shimmy even more, forcing Furquan to wrestle with the steering wheel. Before he could slow down, the car fell hard to one side as his right front wheel popped off and the car skidded to the side of the road.

"What the fuck!" Furquan shouted as his car plunked down loudly, cracking the chassis. Furquan put his flashing lights on and stepped out of the car. Seconds afterward a car pulled alongside him.

"Yo, old head, you alright?" a young kid asked.

"Yeah, I'm alright. I think I just—" Furquan was about to tell the kid that he thought he had broke his chassis when the kid suddenly ducked down. Furquan was suddenly looking at the driver of the car. And the driver looked vaguely familiar, like maybe he knew him from off the block. In that instant Furquan noticed that the driver of the car was pointing a gun at him. Furquan turned to run or at least duck back into his car, but the driver in the car fired quickly and the impact of the bullet from his Glock pushed Furquan up against the side of the car.

"What the fuck!" Furquan screamed before four more bullets fired in rapid succession hit him, the last one slamming into his throat and ripping apart his larynx.

Rah Rah punched hard on the accelerator and was thirty or forty yards down the highway before he heard Antwan hollering for him to stop and back up.

"Back up, Rah. Back up for a minute," Antwan screamed. Rah turned in the seat and looked at him as if he'd lost his mind.

"Back up for what? Nigga, are you fuckin' crazy?" Rah Rah shouted as he slowed the car down.

"Man, back up," Antwan said more evenly.

Rah Rah threw the car into reverse and backed down the empty strip of highway. When the car pulled even with Furquan's Benz,

Antwan hopped out, ran over to where Furquan lay slumped against the wheel of his car, bent over Furquan's lifeless body and emptied the clip of his 9mm into Furquan's face. Then he hopped back into the car and Rah Rah pulled off.

"What the fuck was that all about?" Rah Rah asked, exasperated. "The nigga was already dead."

"That was about my brother," Antwan replied, staring off into space as they sped down the highway. "That was about my brother."

FIVE

DUJUANNA WAS in the Golden Comb Beauty Salon having her hair French permed when Sherrie, from the Little Brick projects, came though the door.

"Baby, did you hear about Furquan?" Sherrie asked no one in particular, but loud enough for everybody in the salon to hear her.

"Uhn-uh, girl. What Furquan and his fine ass done did now?" Nette asked, taking the rollers from her tray and starting to curl DuJuanna's hair.

"Girl, that nigga ain't fine no mo. Somebody smoked his ass two days ago down by Shanaynay's house in Metuchen. Perry's got his body. His funeral s'pose to be Friday."

"Get the fuck outta here. I know that bitch Shanaynay bout to pull her muthafuckin' weave out worrying bout how the fuck she gon' pay the rent on that house now. Her stupid ass gonna hafta move back to the projects 'cause that bitch sho can't afford to pay the rent on that fuckin' town house," Nette smirked, slapping five with the stylist in the station next to her.

"Somebody said that Furquan was s'pose to have paid for that house cash," Naderia said, as she rinsed out a customer's hair in the sink.

"Oh," Nette said, disappointed. Then she suddenly brightened. "Shit, but if Fu's wife finds out about that house and it's in Fu's name, she gon' get that shit from Nay's dumb ass."

DuJuanna heard very little of what any of the girls said after Sherrie said that Furquan had gotten killed. Her stomach was suddenly queasy, and for some reason she was feeling real nervous. When Malik had gotten killed, she had marked his death up to chance. After all, Malik was a deacon in the church. Some muthafucka was probably trying to rob him and Malik must have bucked. But Malik and then Furquan back to back was looking less like a coincidence and more like a pattern. Still, she attempted to reason with herself. She was probably just being silly and paranoid. That shit was almost fifteen years ago. Besides, now everybody but her that was either part of the robbery gone bad was dead.

Then she thought about the little boy she had seen under the quilt with the big, pretty but sad eyes and a quiver ran through her body. How old would he be now, she thought as Nette put the last roller in her hair and pointed her toward the line of dryers along the wall. Shit, fifteen years ago, DuJuanna mused as she set under the dryer and Nette snapped on the hood. Damn, he might be eighteen years old by now, and I don't even know what the fuck he looks like.

Twenty minutes later, Nette tapped DuJuanna and DuJuanna jumped.

"What the fuck's wrong with you?" Nette asked. "Your ass jumped like you been hit by a car."

"Nothin'. I'm straight," DuJuanna said, trying to regain her composure. "I'm just tired of Newark and all this killing and kidnapping shit. I'm seriously thinking about moving to New York with my sister."

* * *

DURING THE NEXT six months, between some wet work for Big Farook, Antwan and Rah Rah opened a crackhouse in the Seth Boyden projects and looked intermittently for DuJuanna. Nobody seemed to know where she lived in New Jersey. However, those that did know her were in agreement about one thing, the bitch hadn't aged since she was a teenager. She was still fine as hell, her beauty bolstered by her green eyes and a small beauty mark on her chin. She also had an ass like a Budweiser Clydesdale and lips that appeared able to suck a golf ball through a water hose. With such a detailed description, Antwan was sure he'd know her when he saw her. That and the fact that the vision of her was embedded in his head.

DUJUANNA LOOKED at herself in the full-length mirror behind her bedroom door when her sister Katrina walked past and looked in. Six years older and perhaps thirty pounds heavier than her younger sister, Katrina was a beautiful woman, too. Katrina never regretted moving from Newark to Strivers Row, so when her baby sister had called her up and said she wanted to stay with her for a little while, Katrina welcomed her. And even though the little while had now turned into six months, Katrina cherished every day of them living together. Katrina paused, looking at her for several minutes, and DuJuanna suddenly looked up and smiled.

"What's up, Trina?" DuJuanna asked as she stepped into a hip-hugging micro-miniskirt that matched her black knee-length boots and black, calfskin waist-length North Beach leather jacket.

"Nothin', D. Where you going in your skintight 'fuck me' outfit?" Katrina asked, smiling.

"Probably down to the Garage Club," DuJuanna replied as she took a bottle of White Shoulders perfume and sprayed it liberally over her arms and dabbed a little behind her ears. "Somebody said that Missy Elliot is supposed to be there to celebrate the release of her new album. The shit is s'pose to be off the hook, girl, so you know I gotta be there."

DuJuanna took one last glance at her profile in the mirror.

"Just be careful," her sister warned her. "It's crazy out there. Have fun. Just be careful."

RAH RAH AND ANTWAN decided to close their dope spot for the rest of the night. Fridays generally were the fastest day of the week. Fiends couldn't seem to get enough. The spot generally did four or five ounces of dope easy, but tonight traffic was slow as hell. It wasn't just 5-0 and the usual jump-outs that had thinned the crowd out. Since Furquan had gotten smoked, homicide had been stopping niggas at random as they came out of the building, trying to shake loose some information from some of the crackheads or dope fiends.

"Yo, Rah, we might as well close this shit down for today," Antwan said as he counted a small stack of bills in front of him. "It's eleven o'clock, and this here ain't even fifteen hundred."

"Bet that," Rah Rah replied as he walked to the back of the cluttered apartment to give $50 and a few rocks to the crackhead woman who rented the apartment. "When I went downstairs earlier to get something to eat off the truck," Rah Rah continued as he stepped back into the small living room, "I saw two homicide detectives coming out of two-twelve. Them muthafuckas had me 'noid as shit."

"All right, let's raise," Antwan said, tucking the small stack of cheddar into his pants pocket. "What you gon' do, Rah?"

"I think I'm going over to baby momma's house and catch the Tyson fight tonight on Pay-Per-View. Why? What's up?" Rah Rah asked as he picked up his nine off the table and stuck it in his belt.

"Why don't you let me use the car, man? I don't feel like going in. I think I want to go over to New York to the Garage. Missy Elliot s'pose to be having a promotional party there for her joint that bout to drop. Anyhow the shit is s'pose to be off the hizzy," Antwan said.

"Alright," Rah Rah agreed. "Sounds like you gon' kick it. Should be a night to remember."

THE GARAGE WAS jam-packed, and as usual, there were as many people outside the club hanging out, slinging E pills, reefer, and coke, as there seemed to be inside partying. Beemers, Benzes, and a few Bentleys were double-parked in front of the club. Most of the owners of the exotic automobiles were sitting in their cars smoking blunts and trying to cruise themselves up on a one-night flava of the night.

Inside, DMX's joint, "What You Want," boomed from the gigantic speakers. Antwan had been in the club for a little over an hour, dancing off and on with three chickenheads from uptown, when he excused himself and started walking toward the men's room. As he walked past the bar, he heard a girl standing in front of him call out a name that made his heart nearly stop in his chest.

"DuJuanna, you done sweated your fuckin' hair out," she said, talking to a girl walking off the dance floor.

As Antwan turned to see who the girl's remark was directed to, he looked into the face that had haunted his dreams and nightmares for the last fifteen years. The face hadn't changed much since he last saw it from beneath the quilt on that fateful night. There were a few laugh lines now and the hair was different, but it was the same bitch—the bitch who had stood over his father and pumped four bullets into him while his mother lay handcuffed and his brother's lifeless body lay in a pool of blood.

"DuJuanna, don't look now, but there is a fine young nigga staring at you, girl. His ass is hypnotized," the other girl said.

"Bitch, where at?" DuJuanna asked, laughing and turning in the wrong direction.

"Not over there, bitch," she said, pointing slightly with her head to the left. When DuJuanna turned she was staring at Antwan.

"Damn, he's fine," DuJuanna whispered, all the while never taking her eyes off the cutie pie standing across the small expanse of floor with his eyes locked on her. DuJuanna smiled at him.

Antwan felt perplexed. In each instance when he had finally caught up with the killers of his family, he was about slumping their asses. Now one of the killers stood across a dance floor smiling at him and he found himself doing everything to contain his rage. He'd waited fifteen years for this, he told himself, fighting to control the anger that was coursing through him.

I got to calm down at least long enough to rock her ass to sleep, Antwan thought, allowing a smile to slowly spread across his face, revealing even, white teeth.

"Girl, 'scuse me," DuJuanna said as she walked away from her small knot of friends. "I'm gon' get me some of that," she whispered over her shoulder, walking toward Antwan.

"What's up, cutie?" DuJuanna asked, smiling.

"Nothin' really," Antwan responded.

"You must not come here a lot," DuJuanna remarked, "because this is the first time I've ever seen you here and I know I would have remembered your fine ass if I had ever seen you before." Then she flashed a playful smile.

"Nah, not a lot," Antwan responded, trying to loosen up. "I'm just hanging out."

For the next hour or so, DuJuanna and Antwan stood off to the side of the dance floor talking while DuJuanna ordered one small bottle of Piper's after another.

"Shit. I'm getting drunk, baby," DuJuanna admitted and leaned suggestively against Antwan. "I better get my ass home."

"I'm about to leave if you want a ride," Antwan said, putting down his bottle of Red Bull.

"Let me tell my girlfriends I'm going, baby, and I'll be right back." She walked off and chatted with her girlfriends. "All right, baby, I'm ready," DuJuanna said, walking back up to the bar and running her fingers through her moist hair.

"Let's roll, then," Antwan said as they headed to the exit.

Relax the bitch, Antwan thought, hitting the door locks on the car, watching DuJuanna hop in.

"Do you have to go straight home?" Antwan asked, pulling the car away from the curb.

"Not really, baby. Why? What did you have in mind?" DuJuanna asked with a knowing smile as she lifted up the armrest and snuggled close to Antwan.

"I was gonna drive down by the waterfront, if it's cool with you."

"Yeah, baby, it's cool with me," DuJuanna replied, reaching over and turning on the radio where a "Quiet Storm" oldies but goodies show was playing the Undisputed Truth's old hit "Smiling Faces."

As Antwan drove toward the pier, DuJuanna unzipped his pants and gently massaged his dick. By the time they got to the pier, DuJuanna was giving him some of the best head he had ever experienced in his short life.

For a minute, Antwan got caught up in the moment, but then he snapped out of the sensational feeling. "Stop, bitch!" he yelled.

"Baby, what's wrong?" DuJuanna asked. She raised her head out of Antwan's lap and looked at him with passion-glazed eyes and beads of perspiration on her forehead. As DuJuanna looked into Antwan's eyes, she realized she was seeing a look she had never seen before. She was seeing real anger, bordering on hatred. She had been with more than a few niggas that liked to talk dirty when they made love. She had even been with one real freak shit that liked to choke her when he started to come. That shit had really turned her on, but cutie pie looked to be somewhere beyond all that. Cutie looked like he was mad for real. "Baby, what's wrong?" she asked again.

"Do you remember me?" Antwan asked with a hard edge to his voice.

"Remember you from where, baby?" DuJuanna asked, forcing a fake smile. "Where do you live at, uptown?"

"I'm not from New York," Antwan said, staring evenly at Du-Juanna.

"Where are you from?" DuJuanna asked nervously, realizing for the first time, as the liquor began to wear off, that she was in the car on an isolated street with some nigga and not only did she not know where he was from, she didn't even know his name.

"I'm from Newark, DuJuanna," Antwan said softly, his eyes never leaving DuJuanna's face.

The words, spoken slowly in the stillness of the car, fell like a thousand-pound weight on her chest. DuJuanna could feel her heartbeat quicken as pearls of sweat suddenly dripped from her armpits.

"I don't think I know you," DuJuanna said, trying to control the nervous tremor that invaded her voice.

"Yeah, you remember me," Antwan stated, turning the radio back on. "It's just been a long time."

"No, I don't think so. How old are you anyway?" DuJuanna asked, slowly inching closer to the door, dreading the answer she knew she was about to hear.

"I'm eighteen," Antwan responded, reaching under his seat.

At that moment DuJuanna reached for the door handle and pushed the door open. She fell to the ground outside the car, her heart pounding in her chest. Suddenly she heard two loud claps as bullets tore into the door panel where she had been sitting only seconds before.

"Oh my God," DuJuanna screamed, jumping up and attempting to run. She only made it ten or fifteen feet before a bullet slammed into her shoulder, knocking her to hands and knees on the ground.

"Baby, please, don't kill me," DuJuanna pleaded, looking at Antwan, who was standing over her with the gun pointed at her face. "They made me do it. I didn't wanna kill nobody," DuJuanna babbled, feeling blood run down her back from the bullet lodged in her shoulder.

"I don't want to kill you," Antwan mumbled, looking at DuJuanna's pleading tear-filled eyes.

"Then, baby, don't. Please, baby, have mercy," DuJuanna begged, trying to sit up, but falling over once again.

Antwan thought for a moment as he stared down at the helpless female. "Nah, baby, no mercy," Antwan said as he raised the gun and fired. DuJuanna heard the first shot. Then everything went black.

AS ANTWAN DROVE back to New Jersey his thoughts were on that fateful night fifteen years ago. He thought about his parents and his older brother and wondered how their lives would have turned out if they had not been murdered. There was nothing he could do or could have done to change any of it. These thoughts filled his head as he drove down the turnpike and watched the sun come up. But now, finally, he had gotten revenge for their murders.

As he drove on in silence, he realized he was doing something he had not done in over fifteen years. He was crying. And as he drove with tears flowing, he realized he was crying as much for himself as he was for his murdered family. He knew now, on reflection, that their murders had made him who he was. At just the age of eighteen, he had killed several people. He had maimed countless others. This was not the hand he wanted or would have chosen, he thought as he turned off the highway and drove into Newark, but it was the hand that fate had dealt him. So this was the one he had been forced to play out.

His thoughts turned to the girl he had just killed, how she had begged for her life, how she had constantly called him "baby" and "cutie" and had sucked his dick better than anyone had ever done before in his life. This made him realize that in some ways he was crying for her, too—that, like him, she had simply done what she had to do. She had played the hand that fate had dealt her.

As the sun rose in the sky, Antwan made a resolution. He was going to put the murdering and mayhem behind him. He would keep his spot rocking. He might even open up another one down the road. But that night was the last chapter of his "no mercy" killings. Either for revenge or money. He was going to make a new life for himself.

SIX

OVER THE NEXT COUPLE of years, Rah Rah and Antwan stacked cheddar. They opened another crackhouse on High Street and generally just hung out. Although Rah Rah was now caked, he still enjoyed the adrenaline rush of a well-executed hit or stickup from time to time.

Rah Rah's fortunes would soon take a turn for the worse. During the winter of 2001, Rah Rah was killed in a blazing gun battle with members of the Millburn Police Department working in conjunction with the state's SWAT team.

Antwan was home watching the six o'clock evening news when the story of a jewelry store robbery and hostage crisis broke. Rah Rah had told him his heist plans earlier and Antwan watched as the event unfolded. Antwan knew Rah Rah would never surrender. Rah Rah had always said that if push came to shove, he would hold court in the streets.

Antwan watched as Rah Rah and his crew gave as good as they got with Millburn's finest. He watched with growing dread as sharpshooters with infrared scopes took up positions on area rooftops and waited for a clear shot. Antwan held his breath and his heart pounded in his chest as Rah Rah's head came into view from behind a parked car. Then he watched as the head of the kid he had known from childhood exploded from the impact of a high-velocity bullet, fired from the rifle of a sharpshooter whose motto was one shot, one kill.

Rah Rah's death would be a defining moment for Antwan. Antwan retired from the game and opened up two self-service Laundromats, one in East Orange and the other in Newark, with his stash. There would be no more what had seemed like easy money at the time. Antwan vowed to himself and on his family's graves that he would never live the life he had once lived, and in an unfortunate way, he had Rah Rah to thank for that.

Ironically, it was Rah Rah that brought him into the life he had formerly lived and it was Rah Rah who brought him out.

SEVEN

ANTWAN MET Michelle Anderson, a girl who, like him, had grown up in foster homes and orphanages. However, unlike Antwan, Michelle had finished high school and graduated from Hampton University with a degree in business management.

From the onset they had been an unlikely pair: one a graduate from a prestigious university, the other from the school of hard knocks. But Antwan and Michelle filled some deep personal need in each other, and soon they were inseparable.

In the fall of 2002, Antwan bought a house in Hillside. A few months later Michelle moved in with him. About a year later, Michelle gave birth to an eight-pound, twelve-ounce son that she named Antwan Mickel Dawson. They married three months later.

The following year Michelle gave birth to a second son, who they named Carl in honor of Antwan's father and brother. The businesses went well and by spring 2004, Antwan had a grand opening for his third Laundromat.

Michelle could not have been happier. She knew, or had heard on the streets, about Antwan's past. But as far as she was concerned, it was just that, the past. Michelle didn't care; she had the life she had always hoped for. She and her husband had two beautiful sons and a successful business.

"Baby, where do you want to take the kids for the picnic?" Michelle yelled from the kitchen. "I'm getting tired of Central Park and all of that traffic when we drive back to the house."

"Wherever you want to go, boo," Antwan told her as he dressed Little Carl.

"How about Roselle Park? It's supposed to be nice and the boys haven't been there before," Michelle responded as she stuffed a large bowl of hot wings into the picnic basket.

"That's cool," Antwan said as Carl, with one shoe off and one shoe on, pulled away from his father and ran laughing into the kitchen.

As Antwan and his family made final preparations for their picnic at Roselle Park, a family of another sort was making final preparations, leaving the Pioneer Homes projects in Elizabeth en route to Roselle Park.

Bilal was the leader of the Pioneer Homes Crips. Sixteen years old, Bilal had been sticking up and gangbanging since he was thirteen. Last year when Big Hussein, the gang's leader, had gotten smoked by some kids from the Stella Wright projects in Newark, Bilal had taken over the gang.

Seeking to expand their turf, Bilal and his crew had taken to going to Saint George Avenue in Linden or Roselle Park, where they would go through the park wildin' out or from time to time staging some impromptu broad-daylight stickups.

Antwan, Michelle, and the two boys had been lying on a blanket on a grassy slope, which overlooked the park's lake. For the last several hours Antwan and his family had eaten hot wings, drunk homemade lemonade, and listened to Alicia Keys's latest CD.

"Baby, it's starting to get a little dark," Michelle remarked as she rose up off the blanket, looking around. "It's probably time to get the boys home."

"Alright, boo," Antwan agreed, sitting up and looking across the slowly emptying park. "Let me listen to this last song. You and the boys start taking the stuff down to the car. I'll be down right behind you."

"Daddy, let me wait with you," Little Antwan begged, looking up at his father with his mother's eyes.

"All right, shorty," Antwan said, looking across at Michelle, who nodded her head, smiled, and started gathering up the picnic basket and blanket.

As Michelle walked hand in hand down the slope with her son, she thought about her life now and a smile crept across her face. She had never dreamed that she could ever have been so totally happy. In her youth, as she moved from foster home to foster home, she had never thought that she would ever enjoy the life that Antwan and she had made for themselves and their children.

As Michelle neared the car, she noticed a group of young boys wearing blue bandannas talking loudly and walking in her direction.

"What's up, boo?" said a light brown–skinned kid who didn't look to be any more than fourteen years old.

"Nothing at all," Michelle replied as she gripped Carl's hand tightly and continued walking, trying to pass the rowdy group.

"Hold up a minute, boo," the kid said, smiling and stepping in front of Michelle to block her path. "Why don't you drop us off?" He reached to grab Michelle's hand.

Michelle pulled away and began to yell for Antwan.

"Shit, bitch, you better chill the fuck out," Bilal snarled as he stepped to the middle of the crowd. "We'll jack your fuckin' chicken-head ass, you keep on running your fuckin' mouth," he said, pointing his finger in Michelle's face.

Antwan and Little Antwan were walking down the slope of the hill when he spotted his wife and son surrounded by the crew of young dudes. As Antwan came nearer, he noticed that one of them had just tried to snatch his wife's car keys.

"Get your muthafuckin' hands off her," Antwan shouted, pushing his way through the small crowd. "Baby, you all right?" Antwan asked Michelle, while keeping his eyes on the crew of young gangstas that now surrounded him and his family.

"Fuck you, nigga," a dark brown–skinned kid with cornrows said, stepping up to Antwan. "We'll jack your bitch ass, too."

"You'll do what?" Antwan questioned, his eyes wide in disbelief as he stepped closer to the kid.

"Baby, please. Antwan, let's go home," Michelle pleaded as Antwan's eyes burned into the eyes of the kid standing directly in front of him.

Antwan stared into the laughing eyes of the kid in front of him. It had been years since he had worn a vest, carried his burner, or dealt with any street drama. A few years ago he would have murdered this little muthafucka just for looking at him. That was a few years ago. Another time, another life, another Antwan. He was married now and had two kids and three businesses. He had to let that shit go. Antwan turned to begin getting his family into the car.

"I thought so!" the kid spat out, then shoved Antwan hard as Antwan tried to maneuver around the gang members to his car.

It's said that old habits die hard, that instinct and unlearned patterns of behavior are hardwired into us at birth. Before Antwan could weigh the consequences, before he could even consider the odds, instinct took over and he was on automatic pilot.

Before Bilal's crew could respond, Antwan spun around and fired a hard right, catching the kid high on the temple and knocking him out cold.

"No, please," Michelle screamed as she watched the crew move toward Antwan. And then out of the corner of her eye Michelle saw a gun. From that moment everything else seemed to happen in slow motion. As Antwan slipped under a roundhouse punch thrown by one of the kids and was about to throw a left hook of his own, three shots rang out. Michelle watched as Antwan's body pitched back and crashed into the car's door. The gang members immediately ran off in different directions.

"Oh my God, no!" Michelle screamed as little Carl began to cry. Michelle kneeled down beside Antwan as a river of blood poured from his chest. Antwan lifted his head and attempted to speak but a heavy stream of dark red blood poured from his mouth.

"Don't try to talk, baby," Michelle said softly with tears flowing from her eyes. Antwan looked up at his wife and forced a smile. He wanted to tell her that he was alright, that everything would work out, that now more than ever before he understood karma and just how life worked out, that he even understood the kids that shot him. He wanted to tell her he loved her and to take care of the boys. But he couldn't. He tried to reach for her hand to hold it and look in her eyes one last time, but the darkness was drawing him in and he was tired of resisting its pull. Then everything went black. Antwan's head rolled to one side and fell. Michelle released a scream that continued every night for the next three years in the psychiatric ward of Roselle Medical Hospital.

Little Carl began to cry when he heard his mother scream and that night he cried himself to sleep.

Antwan was standing next to his dad when the bullets exploded like firecrackers in his father's chest. He had tried to holler, to scream, but nothing came out. He would remain that way, unable to speak or cry, until he was eight years old. And for the rest of his young life he would have one recurring dream. And in it he would find them, kill the people that murdered his dad, and when he did he would show them no mercy.

THICKER THAN MUD

Composed by Y. Blak Moore, understood by many

ONE

APRIL 17, 1991, 3:34 P.M.

THE OLDER, TALLER BOY spat sunflower-seed shells on the cracked sidewalk, and his friend snickered as Danny Man approached them.

Daniel "Danny Man" Russell muttered under his breath as he looked over at Tom-Tom and his friend. *Damn, I knew I shouldn't have come this way to this store. I shoulda went to the candy lady. Tom-Tom and them stay on some bully stuff.*

Danny Man looked up and down the street—no adults. At least none that would have deterred Tom-Tom from misbehaving if he wanted to. Danny Man could feel both of the boys' eyes roving up and down his person. He felt rather than witnessed their eyes come to rest on the brand-new pair of Air Jordans on his feet. Silently, Danny Man wished that his feet weren't so big for his age or that there was at least a smudge or two of dirt on his white-and-red leather basketball shoes.

Again Danny Man looked up and down the block, stalling for time.

"Shorty, check it out," Tom-Tom said, summoning him over with a wave of his hand.

"Who, me?" Danny Man asked. Inside he was hoping and praying that Tom-Tom wasn't talking to him, but he knew he wasn't that lucky.

"Yeah, you little mutherfucker," Tom-Tom said gruffly. "Who the fuck else you think I'm talking to?"

Danny Man dropped his eyes as he slowly drew nearer. "I didn't know you was talking to me."

"W'sup with you," Tom-Tom said, trying to lighten up the mood. "You don't know a mutherfucker since I left school."

More like they put yo old ass out, seventh-grade dropout, Danny Man thought. Without looking at Tom-Tom's face, he said, "It ain't like that. I just don't be seeing you no more since you left school."

"You got some squares?" Tom-Tom asked.

"I don't smoke cigarettes," Danny Man stated bluntly.

Tom-Tom turned to his buddy. "Yo, Rell, gimme a smoke."

"Aww, man. I only got one left. You done already smoked up all my pack."

"Nigga, I don't recall asking you that," Tom-Tom said with his eyes flashing dangerously. "What I said was gimme a mutherfucking cigarette. I don't care if it's your first or your last."

"A'ight, man, calm down," Rell said as he pulled a semi-crumpled cigarette from his pack. He tossed the empty carton on the ground and put the cigarette between his lips. As he was searching his pockets for a light, Tom-Tom snatched it from his lips.

Hoping they were distracted, Danny Man tried to slip away into the small neighborhood store behind them.

Tom-Tom turned back to Danny Man. "Little nigga, where you going? I wadn't through hollering at you."

Danny Man wanted to run, but he knew that if he bolted, they would catch him easily. He paused with his hand on the door handle of the store. "I had thought that you was through talking to me."

"Naw, man, I ain't through. Bring yo ass back over here."

Danny Man took several small steps in Tom-Tom's general direction.

Tom-Tom laughed. "Man, what the fuck is wrong with you? Is you retarded or something? Bring yo ass over here, ain't nobody finta do nothing to you. I just want to ask you a question."

"What?" Danny Man asked, his voice cracking slightly from fear.

Tom-Tom draped his arm around Danny Man's shoulder. Danny Man noticeably flinched when he did this, making Tom-Tom laugh again.

"What you jumping for? I already done told you I ain't finta do nothing to yo ass, so quit acting like that."

Danny Man grinned nervously as he hoped that someone, anyone he knew, would walk up to the corner or come out of the store.

As if he was reading Danny Man's mind, Tom-Tom said, "C'mon, let's get up off this corner before old dude that own the store call the law on us."

With his arm still around Danny Man's shoulders, Tom-Tom begin maneuvering the slightly resistant boy around the corner. Rell fell into step behind them.

"Where we going?" Danny Man asked finally as they neared the alley on the side of the store. "I was finta go to the store. Where is we finta go?"

Tom-Tom looked over his shoulder at Rell, giving him a knowing look. "What was you bout to get at the store? You got some money?"

Danny Man thought about it quickly. "I only got two dollars. That ain't nothing. I was just finta buy some chips and stuff, but if you need it I'll give you one of my dollars."

Tom-Tom stopped at the mouth of the alley and took his arm from around Danny Man's shoulder. He looked around and then he pushed Danny Man into the trash-strewn, broken-glass-covered alley.

"Fuck a mutherfucking dollar! I want them Jordans you got on, bitch! And all the cash in yo mutherfucking pocket!"

"Stop playing, Tom-Tom," Danny Man said as he stumbled backward into the alley. "This ain't funny."

Tom-Tom balled up his fist and whacked Danny Man upside the head. "What you think, this is a mutherfucking joke! I know I ain't said shit funny! Do you see me laughing, bitch? Nigga, what size is them shoes?"

"Y-y-you don't need to know my s-size," Danny Man stammered. "I ain't finta give you my shoes. My big brother just bought these for me."

Tom-Tom grabbed Danny Man by the collar of his jacket and slapped him across the cheek. "I wouldn't give a fuck if yo mammy bought them for you with her last dollar, I said take them off! Now!"

Snot began to run from Danny Man's nose and tears leaked from his eyes. "I can't give you my shoes, my brother just bought me these," he whined. "I can't give them to you."

"Rell, get over here and hold this bitch-ass nigga!" Tom-Tom ordered. "Oh, he finta run them there! I bet the fuck he finta take off those Mikes!"

Rell had been content to watch Tom-Tom's back.

"Tom-Tom, man, leave this little nigga alone," Rell said halfheartedly. "He crying like a little bitch."

"Man, you better bring yo faggot ass up in here and grab this nigga! If you don't when I'm through with him, then I'ma get in yo ass, too."

Rell approached. He got behind Danny Man and held his arms. "Tom-Tom, it don't even look like you can fit this nigga shoes," Rell commented.

"What the fuck you say? Nigga, you sound like a mutherfucking shoe salesman or something. Did I ask you what size I wear? Fuck that! Put this nigga in a nelson so I can get them Jordans!"

"No, no!" Danny Man pleaded.

Behind Danny Man, Rell slipped both of his arms under his and locked his fingers behind Danny Man's neck. Danny Man struggled impotently against the incapacitating wrestling lock.

"Hold this nigga!" Tom-Tom roared as he bent down to get Danny Man's shoes. "If this nigga kick me in my fucking face, I'ma beat yo ass after I beat his."

Rell applied more pressure to Danny Man's neck, causing him to bend over as Tom-Tom slipped the shoes off his feet. Tom-Tom stood up and tied the Jordans together by the shoestrings and draped them over his shoulder. Before Rell released Danny Man, Tom-Tom dug through his pockets and pulled out some money. Quickly he counted it.

"Nigga, yo lying ass," Tom-Tom said happily as he slapped Danny Man playfully on the top of his head. "I thought all you had was two dollars. This here is forty-two dollars. I'm finta get higher than a mutherfucka. Rell, let that bitch go."

Rell let him go, causing Danny Man to fall to his knees at his sudden release. Tom-Tom was already leaving the alley and Rell jogged to catch up with him.

"Stop playing, gimme back my shoes!" Danny Man bawled loudly as he stood up. "Gimme my money! Gimme back my stuff! I'ma tell my brother!"

Tom-Tom abruptly turned and rushed back to Danny Man. Using his foot, Tom-Tom foot swept Danny Man's legs, making him fall again. He climbed onto Danny Man's chest and began wildly punching him in the face with both his fists. Danny Man tried to cover up his face and head as much as possible from the blows, but several of Tom-Tom's punches connected well enough to make Danny Man's head slam against the alley floor. The impact made him dizzy.

Tom-Tom stopped hitting him and leaned in close to Danny Man's face. "Now if you want to tell yo brother something, tell him that I whupped yo ass! Yo brother don't scare me! That nigga got to be a punk if he got a punk-ass nigga like you for a little brother! So fuck you and him!" He stood up and slung the shoes back over his shoulder. "Let's go, Rell."

Danny Man laid on the ground sobbing and holding his head as the two boys left with his shoes and money. When he was sure they were gone, Danny Man jumped to his feet and ran home.

TWO

APRIL 17, 1991, 4:18 P.M.

DONNELL "DODO" COFFMAN eased the 185-pound steel barbell back onto the weight bench cradle. He sat up on the padded bench and used his T-shirt to wipe the sweat off his forehead and chest. He looked across the basement at his friend Casey Russell. Casey was sitting on the edge of the couch. In front of him was an old wooden coffee table. Casey's attention was divided between the television set against the wall and a saucer with a small amount of cocaine on the coffee table.

Dodo got up and walked over to the concrete basement sink. He turned the cold water tap on and let the water run for a while. He dipped his cupped hands under the stream of water and took a drink. He wiped his wet hands on his pants. He looked over at Casey again on the couch and shook his head.

"What's up, man?" Dodo asked. "I thought you was about to lift some weights with me. You must be scared of this steel. Nigga scared to hit some of this steel."

"Nall, nigga, I ain't scared, but the only thing I'ma hit is some of this here coke," Casey said. "You need to get off that swole shit and take you a bump or two."

Dodo walked across the basement. He stopped in front of an old, cracked wall mirror and looked at the reflection of his brown chest. He flexed his biceps several times. Satisfied that his workouts had been paying off, he walked back over to the sink and took another long drink of cold water. He joined Casey on the couch. For a while he just sat and watched some talk show.

"Casey, why do you even watch this stupid shit?"

Casey grinned. "Man, I love this shit. Crazy-ass chicks-with-dicks, I-slept-with-my-brother's-wife dudes, and I'm-a-man-but-my-boyfriend-don't-know shit. I mean look at this show. These mutherfuckers is on here to admit to their boyfriends that they is really men. That shit is crazy! How a mutherfucker don't know he dating another man for three months? Man, if a mutherfucker did fool me on some drag queen shit, I would go bananas when that shit came out! The funny thing about watching this show is that you don't never know how the other mutherfucker gon' react when he find out that the person you thought was a girl probably got a bigger dick than you."

"Do you think them fights be for real?" Dodo asked. "I think that whole shit is a setup. They pay them to scrap on here, I bet."

"Shit, they could pay me and I'd be on there straight knocking mutherfuckers out," Casey said.

Just then the basement door flew open and Danny Man flung himself inside. He stood in front of Casey and Dodo in a pair of dirty athletic socks. The pockets of his pants were still inside out. Snot and tears ran freely down his face and he was out of breath.

Quizzically Casey looked at his younger brother. "Man, what the fuck is wrong with you?"

"They—they took my—my Jordans and my—my money. They j-jumped on me and r-robbed me. I-I told them that-that you was my brother and they said they did—didn't care!"

"Who?" Casey asked as he jumped to his feet.

"It was Tom-Tom and Rell. They grabbed me by the corner store and took me in the alley and jump—jumped on m-me. They—they used to go to my school. They always be up—up on the—the corner starting stuff with people, trying to take people money and stuff."

Casey picked up the saucer of coke from the coffee table and snorted a healthy portion as he began to pace back and forth.

"You know these niggas, Casey?" Dodo asked.

"Nall, it sound like some shorties. I don't give a fuck though. Danny Man, where these niggas from? Where they be at?"

"They from the other side of the Avenue. They either be up at the store or they be right there at the playground up at the school or up at the park."

Dodo looked at Casey and noticed that the cocaine had Casey's eyes wide open. "So what you want to do?"

"What the fuck you think I want to do!" Casey exclaimed, a little too amped. "Man, we finta fuck these niggas up and get my brother his shoes back! Don't nobody take nothing from us! We finta push on these marks! They think we some hos! I'm finta get my shotgun! Let's go!"

"Hell nall, man," Dodo said. "We ain't finta ride with that big-ass shotgun. Give me a minute to go get my pistol. Danny Man, you go put on some shoes."

While Danny Man went to get some shoes, Dodo slipped out of the basement and made his way home to get his gun. Casey sat back down on the couch and snorted the remainder of the cocaine. When he was through, he dug through a pile of clothes by the washing machine and found a black hooded sweatshirt. He snatched the hoodie on over his head. When he heard a car horn honk outside, Casey ran out the back door of the basement, almost knocking down Danny Man.

Heavy, cold raindrops had started to fall as they rushed over to Dodo's car, an ancient, beat-up four-door Chevy Caprice. Dodo slid out from under the steering wheel to the passenger seat and motioned for Casey to come around the vehicle to the driver's side. Danny Man got in the backseat, and Casey climbed behind the wheel.

"Casey, you drive just in case we get pulled over 'cause you got a license and I got this missile."

Casey rocketed the car out of the driveway and fishtailed when he hit the street. He straightened the car up and sped up the block.

"Man, slow this mutherfucker down," Dodo snapped as he braced himself against the dashboard. "You gon' get us popped off driving like that. That's the reason that I let you drive, so we could look halfway legit."

Casey slowed down, just a bit. "Let me do this here. I drive the way that I want to. Nigga, we on this business. And I am the one with the license so let me milk this cow."

"I ain't trying to hear that shit. Like I said, slow this mutherfucker down." Dodo turned around to Danny Man. The younger boy was still sniveling. "Danny Man, what these dudes look like?"

"Tom-Tom he kinda tall. He like almost y'all height. He light-skinned with a short Afro. He think he cocky. Rell, he about my height and my color. He got on a Bears jacket and he got a fade. Rell kinda brown-skinned and skinny."

Dodo turned back around in his seat in time to notice that Casey had started speeding again. He just shook his head. That's that fucking coke got this nigga speedballing, he thought. The car was half a block away from the traffic light in front of them when the signal turned yellow. Instead of applying the brakes in preparation to stop at the inevitable red light, Casey stomped the accelerator. He was still several car lengths away when the signal turned red. Still gunning the old car, Casey barreled into the intersection. They broadsided the rear flank of a Chevy Blazer, causing the small SUV to flip over as their car careened off in the opposite direction.

Casey had time to brace his arms hard against the steering wheel before they slammed into a light pole. The steering wheel slammed into Casey's, chest causing him to pass out. Dodo's knees hit the dashboard and his head slammed into the windshield on impact. Out for the count, he sprawled against Casey. Only Danny Man's legs were visible in the backseat—he was upside down.

Danny Man righted himself in the backseat and looked around. His eyes fell on his older brother's unconscious form. "Casey! Casey! Wake up, Casey!" he yelled as he shook him from the back.

Casey began to come around. He drew in a breath and pain exploded in his chest.

"Ahhh," Casey cried out. "I think my ribs is broke!" He noticed Dodo leaning against him for the first time. "Oh shit, Dodo! Get up, Dodo! Dodo get up!"

Danny Man looked over the seat at Dodo. "Casey, his bones is sticking through his leg, look!"

The bone in Dodo's left leg was easily visible and the cuts on his head and in his face had begun pouring blood. Casey reached over and pushed the driver's door open. It protested but gave way. He stifled another scream.

In the rear seat, Danny Man was panicking. "What? What? What's wrong, Casey?"

"My goddamn wrists hurt like hell! Shit, mutherfuck!"

Grimacing in pain, Casey pushed Dodo off him and rolled his body out of the car. As he stood and looked around, he got his first view of the Blazer he'd collided with—it had flipped over several times and came to rest against the curb. The occupants of the truck had spilled out in the street.

"Casey, what is we gone do?" Danny Man whined. "Is Dodo dead? What is we gone do, Casey?"

Casey leaned in the car and took a good look at Dodo. He saw his friend's chest and stomach rise and fall. "Nall, he ain't dead," Casey announced. "I can't carry him and I know he can't walk on that drumstick in no type of way. I don't know what the fuck we gon' do."

Cars had begun to slow down and stop in the rain. Casey heard sirens in the distance, making up his mind for him. He turned to his younger brother. "C'mon, Danny Man, we got to get the hell up out of here."

"What about Dodo?" Danny Man asked.

"Them people that's on they way can do more for him than we can. We outty five thousand."

THREE

FOURTEEN YEARS LATER Dodo walked up to the guy sitting on the hood of the old car. He looked at his old friend Casey and could easily tell that he was high. Casey's shirt and jeans were name

Y. BLAK MOORE

brand, but filthy; his shoes were run over and greasy-looking. His beard and hair were both matted bunches of nappy hair. A thin line of drool had escaped from the corner of his lips and was attached to his knee.

"Yo Casey," Dodo said. "Casey, w'sup, man?"

Casey came out of his nod and looked up at Dodo. He jumped back like he had seen a ghost.

"Casey, w'sup? It's me, Dodo."

"Dodo, that you, man?" Casey asked, his voice scratchy with heroin. "My nigga, Dodo."

Casey lifted his arms and gave Dodo a big hug. Because of his unwashed smell, Dodo broke off the hug quickly.

"Dodo, my nigga. How you doing? Hold on, you ain't come over here for no rocks or blows, did you?"

"Hell nall. Why you ask me that?"

"Nall, I just was gon' show you who got the bomb on that diesel and I know who got some butter on the cracks. I'm a diesel man myself, but I don't discriminate when it's free."

Dodo took a seat on the car hood beside Casey. "I don't fuck around with that shit. W'sup with you, though? What you doing out here?"

"Man, I'm hustling."

"You hustling?"

"Hell yeah. This shit is sweet. I ain't got to do nothing but sit out here and watch for the law and call out the name of the dope who I'm on security for."

"Don't look like you would have been able to call out nothing the way you was nodding when I walked up."

Casey laughed until he began coughing. "Gimme a square."

"I ain't got none, really. I was on my way to the store to grab me some rollups when I remembered that somebody told me that I could probably find you over here. Who you out here working for?"

"One of these fucking shorties. I don't care who I get down with as long as I get a wakeup blow in the morning, a lunchtime blow, a go-home blow, and twenty dollars a day. What you finta do? You bout to set you up a crew and get down out here?"

"Selling dope? No thanks. Nigga, I'm just out the damn joint and I ain't finta do nothing that can send my ass back."

"I heard that shit. Well, this ain't it for me. I'm just biding my time until I can hustle me up a few dollars so I can get me a few grams of my own and then I'm off and running. Getting some of that big dope money. Since I already blow myself I know I can put the best shit out here on the streets 'cause I'll be testing it myself. Once I get me a nice piece of dough, then I'm out of here. Probably go get clean and then go out to the coast or something. Spend the rest of my days walking me a big pretty dog on the beach with some pretty-ass white wife."

"Sounds like you got it all planned out. Me, I don't think I managed to think that far ahead, Casey. Right now I'm just enjoying my freedom."

"Got to have a plan, man. If you fail to plan, then you plan to fail, baby boy. But look, let me get back over here and start yelling out this name for these niggas. We'll be getting off soon and they'll try to dock my pay if they don't see me yelling out that name. When we get a chance we need to hang out."

Both men stood and Dodo managed to suffer through another of Casey's funk-laced hugs.

"Take it easy," Dodo said as he walked away.

"Dodo!" Casey called out.

Dodo stopped. "Yeah?"

"I thought you was gon' try and come at me when you got out 'cause I couldn't carry you, man. I broke one of my wrists and bruised my ribs up. I couldn't pick you up and you was in bad shape. The best place for you to be was still there when the ambulance came."

Dodo looked at Casey for a long moment. "It's all right. I survived, didn't I? Ain't nothing I could do to you that would be worse than what you doing to yourself, so don't worry about it. Like one of the enlightened brothers in the joint used to tell me, the universe has a way of balancing itself out. I'll try to get back this way and holler at you. Take care of yourself."

Casey grinned, revealing several missing teeth. "I'll do that, Dodo. Love you, baby boy."

FOUR

AS DODO APPROACHED the corner store someone called out to him. "Dodo, w'sup, nigga! Hold up for a sec!" shouted the driver of a creamy white Cadillac SRX. "Hold on for a minute, I'm finta swing around and park."

Dodo looked at the hybrid SUV, but he didn't recognize the driver or his voice. Cautiously he stepped up on the curb in front of the corner store and waited for the driver to park his vehicle.

The driver whipped into a U-turn and glided the car into a no-parking zone in front of the store. The driver climbed out of the car and came around to the sidewalk, smiling all the while. The heavyset man grabbed Dodo's hand and gave him a handshake hug.

"What's happening, nigga?" the man asked. "It's good to see one of the old-school fools out here on the bricks. You looking good, too. All healthy and shit. Nigga was lifting some weights in the joint."

Dodo stood there looking at him blankly.

"Don't tell me that you don't know who I am," the man said. "Nigga, look at me. You tell me you don't know me?"

"My fault, homie, but I can't even lie, I'm clueless."

The man laughed. "Damn, it's been that long, huh? I know that I gained some weight and grew some face hair, but look at me. Take a good look."

Dodo started shaking his head slowly, and then recognition crept into his eyes. "Danny Man? Casey's little brother."

"The one and only. I'm all grown up now."

"Yeah, I can see that," Dodo commented as he glanced at Danny Man's huge potbelly. "You done grown out, too."

Danny Man laughed as he rubbed his large stomach. "Nigga, that's that good living. Steak and lobster, living like a mobster. I see you lost yo hair up in that place, huh?"

Self-consciously Dodo rubbed his head. It was shaved clean, but a close observer could see that on top no follicles would ever grow again.

"Yeah, twelve years in the joint will do that for you," Dodo said. "You'd probably lose more than your hair in there."

Danny Man rankled a bit at the slight insult, but just as quickly he let it go. "You ain't even got to act like that. Nigga, you just did all that time, you a real old gee now. We need to be celebrating that you back among the land of the living."

"You look like you on your way to go celebrate now," Dodo observed. "What you all dressed up for?"

Danny Man looked down at his tailor-made white linen suit and matching white shoes. "Tell me I ain't killing them with this here. I'm on my way to my boy's engagement party. He finta propose to his lady on a cruise on Lake Michigan and everybody that's coming got to wear all white. Yo, have you seen Casey in the coupla weeks since you been out?"

"Actually, I just came from over there hollering at him. What happened to that nigga?"

"Well, you know, Casey always liked to put something in his

nose. He started getting a little money on the heroin side and the next thing I knew he was putting more of it in his nose than out on the streets."

Dodo raised an eyebrow. "Hold on, hold on. You said that I been home for a coupla weeks. How did you know that?"

Making a sweeping gesture with his arms, Danny Man said, "This is my hood. Ain't shit I don't know about. I know while you was in the joint niggas was coming in there talking about DM. I'm DM. Ain't no more of that little Danny Man shit. I'm that nigga now. This is my shit around here, and I always know what's happening."

"Yeah?" Dodo asked skeptically.

"Yeah," Danny Man assured him. "You can check my files. Them niggas that robbed me, they mamas go visit they graves on they birthdays. Now, I got this shit on lock. The neighborhood ain't split up no more, niggas fighting over blocks but ain't getting no money. Them days is over now. We put that shit behind us. It's all about that paper. Cash rules, smack fools. I got the paper so I got the say-so."

"Is that so? Well, I wish you woulda sent me some paper while I was down in the joint."

"Man, they hit you hard, too. Manslaughter, wadn't it?"

"Two counts 'cause I didn't have no license. Old girl that was in that Blazer was pregnant when she died. That plus the pistol and I had a probation warrant."

"Whew, that was way fucked up that day. We tried to get you up out the car, but yo leg was messed up and Casey was fucked up. How's yo leg?"

"Pins in it to this day. Since I was the only one there when the cops got there, they tried to hang my ass in court."

"Man, we thought you was dead, so we got up outta there. It

ain't like neither of us knew no lifesaving techniques or shit. We didn't know what to do so we ran. It ain't my fault."

"Yeah, y'all ran and left me to take the weight," Dodo said with a heavy scowl on his face. "So don't stand up there and act like it didn't happen like that. I wouldn'ta been there if we wadn't trying to catch the niggas that robbed you."

"Man, I told you . . . !" Danny Man exploded. He paused to give himself a second to regain his composure. "Man, I told you that you was so fucked up wadn't nothing we could do but leave you. Don't be up here acting like you wouldn't have done the same thing if the shoe was on the other foot."

"Yeah, that's true, but I didn't make yo brother run that red light."

"You the one told that nigga to drive knowing that he was high off that raw cocaine. That shit had him speedballing. I think that nigga was born to be a dope fiend or something. I don't fuck with that nigga in no type of way. I'm sick of that nigga stealing from me. That dude would steal the paint off a wall. He been to the joint a couple of times for petty shit."

"He ain't come behind the wall," Dodo commented. "Back in the early years of my bit, I would have loved to bump into him in maximum security."

"What you mean by that?" Danny Man asked with a raised eyebrow.

"Oh nothing. Just that if he would have come behind the wall before I managed to get my mind right, then I would have made sure that I showed him the maximum security hospitality that is due such a good friend."

"Whatever that mean," Danny Man said dismissively as he looked at the diamond-encrusted wristwatch he was wearing. "Man, I would love to stick around and chew the fat with you, but I've got to get up out of here. I gotta grab a few things out the store. What you finta do?"

"I'm going in the store, too."

Both men walked to the store's entrance. Dodo pushed open the glass and metal door and walked in, letting the door go behind him. The door almost smacked Danny Man in the face but he caught it in time.

"Damn, Dodo, watch that shit!" Danny Man said.

"My fault," Dodo said dryly without turning around. "The hinges must be loose or something."

They both got in line behind several other patrons. It was a small store crowded with all types of merchandise. As they waited their respective turns to make purchases at the wood-and-Plexiglas counter, the store's door burst open and a trio of boisterous little girls walked in. Oblivious to their surroundings the girls yammered among themselves as they collected potato chips, snack cakes, and juices from the store's aisles.

"I'm gon' get me a dollar worth of cheese on my Flaming Hots," one of the girls said. She was walking backward as she talked to her friends and she almost stepped on Danny Man's shoes, but he stiff-armed her.

"Watch my shoes, shorty!" he said sharply. "These here cost four hundred dollars. I wouldn't let my moms steps on these without going bananas."

The girls fell silent as they got in line behind Danny Man. Behind his back they rolled their eyes.

Dodo peeked back over his shoulder at Danny Man's feet. "Them shoes cost four hundred?"

"Plus tax," Danny Man said proudly.

"What kind of shoes is them?"

"Prada."

"What they do that make them cost that much damn money?"

With a look on his face that said Dodo was asking a stupid question, Danny Man said, "Man, I can tell that you been gone for a long time."

"Yeah, I missed out on the four-hundred-dollar shoes," Dodo said wryly as he stepped up to the counter. "Unlucky me. A homie, give me a pack of Kite's and a today's paper if you got one left."

Dodo tossed two crumpled singles on the counter to pay for his purchases. Danny Man stepped up to the counter next to order as Dodo was leaving out.

"Dodo, don't go nowhere for a sec. I want to put a bug in yo ear before you leave."

Outside in front of the store, Danny Man put his hand on Dodo's shoulder. "Heard you been looking for work since you got out."

"How the fuck you know what I been up to since I got out? Oh yeah, I almost forgot you told me this is your hood. Yeah, I been looking for a gig. I learned a couple of trades in the joint."

"Well, when you get tired of filling out applications for bullshit jobs that they ain't gon' give you, then come holler at yo boy," Danny Man said smugly. "I always need some good dudes that I can trust to work for me."

Contempt was evident on Dodo's face. "Man, what you just say to me? Are you asking me to sell drugs for you?"

Danny Man withdrew his hand from Dodo's shoulder. "You ain't got to say it like that, like I'm trying to send you off or something. I wadn't saying that I wanted you to sell nothing. I got enough people doing that shit. I need people that I can trust to do other shit. Run the bundles, bag up shit, pick up money, or take care of anybody that get in the way of my getting down. That type of shit. I don't need you on the front lines. I know that you old school. I got more respect for you than to try and stick you in a dope spot. Gimme some credit."

"Do I look like a mutherfucking errand boy to you?" Dodo snarled. "I ain't one of these young-ass street punks! You must be losing yo damn mind. Nigga, I was running these streets around here when you was still in diapers."

"That's ancient history, Dodo," Danny Man said arrogantly. "Today is a new day and I'm the mutherfucking man around here. I was trying to put you down 'cause I know you just come home from doing a ugly bit. I was trying to make sure that you get some of this paper. A mutherfucker told me a long time ago, everybody want this money, but very few people know how to get it. Since I first hollered at you, you been talking jazzy. It sound like you mad 'cause while you was in the joint and Casey was snorting away his life, I was out here getting this money and making this shit go my way. Them days of that shorty following up behind you and Casey is long gone. I ain't no shorty no more and you need to quit trying to talk to me like I'm one."

"Man, you better get up out my face with that bullshit!" Dodo snapped. "You might be a heavyweight to these new-school niggas, but you still little Danny Man to me, my man."

Danny Man bit his lower lip as his plump face flushed with anger. Just then the door of the store swung open as the little girls exited. The girl leading the way was carrying a 99-cent bag of Flaming Hot Cheetos. Nacho cheese dripped down the side of the bag. As the little girl was walking out of the store, an uneven piece of the sidewalk caught the toe of her shoe and she stumbled forward. Her bag of cheese snacks sailed from her hand. The plastic sack of Cheetos landed upside down on Danny Man's shoe, but not before the majority of the bag's contents splattered against his pants legs.

In horror Danny Man looked down at the red and orange stains on his pants and shoes. The girl regained her balance and looked at Danny Man. Her hand came up to her mouth in pure terror.

"You stupid little bitch!" Danny Man roared as he kicked the bag off his shoe. The stains on his outfit began to worsen as the red spices from the Flaming Hot Cheetos mixed with the orange nacho cheese began to set in. He stormed over to the girl and grabbed her shoulders. The multicolored barrettes in her hair rattled as he violently shook her back and forth.

"Yo little dumb ass!" Danny Man yelled. "I should break yo mutherfucking neck for this bullshit!"

Dodo stepped up and put his hand on Danny Man's arm. "Man, what's wrong with you? That's a little kid. She ain't try to do that. Let her go."

"You better let me the fuck go!" Danny Man raged.

"Who the fuck you think you talking to? You better get yo damn hands off that little girl, nigga!"

"Dodo, you better mind your business, bitch!"

Dodo took a step back and dropped his newspaper on the ground. "Bitch. Who the fuck you calling a bitch?"

"You! Bitch!"

Dodo hauled off and punched Danny Man solidly in the jaw. The blow made Danny Man release the girl to try to defend himself, but Dodo pounced on him like a tiger. He rained blows on Danny Man's head with both fists, and he easily got the best of the softer, fatter Danny Man. He gave him a body shot to his paunchy midsection, causing Danny Man to double over. Next he launched an uppercut to the underside of Danny Man's chin immediately following the body shot that lifted his head. An overhand right to the bridge of Danny Man's nose put him down for the count. As he lay on the ground, Dodo kicked him in the ribs a couple of times.

"Next time you decide to call somebody a bitch, make sure they really are a bitch," Dodo said to Danny Man as he stood over him. As he picked up his newspaper, he said to the little girls, "Y'all get up out of here."

After kicking Danny Man one more time he crossed the street

and headed for home. The last he saw of Danny Man the store owners were standing over him as one of them made a call on a cell phone.

FIVE

DODO KNOCKED on the back door of his sister's apartment. He winced as a sharp pain shot through his hand. He looked at the back of his hand in the dim hallway light and saw swelling around his knuckles. Inside the apartment he could hear children playing and the television set. He rapped again on the door. This time he used his other hand.

"My momma said, who is it?" his nephew yelled from inside the apartment.

"It's your uncle Dodo."

"It's Dodo, Momma," the boy said as he unlocked several locks on the door. As the door swung open, the chubby six-year-old grinned at his uncle. "W'sup, Uncle Dodo?"

Dodo stepped inside the apartment and closed the door. "W'sup with you, Laheem?"

"Nothing. We was wondering where you was when we got home from school. I need help with my homework, and my momma said to wait on you."

Dodo tickled his nephew. "Where yo momma at?"

Laughing, Laheem said, "In her room on the phone. She putting Mulan to sleep. Latrice is in the front room watching TV with me."

"What you mean watching TV? I thought that you need help with your homework."

He grabbed his nephew to tickle him again, but Laheem broke loose and scampered through the kitchen to the living room, almost knocking over his mother, Crystal. Wearing a silk scarf on her head, jogging pants, and an old T-shirt, she came out of her bedroom with the telephone tucked between her ear and shoulder. She easily side-stepped her son and looked into the kitchen at Dodo.

"Hey, Dodo. Would you help the kids with their homework for me?"

Dodo locked the back door. "Yeah, as soon as I fix me a samich or something."

Crystal turned to go back to her room. "And make sure that you make Laheem read out of his workbook. His teacher said that he need to read at least thirty minutes a day until he get better."

"Was the teacher talking to you or me?" Dodo asked as he pulled open the freezer and got out an ice tray.

"Huh?"

"Nothing, Crystal," Dodo said as he put a few cubes of ice in the dish towel and wrapped it around his swollen knuckles. "Laheem, you and Trice turn that television off and bring y'all homework in here to the table. Y'all hungry?"

Laheem appeared with his Spider-Man book bag dragging on the floor behind him. "What you finta make?"

Crystal reappeared with baby bottles in her hand, which she dumped in the sink. "They don't need nothing now. I done already cooked dinner and the stuff you make will spoil their appetites. Plus they came in the door eating junk. Latrice got something all over her new white Rocawear jacket. What's wrong with your hand, Dodo?"

"Nothing. I just hit it on the wall by accident. The phone ringing."

Crystal ran back to her bedroom as Latrice joined Laheem at the kitchen table. Dodo fixed a couple of fried-salami sandwiches and then assisted the children with their homework. When they were finished, they went to the living room. Laheem turned the big-screen television to the Cartoon Network as Dodo settled down on the couch with his newspaper. Crystal came back out of her room. The silk scarf was gone from her head and her jogging pants and T-shirt had been replaced with a skintight pair of Lady Enyce jeans, and matching baby doll T-shirt. She wore a pair of Pumas that matched her outfit.

"Dodo," Crystal said sweetly.

Dodo didn't look up from the newspaper. "What you want, Crystal?"

"Are you finta do something?"

"I'm already doing something. I'm reading the paper."

"Stop playing, Dodo. You know what I mean. Are you bout to go out?"

Dodo folded his newspaper and pulled his tobacco out of his pocket. He wet the glue strip on a rolling paper with his tongue, stuck them together, and twisted a cigarette.

"Why you still smoking them rollups like you in the joint?" Crystal asked. "I'll give you some money to get you some real cigarettes."

"I been smoking these so long, regular cigarettes don't taste like nothing and they cost too damn much. Now I know that you didn't interrupt my job-hunting to ask me about no rollups. What you want?"

Crystal walked over and perched on the arm of the couch next to Dodo. "Since you ain't going out, I just wanted to know if you would watch the kids for me while I go out and get some air?"

Dodo lit his cigarette. "What you mean by get some air? You can open a window to get some air."

"I mean that I wanna go over by the park where everybody be hanging out for a few minutes. My girls is over there and I just put Mulan to sleep. She ain't had a nap all day so she gon' be sleep for a minute. Please?"

"Gon' head, Crystal, but don't be all night."

"Thanks, Dodo." Crystal darted to her room and grabbed her leather jacket, purse, keys, and cell phone. Back in the living room, she said, "La and La, I'll be back. Be good and make sure you listen to your uncle Dodo. Take y'all baths at eight o'clock on the dot and get in that bed by nine. I'll be back. Love y'all."

" 'Member what I said, Crystal. Bring yo butt back in tonight."

"I got you," Crystal said as she slipped out of the door.

CRYSTAL DROVE her Camry, slowly scanning the faces of the men and women standing and sitting along the block or in the cars lining both sides of the street. Halfway through the block, a car stopped in front of her and its occupants began talking to someone alongside them in a parked car. Crystal pulled out her cell phone and pushed speed dial.

"Where y'all at?" she said into her cell. "I'm on the block. I'm in the middle right behind one of these fools. Hold on."

Using the heel of her hand, Crystal pushed hard on her car horn and didn't release it until the driver in front of her cruised away.

"I see y'all," she said into her cell. "Let me park."

She maneuvered her car into a parking space and got out.

"What's up, y'all!" she shouted to her two friends.

"Crystal, hey bitch!" Shanté exclaimed. "We thought you wadn't gon' make it. Everybody out here tonight."

"You ain't lying," Crystal said as she snapped her cell phone into the holster on her belt. "It's off the chain out here. Everybody is out here today. It some people out here I ain't seen since I don't know when. I thought I was bout to be stuck in the crib with my kids, but my brother is watching them for me."

"I know you glad you ain't have to miss this," Trina said. "These niggas is out here checking for us. They must want to spend some of that paper that they got before they get ready to settle down for the winter."

Shanté slapped Trina a high five. "I know that's right. Sweetest Day right around the corner, too. I think the cost of my pussy done went up the same way the cost of living did."

The three friends laughed as another of their friends joined them.

"Bam-Bam, what's up, bitch?" Trina asked. "That nigga Gilly let you out, huh?"

Bam-Bam smiled. "I do what I want to. Don't act like y'all happy to see a bitch. Y'all know you bitches don't get no action when I'm on the set."

"You ain't blocking no action," Crystal said. "Plus ain't nobody around here gon' say shit to yo ass as long as they know Gilly crazy ass be stalking like that."

Crystal and Shanté high fived this time.

"I don't know what you two bitches is giving each other five for," Bam-Bam said, "not with all that free fucking that Shanté be doing."

"Yeah, whatever," Shanté retorted. "If I do do some free fucking it's cause they packing. And I can't count the niggas who done paid for it and ate it."

"Yeah, I know that's right," Trina agreed. "But I wonder do you let the ones with the little peepees hit it for half price?"

"Fuck you, too, bitch," Shanté said with a smile. "What, you bitches must be broke—y'all ain't sipping on nothing? I knew I shoulda stopped at the store. Let's ride to the store and get something to drink."

"We ain't got to go nowhere," Crystal sang out. "I still got some of that apple vodka from last time in the trunk. We just need some cups." She unlocked the trunk of her car and held high the bottle of alcohol. "One of y'all go ask some of those niggas over there if they got some extra cups."

"I'll be right back," Shanté said. She sashayed over to a group of men across the street, who were listening to the music streaming from the rear of a dark blue Envoy while they sipped beers and liquor. Moments later Shanté returned with a stack of cups.

"Mario and his guys said to tell y'all w'sup," Shanté told them.

"You should have told that nigga 'not a damn thing,'" Trina said. "He need to take his momma back her truck 'cause she got to go to work in the morning."

"You stupid girl," Crystal said as she poured herself a shot of vodka. She passed the bottle around.

As the sun sank, the crisp Chicago night air caused everyone to begin zipping and buttoning their jackets, but no one left. A few incidents arose to gain everyone's attention such as a woman dumping clothes on the ground in front of her man as he talked to another woman, and a drunken shoving match between a couple of the guys, but other than that the night was chill.

Around eleven P.M. a glistening black Cadillac Escalade glided onto the block. As it pulled alongside Crystal's car it stopped and the tinted driver's window slid down.

"Ah, Crystal, DM wanna holler at you," the driver said.

Crystal saw the driver was Gilly, Danny Man's best friend. "Gilly, w'sup? Where DM at?"

"He in the back, get in," Gilly said curtly. "Bam-Bam, take yo ass home now!"

Bam-Bam started to protest, but a stern look from Gilly stopped her in her tracks. She went down the street to her car and left.

"I'll be back, y'all," Crystal called out to her remaining friends. She opened the back door of the Cadillac truck and climbed in.

The scent of witch hazel almost overpowered her in the close confines of the rear seat. Gilly pulled into a parking space a little farther down the block. Danny Man was lying back with a towel covering his head and most of his face.

"DM, what happened to you?" Crystal asked. "Did the police jump on you again?"

"Cut the dramatics, bitch," Danny Man growled. "Where the fuck is yo brother?"

"Dodo?"

Danny Man leaned over and grabbed Crystal by the collar of her leather jacket, pulling her inches from his face. The towel covering his face slipped and for the first time Crystal saw the full extent of his injuries, causing her to gasp.

"Bitch, who the fuck you think I'm talking about? Where the fuck is he at?"

Crystal hesitated.

"Crystal, I ain't playing with you! Where the fuck is Dodo at?"

"I don't know, DM. He ain't been to my house today. I don't know where he at."

Danny Man eyed her closely through his swollen eyes for a moment and then pushed her back against the door and readjusted his towel. "Crystal, you bet' not be lying to me. You sure you ain't seen Dodo today?"

"I told you nall, DM. I ain't gon' lie to you. What you looking for him for? Did he do that to you?"

"What the fuck you think I'm looking for him for?"

"I didn't know. How y'all get into it?"

"That nigga was on some bullshit back-in-the-day shit. He mad 'cause he been locked up all that time, while niggas like me was out here getting that money. Jealous-ass hating shit! I'ma fuck that boy up!"

"Can't y'all squash that shit?"

Danny Man laughed. "C'mon, Crystal, I thought you was

smarter than that. Look at my mutherfucking face. That nigga stole on me on some sneaky-ass penitentiary shit. I can't go out like that. I ain't squashing shit."

Danny Man fell silent, and they were both silent for several minutes.

"DM, I gotta go," Crystal said finally.

"Where the fuck you gotta go?"

"I gotta get the kids from the baby-sitter before she get to tripping and won't watch them for me no more."

Danny Man peered at her from under his towel. "What baby-sitter?" he asked.

"My neighbor," Crystal said quickly. "You don't know her."

For a second, he looked like he didn't believe her, but then Danny Man said, "You better take yo ass straight home, too."

Crystal put her hand on the door latch. "Are you coming over later?"

"Why?"

"Well, just so I can make sure you straight. You know, nurse on you."

"I don't know. I'll call you."

Crystal opened the car door.

"If you see Dodo, you better let me know, girl," Danny Man warned. "I don't want to find out that you was bullshitting me. You hear me?"

"Yeah, I hear you. I wouldn't bullshit you," Crystal said. She closed the car door and quickly walked to her own vehicle.

"I gotta go, y'all," she yelled to her friends. Crystal ignored their protests as she climbed into her car and left.

DODO WAS LYING on the couch watching television with Mulan sprawled across his chest when Crystal came in the house.

"Dodo, what did you do?" Crystal shouted.

"What? Girl, you better lower yo doggone voice. It just took me an hour to get this baby to sleep."

"Gimme her," Crystal said. She plucked Mulan from his chest and took her in the bedroom, depositing her in the playpen. She pulled a blanket over the sleeping infant and then rushed back to the living room.

Dodo was sitting up by now. Crystal came and stood over him.

"What the hell was you thinking, beating DM up like that?"

Television remote in hand, Dodo tried to look around Crystal at the television. "Girl, you better sit down somewhere. Ain't nobody thinking about Danny Man punk ass. He shouldn'ta been talking that shit."

Crystal threw her hands up. "Dodo, you don't have no idea what you done done! You can't just whup a nigga like DM 'cause he was talking shit! DM can talk shit to whoever he want to around here 'cause this is his neighborhood! He run this shit!"

"That nigga don't run shit but his mouth. And quit calling that faggot-ass nigga DM. His name is Danny Man. These new niggas might think he hot shit, but I know he still the same little punk-ass nigga that used to follow behind me and Casey. He ain't have no business talking greasy to me. That nigga ain't no heavy. I was in the joint with real heavies. If we was in the joint . . ."

Crystal sighed as she walked over and dropped down onto the love seat. "You ain't in the joint no more, Dodo," she said in a tired voice. "A lot of time has passed while you was locked up. Remember I was still jumping double Dutch when you went away. That big-chest penitentiary shit don't float on the streets no more. It's a certain way that things is out here and the way things is, is that DM is that nigga around here. It's that simple."

Dodo laughed. "How that nigga get respect and can't even fight?"

"Niggas don't even fight like that no more. They be shooting out here. That's the old days you thinking about. Niggas with they shirt off going toe-to-toe in the street. That shit is dead. Niggas is running to get them pistols. Get yo mind off them old days and that joint shit. DM got more power than them niggas in the joint."

"You talking like you fucking that nigga," Dodo said with a heavy scowl on his face.

Crystal rolled her eyes. "That's Mulan's daddy. That couch you been sleeping on, he bought. This big-screen TV you be watching, he bought."

"Stop playing with me, Crystal."

Crystal sank back on the love seat like she was exhausted and put her hand on her forehead. "I know I should have told you, but I didn't think that it would matter. How would I know that out of all the people around here you would manage to get into it with him? Damn!"

Dodo realized that was how Danny Man had known his personal business. Feeling betrayed, he jumped to his feet. "How could you fuck with a nigga like that? You be on some bullshit, Crystal. I just left a place surrounded by enemies day and night where I couldn't let my guard down and you telling me that my sister is fucking with one of my enemies!"

"So I guess you think I'm yo enemy? They sho fucked yo head up in prison. I'm the only one out the whole family who gave a fuck that you had a place to go when you got out. I tried to make sure that you had someplace nice to lay your head until you got on your feet. My personal life wasn't supposed to have nothing to do with you. Who I'm fucking is my business. I'm grown."

"You know what? That shit don't even matter. What is you trying to say?"

"I'm saying that you got to leave. You got to get out of here. Go stay at Johnny's house with Momma in Glenwood. Either that or go stay with Kent out in San Diego."

"You know I can't stay with Johnny and his wife. They on that super-religious born-again stuff. Momma can barely live with them. And I can't go to San Diego 'cause I'm on parole. Hold the fuck up! I just realized that you got me talking about running and hiding from Danny Man. I ain't finta be dodging that soft-ass nigga. He got to come on with it. Fuck that nigga!"

"Dodo, I'm doing this for your own good; you got to go," Crystal said quietly. "Now. DM could come over here at any time and you can't be here. Him and his people are going to try and hurt you."

Dodo sat back down on the couch. "You really for real, huh?"

"I'm really for real," Crystal said as she dug into her purse and pulled out several hundred dollars. "You were gone so you wouldn't know, but DM and his people don't play fair. Them niggas is straight wild. Take this money and go get you a room for a couple of nights and then you gon' have to go out to Johnny's house and stay out there until this shit die down."

At first Dodo's pride wouldn't let him take the money. I can't believe that she is really honoring this pussy-ass nigga, he thought. *She got to be fucking kidding me. I ain't finta be taking no money from my little sister to run from no Danny Man. I don't believe this shit. She must really be scared if she telling me to get up outta here. That soft-ass nigga already done tried to hit a kid up at the store; he fuck around and try to come through here and try some shit and one of the kids be done got hurt. Yeah, it would probably be better if I got up outta here and thought this shit through. I ain't got nowhere to go though. Fuck it, I'm gon' take this little cash and get me a room till I figure out what to do.*

He pulled his boots on his feet and stood up. "Just let me grab a few things. I ain't got much of shit no way."

Dodo grabbed his clothes and his toilet articles from the bathroom and packed them into a bag. When he returned to the living room, Crystal was sitting with her head in her hands.

Without looking up, she said, "Dodo, please don't be mad at me. I love you, but you know I got kids, man."

Dodo stood at the door. "I'ma go along with what you saying, but I got to tell you that I ain't liking this shit one bit. But I got to admit that you is right about some things you said. While I was locked up, y'all was out here living y'all lives and I'm gon' respect my nieces and nephew, but remember that blood is thicker than mud. As for your little boyfriend, I spanked that nigga ass 'cause he needed it. I'll call you when I get situated."

Dodo left the apartment, leaving Crystal sitting on the love seat where she stayed until Mulan began crying for her late-night feeding. Crystal sighed again as she took off her jacket, locked the deadbolt on the door, and went to get a baby bottle.

SIX

DODO GOT UP off the bed and walked over to the dresser to inspect the few groceries that he had purchased before checking into a hotel room. The decaying hotel mainly catered to transients, cheating husbands, and drug abusers. Dodo grabbed a bag of Doritos off the dresser and settled down in a vinyl chair to watch television. He realized that the last two nights he had slept surprisingly well here. Mainly it was because the late-night rabble-rousing of the hotel's numerous patrons reminded him of being in prison, where the inmates sang, cracked jokes, and talked from cell to cell at all hours of the night. The hotel was relatively close to the neighborhood but far enough that he shouldn't bump into anyone looking for him. It still didn't sit right with him that he was hiding from Danny Man.

After crunching his way through the bag of Doritos, Dodo drank the remainder of a lukewarm, flat two-liter of Pepsi as he continued to watch television. An hour passed and he moved to the side of the bed and picked up the telephone and placed a call.

"Crystal, it's me," he said into the receiver. "Yeah, I'm all right. . . . Nall, I ain't doing nothing, just laying back trying to get my mind right. . . . Now remember if my PO call tell her I still live there. If it's daytime say that I'm out job hunting. If it's at night tell her I'm over at my girlfriend's house and that I'll be back later. . . . Yeah, I got the number to Johnny's house, I'm bout to call out there to see how Momma doing. . . . Do me a favor, I left a piece of paper on top of the fridge with a number on it, see if you see it. . . . It say Mary on it. . . . Don't worry bout all that, just give me the number."

Dodo looked around for a pen but couldn't locate one; instead he traced the number in the dust on the nightstand with his fingertip.

"Thanks. . . . Yeah, I got enough money for now. I didn't run through what you gave me yet. . . . Yeah, I appreciate it and if I need something else, then I'll give you a call. . . . Tell La and La I said w'sup, and kiss Mulan for me. . . . All right, I'm gone."

Dodo pressed the button to hang up and held it down for a few seconds to get a dial tone and then he dialed another number.

"Hello," Dodo said when his party answered. "It's Donnell. . . . Praise the Lord, Johnny. How are you doing? I'm blessed, too. . . . Yeah, I know God is good all the time. . . . Of course. As soon as I get a chance I'ma get out there to your church for one of these Sundays. . . . Right. I know that I have to have fellowship with God's people for him to forgive me for my sins. . . . I know that Jesus died on the cross for my sins." Dodo's eyes rolled to the ceiling. "Not to cut you off, Johnny, but is Ma there? . . . Sorry I missed her. Why don't you tell her that I called when she come back and that I'll call back later. And tell your wife I said hello. . . . All right, Johnny, I gotta go. . . . I'll keep you in my prayers, too.

"Whew!" Doda exclaimed as he hung up the phone. "I don't know how Momma do it."

Dodo knew that his eldest brother had had his own share of struggles in his life, but he wondered what could have made Johnny so religious. He decided to make one more call.

A small child's voice answered. "Hello. Who this is?"

In the background, Dodo heard a woman ask, "Kenshawn, who is that on my phone? I keep telling y'all asses to stop answering my gotdamn phone if you don't know what you doing! Now bring it here! Hello, who is this?"

"It's Dodo."

"Who? I don't know no damn Dodo. And if you one of my sorry-ass ex-husband's friends don't call here no more 'cause he don't live here!"

Dodo chuckled. "This is Dodo, Mary. You gave me yo number a coupla days ago at the Laundromat."

Mary's voice instantly sweetened. "Hey, Dodo, w'sup? I thought you wasn't gon' call. How you been doing?"

"My back still hurt from carrying yo heavy-ass bags, but other than that I'm good. What you up to?"

"I know you ain't hurt yo'self, not with all them muscles you got. You had a sister looking real hard. You almost got me a little wet seeing you flexing like that. I ain't had none in a minute neither, shid."

"That's what I like about you, Mary. You ain't scared to say nothing."

"Dodo, life is too short to be scared to say how you feel. Especially when I see something as fine and chocolate as you."

"What you doing later on, Mary?"

"Me, my cousins, and a couple of my friends is playing cards tonight if you want to stop over. Around eight or nine. Bring yo own beer and bring me a Boones Farm Strawberry, would you? It's the little gray house, second from the corner."

"All right, I'll see you in a couple of hours then."

Dodo hung up the phone for the third time. As he did he thought about Mary and their chance meeting at the Laundromat. In the penitentiary he had grown accustomed to washing his clothes and underwear every Thursday and it was a habit that he continued now that he was on the outside. He had helped Mary and her two teenage daughters with several huge laundry bags. When he introduced himself to Mary, she said that she remembered him from high school before he dropped out. He didn't remember her, but that didn't deter him from asking for her telephone number after she told him she didn't have a man and lived alone with her two daughters and her only grandchild. To him Mary was quite attractive. Dodo had always liked big legs on a woman and Mary wasn't shortstopping in the hips department.

Dodo went to take a shower and prepare himself for his date.

WHEN DODO CLIMBED the porch steps to Mary's house, he noticed that several steps and the banister were loose. There was no doorbell, so he knocked on the door. One of the girls who had been with Mary when they met opened the door and walked back to the couch and plopped down and reattached herself to the television remote control.

"They on the back porch," she said uninterestedly as she turned to the videos. "Straight through there."

Clutching the bag that contained his six-pack and Mary's wine, Dodo followed her instructions to the enclosed back porch. The moment Mary saw him standing in the doorway, she jumped up and rushed over and hugged him.

"Everybody, this is Dodo," Mary announced as she pulled him into the kitchen and took the bag from him. She handed him a beer and put the rest in the fridge. "I thought you wadn't coming. Had me get myself together for nothing."

Dodo smiled at Mary as he admired her tight jeans and even tighter sweater. "You got it together real good, too."

Mary grinned. "This ain't nothing. You just caught me on laundry day. A sister don't care what she look like when she at the Laundromat."

"Yeah, y'all be all up in there wearing rollers and nightgowns and walking on the back of a pair of old shoes."

Mary pursed her lips. "But you still wanted to holler though."

"Ah, Mary, c'mon!" a female voice called out. "Bring Dodo back out here. We ain't gon' bite him. We ready to play some cards! Matter of fact we'll kick you and his ass in some spades!"

"Here we come!" Mary yelled back. To Dodo, she said, "You do know how to play spades, don't you?"

"I'm all right. Let's make a little bet."

Mary put her hands on her hips. "What you wanna bet?"

"If we win I get to spend the night with you."

"We'll see," she said as she switched toward the back porch. "Deal them cards, big mouth, 'cause we bout to kick y'all ass."

MARY ROLLED OVER and shook Dodo's shoulder. Instantly he woke up.

"You got to go before my daughters get up for school," she rasped.

Dodo sat up and reached for his boxers and pants. "What time is it?" he asked hoarsely.

"Five thirty."

He dressed quickly in the darkened bedroom. When he was dressed, Mary shrugged the covers off her nakedness and pulled on a housecoat. They crept past the kids' bedrooms and made their way down the stairs. At the front door, Mary wrapped her arms around Dodo's waist and kissed him on the neck.

Clutching her housecoat, she opened the door. "Call me later."

Dodo nodded and stepped out on the porch. The crisp morning air felt exhilarating as he pulled his thin jacket closed and buttoned it. Hands in his pockets with his shoulders hunched against the cool air, Dodo headed for the hotel.

SEVEN

"GILLY, LET THEM niggas in," Danny Man ordered, covering the mouthpiece of his cell phone. "Bring y'all asses in here and sit down. I'll be with y'all in a minute."

The three men trooped into the apartment and sat down. They surveyed Danny Man's face—he was looking much better. The swelling was gone from his eyes; only green and purple bruises remained.

"Alright, Crystal," Danny Man said in an exaggerated tone. "I'll talk to yo ass later. . . . I don't know if I'm coming over. Quit asking me that shit! Alright, I'm finta go!"

Danny Man pushed the button to end his call and slammed his telephone on the couch next to him. The jarring made the phone redial Crystal's number.

Danny Man directed his attention to his guys. "Timo, Kenchy, and Bogart, my heavy hitters," he said with a hint of sarcasm. "You niggas is 'sposed to be my problem solvers right?"

"You know we take care of shit for you, DM," said Kenchy.

"Whenever you got a problem we stand straight on that shit for you."

"What you saying, we don't hold you down, DM?" Timo asked.

"You hear this shit, Gilly?" asked Danny Man. "These niggas say they hold me down. Out the whole crew they got the sweetest jobs. They ain't got to touch no merchandise. All they got to do is take care of mutherfuckers who don't want to go by what's going on. Now since niggas so rarely fuck up these days, that mean you niggas get free money. Now tell me is there a such thing as free money? I ain't never heard of that. So I must be paying y'all for something. So tell me what I'm paying y'all for if you can't get rid of one nigga for me?"

"Man, we can't find this nigga," Kenchy said. "First of all we really don't even know what this nigga look like."

"How many cocky-ass baldheaded niggas could there be around here?" Danny Man asked disgustedly. "The nigga look like he just got out the joint."

"We been on point," Bogart said. "We ain't been slacking. We been watching Crystal crib, but the nigga ain't showed. Believe me, DM, when you call on us you calling on the pit bulls and we ready to lock on a nigga ass. If this nigga would have showed his ass once he would be leaking right now."

"I don't even want that no more," said Danny Man with an air of finality.

Gilly looked at Danny Man questioningly. "Is you saying let that nigga ride with the bullshit he pulled with you?"

"What the fuck I look like? You saw what that nigga did to my face. It's just that when I first called for this nigga's head I was mad. I had to rethink this shit. I got to handle this shit a bit more delicately than that. So really it worked out for the best that you sorry-ass niggas couldn't take care of him."

"So, DM, now you telling us not to burn this nigga up?" asked Timo.

"That's exactly what I'm saying."

"So what you want us to do then?" Kenchy asked.

"Nothing, nigga. Just play the low unless I tell you different. Me and Gilly gon' handle this one. I figured that Dodo might be a little too slick for y'all to catch. Now just 'cause I'm taking y'all off this one, don't disappear. I still want y'all out and about so niggas don't think shit sweet just 'cause I ain't get up with Dodo yet. All right, I'll holler at y'all."

The three killers, slightly disappointed at being deprived of hunting an elusive prey, cleared out quietly. Danny Man looked over at Gilly, who was sitting on a bar stool looking rather grumpy.

"Nigga, what's wrong with you?" asked Danny Man. "You been looking crazy all night."

"It's this bitch Bam-Bam. She ain't answering her phone. If I find out she on some bullshit, I'ma kill her and the mutherfucka she with! That bitch ain't got but one time to get caught and it's curtains! I ain't one of these sucker-ass niggas that be letting they bitches disrespect them. I can't go out like that. I'ma fuck that bitch up and that nigga!"

"How you gone fuck the nigga up though?" Danny Man asked. "It ain't his fault, especially if he didn't take the pussy. That is some unplayerlike shit you saying. Don't hate the player, hate the game."

"If the nigga know me, then he know that's my bitch. If he knew that was my bitch and he still fuck with her, then he saying fuck me. I don't let nobody say fuck me. I would rather die or do life in a box before I let a bitch or a nigga disrespect me or dishonor me. Forget all that though, what you gon' do about Dodo and why you call them niggas off the job?"

"Man, I told you this shit got to be handled delicately. And delicate them niggas ain't. As bad as I want to fuck Dodo up, I still got to realize that that is my 'sposed-to-be baby momma's brother. Even though she ain't seen him in a long time and he ain't never done nothing for her, she might decide to get sentimental and shit. Blood is blood. Plus I know that nigga done holed up somewhere and I might have to use that dumb-ass bitch to pull him out of his hole without her knowing it."

"Man, you a cold nigga. After me and you killed her baby daddy over that cash he owed us, I thought you was crazy when you started laying up with that bitch. She didn't never suspect shit, huh?"

Danny Man laughed. "I told you she was a dumb bitch."

"Dumb bitch," Crystal repeated as she shut off her phone. She had heard enough. At first when Danny Man's phone called her back, she had happily answered it, thinking it was him calling back to say he was coming over. When she heard his voice talking to someone, she had instinctively listened instead of hanging up. The contents of the conversation she'd overheard shocked her to the core of her being.

"If this punk-ass nigga think I'm gone help him kill my brother, he must be losing his damn mind!" she raged. "Dodo was right, he is a punk! I got him! I don't believe this shit! He killed Laquan! I been fucking with this nigga and he killed my man! All the shit I put up with from this nigga! I got him!"

Crystal stormed over to her bedroom closet and threw open the door. She was crying as she struggled to drag a large packing trunk into the middle of the bedroom floor. She flipped open the trunk and looked at the countless stacks of money in it. On her dresser was a bottle of fingernail polish remover. She grabbed the bottle, unscrewed the cap, and emptied it on the money.

"Dumb bitch, huh?" she snapped as she rifled through her purse for something to ignite the money. "Well, this dumb bitch about to show you that you ain't so mutherfucking smart!"

When she couldn't find matches or a lighter in her purse, Crystal slung the purse on the bed in frustration. The purse hit Mulan on her back; she had been napping on the bed. Mulan awoke and began howling, bringing Crystal back to reality. Horrified, she realized that she was about to start a fire in her bedroom with her baby a few feet away on the bed. Mortified at her own behavior, Crystal raced over to the bed and picked up Mulan to comfort her. She rocked her crying baby in her arms and cooed to her. While she was doing this, Crystal's thoughts became clear and concise.

Eventually Mulan went back to sleep and Crystal laid her back on the bed. For several hours she sat and looked at the chest of money. The shame and humiliation she'd felt after Danny Man had said those terrible things was gone—replaced by scorn and a thirst for revenge.

Crystal was still wide awake when Mulan woke up for her late-night feeding. She fed her baby and put her back to sleep. Finally she undressed, pushed the trunk back into the closet, and lay down beside her baby on the bed, but she didn't fall asleep.

The sun had begun to rise and she was still awake, but in her mind she had the formation of a plan—a plan to pay Danny Man back for his transgressions. She heard her kids stir in their room as the alarm clock went off. Crystal pulled on her bathrobe and got up to help her kids get ready for school. She decided to make breakfast for the kids, and by the time Laheem and Latrice took their places at the table, the aroma of pancakes, eggs, and sausage hung heavy in the air. As she served each of the children their food, she kissed them on the forehead.

"What was that for, Mommy?" asked Laheem as he wiped his forehead with the back of his hand.

"That's just to show you both that I love you and blood is thicker than mud."

Crystal didn't see the bewildered look on her children's faces as she opened the fridge to get them some orange juice. "Y'all make sure that y'all come straight home from school. I'm taking y'all out to y'all uncle Johnny's house for the weekend. And, yes, y'all going to church."

EIGHT

BAM-BAM WAS DRUNK as she got up off Crystal's couch and slightly weaved her way to the living room window and raised it. She turned back around, fanning herself.

"Damn Crystal, it's hot as hell in here," said Bam-Bam.

Trina giggled. "Bam-Bam, bitch, it ain't nowhere near hot in here. You just drunk and that Smirnoff got you hot."

"You ain't lying," Bam-Bam said, rubbing her stomach suggestively. "But it ain't like I'm gon' be able to get me some the way I want it. I got to go home to Gilly stalking little dick ass. When he do finally get around to changing my oil, he got to get into that lovey-dovey shit. Licking my back and my knees and shit. He got to light candles and play soft music and all that bullshit. Then he go downtown for like thirty or forty minutes. When he finally do come up for air, he want to get on top of me and be going all slow and shit, trying to look into my eyes." Bam-Bam shuddered.

Trina was looking slightly flushed as she said, "Bitch, I don't know what's wrong with you, but that shit sound good! I wish I had a mutherfucker that would treat me like that! Hell, he wouldn't have to do that shit for me but a coupla times a year if he wanted to. Special occasions and holidays."

"Fuck that, I need a nigga that's gon' thug me!" Bam-Bam shouted. "I want a nigga with a big dick that tear my panties off, bend me over, pull my hair, and bang my back out. A nigga like . . ."

Bam-Bam fell silent and snuck a glance at Crystal, who was sitting quietly nursing her drink.

Trina wouldn't let Bam-Bam off the hook. "A nigga like who, bitch?"

"You don't know him," said Bam-Bam quickly. "He ain't from around here, Trina, so mind yo business, bitch."

"Don't let that nigga fuck around and pull that weave out yo hair. If you come up in the crib with bald spots in yo hair, Gilly gone fuck around and hire a forensics team to find out what happened."

"Yeah, whatever, bitch. Don't be mad at me 'cause you ain't got no comeback."

Trina fell all over herself laughing. "Bitch, that ain't comeback between yo legs—that's stay back."

Slightly angered, Bam-Bam looked at Crystal again. "What's wrong with you, Crystal? Bitch, you been too damn quiet tonight."

"I'm cool, just got something on my mind," said Crystal through a weak smile. "I'm wondering if I got the heart to do some shit that I know needed to be done for a long time."

Trina looked at Crystal after she made such a sobering statement. "Bitch, whatever's wrong with you, keep it to yourself, you blowing my high."

"Yeah, Crystal," said Bam-Bam. "Bitch, yo kids gone. You should be partying. You need to get you some. Get some of that starch out yo back."

"I'm gon' get some, whatever that means, when my guy comes over later," Crystal told them. She got up and went to the bathroom. She closed the door and pulled a cell phone from her pocket. Quickly she went through the phone's directory. She pulled her own cell phone from the holster on her belt and using the first cellular phone for a reference, Crystal locked a number into her phone and returned it to her waist. In the cell phone still in her hand, she chose another number from the directory and text messaged, I NEED SUM! YOUR PLACE 2MORROW @ 6. After sending it, she erased the message from the outbox and waited. Minutes later the cell phone beeped to alert her of an incoming text message. It was from Danny Man and read, WEAR A THONG, I'MA BLOW YO BAK OUT! Crystal erased Danny Man's reply and cuffed the cell phone in the palm of her hand. She flushed the toilet and went back to the living room, where Trina and Bam-Bam were still trading insults.

"Y'all, I'm tired," Crystal announced. "Why don't y'all bounce so I can get me some rest before my guy get here."

Trina hoisted herself off the couch. "Bitch, I know you ain't trying to put us out. That's all right. I been put out of better places. C'mon, Bam-Bam, you drunk bitch, we getting evicted."

"Hold up," said Bam-Bam. "I got to call my stalker and let him know I'm on the way. That nigga got to know where I'm at every minute. Anybody seen my phone? I had it when I came in, didn't I? Don't tell me that I done lost it. Gilly gone act a damn fool if he can't reach me!"

Crystal extended her hand with Bam-Bam's cellular phone. "Here go yo phone. You dropped it when you went to the kitchen a while ago. I picked it up but forgot to give it to you."

"Thanks, Crystal. You just saved my life. I already got to go home and get interrogated anyway. Long as I got this phone, he just might smell my panties and let me alone."

Trina and Bam-Bam grabbed their purses and jackets and left out the door.

"Call me," Trina said. "C'mon, Bam-Bam, you drunken whore."

Crystal closed and locked her door and took her seat on the couch again. She watched television for an hour until her phone rang.

She answered the phone and paused, then she said, "Ain't nobody up here. C'mon up."

She got up and unlocked the door locks and sat back down. There was a double knock at the door.

"It's open," Crystal called out.

Danny Man stepped inside the apartment. He walked straight through to the kitchen and returned drinking from a carton of orange juice. He plopped down on the couch beside Crystal and picked up the remote control and began flicking through the channels.

They watched television in silence for a few moments.

"The kids here?" asked Danny Man without taking his eyes off the television.

"Why? What, you want to see Mulan?"

"Girl, is the kids here or not?"

"Nall, they ain't here."

A few more minutes passed and Danny Man dropped his hand between Crystal's legs. With the heel of his hand he started massaging her there. He removed his hand and slipped it under her shirt to rub on Crystal's braless breasts. He kicked off his shoes and stood up.

"C'mon," Danny Man said as he led the way to her bedroom.

Later when Crystal was sure Danny Man was sound asleep she slipped out of bed. From his pants on the floor, she removed his cell phone from its pouch on his belt. She tiptoed out of the bedroom and into the bathroom. Seated on the side of the bathtub, Crystal checked the inbox of Danny Man's text messages and found the text she'd sent him from Bam-Bam's cell phone. In his outbox, she saw his reply, too.

She selected Bam-Bam's number and text messaged, BLOW YO BAK OUT! MY CRIB @ 6. WEAR A THONG. She didn't have to wait long for Bam-Bam's reply. It read, I'M THERE. I NEED SUM 2.

Crystal erased the text messages she'd sent and received. She slipped out of the bathroom and returned Danny Man's cell phone. She slid back into bed, taking care to make sure that no part of Danny Man touched her.

NINE

GILLY WAS STANDING in the lottery line at the gas station when his cell phone buzzed on his side. Pulling it loose from the clip he looked at the number and saw PRIVATE displayed. He answered it anyway.

"Who is this?"

"Don't worry about that," said an obviously disguised voice. "Just shut up and listen. If you want to know who Bam-Bam been fucking go over to yo boy DM's apartment right now. The key is over the door on the ledge. Hurry up."

"Who the fuck is this?" Gilly repeated. "Quit playing with me. I don't play that kid shit."

"I ain't lying. Nigga, shut up and go see."

The line went dead.

"Hello, hello," Gilly said, but whoever it was, was gone.

Gilly looked at his watch; it read 6:06. He got out of the lottery line and ran outside to his Escalade. Driving at breakneck speed, Gilly made it to Danny Man's apartment in nine minutes flat. Gilly pulled his pistol from under the seat and jumped out the truck. He pelted up the steps to the second floor and snatched the key down from the ledge over the door. He held his breath as he unlocked the door and entered the apartment. Stealthily he stole upon the bedroom.

In the bedroom, Bam-Bam was naked sitting on the corner of the bed performing an obviously expert act of fellatio on a completely nude Danny Man.

Without a word, Gilly started shooting and had emptied the clip before he knew it. He dropped the smoking gun and staggered to the couch and sat down.

TEN

CRYSTAL AWAKENED to loud banging on her apartment door. She sat up on the couch. "Who is it?"

"Open the door! It's Trina, girl! Crystal, come to the door!"

Crystal unlocked the door and opened it. Trina burst into the apartment.

"Girl, why you ain't been answering yo phone?" asked Trina breathlessly. "I been trying to call you for an hour!"

Crystal picked up the cup she'd been drinking out of and started toward the kitchen. "I was sleep. What was you calling me for?"

Trina ran in front of Crystal and put her hands on Crystal's shoulders.

"What's wrong with you, girl?" Crystal asked.

"DM is dead."

"What?"

"Crystal, DM is dead. Gilly killed him."

Crystal's hand flew up to her mouth. "What happened?"

"Gilly killed him 'cause . . ."

"What happened? Trina, what the fuck happened?"

"Gilly caught him and Bam-Bam together and shot them up. Bam-Bam gon' make it though. Danny Man got the worst of it. The police got Gilly. He didn't even try to run. He just waited until they got there and gave himself up. Get yo jacket, girl. C'mon!"

Crystal shrugged Trina's hands off her shoulders and went on to the kitchen. Not quite sure what was going on, Trina followed her. She watched in utter disbelief as Crystal filled her cup with vodka and took a sip.

"Crystal, I said c'mon, girl. We need to get over there."

"Why I got to go over there?"

"Because that was yo dude! That's Mulan's daddy!"

"That nigga fathered more than his fair share of children, but that don't make him no daddy. Did he come to the hospital when she was born? You was there, did you see him? Has he ever picked up his baby and just spent a couple of hours with her? Not once. Why the hell should I run my ass over there? Ain't his fat-ass wife over there?"

Trina was furious. "Fuck that bitch! DM was yo man! If she say something greasy, we'll whup her ass out there!"

"That was DM's wife and the mother of three of his kids. I was just his little dumb bitch. So no thanks, you gon' 'head without me. I'll play the crib on this one. Just let me know what happened. And find out what hospital that bitch Bam-Bam gon' be in so I can send her some flowers. I'll see you later."

Crystal ushered a nonplussed Trina out the door. After locking the door, she leaned against it. Her drink fell from her hand and she slid down to the floor. Heavy sobs racked her body as she set her pent-up angst free.

ELEVEN

"DAMN, DODO, slow down, it ain't going nowhere," said Crystal as she flipped pancakes at the stove in a black cast-iron skillet.

At the kitchen table, Dodo held up one finger because he had a mouthful of omelet and breakfast sausage.

"Sorry," he said when he was finally able to swallow. "Girl, when you learn to cook like this? I thought all you could make was cereal. This here omelet is good as hell."

Crystal came to the table and served Dodo a stack of golden pancakes. Her own pancakes she put on a plate and set on the table across from Dodo. When she took her seat, Crystal asked, "How soon did you know about Danny Man?"

"I heard a couple of days ago. I really wanted to give you some time to get yourself together. Even though I didn't like him for all that Nino Brown–ass shit, I had to respect that you cared about old dude, being that he was Mulan's daddy and all."

Crystal cut her pancakes into sections and poured syrup on them. "That nigga wadn't no daddy. He ain't sign no birth certificate or shit. When I really think about it, all that nigga did was buy me a few things and come over once and a while to fuck me."

"Damn Crystal, you sound cold as hell," Dodo commented as he carved up his pancakes.

"That ain't cold–that's real. It took me some time, but I finally woke up. Don't nobody really matter in this shit but family. That's you, Momma, my kids, Johnny, and Kent. Fuck everybody else. Blood is thicker than mud."

"I feel you. I found that shit out a long time ago in the joint when I couldn't get a letter or visit from nobody but my family."

They both ate their pancakes in silence for a while. Dodo's pancakes, however, disappeared at a much faster rate than Crystal's.

"Dodo, I got good news and bad news," Crystal announced.

"Gimme the good news first."

"I'm bout to buy a house and you know that you got a room in it if you want it."

"That's tight. I was kinda thinking about trying to move in with my lady friend, but I wasn't so sure. After all I just met her."

"What lady friend?"

"Her name is Mary and she real cool. We ain't serious or nothing, but she fun to be around. Right now we just kicking it and having a good time, but she is good peoples."

"Well, like I said, you got a room at my house and the kids is missing you. They got used to having you around the house. Ain't nobody been there on the regular since they daddy died. He was always in the streets, but he always made time for them."

Dodo looked up from the little bit that was left of his food. "Hey, you getting off track. What's the bad news?"

"I don't know how to tell you this. . . ."

"Spit it out, Crystal."

"The house I'm buying is on the same block as Johnny's house."

"Shid, Mama gone love that. The only problem is that Johnny'll probably be out there watering your lawn with holy water."

They both laughed.

"What you doing today?" asked Crystal.

"Nothing much. I was thinking about heading over to Mary's house and lift some weights with her nephew and cousins. I be working them little niggas out. Plus I'm making sure that I don't lose my muscle tone. The ladies won't like that."

"The ladies? You need to stop it. It sound like this Mary already got you going."

"Never. She just good peoples and I was running out of money for my hotel room. So it was either Johnny's house or try to move in with her."

Crystal got up to put her plate in the sink. "Well, if you bypass a day of working out, I don't think you'll lose too much muscle mass. I need you to go somewhere with me."

"Where?" Dodo asked as he got up out of his seat and put his plate in the sink.

"Well, I wanted to take you shopping and see if we can't find you a little putt-putt so once we move you can get back and forth to see Mary from the new house."

Dodo was taken aback. "Crystal, you can't do that. I'll be all right. You need to be thinking bout them kids. You got to make sure that y'all alright."

"Oh, we gon' be alright. I had a nice insurance policy on DM, I mean Danny Man," Crystal said, referring to the packing trunk full of money in her closet. "That nigga was worth more to me dead than he was when he was alive. Let's go."

GOTTA HAVE A RUFFNECK

Told by Nikki Turner, desired by many
A Nikki Turner Original

ONE

Who'da Thought It?

DAMN! WHO WOULD'VE ever thought I'd end up being a ride-or-die chick? That bottom bitch? Or a down-ass chick, a gangsta's girl, a hustler's wife, or any of that shit that I had always read about. No, no, not me. Not Angel Delaney, a twenty-eight-year-old journalist, already set in her ways. But let me be the first to say, that shoot-'em-up bang-bang type of drama just gets my pussy wet. As a matter of fact, my pussy is dripping as I sit here in this souped-up vehicle just as nervous as the day is long. Never in a million years would I imagine myself caught up in the middle of some real-life gangsta shit. But I should have known it would be only a matter of time before reading about the street life wouldn't satisfy my curiosity. Just getting wet wasn't enough for my needs. It was time to climax!

I lost my virginity with my boyfriend, my high school sweetie,

Brandon Fetch. Any woman who wonders where all the good men are would be honored to have him as their man. I guess I should be, but right now, I can't even think about Brandon. All I can think about is the nigga I'm holdin' it down for right here, right now. A man I haven't even known a full twenty-four hours. I know I'm not acting like the adult woman I am, but the shit is just so intense that guess what? I don't give a fuck!

I know good and well my ass shouldn't even be here. I should've been long gone, like a speeding bullet, ten minutes ago when the shit first hit the fan. I kept telling myself to leave and don't ever look back. I guess it's that edginess, the unknown, the adrenaline pumping boldness through my body that's keeping me sitting here with my hand on the gearshift and the engine running, waiting. Waiting on him.

As I sit here, I can't help but think about how that chick Bonnie must have felt when she was riding off into the sunset with Clyde. On the real, though. How about I ain't mad at that bitch because I'm about to do the same daggone thing for my man. My heart is racing. Every second seems like an hour, but I can't leave. Not yet, not without my man. So I'm steadfast, waiting patiently with no fear at all in my heart although butterflies should be in my stomach and fear should be rattling every bone in my body. But how crazy is it that I'm not scared? I'm a little nervous as to what's taking him so long, but not scared. If my friends were here, hell, those bitches would be scared to death, probably pissin' their pants. Back in the day, or even a few weeks ago, hell, even twenty-four hours ago, I just might have been, too. Why? What is so different about me now from then? Well, I'll tell you what changed in a day.

I'm not used to this ghetto type of mess right here. You know, some ol' gangsta shit right out of a Quentin Tarantino flick. I always walked the straight and narrow. I never did anything that would get me into trouble. I always hung around the right crowd, and I always dated clean-cut, honest men, like Brandon. Brandon and I were homecoming king and queen at our prom. I was even a debutante. I had the picture-perfect life, and everything came easily to me. So I guess it was only a matter of time before I would become attracted to the razor's edge.

From the first moment I ran my tongue across the sharp scalpel, getting a taste of the salty blood, I was hooked like a vampire. Addicted like a crack addict. Dick was the razor's edge for me. Not *a* dick, but Dick, the tall, dark handful of a man I called Dee for short. From the moment I saw him, there was just something about him that made me want to do things that I had never imagined doing and experience things that I never dreamt about even in my wildest dreams. He was that nigga, the one I had read about, the one I had seen in gangsta flicks. He was my Nino Brown, my Scarface, my invincible, hard-to-kill type of cat.

I was at the courthouse doing research when I encountered him. I've been working as a reporter covering the crime beat ever since I got my degree in journalism from the University of Richmond. Because of the nature of my work, I've seen all kinds of street-life cases. When I'm not working on articles for local newspapers and magazines, I gather data and statistics for one of the largest crime data–reporting agencies in the country. I used to just gather stats on pedophile cases until one of my coworkers, who also happened to be black, went on maternity leave and never came back. She covered street life—you know drugs, prostitution, racketeering, murders, anything that has to do with the fast life. So I guess they figured that since I was black with just as much, if not more, experience than she had, who else better to put on the street-life stuff but me?

After a few months, I became intrigued by the lifestyle of the ruffnecks, thugs, drug dealers, ballers, and gangstas and the spunk and boldness that they all seemed to possess. That type of living never seemed real to me. It felt more like fiction. All the killing, stealing, and drug dealing seemed a bit too much for a small town like Richmond. But my reality check came one day when I was at the courthouse gathering some information on a high-profile murder trial. That's when I ran into Dee. I was walking out of the clerk's office with my nose buried in the case file, thumbing through copies of the court transcripts I had just copied. Not paying attention to where I was walking, I ran smack into Dee.

"Excuse me, Miss Lady," he said, his smile blinging like Frosty the Snowman with all that ice.

I looked up, and the first thing I saw was my own reflection in his teeth. His top front four teeth were platinum capped. Then I tuned in to his features. He had mocha latte skin with the bone structure of a Sean John model. I couldn't take my eyes off him. He wore his hair straight back in thick jailhouse braids. They weren't raggedy either but neat as hell, as if he had just gotten up from between the legs of the girl that braided them. He had a tattoo on his hand and a pair of diamond earrings that the sun's shine didn't have shit on.

I slowly and gently rubbed my hand across the case file I had under my arm as my mind began to go to work. *I wonder if he's ever murdered anybody. Nah, he's probably just a small-time pusher who spends all his profits on clothes, jewelry, and tennis shoes. Hell, he probably lives in his Momma's basement.*

The next thing I noticed was his apparel. He wore some baggy Sean John jeans and a button-down shirt with a wife beater underneath. A platinum chain with a cross medallion hung from his neck.

"No, excuse me," I said, still somewhat dazed by our abrupt encounter.

"Do you happen to have change?" he asked, pulling out a wad

of cash and peeling a bill from it. "You know they don't let you bring cell phones up in here. I gotta hit my boy back, and I ain't got no change for the pay phone."

"Hit your boy back?" I said with a perplexed look on my face. See, I'm a college graduate and so are all of my friends. We live in condos or suburban family homes, far removed from the streets; therefore, I was completely ignorant to real live street lingo.

"Call him back," he said. He smirked at my ignorance. "Never mind," he said, shooing his hand at me and proceeding to walk away.

"Wait!" I said. For some reason, I just couldn't let him walk away that easy. I was far too intrigued by his savoir faire. "Uh, wait! Hold up. I do believe I have change for a dollar." I began nervously fumbling around in my purse for change while trying to balance the court files.

"Let me take those for you, Miss Lady," he said, lifting the files from my hands. When he did that, his hand grazed mine. As rough as his exterior seemed to be, his hands were as soft as butter. Suddenly my arms were covered with goose bumps. Brandon's touch never gave me goose bumps.

"Thank you," I said as I located a dollar's worth of change. "Here you go."

We made the transaction. I handed him the change. He handed over my files and gave me the bill. I balled up the bill and put it in my suit pocket.

"Good lookin'." He nodded, winked, and then headed over to the pay phone.

I watched this dude walk, and his swagger was fierce. I was absolutely mesmerized. I felt as though the world had been silenced, and all I could hear were his footsteps walking over to the phone. Loud and clear I heard the clink of the change making its way through the phone and him pounding the keys to the phone number. Then, as if everything was in slow motion, I watched his lips move.

"What up, my nigga?" I read his lips as I stood there licking mine. A smile crept across my face. And I don't know why, but I stepped out of the box for once in my life. And then I did something that I would have never ever done.

I took a deep breath, straightened my posture, and walked over to him. I stood two feet away, waiting for him to complete his call. Once he noticed me, he never took his eyes off me. He stared me up and down as he carried on his conversation. I stood my ground, knowing that there was something in front of me that I wanted a taste of. I don't know where in the hell I got all this courage. It was like I was somebody else, living somebody else's life. I was a fly on the wall, watching myself. Finally, he ended his call.

"Uh, is there something I can do you for, Miss Lady?" he asked, walking closer to me. "You all up in my grill and shit like I stole something from you."

"Well, actually, uhh . . ." I was at a complete loss for words. I wanted this man's phone number or I wanted him to have mine. Either/or, I just wanted us to connect. For some reason I felt the need to experience him, if only for one night, but I didn't know how to approach him without sounding corny. I mean, I wanted to test-drive this baby as if I were Richard Petty, but how could I just come out and say that? So I started speaking.

"I'm a journalist. I focus primarily on criminal-justice cases," I said.

"Let me guess." He laughed. "You think I'm a criminal? What? You wanna interview me or something?"

"No, no. Not that at all," I quickly said. "I just, uh . . . Look, here's my card." I fumbled around and dug up one of my business cards and handed it to him. "I don't know. You look like you've seen a lot, you know? Maybe you might come across a story that might interest me."

He looked down at the card, read my name and information, licked his lips, and then smirked. "Angel, huh?"

"That's me. Angel Delaney," I said, taking a deep breath. Then I threw him a professional smile, but I think he could see right through me.

At that point he stepped up to me as close as he possibly could. "Well, Angel," he said. "You might want to be careful who you run around handing your card to. It might end up in the devil's hands." He winked, tucked the card in his pocket, and walked past me without looking back.

I just stood there with my back to him. It took everything in me not to turn around and watch him walk away, to make sure he had really been there and that my imagination wasn't playing tricks on me. I stood long enough for him to be long gone, and then I let out a deep sigh. What the hell did you just do? I asked myself. He knew as well as I did that the last thing I wanted out of him was a lead on a story. I could have come up with something better than that. Oh, well, that's water under the bridge. It was too late to turn shit around now. I composed myself and headed out to the underground parking garage. I hopped into my gold Audi A-4 convertible and headed for the garage exit. I fumbled around for my parking ticket, locating it by the time I got to the exit, and handed it to the woman in the booth.

"Six dollars, please," she said. It was the usual woman who was there most of the time whenever I came to the courthouse. I pulled out my wallet and discovered that I only had $5. Then I remembered the balled-up dollar in my jacket pocket. I pulled it out and handed it to the woman, then waited for her to lift the gate so that I could exit.

"Here, ma'am," she said, handing back the wrinkled-up bill.

"We can't break this, so I'll just let you go with the five dollars. You can just pay the dollar the next time you come back."

"Pardon me?" I asked, confused. I looked down at the bill, and my eyes widened.

"We don't have change for a hundred-dollar bill," she said. "The five dollars will be fine today." She then proceeded to raise the gate as I drove off, stunned.

I couldn't believe this man had gone and given me a hundred-dollar bill just for change to use the pay phone so that he could *hit his boy back.* So that's how they do it, huh? That's how the so-called ballers rolled? From that moment on, curiosity for sure got the best of my ass.

I raced home and literally sat and watched the phone, waiting for it to ring. I hoped and prayed that he'd call. I guess the devil couldn't resist this angel because my prayers were soon answered. He called, and I agreed to hook up with him that very same evening.

There was a carnival going on in town, and since I was feeling like a high school teenage girl anyway, I decided to convince Dee to go to the carnival. Most first dates are the movies or dinner, but this wasn't most first dates, as I would soon learn.

As soon as I hung up the phone with Dee, I headed to the mall to buy some fly hip-hop street gear. It's funny how things can change in a matter of minutes. One minute I'm this uptight woman who wears black, gray, and navy blue suits, and the next minute I'm transformed into this gangsta's bitch, rockin' skintight Baby Phat with cleavage peeking out.

But now as I sit here ready to put the pedal to the metal, I'm thinking about how when you're dealing with these types of dudes, dem soldier boys, the golden rule should be always to expect the un-expected. I mean just five minutes ago, Dee and I were having a ball at the carnival. He was shooting basketballs, trying to win one of those big-ass teddy bears for me. You know, the ones girls always want their dudes to win for them at the fair. The ones that chicks act like mean so much to them. Like a big-ass teddy bear is a major achievement, a badge of courtship or something. Broads be so happy when those bears are handed over to us by the usual redneck with dirty fingernails who hosts the games at those little bullshit-ass carnivals. We treat that bear like we just spit the mutherfucker out of our pussy, gave birth to it. Then we walk around with our arm wrapped around the stuffed teddy bear, our other arm wrapped around our real live teddy bear like we the shit. The fellas know this, too. It's a macho thing. They spend so much money, energy, and effort trying to win that damn bear for their girl, and we are so happy when they do. But it won't take long before that bear is thrown into the attic or storage room a week or two later because there's really no place to sit that big motherfucker and it damn sure doesn't match the decor in the apartment.

But anyway, Dee was making hoops left and right. He had already won the medium-size bear for me, but of course his male ego wouldn't let him stop until he won the biggest one they had, the one that was damn near bigger than me. He was just about to make that last shot when he looked back over his shoulder at me in order to get my good luck smile. Licking my pouty lips, which glowed with a shimmering cotton candy lip gloss, I threw him that lucky smile. He didn't smile back, wink, or do shit. All of a sudden I realized that he wasn't looking at me at all. In fact, he was looking over my shoulder right past me. Whatever it was, it really had his attention. I folded my arms and began tapping my female claws, you know, the one-inch-long French manicured acrylics that I had gotten that day at the mall. I needed to know what had gotten him sidetracked from winning my goddamn teddy bear. Not only that, but what in the fuck was more important than gazing at my good luck smile, the smile that had been equivalent to his four-leaf clover? Then my woman's intuition kicked in. I turned around to see what it was that had his attention, and the first thing I saw was this big ol' ass in some Apple Bottom jeans. I mean this girl's butt was so big that I am positive when Nelly and his camp came through town to scope out a spokesmodel for their Apple Bottom clothing line, she must have been nowhere to be found. Well, she missed out on her ticket up out of this raggedy-ass town, dumb bitch.

Every dude up in there was trying to catch a glimpse of that ass. No one seemed to even care that she was there with her man, clinging to his arm. At that moment I couldn't be mad at my dude. Shoot! That bitch's ass wasn't nothing to play with, and no man, woman, or child could deny it. I mean I ain't gay or nothing, but this girl's ass even had my attention for a minute. So I took the situation lightly—treated it like lint and brushed it off. But then I thought that I shouldn't take the situation *too* lightly. Why would he settle for the bottom of the apple when he got the apple of his eye right in front of him? I mean, I ain't going to sit here and say I'm a straight dime piece to the third power, but guess what? On a bad day I could give Serena Williams, Beyoncé, and, that's right? . . . I said it, J-Lo a run for their money.

Just like Serena's father had her running around the tennis court for years and years, and Beyoncé's dad had her practicing dance steps from sunup to sundown, and I don't know about J-Lo's daddy, but I'm sure he pointed out the right men for her to get with, my daddy had me running track for as long as I could remember, so my body was always fit and tight. Daddy would say that with my height and petite build, if I'd been at the right place at the right time, I could've easily become a runway model. I knew in my heart that with my big butt, small waist, and firm breasts I had truly missed my real calling as a video chick. Daddy knew it, too, but what daddy wants his sweet, darling little girl to grow up to be a video chick?

My momma did her part, too. Her number-one priority was my

appearance, and my hair was at the top of her list. She made sure that I had a standing appointment with the hair salon every Saturday so my hair was never out of place. I grew accustomed to a weave from the time I could damn near piss the pot. By the time I was nine years old, I thought all that hair sewn into my head was mine. Mama had this thing for long hair. She thought it made a woman. She said that teachers and white people even treated her better than they did the black girls with short nappy hair. My momma has always had hair down her back, as did her mother, and her grandmother, who was 100 percent Cherokee Indian. So, when I say that I have Indian in my family, I mean it. It's just too bad my daddy's genes were more powerful than my momma's when it came to my coarse hair.

My daddy was 100 percent black, straight Zulu. I mean my daddy is as black as the night sky with no moon and no stars. But a beautiful man he is, a black, sexy, dark chocolate specimen. Although I love a dark-skinned brother, in a way, I'm glad I did get Momma's reddish caramel complexion. But I got Daddy's side of the family's hair. Nothin' but naps. Mama didn't know what to do with my kinky locks, but just as soon as my hair got long enough to latch to a horse's tail, my momma took control of the situation and started having extensions braided onto it. All through school and college, my signature hairstyle was long braids down to my ass. Over the years, I think Momma spent more on my hair weave than she did on my college tuition. But I guess it did help that I got a partial scholarship.

My parents always told me that I could be and do anything I wanted. They worked hard at giving me the best of everything so that I could achieve the best things that life had to offer. Never would they have ever imagined that Dee was what I wanted life to give me or that I would want whatever it was that Dee could possibly have to give me, even if it was only a teddy bear from a carnival.

Speaking of my teddy bear and the big ass that put a halt to my getting it, when Dee saw that I was peeping him checking out that girl's Apple Bottoms, he immediately turned his attention back to the basketball that was in hand. He quickly threw the ball, then walked over to me and took me in his arms. He then softly whispered in my ear, "Shawty, do you wanna ride wit' me?" He said it with such intensity that I knew there was more to his words than just a simple question.

With him being taller than me, I met him at his neck. Without saying a word, I embraced him back. I wanted my actions to do all the talking. I could smell the faint odor of Creed cologne combined with the smell of weed on him. Although I hated the smell of weed, it turned me on at this particular moment. But what really got me aroused was the fresh war mark on his neck. Yeah, that cut on his neck gave me confirmation that I had a certified ruffneck on my hands. If you ever cross paths with a thug who doesn't have any kind of war marks, stab wounds, gunshot wounds, or something, then bet your last piece of change that he's an impostor. He ain't who he says he is, because trust me when I tell you, every real soldier done been to war.

I hugged him tight, and he asked me again, "Do you wanna ride wit' me? I'm talkin' some ride-or-die shit. A bitch down for her nigga type shit." This time there was a deep sincerity in his tone.

"Of course," I said, ignoring the fact that less than twenty-four hours ago I was somebody else's bitch. Or should I say woman— Brandon's, that is.

"You just saying that shit. You ain't trying to be wit' me fo' real, are you?" he said, gripping my ass.

"Yes, I am," I said, my voice going hoarse with desire.

"So you trying to be wit' me?"

I nodded yes.

"I ain't just some experiment, some story idea?"

I shook my head.

"For how long?" he asked.

That shit threw me off totally. I mean, what in the hell was I doing here? With him? At this time? At this place, all out in the open, setting myself up to run into somebody Brandon knew or worked with? What was I thinking? Had I lost my damn mind? I was completely out of my element, out of my league. This was a game to me, something I could start and finish and maybe even hit the restart button, but now here Dee was, testing me—or should I say initiating me?

"For how long?" I repeated, stalling. "Ummm." I hesitated for a minute, trying to think of something slick to say that any other down-ass chick would let fly off of her tongue. He was looking at me dead in my eyes, and it caused me to go blank. I couldn't be quick on my feet. His gazing into my eyes had me weak at the knees, so I just said the same corny shit that the rest of them chicks probably told him, but I didn't care. Why? Because my words came from the heart, and he knew it, too. "For however long you want me to be." At that moment, not caring if he meant one night or an eternity, I proceeded to tongue him down like we were the only two people left on earth.

"Then you gon' ride till I die? You gon' be my bottom bitch?" he asked.

"Yes," I responded, although I hadn't the foggiest idea what a bottom bitch was. Looking into his strong eyes, vibin' off that aura that just reeked with authority, I knew that whatever a bottom bitch was, I wanted to be it. I knew it meant being in his stable. And once I got my foot in the door, I believed without a doubt that I could be his thoroughbred.

He stared at me for a moment and then he chuckled. "You don't know what a bottom bitch is, do you?"

I put my head down. "Nope, not really," I said, giggling a little because I felt green, but then I lifted my head up and hoped to earn a few cool points with my next comment. "But I know you gon' school me, right?"

"School you?" He laughed. "You learning. I feel that." He rocked his head back and forth, admiring my eagerness to learn more. "You know I got you," he proceeded. "A bottom bitch is a nigga's main chick. That number-one broad. She might not be the only one, but she damn sho number one. And she know that no other bitch can fuck with the bond they got, no momma, sister, baby momma, great-great-granny, no trick . . . just nobody. No bitch ain't got shit on dat bottom bitch. It's da chick that no matter what, a nigga know without a shadow of a doubt that she got him. Rain, sleet, hail, bright and cloudy, win, lose, or draw, she got him. It don't matter what, he could be blind and stinky with a glass eye and he know she got him. As long as he know he got her, he know he gon' be a'ight. That's what a bottom bitch is, a nigga's muh-fuckin' lung, his life support, and if a bitch pulls the plug, he could damn near lose everything. You feel me? Now, do you think you can handle that?"

I took in everything he was saying. The woman in me translated that street shit to a language that I could understand. I didn't need a minute to think it through. I had already started the game now. It was time to keep playing. "I do," I said like I had just been asked to take the hand of the man I longed to be with in marriage. For some unknown reason, I felt like it was a privilege to be his bottom bitch. Trust me, I am not insane; I was just mesmerized, caught up in the moment of wanting to live on the edge. I was well aware that we came from different sides of the tracks and we would never see each other again. So today, just for this one day only, if I never lived on the edge another day in my life, then this day, I would.

"You fo' real?" he asked with slight disbelief.

I nodded Yes. He smiled as he began to kiss me.

"You sho, 'cause the shoes is big to fill?" he asked, tongue kissing me down. It wasn't one of those neat little kisses that Brandon placed upon me. It was a wet, juicy, sloppy, wild-out kiss. I felt like I was in heaven. The only thing that ran through my head was the old Keith Sweat song, *"Make It Last Forever."* I was corny like that. For better or worse, I hadn't figured all that out yet, but shit was definitely about to change.

"I'm sure," I answered. "I mean, I'm sho."

He held my face with both his hands and looked me in my eyes. "Then understand this: We gon' have to leave here right now 'cause I gotta handle some B-I." Observing the puzzled look on my face, he said, "Business. I gotta handle some business." He kept talking before I could even respond or get my two cents in. "I promise I'ma bring you back out here this weekend and win you some mo' bears, but something's come up and we gotta go. Here's what I need you to do. I need you to go get the car," he said, handing me the keys to his truck, an oriental-burgundy-with-metallic-flakes Porsche Cayenne truck with custom twenty-two-inch rims. "Pull around on the back side of the carnival in the A&P parking lot. Leave the lights off until you see me and wait for me to come through the cut."

I stood there listening intently. Before I could ask any questions, he smiled, looked in my eyes and said, "Put that bottom bitch position on lock."

I was sure by the expression on my face he knew that comment was like music to my ears. I knew what it meant. This was my tryout to be the head cheerleader on his squad. There wasn't any application process; there were no presentence reports, background or reference checks. None of that. Just like that I was in. And to secure my position, I had to do what I was told. I never thought twice about it even though what he was asking me to do went against what I believed in, what I had been taught, and my better judgment.

He kissed me on the cheek and turned to walk away.

"Excuse me, sir," the guy running the basketball game called to him. "You gonna pick out your prize?" Dee and I looked at him, and he pointed to the extra-large teddy bears. "You made your shot."

Dee and I were both so involved in our conversation and this B-I that suddenly came up, neither of us even noticed that when he threw the ball, he made the shot. Dee looked over at me and nodded for me to pick out my prize.

"I'll take that one," I said, pointing to a huge white teddy bear holding a red silk heart.

"You heard the lady," Dee said to the man.

The man handed me the bear. Dee winked at me, and then he was on his way. For a split second I felt like Lois Lane when Superman went off to save the world. All I could do was wait for him to go do whatever he had to do in order to handle his business. He walked away quietly, never looking back at me. I watched every move he made. He walked as if he had something in his pants that might have been weighing him down. Maybe God had blessed him in a way that every man wants to be blessed. Him leaning to the side with that gangsta pimp just added to his attraction.

His whole package wasn't like anything I had ever experienced before. See, I was always used to a man in a suit, preferably an Armani, Zanetti, or a Valentino. Surely not a sweatsuit or a denim suit, and especially not one with his pants sagging off his ass. The way that his pants hung, showing the rim of his Ralph Lauren boxers, was so new and sexy to me. Usually I love a clean-cut man, low haircut or a bald head, definitely not braids. I mean Dee's braids were almost as long as my weave and his facial hair almost looked like Wolfman Jack's, but only he could do it and get away with it. Any other day in my typical bourgeois life, I would have said "Hell no" to this type of guy, but for some reason this day I was saying "Hell yes!"

As Dee crept through the carnival, he was all slick acting like he was on some MacGyver shit. Then suddenly he slid his hand to his waist, and I watched him pull out a gun. The way he moved swiftly through the crowd, as if he had rehearsed the scene many times before, mesmerized me. Then he aimed.

Boom! Boom! I jumped as I heard the shots fired.

Once the gunshots roared through the air, people started running and screaming. It was at that very moment I realized it wasn't the Apple Bottoms that had his attention. It was her dude he was after. Dee's gun jammed. Mr. Apple Bottom ducked and dodged and ran.

Although Dee was a big guy—six feet, 270 pounds—he was fast. He wasn't trailing far behind Mr. Apple Bottom. What kept Dee from catching him was that the guy started running in a zigzag through the crowd. He was a real bitch-ass dude, trying to latch on to old folks, women, and children to keep Dee from shooting. Coward! When I saw how he was using kids, women, and the elderly for his shield, I secretly wanted Dee to hunt him down like wild game and give him whatever he had coming.

Nigga, just take it like a man, I caught myself thinking. I wanted to see some action. Selfishly, I no longer wanted to live vicariously through court transcripts. The life I had speculated about was happening right here before my very eyes. Only I could tell that ol' dude that was running wasn't a real gangsta. These modern-day Negroes kill me, talking about they gangstas. Did you ever see Jesse James running? Hell no! Now those were some real gangstas. Met in the damn saloon at high noon and shot that shit out right then and there. Ain't nobody have to chase nobody in the Wild Wild West.

When he was no longer in my sight, I started to worry about Dee. But it wasn't the loud, roaring gunshots or the people running for cover that forced me to step up and play my position. It was a security toy cop who stepped on my foot and damn near knocked me down. That's when I put the pep in my step. I started running, too, just as fast as I could, like the track star that Daddy had trained me to be, but it wasn't for cover. The police may have been onto my dude but as long as he made it to the car, it was one thing for certain and two things for sure: I was about to be the getaway driver for my man just like any bottom bitch would.

I quickly jumped in the truck and waited in the designated area as instructed. Once I saw Dee coming, I cut on the lights, put the car in drive, and scooped him up. As soon as he heard the sirens and saw the blue lights coming toward us, he ducked down in the seat.

My Momma always said, How something starts out is usually how it ends. So all I can say is the best is yet to come. If this is the first date, damn, I wonder what will happen in the days to come. Brandon has never, ever been able to get my blood pumping, heart throbbing, and adrenaline going like this even during our wildest sexcapades. This right here confirms that I, Angel Delaney, from this day forward, gotta have a ruffneck.

TWO

The Stash Box

"DAMN! AIN'T THIS a bitch?" Dee raised his voice as I looked up at him to see what was wrong. "I must have dropped my fucking cell phone somewhere at that goddamn carnival when I was chasing that sucka-ass nigga," Dee said, checking his pockets. "Goddamn. Where your phone at? I've got to make some calls."

As I handed him my phone, I asked him, "Where you want me to go, baby?"

"Hold up. I'm trying to see now. Don't go home or nothin'. Just drive across the water or something. I need to holla at a few people.

After I do that, I'ma concentrate only on you. But I gots to handle some real small B-I first."

I sighed, not budging. "Is it going to be *B-I* like a few minutes ago?" I just had to ask. I mean, do you blame me? Who would have thought that my first date with a ruffneck would include gunfire? I shouldn't be surprised because I knew from the gate that I was dealing with a thug, but goddamn. Did I really have to be the getaway car driver for real?

He snickered and stroked my cheek. "No, baby. It ain't nothing like that. Matter fact, I'm sorry that shit had to go down like that, but opportunity was knocking, you know? A nigga had to say what up to it and answer." He began dialing a number and put the phone up to his ear. Although he spoke in code, I knew from court transcripts that it meant some kind of drug deal was going down. And if I knew it and my cell phone had been wired, the police would have known it, too. He made a few more calls and set up some meetings, all of which were ten minutes apart. Between phone calls he managed to tell me, "All I need is an hour to do what I got to do. You ridin' wit' me, right? Because this date ain't over yet."

At this point, my brain wanted to say no. But then I started thinking about the music video we had watched on the sun visor television on the way to the carnival. It was by some rapper named Young Buck called "Shorty, Wanna Ride?" I remember him saying to the girl in the video, "You said you wanna thug. Don't be scared now."

"Yes." I nodded. I didn't know what I was getting myself into, but I knew that it was too late to get scared now. So I rode, driving to every destination he instructed me to. After we made the last stop, I could sense his disappointment with the final guy we went to see.

"Shit," Dee said, getting into the car and slamming the door.

"You okay, baby?" I asked with concern, putting my hand on his leg.

"Yeah." He sighed, picking my hand up, kissing it, then letting it go. "It just that that punk-ass nigga was short on my money and he knew from the get-go that he didn't have all my money for all the shit he wanted. He gon' tell me to bring one thing thinking that I would just be like a'ight, you can owe me, but it ain't go down like that. I ain't on no consignment type shit."

"Oh, does he have bad credit or something with you?" I asked.

"It ain't the point of him getting credit. It's the principle. Clear that shit before I come through. Niggas kill me assuming."

"I understand," I said in a comforting manner. "They take the first three letters of the word assume and that's what they make of themselves," I added, referring to that old wise cliché.

Dee put his hand on my leg and kissed me on the cheek. He just sat there looking at me, and then in a somewhat proud tone, he said, "Damn. My baby girl was holding me down today. You was rolling for your man today, huh?"

Hearing him refer to me as his girl and him as my man made me feel like I had been riding with him for ages. It also made me feel special, like I had won him over that quick. But in reality, I think he was pumping me up by praising me like I was a mediocre child who would do even better if motivated. I nodded, feeling good that he had recognized and had not taken me for granted. Perhaps his psychological strategy was worth something, after all.

"I know we don't even know each other like that, but it seems like we go way back. Like we soul mates or some shit, or whatever muh-fuckas call it."

"Yeah," I replied with a smile.

"You seem like a chick that I could really wifey and make you mines."

"I thought I was," I said on the defense. "You told me to put that bottom bitch position on lock, and I did what I had to do. Now you acting like you got Alzheimer's disease or something."

Dee began laughing, but I was dead serious. This nigga had me in the middle of some ol' ghetto shit like it was something regular for me. I felt like Olivia Newton-John in the movie *Grease*. One minute I'm Sandra Dee, and the next minute I'm some hot girl at a carnival.

He pulled out a blunt, lit it up, and began to smoke. As he took a deep pull on the blunt, he just looked over at me and blew rings of smoke. He said nothing, just looked. He could have stared a hole in me. It was making me uncomfortable. What was running through his head? What was he thinking? Did he like what he saw? And most of all, was he feeling me at least half as much as I was feeling him?

I guess to kill the awkwardness that I knew he could sense, he extended his hand out to offer me a hit of the blunt. I declined by shaking my head. I don't do drugs and even if I did, I wouldn't do them with a crazy mutherfucker like him. Shoot, somebody had to be sane in this relationship.

Still chauffeuring ever since the incident at the carnival, I drove off without knowing where our next destination was, or even caring. Dee sat in the passenger seat puffing away, staring into space.

"What you thinking about?" I finally asked him.

"You want to know what's on my mind?"

"I asked, didn't I?"

He sucked his teeth, poked out his lips, then scratched down his neck a couple of times. "I was thinkin' bout how someone like yourself, Miss College Degree, got your little position of power at yo high sidditty job, I want to know how a nice girl like yo'self, who seems like she never been exposed to anything outside of dandelions, could be wit' a nigga like me today from start to finish and never, not one time, demand any details or bitch up on me."

I shrugged my shoulders. "I don't know. I keep asking myself the same questions. As far as not asking you for any details, I figured, if you want to give me an explanation, then you would." This is what I told him, but on the real, I wanted to know what would make a person want to take another person's life. What would make a person want to flip and put everything at stake? Jeopardize everything, including their own life and freedom? I don't know if it was the journalist in me or the sane human being, but I wanted to know. But I wouldn't dare ask.

"If you don't know nothing, then when the police come to question you, you can't tell 'em nothing." Dee said confidently.

"Accessory after the fact, huh?" He nodded. "What makes you think the bottom bitch is going to tell anything on her man in the first place?" I said, trying to sound like I was a real gangsta's bitch.

"You see this?" he asked, pointing to the mark on his neck.

"How did you do that? What happened?"

I examined it until the car behind me blew his horn to notify me that the red light where we were sitting had changed. I looked in the rearview mirror and waved to apologize as I put my foot on the gas. This jerk still would not let off of his horn. He was upset, and when I looked in the mirror, I saw he was cussing my ass out to the fullest, which only added fuel to Dee's low, always sizzling fire.

"Damn mutherfucker! She said she was sorry," Dee screamed, looking back as if the man behind me could hear him. He looked over at me and said, "Let's fix that mutherfucker. Don't move. Just wait until the light turns yellow before you pull off. Let's really give him something to cry about."

I sat there at the light and waited for it to turn yellow. Once it turned, I waited a couple of seconds then I took it, leaving him with the red light. However, don't you know that motherfucker ran the red light, almost getting nipped by an oncoming car? People are crazy. He jeopardized his driver's license, not to mention his life, driving like a bat out of hell only to catch up with me at the next red light to give me the finger and call me a bitch.

I don't know what he did that for. He must not have realized who in the hell I was rolling with. Now, let me let you in on a little secret. Well, I don't know if it's really a secret. I think it's public information, something anybody with any kind of common sense would just know. Some things you just don't do, and calling a ruffneck, thug, or major player's girl, especially his bottom bitch, a bitch, and not to mention in front of him, too, is something you just don't do. It was definitely common sense, even to me. Oh, trust and believe that fool of a driver had fucked up big-time.

"Bitch, pay the fuck attention," the driver said after angrily rolling down his window.

And before I or the wise ass knew it, Dee had reached for the old Coca-Cola bottle that had been rolling around on the floor of the car from earlier that day, and hummed it at the wise ass. Before he could react, it hit his car and shattered everywhere. It was pure entertainment, watching that dude run the red light to try to get away from us. He went from the big bad wolf to Little Red Riding Hood.

"Punk mutherfucker!" Dee said. He continued poppin' junk for a while about the wise ass until finally calming down.

I laughed at some of the slick shit that was sliding off of his tongue. I made a mental note as well. I never knew when and if I might find myself in a situation where I needed to prove my hood credibility with my tongue. Soon after my laugh faded, I got back to the subject at hand. I don't know if it was curiosity or the chance that the story would get me all worked up in my panties. Probably a little bit of both.

"So, baby, what happened to your neck?" I asked.

"Oh, yeah," he said, getting back to what he was about to tell me before the road rage incident. "The other night we were in this club called Club Zipendale's at the picture booth. We got it on lock, right? Me and my boys had it on lock for about an hour, just snappin' and shit. Posing and shit. My man, Chicago, had just came home."

"Came home from where?" I asked. I guess the squareness in me came out for a minute because I thought he was going to say the military or something.

"From the penitentiary. He was down ten years."

"For what?" I asked.

"What you think?" He looked at me like, *Damn, Ma, it don't take a rocket scientist to figure the shit out,* and then he said, "Drugs."

"I didn't know. In all the cases I've read, most hood dudes go for one of four reasons: drugs, gun charges, murder, or parole violation. So as you can see, I had several choices."

He smiled. "My baby sharp, ain't you? Got them statistics and shit down packed, huh?"

"I try to stay on my toes," I said. "But anyway, what happened?"

He relit his blunt and continued on with the story. "So we's in the club doing it up real big. It's like bout fifty-leven niggas with us from around the way, trying to show Chicago a nice time." He used his hand to motion to me to turn left.

"So, these dudes from across the water get tired of waiting to take pictures and go over and address the photographer. The photographer ain't no gangsta. He's what he is, the picture man, and don't want no problems."

"And I understand that," I said, listening closely, waiting for the foreseeable drama.

"Me, too," Dee agreed. "I admit, we was hogging up shit, but still. So the picture man sent the dudes over themselves to holla at us. I guess the picture man figure he making money, he don't care who in front of the camera. So, they came and threw a wad of money in our face, telling us to let up off the picture booth."

"Did you?" I didn't have to ask. I should have known better.

"Baby, I ain't no ho! A nigga can't just throw no money in my face and 'spect me to move." Dee took a pull on his blunt and exhaled. "I told that nigga to get the fuck out my face. He walked away but the next thing I know, this nigga, Shank, ol' dude from the carnival today, snuck me from behind with a Moët bottle. That's how I got this cut. A bitch-ass nigga. We got ta rumbling in that mutherfucker and they had to shut it down."

"Is that the brawl they were talking about on the news?"

"Yup," he said, confirming it with a devilish grin on his face.

This was all too damn much for a virgin to the streets like myself. This nigga could rumble. He slung drugs, and he had the gunplay action on lock. At that moment and for the first time tonight, it finally sunk in that I, square-ass Angel Delaney, was rolling with the big dawg, a real live muthafuckin' ruffneck in every aspect of the word. And I was loving every minute of it. When the thought sunk in, my corny ass wanted to pull the car over on the side of the road and get out and do the cabbage patch. I know it might sound crazy, but that's the kind of effect this dude had over me. He was my aphrodisiac. He took my shyness and squareness away and breathed bravery and boldness into my body like a life-support system, making me wonder how did I ever live without him in my life.

Then it didn't help when Ashanti's song came on the radio, "Baby Baby." Now, I had never been a big Ashanti fan before, but after really listening to how deep she took it in that song, I'm about to be the president of her Richmond-based fan club. Then, as I had the bass pumping in the song, feeling like I had smoked some hydro, high off my ruffneck, suddenly my high was blown.

For the first time all night, my heart finally dropped as I checked my rearview mirror and saw the police behind me. I didn't want to say nothing yet because I didn't want Dee to think he was rolling with a punk. My heart was in my panties as I checked the speedometer. The speed limit was fifty-five and I was doing fifty-eight; I always gave myself five miles over the speed limit. Before I could blink, you guessed it. The blue lights were on.

Dee turned around to look out of the back window, and my gangsta nigga straight panicked.

"Shit! Ain't this a bitch? Boss Hogg is on a nigga's ass," he said, putting out his blunt, chewing it up, and then swallowing it like it was a piece of filet minion. "Guyddamn!" he shouted as something must have come to mind. The next thing I know he reached into his ashtray and pulled out a baggie. This nigga had to have bumped his head somewhere along the way when he turned and said to me, "Yo, put this in your pussy for me right quick." He handed me a bag of heroin, cocaine, or whatever it was that the guy earlier didn't buy from him.

Now, make no mistake about it. I was born at night but not on this night. I may have been mesmerized by the Billy the Kid lifestyle, but for the first time since being a part of his what seemed to be everyday drama, my common sense kicked in. Before I could even think twice, or knew what I was saying, I blurted out, "Hell no! You put that shit up your ass or something. Don't give it to me!"

"Look," he pleaded in the little bit of time he had before I was fixing to pull over. "They ain't going to search you." He looked behind us at the squad car. "It ain't no woman police with them, and once you stuff it in yo pussy they can't detect it up there. It's bad enough I got the gun on me. Shit, I don't need no more charges on me."

I know you're going to think I am lying just to try to justify why I eventually pulled my panties to the side and shoved that shit up in my pussy, but this is the truth, so help me God. As soon as he said that, a city bus rode past wrapped with the PROJECT EXILE ad, promising a nigga a five-year mandatory in a federal prison if caught with a gun. Project Exile wasn't no joke when it came to drugs either. Trust me. I know. I studied this shit day in and day out. I began to think about the Michael Simmons case and how he got ten years for one rock of crack cocaine. I didn't want Dee to get five years for the gun plus whatever else they would give him for the drugs. So, that's right. I let my pussy be the stash box.

I slipped the drugs into my wet canal and slowly pulled over. As the police sat in his car a moment before getting out, Dee was starting to talk crazy.

"I should just shoot this mutherfucker when he come up to the car, huh?"

He was dead serious. And all I could do was look at him like he had lost his mind.

"No, you shouldn't," I said, trying to be the sensible one in this matter. "Where's your registration?" I asked, knowing that was the first thing the police was going to ask me.

Ignoring me, Dee said, "Look, as soon as Boss Hogg get to the window, pull the fuck off."

"Are you crazy?" I asked as serious as a heart attack. "Now where's the registration?"

"In the glove box," he replied. "The car ain't in my name, though. It's in my momma's name."

It's just like a nigga, a grown ass man, to have his $80,000 vehicle in his momma's name.

My brain started churning. "Where does she live?" I asked. "What's the address?" He told me the address and I repeated it over and over in my head. "Let me do the talking," I added, taking authority for the first time that night. He tried to say something else but I just put my hand up and said, "I got this. Let me do this, a'ight?"

I was scared to roll down the window because I knew the weed smell was strong. I told him to reach in my Chanel bag and grab that small bottle of Gucci perfume out of it. "Hand me my wallet, too." He did exactly as I said. Once he had it in hand, he let out a couple of squirts. At the same time he was taking the Gucci perfume out of my purse, he was putting the gun in it. I couldn't believe my eyes, but I couldn't say shit because by now the police officer was on his way to the car.

The police approached the car, and I proceeded to roll down the window.

"Hello, officer," I said in a coy manner. "What seems to be the problem?"

I handed him the registration card and began going through my wallet to get my license out. I made sure the officer saw the card that showed that I was a contributor to the Police Charity Association. You know when those telemarketers call you asking for money to go to their charity? They call you until you say yes or until you cuss them out. Well, my daddy was actually the one who contributed, but he gave me the card. Who knew the shit would ever come in handy? When the officer saw it, he lightened up a little. I located my license, then handed it to the officer.

"Ms. Delaney," the officer said. "Are you *the* Ms. Angel Delaney?"

Under Dee's breath I faintly heard him mumble what sounded like "Don't tell me this bitch is the police or something."

My heart began to beat faster than ever. Where in the hell did this officer know *me* from? Was there an APB out on me or something?

"The reporter Ms. Angel Delaney?" the officer asked.

I let out a sigh of relief. "Yes, that's me," I said.

The officer eagerly began shaking my hand. "It's a pleasure to meet you, Ms. Delaney. Just think, I pull over a car to let them know the safety belt was hanging out of the door. It was swinging and I didn't want you messing up this nice automobile. And looky here. I meet the one and only Ms. Angel Delaney. This is the highlight of my day."

Humbly I said, "Thank you, officer."

"No problem, Ms. Delaney," he said, tilting his hat. Everything was going smooth. But then I noticed the officer noticing Dee. That's when I started to sweat. Ordinarily, I wouldn't want to be caught dead with a thugged out stereotypical criminal-looking dude like Dee. At this particular moment, when life depended on it, this time wasn't any different than any other time.

Small talk with the officer had taken me back to who the real Angel Delaney was, the infamous journalist, that ruthless bitch with a pen. I myself had even forgotten all about Dee sitting over there. I closed my eyes and wished that he was some clean-cut honest-looking fella. You know, the Denzel type. I opened my eyes, hoping that my wish had come true. I looked over at Dee. Nope, no Denzel type. He was still the DMX type all day long.

Fortunately enough, the officer merely nodded at Dee and then directed his attention back to me.

"Ms. Delaney, I hope you don't mind me asking," the officer said as my heart sank into my stomach. "But could you give me your autograph please?"

"Certainly," I said, with yet another sigh of relief. This officer was trippin'. I had written several excellent pieces if I say so myself. But not many folks had ever asked me for my autograph. Nonetheless, I signed my name for him.

"Thank you so much," he said gratefully. "Y'all be safe and y'all have a nice evening," the officer said with a southern twang.

"You, too, officer," I said, watching him walk away.

Dee and I sat in the car silently, not saying a word, until the officer had driven off. Once he was out of sight I quickly opened up the car door and puked my guts out.

I could never make you understand just how much I thanked God for that blessing because I knew that was truly a close call. As I hung out of the door, sick to my stomach, I could only wonder just how much closer shit was going to get.

THREE

Thug Passion

I WAS TIRED and worn out from the evening's events, but I was in no shape to go home. I knew Brandon would probably be there and I wasn't in any condition to be put through the third degree by him about my day. Dee said that he would get me a hotel for the night. I guess that was his way of rewarding me.

The ride to the Jefferson Hotel was silent except for him calling a couple of his homeboys on my cell. My phone rang a few times, but I didn't recognize any of the numbers.

"I don't know anybody from this number," I said to Dee, reciting it.

"Oh, that might be my boy," he said, taking the phone from me. "He's probably hitting me back off of his caller ID. . . . Yo," he said, pausing. "Oh, okay, dukes," he said. "It was the wrong number. They wanted to speak to Marie."

Just then my heart dropped. I don't know how much more of this my poor heart could take. It never dawned on me until that moment that Brandon could have been calling me from anywhere. But when Dee said that someone asked for Marie, I knew it was Brandon calling. He's the only one who calls me by my middle name.

The phone rang again. Dee went to answer it again but I stopped him.

"No!" I shouted quickly, snatching the phone from him. "Don't answer it. Somebody is just playing on my phone. Probably someone pissed off about an article I wrote about them or something."

I knew it was Brandon calling back and I didn't know what to say to him. I would have plenty of time to think up some lie while I rested up at the hotel and gathered my thoughts. Little did I know, rest was the last thing I was going to be getting.

When we arrived at the hotel, the valet parked the truck, and we went in to get a room. I sat down on a sofa in the hotel lobby while Dee got the room. The desk clerk asked for a picture ID, and he must have handed her one that had the name Shawn Michelob on it because she referred to him as Mr. Shawn Michelob.

Had this motherfucker lied about his name when he first called me or what? I thought when I heard the clerk address him. Or maybe it was just a fake ID. Who cared at this point? I just wanted to get to a nice comfy bed to lay it down and get my mind right.

Once we got to the room, we ordered a pizza from my cell phone. I wasn't even able to agree to the total because my cell phone battery died and my cell phone went dead. We tried calling them back on the hotel phone, but it had not been connected yet. Dee was consumed with getting the phone on so he could finish making his calls, handling all that B-I stuff he said he had to take care of before he could give me all of his undivided attention. I was cool with that because while he did his thing, I hopped in the shower. I damn near turned on all hot water and let it beat down on my body as I replayed in my head all of the crazy shit that had happened in the past few hours. I allowed my hands to massage my body, my shoulders, my breasts, and my inner thighs. Then all of a sudden something plopped out of my pussy and hit the shower floor. I almost shitted on myself. My scream rang through my ears. I had forgotten all about the baggie I had stuffed up inside of me.

"You all right up in there?" Dee asked, entering the bathroom.

"Yeah," I replied, turning the water off. "I'm cool." I started laughing to myself.

"Well, I'm bout to head downstairs and see why they ain't cut the phone on yet. I be back. I left da money on the dresser for da pizza."

"Oh, okay," I replied softly. I picked up the baggie, pulled the shower curtain back, and reached for my towel.

As I reached for the towel, I realized that I should have told him to bring us back some drinks out of the soda machine. I sat the baggie on the sink, wrapped the towel around me, ran to the door, and tried to catch Dee. I didn't see him when I peeped out the door, so I just slipped on my clothes, got some change out of my purse, and went to the soda machine myself to get us some drinks.

The closest vending machine was on the first floor, so I took the stairs down a flight. As soon as I got close to the soda machine, I could hear Dee at the front desk laying the front desk clerk's ass out!

"Why you ain't cut on the phone yet? Shit, I paid extra to get it on and it's been over a half hour and that shit ain't on yet."

"Sir, I'm going to take care of that for you in a few minutes," the clerk said apologetically. "I'm sorry. I got busy and couldn't get around to it. But give me a couple of minutes and I'll have it on then."

"Why I gotta wait mo' minutes?" Dee said sharply. "I done already waited thirty minutes as it is."

"Sir," the clerk said, becoming agitated by Dee. "In all actuality, I've been off the clock for fifteen minutes. I had another fire to put out and some paperwork to do. I'm trying to get out of here. I have been here for twelve hours and I am ready to go home."

"So, what the fuck that got to do with me? I'm ready to make my calls and go to sleep. I'm tired, too."

"Well, we're even then," she said sarcastically.

I stood watching, but Dee didn't see me. He picked up the sign, which read CUSTOMER SERVICE IS OUR FIRST PRIORITY and started at the clerk again.

"What da fuck does this mean?" he demanded to know.

"Sir, I'm not going to get into this with you right now," the clerk said. "You are just going to have to understand that I said your phone will be turned on soon. The longer I stand here and go back and forth with you, the longer it will take me to get the phone on."

"That ain't putting me first, the customer. The paying customer at that," Dee said, throwing the sign across the counter.

"Look, Mr. Michelob. I am going to have to ask you to leave," the clerk said sternly.

"Not until my phone is on!" Dee replied, getting in her face so closely that spit accidentally came out of his mouth and got on her face.

The clerk turned red. "Look, Mr. Michelob. I'm going to refund your money and you need to leave the premises."

"I'm not going anywhere. I just ordered a pizza and I am tired. All I want you to do is what you neglected to do, your fucking job. Turn my goddamn phone on, ya hear?"

"As I said, Mr. Michelob, you're going to have to leave," the clerk said.

"Why? Because you's a lazy bitch and don't want to do yo fucking job?"

He was loud and irate. The only thing that stopped him from tearing into the clerk even more was the pizza man walking through the hotel lobby door. He redirected his attention to the pizza man.

"Yo, dude," Dee said to the pizza man. "That's me, right here."

I proceeded to get a couple cans of soda while Dee finished up his transaction with the pizza man. When he turned and saw me, I just shook my head at him. He smiled and threw his head up, acknowledging that he saw me.

We went back to the room and ate every last slice of the pizza. It was safe to say that we had worked up one hell of an appetite. While we ate our pizza, we both were comfortable. Dee was sitting in the chair beside the bed in his boxers and no shirt. Me, I had nothing on except for my panties and my camisole that I had on under my clothes from earlier. I was lying across the bed. We talked and laughed.

"Can I ask you something?" I said to Dee. "What's your real name?"

"Dick, I told you," he said seriously.

"Is that short for Richard or something?"

"Naw, baby," he said, looking down at his manhood. "Ain't nothing short about it. It's just plain old Dick."

"Stop joking," I said, play punching him. "I know your momma didn't name you no Dick."

"I'm telling you, for real though, my name is Dick." He smiled and then chuckled a little bit. "That's how wild my momma was. After she pushed me out and the nurse handed me to her, she looked at my dick and, after having four more boys ahead of me, she knew that I had the biggest dick she ever saw a baby have and she named me Dick."

I laughed at him, but he was serious as a heart attack.

"Why your people name you Angel?" he asked.

I stopped laughing and answered him. "My daddy said that my mother was so evil when she was pregnant that he thought she had been possessed by the devil, that she was probably having Rosemary's baby. But when I was born and they laid their eyes on me, they knew I was far from a little devil and that God had definitely given them one of his angels. So they named me Angel."

"Well," Dee said, "after seeing yo ass in action today, I think yo peoples had it right the first time. A devil in disguise."

I laughed at his little joke, then added to it. "Or perhaps what you saw was just the devil in me that had been longing to get out."

"I guess I can bring out the devil in a girl," Dee said, winking.

You could have cut the sexual tension between us with a knife. "Come 'ere," he said, nodding his head and licking his lips.

As if I was a genie in a bottle and his every wish was my command, I got up from the bed and walked over to him. He patted his lap with his hand, instructing me to sit down. I sat down on his lap like I was a child climbing up onto Santa's lap to tell him everything I wanted.

Dee scooted me over so that my ass was positioned right on his cock. I could feel his hands running up and down my back. Chills covered my body. His touch was so strong and sensual. Brandon had never touched me like that. I don't know, maybe he had, but his touches never made me feel like this.

Dee gripped one of my hips with each hand and started grinding on my ass. I could feel him growing even harder. I thought his dick was going to burst right out of his boxers and up inside of me. He pulled me against him as he grinded me harder and harder. It felt so fucking good. Before I knew it, I was grinding him back. It was as if the shit had been choreographed by Fatima. We were so in sync.

Before I knew it, Dee had stood me up and walked me over to the bed, kissing my neck and caressing my breasts as he walked behind me.

"Take this off," he whispered in my ear, referring to the camisole. "As a matter of fact, let me take that shit off."

The next thing I knew, my $65 Victoria's Secret catalog special camisole was being ripped off of me. I could hear it ripping at the seams as Dee snatched it off of me. Before I could even react, he pushed me down onto the bed. There I was, lying there on my stomach. I attempted to look back at him, but he pushed my head down and started running his fingers through my hair with one hand as he pulled his dick out of his boxers and positioned the tip inside me with the other.

"Dee," I moaned.

"Hush, baby," he said, then in one huge stroke he was inside of me.

I went to scream but he had rammed his tongue into my mouth before a sound could come out. The pain hurt so good as he fucked me wild. He was grinding, swirling, fucking me in and out, and all at once it seemed. I could hear my wetness as he dipped in my juices.

"Oh, baby. You got the bomb-ass pussy," he crooned in my ear as he pumped me.

That buck-wild shit right there turned me on. That's right. Those words sent me into a trance, doing tricks like I was mother-fucking David Copperfield. Before I knew it, I was throwing that ass back at him. My back was arched like a kitty cat as I tooted my ass in the air for him to hit harder.

"Fuck me harder, daddy dearest," I whined like a little girl.

"Oh, shit," he said. "I like a bitch that ain't scared of the dick," he said, as he got up on his hands, extending his arms, and watched me fuck his dick.

I had never worked it like that in my life. I felt like a porn star and I was loving every minute of it. I wanted to do whatever I needed to please him. That's the toll some good dick can put on you. Good dick will have you so caught up in the moment, the next day when you reminisce, you be wondering, "What the fuck was I thinking?"

"Fuck me back," I said to him as he obeyed. "Fuck me hard, daddy. Fuck me like you paying for this," and believe you me he did, just like Long Don Juan. And Dee's momma wasn't lying, she knew just what she was talking about when she named his ass. "Fuck me," I kept repeating. "Fuck me, daddy."

I always wanted to say that, but Brandon wasn't the type of man a girl could say that type of thing to. Brandon was a romantic. He preferred I say something like "make love to me." But fuck all that. This right here was some thug passion. There were no rules, and more important, no preferences. It was just straight-out Erotic City.

I was taking Dee's dick better than any of his skeezers could have. Dee was so huge. I swear on everything I love that I never had anything so big up inside me and I was taking it like a seasoned vet, Vanessa Del Rio, Janet Jackme, or Jenna Jameson ain't have shit on me. Dee flipped me onto my back and ran all up inside me.

"Auull. Ouch! That hurts," I said with no shame in my game as he continued. I guess him knowing that he was puttin' a hurtin' on me only intensified his thrust.

"This is my pussy," he bragged, looking me in my eyes as he said it with authority.

I wasn't about to let him think that I couldn't handle what he was dishing out. I grabbed his ass and wrapped my legs around his back. I opened myself up to him and let myself go.

"Goddamn," he moaned. "Goddamn," he repeated as saliva dripped from the corner of his mouth. That's when I knew I had his ass. He was about to come and so was I.

"Fuck me, nigga," I added, just to see how it would sound. Brandon would die if I ever called him a nigga. But this wasn't Brandon, the soft, sweet gentleman. This was a muh-fuckin' ruffneck. Now I knew what the fuck MC Lyte was talkin' about. And she ain't never lied. That's why I love her to this very day because she kept it real. She tried to warn us, but we thought she was just singing a song. I was getting hooked, this dick was like a drug. I knew I was going to need this morning, noon, and night.

Right as I was about to explode there was a knock on the door.

"Security," someone yelled through the door. "Open up."

Before we could do anything, they were putting the key in the door, turning the knob to enter the room.

I didn't give the embarrassment time to set in before I just hopped up and started yelling, "Rape! Help! Rape!"

"What da fuck," Dee screamed, looking at me in shock.

"Rape," I frantically repeated.

I could see the rage in Dee's eyes as he punched me in the face. "Bitch, you lying. Is you fucking crazy?" I'll never forget the look of complete disbelief that was on his face.

I pulled away from him and began scrambling all over the room for my clothes.

Security approached Dee as he was grabbing his pants and shoes. Dee punched the security guard with a mean-ass right and damn near sent him to his knees. Before the toy cop could recoup, Dee was gone like Flash Gordon.

I snatched my clothes and purse and ran into the bathroom and locked the door. I began to cry at the top of my lungs. Security didn't know if he should try to console me or go after Dee. Honestly, I don't think he really wanted any more parts of Dee, so he chose me. He stood at the door knocking, trying to get me to open it, but I put on the best award-winning performance ever. I cried like a baby— that is, until the paramedics got there. They finally got me to open the door. They took me to the hospital to get checked out. A rape counselor came in and tried to comfort me before the doctor would come in to examine me. I stared off into space with tears rolling down my eyes. I tell you, watching those Lifetime movies really paid off. I had them all fooled. I gave them a fake name and as soon as the counselor left, I grabbed my Chanel bag and slipped out of the hospital like a thief in the night.

I hopped in a cab outside the Medical College of Virginia and went home to my Tobacco Row downtown studio apartment that overlooked the James River. When the taxi pulled up, I was relieved to see that Brandon's car wasn't there. Since he has a key to my place, he comes and goes as he pleases. With one fuckin' thing after another, I still hadn't decided what lie to work up to him about my evening whereabouts.

I changed my clothes to another outfit that I had bought when I went to the mall. It was a one-piece, form-fitting, tight-ass Rocawear denim pants hookup. I grabbed my purse and the keys to my car and was out the door. I drove with one thing on my mind, Dee and that good-ass dick. Okay, so it was two things. I drove past all the places that he had taken me to earlier. Until that minute, I had never appreciated those camping trips that my daddy had taken me on. Those trips gave me a great sense of direction, but in the hood, everything looks alike.

Any other time, rollin' through the hood, I would have looked like a fish trying to survive on land. But I learned quickly. My day's schooling was like a person getting a GED in a matter of months versus the rest of us who had to spend four exasperating years in high school. Well, compliments of Dee's homeschooling, I had gotten my SWU degree (Sidewalk University), which is equivalent to a GED in the hood. The famous slogan was up and down the sidewalks: If you don't learn it in the streets, you don't learn it nowhere!

I didn't see Dee or his truck anywhere in sight, but just when I was about ready to give up I spotted the Porsche truck parked in the alley. You would have thought I'd been a little kid outside of a candy shop the way I smiled. I literally wanted to do cartwheels, but I didn't. I was at the point of no return as I rode up on a zombie-looking dude like I was the police about to lock him up. I rolled down the window and asked the zombie, "You know where Dee at?"

"Er'body over in Tabby's house gambling," he said, then looked at me like I was suppose to give him something.

"Can you go get him for me?" I asked, trying my hand. I didn't know who no damn Tabby was and I wasn't trying to show up on her doorstep unannounced. I don't play that and I know a hood chick wouldn't either.

"You know fair exchange ain't never been robbery," he said.

"Pardon me?" I said, confused.

"You know, a tit for a tat," he said, holding his hand out.

Just then, everything sank in. "Oh," I replied. "You right. So what you need?" I asked, not really caring because I needed him to get Dee for me.

"I'm out here sick as a muh-fucka and I need to get my shot. I need twenty dollars at least to shake this sickness."

"A'ight, no problem. Well, let's make the exchange then. Just make sure you handle your B-I," I said, using the word like I had been saying it all my life.

"A'ight, give me the twenty dollars, den."

I laughed because I had seen this same shit on *The Wire*, I think, or one of them shows, where the clown ran off with the money. All I know is that I needed Dee and he was my only lead. By no means could I let him get out of sight with my $20 and I don't see him no more.

"Look, here go five dollars, hurry up and get Dee. Tell him that it's his cousin that wants him. And soon as you come back, I am going to give you the rest."

He agreed, taking the $5. I watched him like a hawk as he went into a building. He was only in there a minute or so before he came right back out to my car.

"He said he coming," he yelled to me, walking toward my car. "Pull over, cut yo lights off and he coming." He motioned to me with his hands.

I wanted to see Dee coming for myself before I handed over any more money to the guy. A few seconds later Dee came out of the same building that the guy had just exited. Once I saw him, I gave the zombie the $15 that I promised, and he was off to get his shot on.

When Dee got up on my car, he saw that it was me. I didn't know what he was going to say or do to me. I just braced myself.

"Bitch, you got some muh-fuckin' nerve," he said between gritted teeth. "What da fuck you doing round here wit' yo police ass. Get da fuck from around me before I beat da shit out of you." He raised his hand at me and was looking like he was about to turn into the Incredible Hulk.

"Baby, I came around here to bring you what's yours," I said, reaching into my purse and pulling out his baggie and gun. The most puzzled look came over his face, like he was trying his damnedest to figure me out. Then he slid into the passenger side of my car, still watching me suspiciously.

"I apologize for screaming rape but I needed to create a distraction and it was the only thing I could think of," I continued.

"A distraction?" he asked.

"Yes, you needed to get up out of there," I pleaded my case. "I did what any bottom bitch would have done. Even if they caught you, a rape charge wouldn't have been nothing for you to beat if I wasn't around. What's a rape charge with no witness? I had to come up with a way for you to get up out of there so I could get my pocketbook into the bathroom with the drugs and gun."

He thought for a minute and smiled as he digested what I said.

"You know the bottom bitch is down for whatever when it comes to her man. So, that's why I screamed rape. It was to save your ass, not to have a toy cop aid in locking you up. You know I couldn't let you go out like that. I wasn't going to let you go out when that cop pulled you over, was I?" I asked in a firm tone. "Was I?"

Dee sat there and thought for a minute. "Damn," he said, sighing and shaking his head. "I'ma keep it real wit' choo. I figured you was like, 'I just met this nigga, he was all fun and games, but now that da shit is grimy, I'ma turn on his ass.' " He paused. "Baby, you know you's mines for real. I fucks with you sho nuff."

A huge grin covered my face.

He had a sudden thought. "But what if they go back to the hotel room and try to get some DNA or forensic shit or something?"

I giggled. "Nigga, please. You been watching too much crime TV. It ain't like you Kobe Bryant and I'm some little white chick from Colorado."

He laughed and shook his head at me. "Let's get out of here," he said. "I'ma get my truck. Follow me."

"Where we going?" I asked.

"Not to no hotel, that's for sure. Let's go to my house where the phone is on."

He smiled and kissed me on the cheek as I headed to his place.

FOUR

Fuck da Police

ONCE DEE and I got to his place, we didn't even say two words. We just screwed. From the minute we walked through the door, he was all over me. I couldn't even tell you what his living room looked like because we headed straight for the bedroom. It was even more over the edge and exciting than in the hotel room. This time we got to come and come and come some more. I was flushed with the orgasm of my life. I thought his king-size mattress set was a waterbed for a minute there the way I was swimming in juices. Before we knew it, time got away from us, and we fell asleep in each other's arms.

The next time I opened my eyes, the sun was just coming up.

"Damn," I said, looking over at the clock on his night table.

It was seven in the morning, and I was due at the courthouse by nine A.M. It was a hot case and I knew I could get top dollar for articles trailing it. I had to get my ass up and go, but then I looked over and saw him lying there next to me.

I smiled as I sat there, watching his chest go up and down with every breath. I couldn't resist leaning over to kiss him, morning breath and all. Like a sleeping beauty he woke up with my kiss.

"What up, girl?" he said, stretching and yawning.

"Nothing, just sitting here, looking at you, wishing I didn't have to go to work today so I could spend it with you."

"No work today," he said.

"But I have to go," I pouted as I got up out of the bed. "A big trial starts today and I know I'll get paid top dollar for any articles I write on it. After all, I am *the* Ms. Angel Delaney." I mocked the police officer.

Dee got up out of bed and went over and picked up his pants. He dug inside of them and pulled a roll of cash out of each pocket. He peeled off a few bills from one of them and placed them in his jeans. Then he proceeded to peel off each bill one by one, throwing them onto the bed.

"Whatever the most they pay you for those stories, I'll triple that shit," he said with a thuglike cockiness.

I walked over to the bed and began to play with the money, all $100 bills. Needless to say, we lay in the bed all morning long, making passionate love—I mean fucking. I had never fucked on top of money before. I was in complete sextasy.

He told me that lying in the bed all day was something he never did. I started to analyze his comment. Funny, how dudes who hustle, chase the dollars day in and day out. They put in more work than the Donald Trumps and Bill Gateses of the world.

I whipped up something to eat with what I could find in his bachelor kitchen. After eating we fell asleep again in each other's arms. Evening came. I probably could have slept forever if Dee hadn't woken me up with his movement. He was back on the phone checking the messages on his cell phone that he had lost at the carnival.

"Damn, I missed so much fucking money!" he exclaimed.

"I'm sorry," I said.

"Oh, no, baby, not because of you," he lied, not wanting to make me feel bad. He knew good and well that laying up with me was the reason he wasn't out making drug transactions.

I didn't say anything. I just lay there and listened as he made his phone calls. Just watching him handle his business, talking to busters like they weren't shit reminded me of why I was laying up with him, jeopardizing my career.

Out of nowhere I slipped under the covers and made my way over to his hard-on. When I started sucking his dick, just to fuck with his head while he was on the phone, he put the phone on speakerphone to free up his hands while he placed them on my head and bobbed them up and down in sync with my flow. Although my first concern was to make sure he busted a nut, my curious side had me tending more to his conversation than I was slobbin' the knob.

"Like I told you before, Chicago," he said, grunting, then continuing his conversation. "I can only hit you with half because I promised Lil Sam three."

"Come on, Dee," Chicago said. "A nigga need to get this paper, man. I'm starving and I just came home and shit. You know dat."

"I feel you on that, Chicago, but know I'm big on principles. All I have is my word." I looked up at Dee, who was looking down at me. He smiled and I gave him a sexy look then continued handling my business between his legs.

Chicago sighed. "I feel you. You right. So what can you throw me until you get from up top?"

"You wanted four but I can only hit you off with two because I ain't got but five," Dee said to Chicago. He scrunched his face because the shit was feeling good. He wanted to bust, but not on the phone. He mouthed to me to hold up for a minute.

I got up and went to the bathroom to brush my teeth, and Dee never bothered to take the phone off speaker as he continued the conversation with Chicago. Once I entered the room, Dee called out to me. "Hey boo," he said, pointing. "Get that Louis Vuitton duffel bag out of that closet right there."

"Sure thing, baby," I called right back out to him.

"Who dat?" Chicago asked.

"Oh, that's my baby, Angel."

"Oh, that's the new eye candy you was telling us about over at Tabby's. The one you met at the court building?"

"Right, right," Dee said.

Chicago paused. "Man, you up over there talkin' business in front of that broad? You ain't no playa."

"Nigga, you high or something? You know how I get down. And know that I ain't no playa. I'm a pimp. Players get played and pimps get paid."

"Okay, Bishop Magic Juan." Chicago laughed.

"You know it. Well, nigga, I'm about to take flight. So, be at the boarding gate in about ten."

"Okay, my nigga. One!"

Dee hung up the phone and then he started talking to me as if I hadn't been listening the whole time. "I gotta go make this move. Since I've been off da radar for two days, I gotta go hit my little shorty, Chicago, off with some work. I was s'pose to be going up top and I didn't cuz I was wit' you. And niggas ain't got nothing. So, I'm going to go up to New York to re-up first thing in the morning."

All of a sudden I felt like a hoochie that he had used and was finished with. I think he could tell I was disappointed by the look on my face.

"Come here, ma," he said in a comforting tone. I just stood there with the duffel bag in hand. He repeated, "Come here."

I sat down next to him. He puckered his lips, and I leaned over and gave him a kiss. He grabbed me by the face then and kissed me hard and passionately.

"Okay, well, I know you gotta get going and all," I said, as if that would be the last time I ever saw him. "I guess I'll see you whenever."

"You ain't going home." He leaned in and began to kiss and suck on me, quickly making his way down to my titty. "Just stay here until I get back. And just leave and go home from here in the morning when I get up to go to NY."

"Okay," I happily agreed, glad that he trusted me in his house.

"I should be back in an hour or so. Since I don't keep shit here, I gotta go 'cross town and get it. Then I gotta come back this way and meet Chicago."

"I'll be waiting for you," I said softly. "You and I have some business we need to finish up." I winked. "Be careful, baby."

When Dee left, I got up and made something to drink. For some reason, I couldn't help myself. I began snooping through his things. I wanted to know more about Dee. I was basically searching for female items, underwear under the bed, bobby pins, another toothbrush, anything, but I found nothing. The only thing I came across was the gun in his night table drawer. I wanted so badly to find some more things, but I didn't. See, that's us women, always want to find some shit, but when we do, we can't take it. Since his place had passed the ho inspection, all that was left for me to do was to wait for Dee to return home to me.

I lay up in that house like I had been his bitch from day one, walking around the place like I owned that shit. I flipped through the channels thinking that I would be up all night since I had been lying around in the bed all day. However, after sucking and fucking around the clock, I was dog-ass tired. Before I knew it I had fell off to sleep.

BOOM, BOOM. I was awakened by a kicking sound on the door. It sounded like somebody trying to break into the house. Don't you know some dudes was trying to run up in Dee's spot? Was these dudes crazy or what? They were trying to kick the door in like the police.

Now, let me tell you the past couple of nights, I had played the role of gangsta bitch to the fullest, and if I must say so, I did the damn thing, too. But knowing that a nigga or some niggas was on the other side of the door trying to kick it in and do God only knows what to me was something else. I wasn't at home, where I had a baseball bat right beside my bed. I was in a real gangsta's house, where there was a big gun. But the problem was I didn't know how to fire no gun. Daddy took me camping, not hunting.

All that gangsta bitch shit went straight out the window! You best believe that I bitched all up. Let's get this straight, I wasn't born into this. I was sworn into it. I gave an oath, a promise to Dee, but without even thinking, I did what was natural for me, or anybody else with good common sense. I grabbed the phone, and I called 911. That's right! My life was on the line. A square bitch like me wasn't saying, "Fuck da police." Helllll no! At that point, I needed them. I'm a taxpayer, and the police were here to protect and serve. I needed them to be Johnny on the damn spot.

As soon as the operator said, "Nine-one-one operator, what's your emergency?" Boom! I heard the last, final and the loudest sound. I knew the hinges on the door were off. I could hear the door scrape the hardwood floors. Two dudes in black ski masks came charging through the door. For a minute they couldn't see me, but I could see them. I placed the phone under the bed so that the 911 operator could hear what was going on. I tiptoed over to the bathroom that was connected to the bedroom. I quietly got into the bathtub. My heart was racing like two motorcycles. I cried like I had never cried before, only there were no sounds proceeding from my mouth. I was scared and shaking like a leaf. I had not been in the bathtub a good minute before one of the men came in and snatched the shower curtain down.

"Look a here, look a here," he yelled. He snatched me out of the tub mercilessly.

The other dude came into the bathroom and in a cold voice said, "Tie that bitch up."

Following his croney's orders, the first one dragged me into the bedroom, snatched the phone cord out of the wall, and tied me up with it. It was apparent by the way they tied me up in such a flash that this was something they had done before. While I was being tied up, I don't know why, but I guess it was from watching too many Lifetime movies, I said, "You better get out of here. Dee will be back any minute now."

The dude who had found me in the bathtub, the one tying me up, gave me a cunning look. Then he said, with such pride in his voice, "No, he won't because that lame muthafucka is waiting for me somewhere."

That's when I recognized his voice. It hit me, and it really hit home. That shit really blew me away because I realized at that moment it was Chicago, his homeboy, his man, and his friend since the sandbox, who was robbing Dee's spot.

As I sat there tied up, Chicago and his accomplice methodically emptied out Dee's safe. Chicago was the same guy who started the beef in the club. If Dee wouldn't have been in the club showing Chicago a good time, then that fight wouldn't have escalated to the shootout at the carnival. Damn, they always say it's the closest ones that get you every time. I suppose that's why you keep your enemies close and your friends even closer.

Chicago came back in the room and started yelling at me, "Where da flav at?"

Shaking and crying with snot running down my face, I replied, "I don't know."

"Bitch, you lying because when I was on the phone with that nigga, he said he could only give me half and had promised the rest of his shit to someone else, so I know dat nigga got some shit up in here. Where the fuck it at?" I shrugged my shoulders because I really didn't know where the drugs were. "Oh, you gon' play dumb, huh?" he asked. He paused for a moment as if he expected me to reply, so I obliged him.

"He don't keep it here," I said between tears. "He just told me that he had to go get it from where he keeps it, then he had to meet you."

"What da fuck?" he screamed and then paused, shaking his head because Dee was two steps ahead of him. "Guyd damn, that nigga always told me never let yo right hand know what yo left hand is doing. Damn. How da fuck I slept on dat nigga? Can't shit where you eat. Ain't this a bitch?"

I could see that Chicago knew that Dee had played him. He'd thought he had the upper hand on Dee. He'd been sure that Dee was like the average nigga and never took his own advice. I'd been learning over the past couple of days that Dee was far from being the average drug boy.

I was smiling inside, so much that I didn't realize the smile had seeped from my thoughts and covered my face. This must have angered Chicago because the next thing I knew he hit me on the head with the butt of the gun. The pain was like electricity running through my body. By that time it had been a good fifteen minutes, and I had given up on the police. If I hadn't realized that I was in the hood before, I knew that shit now. As I sat there with blood dripping from my forehead, I thought about all those statistics that I had reported. It was really true about the police taking their time to respond to trouble in the hood. They wouldn't do this in the suburbs. Every second felt like an hour because I didn't know exactly what Chicago's plans for me were.

As Chicago joined his accomplice in getting the money out of Dee's safe, I heard sirens, and at that moment I knew I was scot-free. I prayed that they would simply go and leave me alive. I had seen too many movies where they shot the witness just on general principle. The sirens startled them, and they jumped across furniture to flee.

The first officer on the scene called for backup while the other ran to try to apprehend Chicago and his boy. The police officer untied me, and I ran to the bedroom to slip on my jeans because I was only wearing one of Dee's T-shirts. I guess somehow Dee and I really were connected because I don't know why, but for some reason I thought about the gun in the night table drawer. It was a big-ass chrome gun, the same one from the carnival shooting. I wiped it off and went into the bathroom and hummed it out of the window as hard as I could.

As I exited the bathroom, a female police officer entered the room. She wanted to ask me some questions. I told her I was too upset to answer any questions right now. She insisted on escorting me out to the ambulance so that they could check my head where Chicago had hit me with the gun.

Blue lights and blue suits were everywhere. They had even set up a roadblock down the street from Dee's house. Dee had got caught up in the roadblock. One of the fuckin' cops recognized Dee's truck from a description at an incident reported at the Jefferson Hotel. They snatched his ass, and, of course, he was riding dirty because of the sale he had planned on making to Chicago.

The police asked me a zillion and one questions. It was hard for them to believe, hell, it was even hard for me to believe, that I couldn't give them much information on Dee because I had just met him. And even if I had known anything, I wouldn't give them anything on him anyway. I needed him to trust me. I couldn't help thinking about crazy stuff like whether or not Dee would even remember my last name to put me on his visitors' list. Then I realized that fuck, I didn't even know his last name. He had so many of them. I'm not even sure if he really gave me his government name or not. He doesn't know my address so he can't write me. All he has is a cell phone number for me and hell, they can't get collect calls. Damn, how could this be? My girls wouldn't believe me if I told them. I have no proof that the past nights even happened. Hell, did it? Maybe I was just living out one of those court cases I had sat in on. Everything seemed so crazy and surreal.

An officer walked me to my car. He asked if I needed an escort home but I told him that I would be fine. As I got in my car, parked outside of Dee's house, I gazed up at his house, which was covered in crime scene tape. Then I drove off.

On my way home my mind was filled with thoughts. I put on my Kirk Franklin CD. After all I had experienced, I needed Jesus. All I could do was keep thanking God for sparing my life.

In the midst of trying to start one particular song over because it was really touching my heart, I made a mistake and hit the wrong button, putting it on Power 92.1 FM. Blaring from my speakers was "Soldier" by Destiny's Child. You know, every superhero has a theme song and so does a down-ass bitch and that just happened to be mine. I listened to all the words, and it was my inspiration. Once the song went off, I looked at the clock in my car. It read 1:36 A.M. I knew without a doubt that Brandon was probably worried sick about me. I bet he had blown my cell phone up, filling my voice message box. I started to feel bad about putting him through so much worry. He was a good man. Sweet, kind, and gentle. Maybe he was what I needed in my life. Then I thought again.

As I exited the heart of the hood, I drove by a building that had a line down the street. The top of the building had a neon sign that read Club Zipendale's.

I looked in the mirror and fixed my hair to cover up the bruise from the gun. Without even thinking, I busted an illegal U-turn in the middle of the street. I thought that if I hurried up, I could make it inside the club by two a.m. before it closed its doors. I knew that at that particular club I could find what I wanted in my life. Fuck that, what I needed! That move right there proved that I, the new and improved bad-ass bitch Angel Delaney, from here on out, *gotta have a ruffneck!*

ACKNOWLEDGMENTS

Seven I was asked to keep my acknowledgments short and simple. At first I laughed because as a writer it's hard for me not to editorialize. Then I thought, how can I thank everybody without leaving anyone out? Then my Lord and Saviour came to mind. He is the reason for everyone in my life, whether for a reason, a season, or a lifetime. He's blessed me with a strong mother and two beautiful black boys. He's blessed me with friends who love me no matter what. He's also placed situations in my path in order to see how I would handle them, and when I thought I couldn't go anymore, it was God who had my back! Having lost my father, brother, nephew, sister, brother-in-law, and several close friends—all to the streets, and having a brother on lockdown for eighteen years, believe me when I say, there were many times when I thought I was going to lose my mind. But late in the midnight hour . . . He saved me! So, for all that I am, for all that I have, for every gift or talent, for every story I write and sell (regardless of how gangsta), for every character I create, I give all praises to God!

The Ghost I would first like to thank the "Most High" for blessing me with such a wonderful gift. Next, my family and close friends for staying real from the beginning to the end (I got you). "Ms. Lavern," my dear friend. Last but not least, the Queen, Ms. Nikki Turner. When I called, you answered. I thank you for giving me the opportunity to be heard. You'll always have a friend in me.

Acknowledgments

Y. Blak Moore I have to acknowledge The Creator for affording me safe passage thus far. To Lasheka Hasan, Akilah (Killah) Hasan, Briana (Taco) Hasan, Loony, Moo-Moo, and Ham. Thanks, Nikki, for the love. Peace.

Akbar Pray Although I thought it unusual to make acknowledgments for a short story, I nonetheless knew on some level that I would be remiss if I didn't take this occasion to thank a few of the people, though not all of them, who have been the core of my support both personally and professionally in my literary endeavors. Not necessarily in order of importance I would like to thank and acknowledge Khadijah Ahmid. You have been often my staunchest literary critic but have grown to be one of my dearest friends. On both fronts I thank you. To Valarie Paschall. On the other side of the gun tower you have been my eyes and ears and have helped to bring many of my visions to fruition. You have also been a sweetheart and a reliable friend. Thank you, Val.

To Dirtman (my cellee), you read the reread then read once again the various drafts of this story as I tried to pull it together. Thanks for tolerating the glare of the lights as I wrote in the wee hours of the morning. To Yusuf (my homey), I've been away from the streets for a while and the name of some streets and the locals of some places have often escaped me. Yet, they seem to never have escaped you. Thanks, Sef, for helping me keep my facts straight.

To Julia P. Robinson. To say that you have been invaluable would understate all that you have done and continue to do, albeit slowly. (smile) Last but certainly not least, Attorney Cassandra Savoy, without whom none of my literary endeavors would have been possible, as you have been a constant inspiration in my literary endeavors and my legal pursuits. From the depth of my heart, thank you.

ABOUT THE AUTHORS

SEVEN was born the seventh child to one of the most notorious hustlers in Richmond, Virginia. She was raised in the Whitcomb Court housing project by her mother. The author and poet is a graduate of Virginia Union University and currently resides in the DC metropolitan area with her two sons. She is currently writing a novel.

THE GHOST is the new kid on the literary block and plans on becoming a permanent resident. He is currently working hard on his upcoming novel, titled *Tribulations of a Ghetto Kid*.

AKBAR PRAY, an urban legend, is the author of *Death of the Game* and is currently working on his next novel, titled *Brick City*.

Y. BLAK MOORE is a poet and former gang member who grew up in the Chicago housing projects. He is also the author of the novels *Triple Take*, *The Apostles*, and *Slippin'*. He has three children and lives in Chicago.

NIKKI TURNER, formerly the Princess of Hip-Hop Fiction, has graciously earned and accepted her new title of the Queen of Hip-Hop Fiction. Creatively editing each story in this anthology, Ms. Turner, a literary jewel herself, continues to show the world why she deserves to wear her crown. She is gutsy, gifted, courageous, and taking the urban literary community by storm. She is the bestselling author of *A Hustler's Wife*, *A Project Chick*, and *The Glamorous Life*. Visit her website at www.nikkiturner.com, or write her at nikki@nikkiturner.com, or at P.O. Box 28694, Richmond, VA 23228.